D1365366

American Gothic

AMERICAN GOTHIC

Edited by Elizabeth Terry

with Terri Hardin

BARNES
&NOBLE
BOOKS
NEW YORK

1997 Barnes & Noble Books

ISBN 0-7607-0349-3

Book design by Nicola Ferguson

Printed and bound in the United States of America

97 98 99 00 01 M 9 8 7 6 5 4 3 2 1

BVG

Contents

PART II: BLURRED VISIONS

PART III: MIRROR IMAGES

PART IV: THE INWARD GAZE

Introduction:
Landscapes of Darkness

I was a child in Mississippi, where cicadas crawled up trees to split their shells and emerge as large and wet-winged creatures. They had big eyes and flew blindly into our heads as we played swingin' statues. We called them "locusts," Baptists that we were, and we picked their dried brown bug shells off of trees and stuck them to little kids' shirts to scare them. Between the elementary school playground and the house where the only Catholic family in the neighborhood lived, there was a small and benign block of Southern pines that became known as "the woods" (a portentous description that thrilled our little suburban hearts), and soon enough this innocent piece of undeveloped real estate took on an aura almost dripping with primeval mystery. This feeling was only enhanced at cicada time because of their infernal singing, when the buzzing layers of loud and mesmerizing monotones seemed to come right out of the trees. At the end of the bike trail that humped and snaked through the woods, there was an old culvert, large enough to ride through, and dark enough to terrify once the rumors of bats started circulating. The culvert marked the end of the trail, and the only way to get back to the road was to double back through the dark green light of the pines. Being caught at the culvert at dusk meant a rage of sheer terror that grew as the sun went down and the air got cool— spurring a bike ride of panic, the body pushed forward and the back parallel to the bumpy ground, the bell and basket emitting short bursts of tinny jangling noises as the bike banged over rocks in the dirt, big wet locusts smacking into the furiously lined forehead, darkness nipping at the nape of the neck, bats gathering overhead to hurl themselves any moment at the head, that buzzing getting louder and louder, so loud it would drown out any screams, monsters skulking just behind the trees, something about to grab the tire of the bike any second now . . .

    ✴   ✴   ✴   ✴   ✴   ✴

Far to the north, Ichabod Crane, on a horse instead of a bike, never comes out of the woods. And although the hapless Hudson Valley schoolteacher is truly being chased by something, the only demon at work is his feverish imagination, fueled that same night by stories of goblins told around his compatriots' fire. In pragmatic American fashion, Washington Irving left nothing to the supernatural in "The Legend of Sleepy Hollow," except for its impact on the mind. Herein lies the heart of the American Gothic story—that even the fantastic is not without basis in fact.

Looking Back

Being a Southerner fosters an innate notion of gothic, or rather the assumption of such seems to follow the Southerner around. "Southern Gothic" means that one understands the stillness of air and the empty rusted porch swing, that the shadow behind the screen door is pointing with a trembling finger toward a letter pressed between the pages of a Bible, that there's a boy living in a doghouse and a young girl living with the backyard neighbors because of her mama's "sickness." There's an atmosphere of the macabre, an equal passion for both the religious and the secular, and tragedies of misdirected taboos; a sense that a lost civilization still lurks behind the thick waxy leaves of easily bruised magnolias. In fact, the many-tendriled term "Southern Gothic" has been incorporated into the American vernacular, as opposed to its extended family of more specific terms like "gothic architecture" or "gothic period."

"American Gothic" treads on spongier, wider terrain, although Washington Irving, Nathaniel Hawthorne, and Edgar Allan Poe effectively drew the parameters of the genre. Gothic literature originated in Europe, in brooding, dark tales of romantic conspiracies and supernaturalism, such as Horace Walpole's *The Castle of Otranto* (1764) and Ann Radcliffe's *The Mysteries of Udolpho* (1794), played out by stock characters amid the mossy ruins of castles and convents. Usually set in the late medieval period, the genre was wildly popular, and it was only natural that American writers would follow suit, some emulating the style so well that their stories were barely distinguishable from their European forebears.

America, though, offered little in the way of a traditional gothic motif—no dashing barons in exile waiting to reclaim a homeland, no prevalent Catholic "mysticism" fostering fear among the austere and suspicious Protestants, and few, if any, castles. There was a difficulty in relocating such a distinct, place-related style of fiction to a new and unfolding landscape. For the imaginative writer, though, the new land of America was rife with possibilities, from a wilderness so vast it was capable of swallowing a person whole, to a Calvinist doctrine whose emphasis on predestination left little room for the force of individual will. Early American writers like Charles Brockden Brown created a uniquely American sort of terror by basing their suspenseful narratives upon events founded in fact (in *Wieland*, he used spontaneous human combustion to explain the smoky fireball of death that consumed a fervently religious man). Americans looked to logic and science for their explanations, leaving superstition and spirits to their European relatives. And, of course, the potential reality that a hand is waiting to grab the tire is always more horrifying than the improbability that the flimsy and philosophically debatable devil will appear.

This same "horrifying" reality is what will be found in most of the stories in *American Gothic*. Some may have a predilection toward a foggy mysticism, but any palpable fear is derived from what is tangible. Having said that, of course, it seems necessary to poke at the notion of reality with a sharp stick to see whether its eyes are open or not—because, as we learn through unfortunate experience, that which is as clear as day to one may be murky to another. The ability to discern shape and movement by the flickering light of a fire, beyond which lurks pitch blackness, and to decide at which point visibility ends and fear begins, is at the heart of these four groups of stories.

Gathering Darkness

In Part I, "Being Watched and Watching," all of the stories are spun from a common thread, from the fear that comes from being watched for reasons unknown. Though this fear obviously is not in itself a uniquely

American experience, in the early days of the Union several factors may have added to the terror that ensued from feeling the burn of a pair of eyes on one's colonial back. Plunging headlong into the cavernous depths of dark and untested American forests would have given rise to the same sorts of imaginings of mythical beasts that plagued the European sailors who sailed into dark and uncharted waters. Added to this arboreal nightmare was the terror created by a God who was forever poised to drop any unwitting soul into the hot and unforgiving jaws of hell. The concept of predestination was followed to the letter by the Calvinists, but its spirit seeped into the tenets of everyday, run-of-the-mill Protestantism, forging a gnawing, unsettling notion of being forever watched.

In "The Giant Wistaria," Charlotte Perkins (Stetson) Gilman's story that opens the section, a young woman's glowing eyes pierce the dark with an intensity that survives her corporeal form. Darting, conniving eyes hidden in the dark, eclipsed by the feeble glow of candles, hover in the back rooms of George Lippard's "A Night in Monk-Hall." (This story, the only excerpt in the collection, is from his 1846 novel, *The Quaker City, or The Monks of Monk Hall; A Romance of Philadelphia Life, Mystery, and Crime*.) Ambrose Bierce's penchant for the bizarre is clear and dreadful in "The Eyes of the Panther." And a visage of a less heinous breed—that of nature itself— demonstrates its malleability of expression in E. P. King's "A Story of the White Mountain Notch." Here nature's amorphous attitude depends upon who's doing the looking, and the tendency toward trepidation bears witness to one of our earliest literary lessons, that the first of the triad of man's antagonisms ("Man vs. Man," "Man vs. Himself") is "Man vs. Nature."

Safely out of the woods, we join civilization and take on the role as watcher in Part II, aptly titled "Blurred Visions." These stories are of sight that goes awry when the integrity of vision is compromised for the agenda of a larger view. Kate Chopin, in "Désirée's Baby," writes a lyrical and darkly ironic story of a young woman whose fate is decided by people who look but do not see. "An Illusion in Red and White" is Stephen Crane's deceptively folkish tale of manipulated perception. The gothic moniker in Ichabod Crane's world of Sleepy Hollow applies not only to the eeriness of the misty haunts of Tarrytown, but also to the ominous aspect of being singled out, separated from the group, and chased by the villagers.

While Ichabod breathes a (transitory) sigh of relief once he's over the bridge, the poor souls in the stories of Part III, "Mirror Images," have not quite so simple an escape, for they are inextricably connected to their pursuers—some willingly, some not. The opening story, Robert Chambers's "The Yellow Sign," is an astounding tale suspended between an earthiness that smacks of American post-Romanticism and an otherworldliness that hovers on the edges of science fiction. Chambers allows his main character to see himself beyond his own here and now while standing firmly on the ground, much like the young woman in Nathaniel Hawthorne's "The Hollow of the Three Hills" and the susceptible young man in Edgar Allan Poe's "A Tale of the Ragged Mountains." Neither of these stories is among the authors' most famous (a tempting enough reason to include them), but both illustrate, quite dramatically, the notion of the reflected image and its distortions. Hawthorne's grim fairy tale is probably one of the more mystical in the collection, while Poe's story involves an unfortunate trade in the spirit of commerce, the dividend being an overwhelming power of sight that few would desire. Poe shows how terrifying the unexpected glance in the mirror can be—especially when one's vulnerable eyes cannot fathom the difference between reflection and concoction.

The most penetrating scan, though, is the inward gaze, for the eyes bore directly into the soul and see its whys and wherefores, its buried bones and unspoken passions. It is an isolating experience to look inside, whether purposely or not, and the stories in Part IV, "The Inward Gaze," share a sense of desperate solitude. In the first story, "Mrs. Manstey's View," Edith Wharton writes of a woman who has so completely defined her own world that its margins are characterized by comfortable claustrophobia. In "The Diamond Lens," Fitz-James O'Brien sketches a portrait of a scientist so completely possessed by his work that he is rendered blind to all life outside the slide under his microscope. His cold calculations, egomania, and prejudices are clues to the psyche of his character. Finally, Gilman's "The Yellow Wall-Paper," is a suspenseful and atmospheric depiction of the path taken by a woman whose fecund mind is forced to turn in upon itself.

An intrinsic part of American culture is the need to explain, to find a justification and, therefore, an answer. American fiction reflects the need to assign tangibility to the intangible, so it is no wonder that this predilection is found in our gothic fiction, where the unseen begs to be unraveled.

Scarier, of course, is realizing that just about any of the scenarios in *American Gothic* could really happen, but it's harder to say which is more frightening—the shapes that we really see by the light of the fire, or the figures we try to convince ourselves are not out there in the dark . . . waiting . . . and watching.

—Elizabeth Terry
Columbia, South Carolina
February 1997

Part I

BEING WATCHED AND WATCHING

THE GIANT WISTARIA

Charlotte Perkins Gilman

M eddle not with my new vine, child! See! Thou hast already broken the tender shoot! Never needle or distaff for thee, and yet thou wilt not be quiet!"

The nervous fingers wavered, clutched at a small carnelian cross that hung from her neck, then fell despairingly.

"Give me my child, mother, and then I will be quiet!"

"Hush! hush! thou fool—some one might be near! See—there is thy father coming, even now! Get in quickly!"

She raised her eyes to her mother's face, weary eyes that yet had a flickering, uncertain blaze in their shaded depths.

"Art thou a mother and hast no pity on me, a mother? Give me my child!"

Her voice rose in a strange, low cry, broken by her father's hand upon her mouth.

"Shameless!" said he, with set teeth. "Get to thy chamber, and be not seen again to-night, or I will have thee bound!"

She went at that, and a hard-faced serving woman followed, and presently returned, bringing a key to her mistress.

"Is all well with her—and the child also?"

"She is quiet, Mistress Dwining, well for the night, be sure. The child fretteth endlessly, but save for that it thriveth with me."

The parents were left alone together on the high square porch with its great pillars, and the rising moon began to make faint shadows of the young vine leaves that shot up luxuriantly around them: moving shadows, like little stretching fingers, on the broad and heavy planks of the oaken floor.

"It groweth well, this vine thou broughtest me in the ship, my husband."

"Aye," he broke in bitterly, "and so doth the shame I brought thee! Had I known of it I would sooner have had the ship founder beneath us, and have seen our child cleanly drowned, than live to this end!"

"Thou art very hard, Samuel, art thou not afeard for her life? She grieveth sore for the child, aye, and for the green fields to walk in!"

"Nay," said he grimly, "I fear not. She hath lost already what is more than life; and she shall have air enough soon. To-morrow the ship is ready, and we return to England. None knoweth of our stain here, not one, and if the town hath a child unaccounted for to rear in decent ways—why, it is not the first, even here. It will be well enough cared for! And truly we have matter for thankfulness, that her cousin is yet willing to marry her."

"Has thou told him?"

"Aye! Thinkest thou I would cast shame into another man's house, unknowing it? He hath always desired her, but she would none of him, the stubborn! She hath small choice now!"

"Will he be kind, Samuel? can he—"

"Kind? What call'st thou it to take such as she to wife? Kind! How many men would take her, an' she had double the fortune? and being of the family already, he is glad to hide the blot forever."

"An' if she would not? He is but a coarse fellow, and she ever shunned him."

"Art thou mad, woman? She weddeth him ere we sail to-morrow, or she stayeth ever in that chamber. The girl is not so sheer a fool! He maketh an honest woman of her, and saveth our house from open shame. What other hope for her than a new life to cover the old? Let her have an honest child, an' she so longeth for one!"

He strode heavily across the porch, till the loose planks creaked again, strode back and forth, with his arms folded and his brows fiercely knit above his iron mouth.

Overhead the shadows flickered mockingly across a white face among the leaves, with eyes of wasted fire.

    ❈   ❈   ❈   ❈   ❈   ❈

"O, George, what a house! what a lovely house! I am sure it's haunted! Let us get that house to live in this summer! We will have Kate and Jack and Susy and Jim of course, and a splendid time of it!"

Young husbands are indulgent, but still they have to recognize facts.

"My dear, the house may not be to rent: and it may also not be habitable."

"There is surely somebody in it. I am going to inquire!"

The great central gate was rusted off its hinges, and the long drive had trees in it, but a little footpath showed signs of steady usage, and up that Mrs. Jenny went, followed by her obedient George. The front windows of the old mansion were blank, but in a wing at the back they found white curtains and open doors. Outside, in the clear May sunshine, a woman was washing. She was polite and friendly, and evidently glad of visitors in that lonely place. She "guessed it could be rented—didn't know." The heirs were in Europe, but "there was a lawyer in New York had the lettin' of it." There had been folks there years ago, but not in her time. She and her husband had the rent of their part for taking care of the place. "Not that they took much care on't either, but keepin' robbers out." It was furnished throughout, old-fashioned enough, but good; and "if they took it she could do the work for 'em herself, she guessed—if *he* was willin'!"

Never was a crazy scheme more easily arranged. George knew that lawyer in New York; the rent was not alarming; and the nearness to a rising sea-shore resort made it a still pleasanter place to spend the summer.

Kate and Jack and Susy and Jim cheerfully accepted, and the June moon found them all sitting on the high front porch.

They had explored the house from top to bottom, from the great room in the garret, with nothing in it but a rickety cradle, to the well in the cellar without a curb and with a rusty chain going down to unknown blackness below. They had explored the grounds, once beautiful with rare trees and shrubs, but now a gloomy wilderness of tangled shade.

The old lilacs and laburnums, the spirea and syringa, nodded against the second-story windows. What garden plants survived were great ragged bushes or great shapeless beds. A huge wistaria vine covered the whole front of the house. The trunk, it was too large to call a stem, rose at the corner of the porch by the high steps, and had once climbed its pillars; but now the pillars were wrenched from their places and held rigid and helpless by the tightly wound and knotted arms.

It fenced in all the upper story of the porch with a knitted wall of stem and leaf; it ran along the eaves, holding up the gutter that had once supported it; it shaded every window with heavy green; and the drooping, fragrant blossoms made a waving sheet of purple from roof to ground.

"Did you ever see such a wistaria!" cried ecstatic Mrs. Jenny. "It is worth the rent just to sit under such a vine,—a fig tree beside it would be sheer superfluity and wicked extravagance!"

"Jenny makes much of her wistaria," said George, "because she's so disappointed about the ghosts. She made up her mind at first sight to have ghosts in the house, and she can't find even a ghost story!"

"No," Jenny assented mournfully; "I pumped poor Mrs. Pepperill for three days, but could get nothing out of her. But I'm convinced there is a story, if we could only find it. You need not tell me that a house like this, with a garden like this, and a cellar like this, isn't haunted!"

"I agree with you," said Jack. Jack was a reporter on a New York daily, and engaged to Mrs. Jenny's pretty sister. "And if we don't find a real ghost, you may be very sure I shall make one. It's too good an opportunity to lose!"

The pretty sister, who sat next him, resented. "You shan't do anything of the sort, Jack! This is a *real* ghostly place, and I won't have you make fun of it! Look at that group of trees out there in the long grass—it looks for all the world like a crouching, hunted figure!"

"It looks to me like a woman picking huckleberries," said Jim, who was married to George's pretty sister.

"Be still, Jim!" said that fair young woman. "I believe in Jenny's ghost as much as she does. Such a place! Just look at this great wistaria trunk crawling up by the steps here! It looks for all the world like a writhing body— cringing—beseeching!"

"Yes," answered the subdued Jim, "it does, Susy. See its waist,—about two yards of it, and twisted at that! A waste of good material!"

"Don't be so horrid, boys! Go off and smoke somewhere if you can't be congenial!"

"We can! We will! We'll be as ghostly as you please." And forthwith they began to see bloodstains and crouching figures so plentifully that the most delightful shivers multiplied, and the fair enthusiasts started for bed, declaring they should never sleep a wink.

"We shall all surely dream," cried Mrs. Jenny, "and we must all tell our dreams in the morning!"

"There's another thing certain," said George, catching Susy as she tripped over a loose plank; "and that is that you frisky creatures must use the side door till I get this Eiffel tower of a portico fixed, or we shall have some fresh ghosts on our hands! We found a plank here that yawns like a trap-door—big enough to swallow you,—and I believe the bottom of the thing is in China!"

The next morning found them all alive, and eating a substantial New England breakfast, to the accompaniment of saws and hammers on the porch, where carpenters of quite miraculous promptness were tearing things to pieces generally.

"It's got to come down mostly," they had said. "These timbers are clean rotted through, what ain't pulled out o' line by this great creeper. That's about all that holds the thing up."

There was clear reason in what they said, and with a caution from anxious Mrs. Jenny not to hurt the wistaria, they were left to demolish and repair at leisure.

"How about ghosts?" asked Jack after a fourth griddle cake. "I had one, and it's taken away my appetite!"

Mrs. Jenny gave a little shriek and dropped her knife and fork.

"Oh, so had I! I had the most awful—well, not dream exactly, but feeling. I had forgotten all about it!"

"Must have been awful," said Jack, taking another cake. "Do tell us about the feeling. My ghost will wait."

"It makes me creep to think of it even now," she said. "I woke up, all at once, with that dreadful feeling as if something were going to happen, you know! I was wide awake, and hearing every little sound for miles around, it seemed to me. There are so many strange little noises in the country for all it is so still. Millions of crickets and things outside, and all kinds of rustles in the trees! There wasn't much wind, and the moonlight came through in my three great windows in three white squares on the black old floor, and those fingery wistaria leaves we were talking of last night just seemed to crawl all over them. And—O, girls, you know that dreadful well in the cellar?"

A most gratifying impression was made by this, and Jenny proceeded cheerfully:

"Well, while it was so horridly still, and I lay there trying not to wake George, I heard as plainly as if it were right in the room, that old chain down there rattle and creak over the stones!"

"Bravo!" cried Jack. "That's fine! I'll put it in the Sunday edition!"

"Be still!" said Kate. "What was it, Jenny? Did you really see anything?"

"No, I didn't, I'm sorry to say. But just then I didn't want to. I woke George, and made such a fuss that he gave me bromide, and said he'd go and look, and that's the last I thought of it till Jack reminded me—the bromide worked so well."

"Now, Jack, give us yours," said Jim. "Maybe, it will dovetail in somehow. Thirsty ghost, I imagine; maybe they had prohibition here even then!"

Jack folded his napkin, and leaned back in his most impressive manner.

"It was striking twelve by the great hall clock—" he began.

"There isn't any hall clock!"

"O hush, Jim, you spoil the current! It was just one o'clock then, by my old-fashioned repeater."

"Waterbury! Never mind what time it was!"

"Well, honestly, I woke up sharp, like our beloved hostess, and tried to go to sleep again, but couldn't. I experienced all those moonlight and grasshopper sensations, just like Jenny, and was wondering what could have been the matter with the supper, when in came my ghost, and I knew it was all a dream! It was a female ghost, and I imagine she was young and handsome, but all those crouching, hunted figures of last evening ran riot in my brain, and this poor creature looked just like them. She was all wrapped up in a shawl, and had a big bundle under her arm,—dear me, I am spoiling the story! With the air and gait of one in frantic haste and terror, the muffled figure glided to a dark old bureau, and seemed taking things from the drawers. As she turned, the moonlight shone full on a little red cross that hung from her neck by a thin gold chain—I saw it glitter as she crept noiselessly from the room! That's all."

"O Jack, don't be so horrid! Did you really? Is that all! What do you think it was?"

"I am not horrid by nature, only professionally. I really did. That was all. And I am fully convinced it was the genuine, legitimate ghost of an eloping chambermaid with kleptomania!"

"You are too bad, Jack!" cried Jenny. "You take all the horror out of it. There isn't a 'creep' left among us."

"It's no time for creeps at nine-thirty A.M., with sunlight and carpenters outside! However, if you can't wait till twilight for your creeps, I think I can furnish one or two," said George. "I went down cellar after Jenny's ghost!"

There was a delighted chorus of female voices, and Jenny cast upon her lord a glance of genuine gratitude.

"It's all very well to lie in bed and see ghosts, or hear them," he went on. "But the young householder suspecteth burglars, even though as a medical man he knoweth nerves, and after Jenny dropped off I started on a voyage of discovery. I never will again, I promise you!"

"Why, what *was* it?"

"Oh, George!"

"I got a candle—"

"Good mark for the burglars," murmured Jack.

"And went all over the house, gradually working down to the cellar and the well."

"Well?" said Jack.

"Now you can laugh; but that cellar is no joke by daylight, and a candle there at night is about as inspiring as a lightning-bug in the Mammoth Cave. I went along with the light, trying not to fall into the well prematurely; got to it all at once; held the light down and *then* I saw, right under my feet—(I nearly fell over her, or walked through her, perhaps),—a woman, hunched up under a shawl! She had hold of the chain, and the candle shone on her hands—white, thin hands—on a little red cross that hung from her neck—*ride* Jack! I'm no believer in ghosts, and I firmly object to unknown parties in the house at night; so I spoke to her rather fiercely. She didn't seem to notice that, and I reached down to take hold of her—then I came upstairs!"

"What for?"

"What happened?"

"What was the matter?"

"Well, nothing happened. Only she wasn't there! May have been indigestion, of course, but as a physician I don't advise any one to court indigestion alone at midnight in a cellar!"

"This is the most interesting and peripatetic and evasive ghost I ever heard of!" said Jack. "It's my belief she has no end of silver tankards, and jewels galore, at the bottom of that well, and I move we go and see!"

"To the bottom of the well, Jack?"

"To the bottom of the mystery. Come on!"

There was unanimous assent, and the fresh cambrics and pretty boots were gallantly escorted below by gentlemen whose jokes were so frequent that many of them were a little forced.

The deep old cellar was so dark that they had to bring lights, and the well so gloomy in its blackness that the ladies recoiled.

"That well is enough to scare even a ghost. It's my opinion you'd better let well enough alone?" quoth Jim.

"Truth lies hid in a well, and we must get her out," said George. "Bear a hand with the chain?"

Jim pulled away on the chain, George turned the creaking windlass, and Jack was chorus.

"A wet sheet for this ghost, if not a flowing sea," said he. "Seems to be hard work raising spirits! I suppose he kicked the bucket when he went down!"

As the chain lightened and shortened there grew a strained silence among them; and when at length the bucket appeared, rising slowly through the dark water, there was an eager, half reluctant peering, and a natural drawing back. They poked the gloomy contents. "Only water."

"Nothing but mud."

"Something—"

They emptied the bucket up on the dark earth, and then the girls all went out into the air, into the bright warm sunshine in front of the house, where was the sound of saw and hammer, and the smell of new wood. There was nothing said until the men joined them, and then Jenny timidly asked:

"How old should you think it was, George?"

"All of a century," he answered. "That water is a preservative—lime in it. Oh!—you mean?—Not more than a month: a very little baby!"

There was another silence at this, broken by a cry from the workmen. They had removed the floor and the side walls of the old porch, so that the sunshine poured down to the dark stones of the cellar bottom. And there, in the strangling grasp of the roots of the great wistaria, lay the bones of a woman, from whose neck still hung a tiny scarlet cross on a thin chain of gold.

MALHALLA'S REVENGE

Joanna E. Wood

A long lane bordered upon each side by gray weather-beaten rail fences leads from the stone road down to Kaspar Erb's house. It is a two-story white frame house, with one large room in front and two smaller ones at the back and four box-like bedrooms upstairs. It has green-painted shutters, and three drab-painted steps in front.

At the time of Malhalla's first seizure there stood upon one side of the steps a prickly pear cactus, planted in a shilling crock. Upon the other side were two tomato cans, one with a sickly geranium in it, the other with a fuchsia slip, which, instead of putting out a root, had expended all its sap in producing one tiny misshapen blossom. Poor little slip!—in two days it lay a brown shrivelled twig across the can, but it had fulfilled its destiny and matured one blossom.

The last time Mrs. Erb was in the village she had gotten the geranium and the fuchsia slips from the postmaster's wife. The next day, as usual, she rose at four o'clock to go through the dew-drenched fields to bring home the cows. She only got as far as the pasture bars, when she fell. Kaspar, after waiting long, went to seek her, and carried her back to the house. He set her down in the huge old chair facing the window, and from it she never rose. Rheumatism and sciatica had terminated in a paralysis all but complete; the active, wiry little woman sat stiff and rigid, able only to move her left arm, incapable of a change of facial expression, or more than to mumble words indistinctly betwixt shackled jaws.

She had never spared herself. The early and late walks through the long, damp grass, driving the cows to or from pasture; the excursions at dawn to the red raspberry swamps, where her wet skirts clung about her until the

rising sun dried them; the standing for hours up to her knees in the shallow waters of the river's overflow, helping Kaspar secure the yearly spoil of
logs and planks brought down in spring freshets from the lumber camp
and regarded as lawful flotsam and jetsam by all the neighborhood; or the
sudden change from the fiery furnace of the harvest field to the chill damp
of the spring house where she churned and where a single plank, precari-
ously balanced, lifted one above the two feet of icy water in which the
creamery tins stood—any of these unconscious hardships, or the combined effects of all, may have brought about the paralysis, but Kaspar, his
neighbors, and indeed Malhalla herself bestowed no thought whatever
upon causation. They were concerned only with the effect. And their most
dominant feeling was that it was hard on Kaspar. Including Malhalla, they
considered him an ill-used man. He had to hire a boy, and finally a man
to do what his wife had done outdoors, and after trying from economic
reasons to manage within the house alone, he told himself he must get a
woman also. This was hard on Kaspar, but it was bitter to Malhalla, his
wife.

Malhalla was, like Kaspar, of Pennsylvania Dutch extraction, and, like
him, lived in one of the German settlements in Canada. She had been the
best worker in the county, and Kaspar, who was well off but miserly to the
extreme, had married her for that and not for her beauty. She was some
years older than Kaspar, and he was then forty-three. Her thrift had increased his worldly goods. She had given unsparingly of her strength, and
now, when her death seemed the only gift which would be acceptable to
him, she longed inexpressibly for it. And her longing became a resolution
to die.

The doctor had said that the warm coverlets must be closely drawn over
the helpless limbs to shut out even a breath of chill, and that the poor
drawn-up feet must rest on the little square cushion to keep them from the
cold painted floor. Often half the night she worked by little twitchings of
flesh and muscles to shake off the entwining coverlets and to get her helpless feet off the cushion. If she could but die, Kaspar would not have to
spend money, she thought, her little black, bird-like eyes looking out of
her pinched white face after the black-headed, stolid, heavy-built Dutchman. These efforts and her constant worry wore her body to a shadow, and
now and then she felt an awesome premonition that time for her would
soon cease.

Harvest was coming on, and at last Kaspar brought Lizzie Snyder to keep house for him and wait upon Malhalla. Lizzie was a tall, raw-boned woman with colorless hair, lips and cheeks. All the pigment in her cuticle seemed to have concentrated itself in two shining red circles round her eyes. Eyelashes she had none, and the two red rims formed an iris of blood for her light-blue eyes. She worked well and waited well on Malhalla; and Kaspar came and went in his dogged way.

The last of the harvesting was done, the threshing was past, the cider had grown "hard," the apple butter was all made and tied up securely in its brown crocks, itself a deep mahogany tint. The winter approached, the yearly washing was over. The winter deepened. The sap in the maple woods began to flow. The syrup was made, and Kaspar and Lizzie went at night, with the rest of the neighbors, to the "sugaring off." Malhalla, from her chair looking across the turnip field over the pasture and beyond the river, saw in the bush far off the twinkling of the fires which boiled the syrup down. And she longed to die, and felt that death was near.

Spring came fully in, and the freshets brought down their spoils. Kaspar and his man, not Lizzie, worked with might and main at the river's edge.

Summer passed, and one night in autumn when "the frost was on the pumpkin" and "the corn was in the shock" there thrilled through the house of Kaspar and through the heart of Malhalla, his wife, the cry of a new-born child. There had been coming and going through the night, but Malhalla's chair faced the window and she knew naught of it.

The night passed, and in the morning the coverlets were tightly over Malhalla's knees and the cushion beneath her feet. A neighbor's wife came from the kitchen and put Malhalla's food on the broad shelf-like arm of her chair. With her left hand she had ever been able to feed herself, and usually she but ate those morsels which nature imperatively demanded; but this morning slowly and laboriously she ate, crumb by crumb, all the food that had been brought her, and drank, sip by sip, painfully through the all but locked jaws, the cupful of weak tea. The woman came to take the things away, and said, looking at Malhalla curiously, "Lizzie got fine baby now." "Yes," mumbled Malhalla and said no more.

The days passed. Lizzie waited on Malhalla as of old. The cry of the child was often heard, and as winter came again Kaspar and Lizzie looked often at the attenuated form which still lived, and Malhalla from her chair returned their gaze, when her eyes met theirs, with one of impassivity. The winter was gone and the spring, then the summer; the child's first year was past; and Malhalla still lived.

In the eyes of Kaspar and Lizzie impatience lived, and in Malhalla's peace. The three had all belonged to the same church. Kaspar, to use the village expression, was "var' religious;" so was Lizzie. They were thus constrained to give Malhalla plenty of food. But they nightly now closed the green shutters on the window and thus blotted out from the woman's watching gaze the heavenly panorama of the stars. This was a blow aimed by Lizzie, for she had subtly become aware of the pleasure Malhalla took in watching the night through her long wakeful hours. But Malhalla did not murmur, and soon discovered, with a thrill of exultation, that she was granted a greater pleasure; for one night, when the lamps were lit, she noticed that the shuttered window formed a mirror in which she could see all that passed in the room behind her; the supper of Kaspar and Lizzie and the child Susanna at the little square table, their gestures toward herself, their slow smiles at each other. What a joy this was, and what a tonic to stay her fainting will!

One night in the darkness, after she slept, a hand slyly took from her pocket the three horse-chestnuts grown in a single burr that Kaspar had brought her when she was first taken with rheumatics. She had had them in her pocket ever since; for, as every one knows, they have a peculiar virtue of their own against rheumatism and sciatica. Malhalla had a good deal of faith in them, but she said nothing, and still lived. Upon her finger was a lead rheumatism ring. Kaspar had paid a charm doctor fifty cents for it. It had grown too large for the claw-like finger, and was grotesquely fastened on the stiff right hand by a thread to her wrist. One night stealthy scissors cut the thread, and the ring slowly slipped down the outstretched finger and rolled away over the floor. She missed that, too, for such a ring is a sure cure for pains; but she said nothing, and still lived.

One morning when Kaspar and Lizzie came to look at her, as they did daily, her eyes were closed and no breath seemed to cross her lips. "She's dead," said Lizzie, with the terror of joy in her voice. Kaspar strode to the wall, took down the little square looking-glass and held it before her lips; it filmed over, her eyes unclosed, she looked at them—the ghost of laughter in her eyes mocking the hate which slumbered in theirs.

It was winter again, a bitter winter indeed. Lizzie's amber beads, which she wore to cure her rheumy eyes, broke from the string as she came from the cow stable, and were, all but a few, lost in the deep snow. Of course Lizzie's eyes grew worse; the blue faded out of them, and the red rings grew redder. Susanna's eyes were red and rheumy, too. Kaspar was weary to the point of malignity; and still Malhalla lived on.

One night, in her window mirror, Malhalla saw Kaspar with the black cat on his knee. She thought nothing of this until at night when she felt three sharp pulls at her hair; then her heart sank. Kaspar was going to put a curse upon her. He took the three hairs from her head and the three hairs from the black cat's tail and folded them in the charm-written paper. Then he lit his lantern and tramped away through the snow. He reached the bush, sought and found a witch-hazel and cut a twig from it. Then he went to a tree he wot of, very much decayed and rotten to the core. He picked a little hole in the touchwood bark with the point of his knife, and put in it the folded paper; then he hammered in the twig of witch hazel. The tree was soft as punk and the sharpened twig penetrated it easily. This done he took his axe, cut the tree almost through, murmuring cabalistic words of ill omen. When the tree fell the one thus cursed would die. And the form he wished to crush was a feeble, rigid, attenuated frame, which prisoned a spirit strong to endure. His conscience permitted him to put this doom upon a helpless woman, a doom he believed in implicitly, but it would not allow him to stint her in food.

Kaspar returned home with skulking steps, for he felt the deed was evil.

The wind rose in little gusts, and he hurried forward. He dreaded hearing the crash of a falling tree. But the morrow's light dispelled the feeling, and he felt his heart lighter by the prospect of release. He went to the town and bought two amber necklaces, one for Lizzie and one for Susanna.

Now dread lay upon Malhalla's soul, but she fought it off and still lived. A week later the spring winds began to tear through the woods, and after each windy night Kaspar hurried to the bush. Through the window Malhalla saw him go, knew the reason of his going, read the import of his disappointed look when he returned, read also the paleness of fearful joy which sat upon his countenance one morning, and then she knew the tree was down.

But vengeance overcame even the inherited forcefulness of superstition, and she still lived—lived through springs and summers, autumns and winters, lived until Susanna went to school, until she left school—lived on, week by week, month by month, until twenty years had passed since Susanna's first cry had inspired her with the thirst for vengeance. Then one night, her soul sated with vengeance, she laid down life, and slept with the calm of one who has enjoyed triumph until aweary of it.

And two days after her funeral there was a joining of hands—and Susanna had a name. But the lives of Kaspar and Lizzie never emerged from the shadow of that frail, rigid form.

THE EYES OF THE PANTHER

Ambrose Bierce

I

One Does Not Always Marry When Insane

A man and a woman—nature had done the grouping—sat on a rustic seat, in the late afternoon. The man was middle-aged, slender, swarthy, with the expression of a poet and the complexion of a pirate—a man at whom one would look again. The woman was young, blonde, graceful, with something in her figure and movements suggesting the word "lithe." She was habited in a gray gown with odd brown markings in the texture. She may have been beautiful; one could not readily say, for her eyes denied attention to all else. They were gray-green, long and narrow, with an expression defying analysis. One could only know that they were disquieting. Cleopatra may have had such eyes.

The man and the woman talked.

"Yes," said the woman, "I love you, God knows! But marry you, no. I cannot, will not."

"Irene, you have said that many times, yet always have denied me a reason. I've a right to know, to understand, to feel and prove my fortitude if I have it. Give me a reason."

"For loving you?"

The woman was smiling through her tears and her pallor. That did not stir any sense of humor in the man.

"No; there is no reason for that. A reason for not marrying me. I've a right to know. I must know. I will know!"

17

He had risen and was standing before her with clenched hands, on his face a frown—it might have been called a scowl. He looked as if he might attempt to learn by strangling her. She smiled no more—merely sat looking up into his face with a fixed, set regard that was utterly without emotion or sentiment. Yet it had something in it that tamed his resentment and made him shiver.

"You are determined to have my reason?" she asked in a tone that was entirely mechanical—a tone that might have been her look made audible.

"If you please—if I'm not asking too much."

Apparently this lord of creation was yielding some part of his dominion over his co-creature.

"Very well, you shall know: I am insane."

The man started, then looked incredulous and was conscious that he ought to be amused. But, again, the sense of humor failed him in his need and despite his disbelief he was profoundly disturbed by that which he did not believe. Between our convictions and our feelings there is no good understanding.

"That is what the physicians would say," the woman continued—"if they knew. I might myself prefer to call it a case of 'possession.' Sit down and hear what I have to say."

The man silently resumed his seat beside her on the rustic bench by the wayside. Over-against them on the eastern side of the valley the hills were already sunset-flushed and the stillness all about was of that peculiar quality that foretells the twilight. Something of its mysterious and significant solemnity had imparted itself to the man's mood. In the spiritual, as in the material world, are signs and presages of night. Rarely meeting her look, and whenever he did so conscious of the indefinable dread with which, despite their feline beauty, her eyes always affected him, Jenner Brading listened in silence to the story told by Irene Marlowe. In deference to the reader's possible prejudice against the artless method of an unpractised historian the author ventures to substitute his own version for hers.

II

A Room May Be Too Narrow for Three, Though One Is Outside

In a little log house containing a single room sparely and rudely furnished, crouching on the floor against one of the walls, was a woman, clasping to her breast a child. Outside, a dense unbroken forest extended for many miles in every direction. This was at night and the room was black dark: no human eye could have discerned the woman and the child. Yet they were observed, narrowly, vigilantly, with never even a momentary slackening of attention; and that is the pivotal fact upon which this narrative turns.

Charles Marlowe was of the class, now extinct in this country, of woodmen pioneers—men who found their most acceptable surroundings in sylvan solitudes that stretched along the eastern slope of the Mississippi Valley, from the Great Lakes to the Gulf of Mexico. For more than a hundred years these men pushed ever westward, generation after generation, with rifle and ax, reclaiming from Nature and her savage children here and there an isolated acreage for the plow, no sooner reclaimed than surrendered to their less venturesome but more thrifty successors. At last they burst through the edge of the forest into the open country and vanished as if they had fallen over a cliff. The woodman pioneer is no more; the pioneer of the plains—he whose easy task it was to subdue for occupancy two-thirds of the country in a single generation—is another and inferior creation. With Charles Marlowe in the wilderness, sharing the dangers, hardships and privations of that strange, unprofitable life, were his wife and child, to whom, in the manner of his class, in which the domestic virtues were a religion, he was passionately attached. The woman was still young enough to be comely, new enough to the awful isolation of her lot to be cheerful. By withholding the large capacity for happiness which the simple satisfactions of the forest life could not have filled, Heaven had dealt honorably with her. In her light household tasks, her child, her husband and her few foolish books, she found abundant provision for her needs.

One morning in midsummer Marlowe took down his rifle from the wooden hooks on the wall and signified his intention of getting game.

"We've meat enough," said the wife; "please don't go out to-day. I dreamed last night, O, such a dreadful thing! I cannot recollect it, but I'm almost sure that it will come to pass if you go out."

It is painful to confess that Marlowe received this solemn statement with less of gravity than was due to the mysterious nature of the calamity foreshadowed. In truth, he laughed.

"Try to remember," he said. "Maybe you dreamed that Baby had lost the power of speech."

The conjecture was obviously suggested by the fact that Baby, clinging to the fringe of his hunting-coat with all her ten pudgy thumbs was at that moment uttering her sense of the situation in a series of exultant goo-goos inspired by sight of her father's raccoon-skin cap.

The woman yielded: lacking the gift of humor she could not hold out against his kindly badinage. So, with a kiss for the mother and a kiss for the child, he left the house and closed the door upon his happiness forever.

At nightfall he had not returned. The woman prepared supper and waited. Then she put Baby to bed and sang softly to her until she slept. By this time the fire on the hearth, at which she had cooked supper, had burned out and the room was lighted by a single candle. This she afterward placed in the open window as a sign and welcome to the hunter if he should approach from that side. She had thoughtfully closed and barred the door against such wild animals as might prefer it to an open window— of the habits of beasts of prey in entering a house uninvited she was not advised, though with true female prevision she may have considered the possibility of their entrance by way of the chimney. As the night wore on she became not less anxious, but more drowsy, and at last rested her arms upon the bed by the child and her head upon the arms. The candle in the window burned down to the socket, sputtered and flared a moment and went out unobserved; for the woman slept and dreamed.

In her dreams she sat beside the cradle of a second child. The first one was dead. The father was dead. The home in the forest was lost and the dwelling in which she lived was unfamiliar. There were heavy oaken doors, always closed, and outside the windows, fastened into the thick stone walls, were iron bars, obviously (so she thought) a provision against Indians. All this she noted with an infinite self-pity, but without surprise—an emotion unknown in dreams. The child in the cradle was invisible under its coverlet which something impelled her to remove. She did so, disclosing the face of a wild animal! In the shock of this dreadful revelation the dreamer awoke, trembling in the darkness of her cabin in the wood.

As a sense of her actual surroundings came slowly back to her she felt for the child that was not a dream, and assured herself by its breathing that all was well with it; nor could she forbear to pass a hand lightly across its face. Then, moved by some impulse for which she probably could not have accounted, she rose and took the sleeping babe in her arms, holding it close against her breast. The head of the child's cot was against the wall to which the woman now turned her back as she stood. Lifting her eyes she saw two bright objects starring the darkness with a reddish-green glow. She took them to be two coals on the hearth, but with her returning sense of direction came the disquieting consciousness that they were not in that quarter of the room, moreover were too high, being nearly at the level of the eyes—of her own eyes. For these were the eyes of a panther.

The beast was at the open window directly opposite and not five paces away. Nothing but those terrible eyes was visible, but in the dreadful tumult of her feelings as the situation disclosed itself to her understanding she somehow knew that the animal was standing on its hinder feet, supporting itself with its paws on the window-ledge. That signified a malign interest—not the mere gratification of an indolent curiosity. The consciousness of the attitude was an added horror, accentuating the menace of those awful eyes, in whose steadfast fire her strength and courage were alike consumed. Under their silent questioning she shuddered and turned sick. Her knees failed her, and by degrees, instinctively striving to avoid a sudden movement that might bring the beast upon her, she sank to the floor, crouched against the wall and tried to shield the babe with her trembling body without withdrawing her gaze from the luminous orbs that were killing her. No thought of her husband came to her in her agony—no hope nor suggestion of rescue or escape. Her capacity for thought and feeling had narrowed to the dimensions of a single emotion—fear of the animal's spring, of the impact of its body, the buffeting of its great arms, the feel of its teeth in her throat, the mangling of her babe. Motionless now and in absolute silence, she awaited her doom, the moments growing to hours, to years, to ages; and still those devilish eyes maintained their watch.

Returning to his cabin late at night with a deer on his shoulders Charles Marlowe tried the door. It did not yield. He knocked; there was no answer.

He laid down his deer and went round to the window. As he turned the angle of the building he fancied he heard a sound as of stealthy footfalls and a rustling in the undergrowth of the forest, but they were too slight for certainty, even to his practised ear. Approaching the window, and to his surprise finding it open, he threw his leg over the sill and entered. All was darkness and silence. He groped his way to the fire-place, struck a match and lit a candle. Then he looked about. Cowering on the floor against a wall was his wife, clasping his child. As he sprang toward her she rose and broke into laughter, long, loud and mechanical, devoid of gladness and devoid of sense—the laughter that is not out of keeping with the clanking of a chain. Hardly knowing what he did he extended his arms. She laid the babe in them. It was dead—pressed to death in its mother's embrace.

III

The Theory of the Defense

That is what occurred during a night in a forest, but not all of it did Irene Marlowe relate to Jenner Brading; not all of it was known to her. When she had concluded the sun was below the horizon and the long summer twilight had begun to deepen in the hollows of the land. For some moments Brading was silent, expecting the narrative to be carried forward to some definite connection with the conversation introducing it; but the narrator was as silent as he, her face averted, her hands clasping and unclasping themselves as they lay in her lap, with a singular suggestion of an activity independent of her will.

"It is a sad, a terrible story," said Brading at last, "but I do not understand. You call Charles Marlowe father; that I know. That he is old before his time, broken by some great sorrow, I have seen, or thought I saw. But, pardon me, you said that you—that you—"

"That I am insane," said the girl, without a movement of head or body.

"But, Irene, you say—please, dear, do not look away from me—you say that the child was dead, not demented."

"Yes, that one—I am the second. I was born three months after that night, my mother being mercifully permitted to lay down her life in giving me mine."

Brading was again silent; he was a trifle dazed and could not at once think of the right thing to say. Her face was still turned away. In his embarrassment he reached impulsively toward the hands that lay closing and unclosing in her lap, but something—he could not have said what—restrained him. He then remembered, vaguely, that he had never altogether cared to take her hand.

"Is it likely," she resumed, "that a person born under such circumstances is like others—is what you call sane?"

Brading did not reply; he was preoccupied with a new thought that was taking shape in his mind—what a scientist would have called an hypothesis; a detective, a theory. It might throw an added light, albeit a lurid one, upon such doubt of her sanity as her own assertion had not dispelled.

The country was still new and, outside the villages, sparsely populated. The professional hunter was still a familiar figure, and among his trophies were heads and pelts of the larger kinds of game. Tales variously credible of nocturnal meetings with savage animals in lonely roads were sometimes current, passed through the customary stages of growth and decay, and were forgotten. A recent addition to these popular apocrypha, originating, apparently, by spontaneous generation in several households, was of a panther which had frightened some of their members by looking in at windows by night. The yarn had caused its little ripple of excitement—had even attained to the distinction of a place in the local newspaper; but Brading had given it no attention. Its likeness to the story to which he had just listened now impressed him as perhaps more than accidental. Was it not possible that the one story had suggested the other—that finding congenial conditions in a morbid mind and a fertile fancy, it had grown to the tragic tale that he had heard?

Brading recalled certain circumstances of the girl's history and disposition, of which, with love's incuriosity, he had hitherto been heedless—such as her solitary life with her father, at whose house no one, apparently, was an acceptable visitor and her strange fear of the night, by which those who knew her best accounted for her never being seen after dark. Surely in such a mind imagination once kindled might burn with a lawless flame, penetrating and enveloping the entire structure. That she was mad, though the conviction gave him the acutest pain, he could no longer doubt; she had only mistaken an effect of her mental disorder for its cause, bringing into imaginary relation with her own personality the vagaries of the local mythmakers. With some vague intention of testing his new "theory," and no very definite notion of how to set about it he said, gravely, but with hesitation:

"Irene, dear, tell me—I beg you will not take offence, but tell me—"

"I have told you," she interrupted, speaking with a passionate earnestness that he had not known her to show—"I have already told you that we cannot marry; is anything else worth saying?"

Before he could stop her she had sprung from her seat and without another word or look was gliding away among the trees toward her father's house. Brading had risen to detain her; he stood watching her in silence until she had vanished in the gloom. Suddenly he started as if he had been shot; his face took on an expression of amazement and alarm: in one of the black shadows into which she had disappeared he had caught a quick, brief glimpse of shining eyes! For an instant he was dazed and irresolute; then he dashed into the wood after her, shouting: "Irene, Irene, look out! The panther! The panther!"

In a moment he had passed through the fringe of forest into open ground and saw the girl's gray skirt vanishing into her father's door. No panther was visible.

IV

An Appeal to the Conscience of God

Jenner Brading, attorney-at-law, lived in a cottage at the edge of the town. Directly behind the dwelling was the forest. Being a bachelor, and therefore, by the Draconian moral code of the time and place denied the services of the only species of domestic servant known thereabout, the "hired girl," he boarded at the village hotel, where also was his office. The woodside cottage was merely a lodging maintained—at no great cost, to be sure—as an evidence of prosperity and respectability. It would hardly do for one to whom the local newspaper had pointed with pride as "the foremost jurist of his time" to be "homeless," albeit he may sometimes have suspected that the words "home" and "house" were not strictly synonymous. Indeed, his consciousness of the disparity and his will to harmonize it were matters of logical inference, for it was generally reported that soon after the cottage was built its owner had made a futile venture in the direction of marriage—had, in truth, gone so far as to be rejected by the beautiful but eccentric daughter of Old Man Marlowe, the recluse. This was publicly believed because he had told it himself and she had not—a reversal of the usual order of things which could hardly fail to carry conviction.

Brading's bedroom was at the rear of the house, with a single window facing the forest. One night he was awakened by a noise at that window; he could hardly have said what it was like. With a little thrill of the nerves he sat up in bed and laid hold of the revolver which, with a forethought most commendable in one addicted to the habit of sleeping on the ground floor with an open window, he had put under his pillow. The room was in absolute darkness, but being unterrified he knew where to direct his eyes, and there he held them, awaiting in silence what further might occur. He could now dimly discern the aperture—a square of lighter black. Presently there appeared at its lower edge two gleaming eyes that burned with a malignant lustre inexpressibly terrible! Brading's heart gave a great jump, then seemed to stand still. A chill passed along his spine and through his hair; he felt the blood forsake his cheeks. He could not have cried out—not to save his life; but being a man of courage he would not, to save his life, have done so if he had been able. Some trepidation his coward body might feel, but his spirit was of sterner stuff. Slowly the shining eyes rose with a steady motion that seemed an approach, and slowly rose Brading's right hand, holding the pistol. He fired!

Blinded by the flash and stunned by the report, Brading nevertheless heard, or fancied that he heard, the wild, high scream of the panther, so human in sound, so devilish in suggestion. Leaping from the bed he hastily clothed himself and, pistol in hand, sprang from the door meeting two or three men who came running up from the road. A brief explanation was followed by a cautious search of the house. The grass was wet with dew; beneath the window it had been trodden and partly leveled for a wide space, from which a devious trail, visible in the light of a lantern, led away into the bushes. One of the men stumbled and fell upon his hands, which as he rose and rubbed them together were slippery. On examination they were seen to be red with blood.

An encounter, unarmed, with a wounded panther was not agreeable to their taste; all but Brading turned back. He, with lantern and pistol, pushed courageously forward into the wood. Passing through a difficult undergrowth he came into a small opening, and there his courage had its reward, for there he found the body of his victim. But it was no panther.

What it was is told, even to this day, upon a weather-worn headstone in the village churchyard, and for many years was attested daily at the grave-side by the bent figure and sorrow-seamed face of Old Man Marlowe, to whose soul, and to the soul of his strange, unhappy child, peace. Peace and reparation.

THE RIGHT-HAND ROAD

Anonymous

George and I—better known as Mr. and Mrs. Ogden—about two years after our marriage, settled our affairs in the great metropolis, and took our departure for the "far West." George's uncle when dying, had bequeathed to him a farm, of, I really can't say how many acres, situated about fourteen miles from the village of Smokieton, which contained a mill, a blacksmith's shop, and one store. As George was not getting along very nicely—our income amounting to six hundred dollars a year, and our expenditure to but little less than twice that sum—he thought it better to try what he could do on the above-mentioned farm, having no doubt of a speedy increase in worldly wealth; for, as he said, "We wouldn't see any one, and so we need not try to keep up appearances. A very little plain furniture would be all that would be necessary, under the circumstances; and as regards dress, why—we could dress anyhow."

At length we arrived at our new home—and a very small one it was, so far as the house was concerned. There was only one room on the first-floor, which I called the universal room, and a corresponding number upstairs; but I afterwards persuaded George to build a partition, increasing the number of apartments, and decreasing their size in the same ratio—but I have always vowed, that if compelled to sleep in the kitchen myself, I *would* have a spare bed-room in my house. It has never yet been of the slightest use; but I am always hoping it will be, and remain true to my first resolve.

The first year we had very hard work to make both ends meet; but since then, we have had much better success. George goes to Smokieton about three or four times a year, for essentials; and sometimes I accompany him, but not often—for I always have so much to do, that I find it impossible to give up nearly a whole day to mere pleasure.

Before I came here, I used to promise myself an unlimited amount of enjoyment in riding round the country; but I have seldom tried it—never indeed but once, and then my experience was not of a nature to make me wish very ardently for a second trial. It is about this one ride that I am going to tell.

My Story

One evening in the early part of November, as George and I were sitting by the fire—he taking journeys into the land of Nod, and I mending his clothes—I suddenly remembered the empty state of our larder; and at the same time, noticing my husband's condition, by a philanthropic and disinterested effort, I brought him to life again, metaphorically speaking, by asking the following very natural and seemingly harmless question:

"George, when do you intend to go to Smokieton?"

"Well, my dear," replied he, with scarcely recovered faculties, and in a tone of voice that plainly showed he thought it a most extraordinary and highly disagreeable inquiry, "what in the world do I want to go there for?"

I have often noticed, where gentlemen are concerned, that to want a thing done, which is at the same time sensible and inconvenient, is most exasperating and discomposing—I suppose because of their natural willingness to oblige. Therefore, when George answered me sharply in the way I have described, I immediately concluded that some unseen but insurmountable obstacle intervened, and that this and not my simple question ruffled his serene temper; and therefore mildly explained my premises, without any attempt at self-justification, or any outcry at his harshness, thus: "Because there are a great many necessaries to be procured. In the first place, the wheat must be taken to the mill—for we are entirely out of flour." And then followed a list of articles of various descriptions, all really needed; and to leave an impression, I closed by mentioning that I needed the material for a new pair of over-alls for him.

George acknowledged quite reasonably the necessity for going; but added, that he did not think he could, in this instance, yield to necessity. I cannot remember what prevented him, but I know his objections were unanswerable.

Thereupon a bright idea struck me.

"George," said I, "I'll go."

He demurred for a while, saying that he was afraid I could not find my way; but I soon succeeded in making him look at it in a proper light, and the result was, that at about two o'clock the next afternoon, I was in Smokieton making my purchases.

I had not started quite as early in the morning as I had intended doing, and some hours passed while I was waiting for the flour; so that it was five o'clock before I was able to start on my way home. The road was merely a cart-path through the woods; and as several others crossed or joined it in various places, I felt quite timid, being uncertain many times which was the one I was to follow. They were each as like the other as one pea to his fellow; woods, dense and impenetrable, inclosed them; and in addition to these difficulties, I saw that the setting of the sun would soon leave me without the means of distinguishing any road at all. I recollected, however, that George had told me to keep the *right-hand road* all the way; and as I had done so, I must be right—though instinct told both "Dobbin" and myself quite positively, that we were certainly wrong. I am sorry to have to display such a degree of ignorance, but I am forced to confess that I had forgotten that of course if I took the *right*-hand road when going to Smokieton, on returning I should follow the *left*. After riding for what seemed an interminable length of time, I began to look for the light from our house—but no light did I see; and heavy clouds, flying in black masses overhead, threatened rain every moment. With unacknowledged terror, making my heart beat faster and faster, and the hands which held the reins of very uncertain use, I tried to cheer up my old horse, and inspire myself with a little confidence by talking aloud. Little good did it do however; my voice sounded weak and quavering, and could scarcely have been heard by a listener. For nearly an hour longer we travelled wearily along, and at the end of that time I ceased trying to conceal from myself the disagreeable knowledge that I was all wrong, and had lost my way! My heart sunk as the truth forced itself on my mind. I did not know what to do. I could not retrace the road I had taken in such thick darkness as now surrounded me, and to go forward seemed equally useless; but just at this moment, to my surprise and delight, I saw a short distance before me that the woods had been cleared away a little, and began to feel a faint hope that a house might be near, in which I could find shelter. I drove on till I reached the opening; then alighting, tied "Dobbin" to a tree, and commenced picking my way with great care over stones and branches, and through briers and tangled grass. At last my outstretched hands touched something which I could not see, and I found my wishes realized. I was standing by a rough log-cabin, and who could tell what comfort and hospitality might await me within? I felt along the sides of the house till I discovered the door, then knocked most emphatically, but received no answer. I turned the latch, opened the door, and looked in. Darkness reigned supreme there as elsewhere. No sound could be heard to show that it was inhabited. I felt very much disheartened, and immediately gave up all idea of taking refuge there. I am naturally timid, though generally very loth to acknowledge it. I have a natural aversion to darkness, and a horror of passing the night in any house alone; so I returned to the wagon, with the intention of driving around until day-light, with the satisfaction of having a companion at least in the poor horse, who I think disliked the place and circumstances quite as much as I did.

I was just stepping in when I felt a large drop of rain fall on my hand; and soon after, other drops commenced falling all around on the dried leaves. I could have cried with fright and vexation; but collecting all my courage and common-sense, I tried to look at things in the right way, and soon decided it would be perfectly useless for me to go further. That I reached this house so unexpectedly, immediately before it commenced raining, was surely a very providential occurrence, and one which I could not do better than avail myself of. I would at least be saved a good drenching; and passing the night in a solitary house was not so much worse, after all, than passing it in a dreary, wet ride, through unknown regions of forest. Fortifying myself in this way, I again alighted; and leading old "Dobbin" to the back of the house, where I thought he would be protected from some of the wind and rain, and covering him with a blanket, I entered the forsaken dwelling.

Would that I had done anything but that!

Fortunately I had matches with me, which I had bought that day; and tearing off some paper from a bundle, I made an extempore candle, which I lighted, and which, though it flared dreadfully and burned down to my fingers too soon, enabled me to make a cursory examination of the abode. I first directed my attention to the board shelf that served for a mantel-

piece, and there to my surprise I discovered a candle. I immediately lighted
it, and proceeded to inspect the room more leisurely. At present I certainly
was the only occupant—though there were many proofs that some one had
been there recently. It was a small house—smaller even than ours, for it
contained but one room, and no "upstairs." Some one of refined tastes had
evidently lived there, for there were attempts at more than mere comfort in
some of the arrangements. The bed, in one corner of the room, was cur-
tained, and reminded me of those one sees at hospitals. I looked in it and
under it, but saw nothing. A rough deal table stood on one side of the
room, and upon it was a singularly inappropriate rosewood writing-desk,
beautifully finished, with silver mountings, and two or three books, in
plain but handsome bindings, lay near. "And now," said I to myself, "if I
could only have a fire, I should be quite comfortable."

Were all wishes as easily gratified as this, but little would be left to wish
for. A basket, filled with kindling-wood, was standing in the chimney-
corner. Going to the door, I shut it tight; and was about to fasten it, when
the upper hinge broke, and it sank down below the step to the ground. I
left it as it was, knowing that I could not lift it, but thinking that I could
easily push it open in the morning. It was raining very drearily; and the
wind, howling among the trees, made me miserably frightened and lonely. I
took the most sensible means I could think of to cheer myself, and lighted
the fire, which soon crackled and blazed joyously in the fire-place. It threw
out little ruddy jets of flame, whose brightness penetrated the mysterious
dark corners, and made them seem as open to inspection, and as free from
all intention of concealing things I would not like to see, as the ordinary
corners I saw every day at home—which never hid any thing worse than a
handful of dust, and never even that for a very long time. When I grew
melancholy, the merry blaze laughed at me; and the shadows on the wall
gambolled in all sorts of odd ways, to show me that they didn't mind being shut up there, protected from the rain outside. It was scarcely possible
to feel superstitious where there was such a fire; and accordingly, after wandering around uncertainly for some time, and finding by my watch that it
was only eight o'clock, I seated myself by the side of my agreeable companion, and took up one of the books to while away the time. To my surprise, it proved to be a volume of Tennyson's poems. "Walter Talbot" was
written on the fly-leaf—evidently by a lady; and underneath, in a bold and
manly hand: "From his dear Rachel." It was, certainly, a well-read book;
many passages were marked; the leaves were turned down in various places;

and on some pages were traces of tears. I read until eleven o'clock, though my eye-lids were heavy with sleep, and my eyes saw the letters indistinctly through a haze of drowsiness. Then I tried to settle myself in a comfortable position on the floor, using my bench for a pillow; and there I continued, dropping off into short naps, and waking up occasionally to find my head bobbing up and down merrily, and threatening a speedy dislocation of my neck.

At last, in despair of really resting, I arose, and walked up and down the room, trying to awake myself, but all to no purpose. The wailing wind sung a lullaby, which I was unable to resist; and the accompaniment on the roof, played by the pattering rain, only increased the spell, while even the bright fire-light turned against me, and flashed so dazzlingly straight in my eyes, that I was forced to close them. And so it came to pass that I finally decided to lie down on the bed. It was not such a curious resolution, after all, for it certainly looked like a most comfortable resting-place—neat and clean, and, moreover, soft and well-made. But still I felt a strange repugnance to it, which only the most overpowering drowsiness would have enabled me to overcome. However, I made another minute examination of it inside and out, to see that there were no concealed mice, with well-built nests, hidden between the covers, who would come out after I slept, and regale themselves on my fingers and toes; and then I threw myself down, closed my eyes, and in less than five minutes had fallen into a deep slumber.

I think I must have slept about an hour in this dreamless way, when I began gradually to grow restless. Horrid visions of robbers, wild beasts, mangled human forms, and wandering ghosts, mingled in dire confusion in my brain, until I awoke with a half-suppressed scream, and tried to realize where I was, and what made me so wretchedly nervous. Then I tried to compose myself again. I thought of home, and of the interesting adventure I would have to tell George about, when I arrived. I retraced the road from the house as well as I could, remembering but dimly the way I had come; decided the precise point where I commenced going wrong, and thought of George's half-triumphant pity at my misfortunes, and regrets that he had consented to my going to Smokieton alone. But the longer I thought, and the more I tried to go to sleep, the more restless I grew. I turned over and over, but could not lie comfortably. The top of my head felt cold, and it seemed as though there was something terrible near me, which made my hair stand on end, and opened my eyes the moment they were closed. I raised myself, and looked at the head of the bed, but saw only the white curtain. I tossed about for some time longer, but still the dread horror continued, and the fearful cold kept creeping more perceptibly over me.

At length I jumped up, thinking it was a draught of wind which chilled me, as the bed was standing some little way from the wall. I attempted to push it nearer, but it only moved a little way, and then stood fast. I made another effort, it moved again, and the outlines of a human form were discernible behind the curtain. I stood motionless, with starting eyes gazing at it. I could not distinguish the whole figure—it was not all there. I could not see the head—the shoulders were even with the top of the bedstead; then the arms and body were easily traced; the feet must be below the curtain, but surely they could not touch the floor!

I gazed fascinated by that strange sight, until a great dread came over me, and with a piercing shriek I rushed to the door, my only thought, my only wish being to get away from the place. I pushed against it with my whole strength, but it only sunk lower and lower in the mud, below the step. I could not raise it. My arm was nerveless; all power had left me. I could do nothing, but remain where I was, shut up with that spectre behind the bed, till some one came to release me. I shrieked again and again, but no one could hear me, I knew. The rain pattered on the roof, the wind howled mournfully around the corners, the fire sunk lower and blazed more fitfully, and it grew colder all the time. I turned wildly around, and then sank on my knees in abject horror, as I saw, by the flickering light of the dying embers, a human face—purple and swollen, with starting, bloodshot eyes—staring at me over the top of the bedstead. Above the head was a beam, which ran across the house, and from the beam a rope came down, and there the body hung.

I contemplated the sickening sight, till the bursting eye-balls seemed forcing their way into my brain; and the discolored face made fearful grimaces, laughing and grinning at me, as I knelt there, crouching like some abject petitioner before it.

Soon a change seemed to come over every thing. I was no longer in this deserted house in the far West, but in a bright and pleasant room, in some gentleman's country-house. I think it was a library, for there were shelves filled with books, around the walls. Near a table, in the centre of the room, stood two persons, a man and a woman. I could not see the face of the latter, but she was writing on the fly-leaf of a book the name, "Walter Talbot."

I looked at the man. His face was strangely familiar. Surely I had seen it before; but not then as now. I remembered it swollen and discolored, with bleared and bloodshot eyes starting from their sockets. There was but little similarity between them. This young man's cheek was brown and ruddy; his bright dark eyes were softened by the light of love, a smile of winning sweetness played around the full-curved lips, while the dark curls, clustering around his forehead, contrasted strangely with the matted hair that fell over the brow of the other.

When his companion ceased writing, he motioned her to proceed, but her merry laugh rang out a denial, as she threw down the pen. He took it, and stooping forward, traced a few words; then he handed her the book, and I saw that underneath his name, he had written, in a bold, manly hand: "From his dear Rachel." That was all.

In the whole interview, no word had been spoken. It was a mysterious vision, which was passing rapidly away. I tried to pierce the mist of oblivion that was hiding it from my view. I saw them standing by the window, looking out at the bright autumn sun-set. He had taken her hand in his, and his arm encircled her; though they were speaking, I could not hear their words; but I saw that as he drew her closer to him, a mournful farewell glistened in the tears that filled her eyes, while his right hand was pointing to the western sky.

A dark void succeeded this strange dream. When I recovered my senses, I was at home, lying on my own bed, with George sitting beside me.

I will not make my story longer. I suppose I must have fainted after my distempered fancy had presented that life-like picture to my mind.

George said he had expected me until nearly twelve o'clock, and had then given me up for lost; but knowing how useless any search for me that night would be, he had waited until morning, when, with one of the farm-hands to render any assistance that might be required, he had explored all the roads for miles round. Late in the afternoon they arrived at the house I had taken refuge in, and knew I must be there, when they found old "Dobbin" tied where I had left him. After vainly endeavoring to make me answer their calls at the door, with difficulty they forced it open, and found me lying on the floor perfectly senseless.

George soon discovered what had caused my swoon, and while he was occupied in restoring me to consciousness, the man who was with him examined the writing-desk, to see if any papers could be found which would throw any light on the subject. He found a letter, without any address, in which the deceased stated his intentions of committing suicide, and gave as his reasons for the crime, that he had forged to a large amount to meet pressing necessities; and that when it was discovered, he fled to the West, hoping to escape from punishment. He had trusted that he might outlive his disgrace, and be enabled to commence a life of honest industry; but hearing through a letter from an accomplice, that the officers of justice were on his track, he had in despair resolved to anticipate retribution, and place himself beyond their power. His only regret was the grief it would occasion one very dear to him; but he had explained all in a letter to her, and he hoped she would forgive him. The letter closed by requesting the finder not to make his disgrace public. He also desired that he might be buried there, where he had intended to regain his honorable name; and that his few possessions might be sent with the letter in his desk, to Miss Rachel Staunton, the only one whom he felt still loved him. I suppose it is hardly necessary to say, that his wishes were complied with, as far as it was practicable. Under the dark forest trees now repose the remains of Walter Talbot. His name is forgotten among men. He sleeps in oblivion. But not thus can the memory of that dreadful night perish. There is no grave in which I can bury that. It always haunts me. Ever as night comes, and I lie down on my pillow, I seem to see a human form behind the curtain; and from above, a disfigured face looks down at me.

THE HAUNTED HOUSE

John G. Whittier

The beautiful river, which retains its Indian name of Merrimack, winds through a country of almost romantic beauty. The last twenty miles of its course in particular, are unsurpassed in quiet and rich scenery, by any river in the United States. There are indeed, no bold and ragged cliffs, like the Highlands of the Hudson, to cast their grim shadows on the water—no blue and lofty mountains, piercing into the thin atmosphere, and wrapping about their rocky proportions the mists of valley and river—but there are luxuriant fields and pleasant villages, and white church-spires, gleaming through the green foliage of oak and elm—and wide forests of Nature's richest coloring, and green hills sloping smoothly and gracefully to the margin of the clear, bright stream, which moves onward to the Ocean, as lightly and gracefully as the moving of a cloud at sunset, when the light wind which propels the ærial voyager is unfelt on earth.

It was on the margin of this stream, during the early times of Massachusetts, that a stranger—a foreigner of considerable fortune—took up his residence. He had a house, constructed from a model of his own which, for elegance and convenience, far surpassed the rude and simple tenements of his neighbors; and he had a small farm, or rather garden, which he seemed to cultivate for amusement, rather than from any absolute necessity of labor. He had no family, save a daughter—an interesting girl of sixteen.

Near the dwelling of Adam McOrne—for such was the stranger's name—lived old Alice Knight—a woman, known throughout the whole valley of the river, from Plum Island to the residence of the Sachem

Passaconaway, on the Nashua,—as one under an evil influence—an ill-tempered and malignant old woman—who was seriously suspected of dealing with the Prince of Darkness. Many of her neighbors were ready to make oath that they had been haunted by old Alice, in the shape of a black cat—that she had taken off the wheels of their hay-carts and frozen down their sled-runners, when the team was in full motion—that she had bewitched their swine, and rendered their cattle unruly—nay, more than one good wife averred, that she had bewitched their churns and prevented the butter from forming; and that they could expel her in no other way, than by heating a horse-nail and casting it into the cream. Moreover, they asserted that when this method of exorcism was resorted to, they invariably learned, soon after, that goodwife Alice was suffering under some unknown indisposition. In short, it would be idle to attempt a description of the almost innumerable feats of witchcraft ascribed to the withered and decrepid Alice.

Her exterior was indeed well calculated to favor the idea of her supernatural qualifications. She had the long, blue and skinny finger—the elvish locks of gray and straggling hair—the hooked nose, and the long, upturned chin, which seemed perpetually to threaten its nasal neighbor—the blue lips drawn around a mouth, garnished with two or three unearthly-looking fangs—the bleared and sunken eye—the bowed and attenuated form—and the limping gait, as if the invisible fetters of the Evil One were actually clogging the footsteps of his servant. Then, too, she was poor—poor as the genius of poverty itself—she had no relatives about her—no friends—her hand was against every man, and every man's hand was against her.

Setting the question of her powers of witchcraft aside, Alice Knight was actually an evil-hearted woman. Whether the suspicions and the taunts of her neighbors had aroused into action those evil passions which slumber in the seldom-visited depths of the human heart—or, whether the mortifications of poverty and dependence had changed and perverted her proud spirit—certain it was, that she took advantage of the credulity and fears of her neighbors. When they in the least offended her, she turned upon them with the fierce malison of an enraged Pythoness, and prophesied darkly of some unknown and indescribable evil about to befall them. And, consequently, if any evil *did* befall them in the space of a twelve-month afterward, another mark was added to the already black list of iniquities, which was accredited to the ill-favored Alice.

With all her fierce and deep-rooted hatred of the human species—one solitary affection—one feeling of kindness, yet lingered in the bosom of Alice Knight. Her son—a young man of twenty-five—her only child—seemed to form the sole and last link of the chain which had once bound her to humanity. Her love of him partook of the fierce passions of her nature—it was wild, ungovernable and strong as her hate itself.

Gilbert Knight inherited little from his mother, save a portion of her indomitable pride and fierce temperament. He had been a seaman—had visited many of the old lands, and had returned again to his birth-place—a grown up man—with a sun-burned cheek—a fine and noble figure, and a countenance rude and forbidding, yet marked with a character of intellect and conscious power. He had little intercourse with his mother—he refused even to reside in the same dwelling with her—and yet, when in her presence, he was respectful, and even indulgent to her singular disposition and unsocial habits. He had no communion with the inhabitants of his native town—but, stern, unsocial and gloomy, he held himself apart from the sympathies and fellowship of men, with whom indeed, he had few feelings in common.

Mary, the daughter of Adam McOrne, seemed alone to engage the attention of Gilbert Knight. She was young, beautiful, and, considering the condition of the country, well-educated. She naturally felt herself superior to the rude and hard-featured youth around her—she had tasted enough of the sentiment, and received enough of the polish of education, to raise her ideas, at least, above the ignorant and unlettered rustics, who sought her favor.

Despised and spurned at, as the mother of Gilbert Knight was, still her son always commanded respect. There was something in the dignity of his manner, and the fierce flash of his dark eye, which had a powerful influence on all in his presence. Then, too, it was remembered that his father was a man of intellect and family—that he was once wealthy—and had suddenly met with reverses of fortune. These considerations gave Gilbert Knight no little consequence in his native village; and Adam McOrne, who ridiculed the idea of witches and witchcraft, received the occasional visits of Gilbert with as much cordiality as if his mother had never been suspected of evil doings. He was pleased with the frank, bold bearing of the sailor; and with his evident preference of his dwelling, above that of his neighbors—never so much as dreaming, that the visits of Gilbert were paid to any other than himself.

It was a cold, dark night of Autumn, that Gilbert, after leaving the hospitable fire-side of McOrne, directed his steps to the rude and lonely dwelling of his mother. He found the old woman alone;—a few sticks of ignited wood cast a faint light upon the dismal apartment—and an old and blear-eyed cat was at her side, gazing earnestly at her unseemly countenance.

"Mother," said Gilbert, seating himself, "'tis idle—'tis worse than folly to dream of executing our project. Mary McOrne will never be my wife."

"Ha!" exclaimed Alice, fixing her hollow eye upon her son—"Have I not told you that it *should* be so, and *must* be? You have lost your courage; you have become weaker than a woman, Gilbert. I tell you that Mary McOrne loves you, as deeply, as passionately as ever man was loved by woman!"

Gilbert started. "I do believe she loves me," he said at length, "but she will never be my wife. She dreads an alliance with our family. She has said so—she has this night solemnly averred that she had rather die at once, than become the daughter-in-law of—of"—Gilbert hesitated.

"Of a witch!" shrieked Alice, in a voice so loud and shrill that it even startled the practiced ear of Gilbert. "'Tis well—I will not be stigmatised as a witch with impunity. That haughty Scotchman and his impudent brat of a daughter shall learn that Alice Knight is not to be insulted in this manner! Gilbert, you shall marry her, or she shall die accursed!"

"Mother!" said Gilbert, rising and fixing his dark eye keenly on that of his mother—"I understand your threat; and I warn you to beware. Practice your infernal tricks upon others as you please—but Mary McOrne is too pure and sacred for such unhallowed dealing; and as you dread the curses of your son, let her not be molested."

He turned away as he ceased speaking, and instantly left the dwelling. He had seen little of his mother for many years—he knew her disposition but imperfectly; and, while in public he ridiculed the idea of her supernatural powers, he yet felt an awe—a fear in her presence—a certainty that she was not like those around her. He knew that the breath of her displeasure operated to appearance like a curse—that she *did*, either by natural cunning, or supernatural power, mysteriously distress and perplex her neighbors. He saw that her proud spirit had been touched; and that she meditated evil against McOrne and his daughter. The latter, Gilbert really loved—as deeply and devotedly as such a rude spirit could love; and he shuddered at the idea of her subjection to the arts of his mother. He therefore resolved to press his suit once more, and endeavor to overcome the objections which the girl had raised; and, in the event of his failure to do so, to protect her from the wrath of his mother.

But Mary McOrne—much as she loved the dark-eyed stranger, and his tales of peril and shipwreck in other climes—could not associate herself with the son of a witch—the only surviving offspring of a woman, whom she verily believed to be the bond slave of the Tempter. And so she strove with the strong feeling of affection within her—and Gilbert Knight was rejected.

A short time after, the tenants of the dwelling of McOrne were alarmed by strange sounds and unusual appearances. In the dead of the night they would hear heavy footsteps ascending the stair case, with the clank of a chain—and groans issued from the unoccupied rooms of the building. The doors were mysteriously opened, after having been carefully secured— the curtains of the beds of McOrne and his daughter were drawn aside by an unseen hand; and low whispers of blasphemy and licentiousness, which a spirit of evil, could only have suggested, were breathed, as it were, into their very ears. The servants—a male and female—alike complained of preternatural visitations and unseemly visions. They were disturbed in their daily avocations—the implements of household labor were snatched away by an invisible hand—they saw strange lights in the neighborhood of the dwelling. They heard an unearthly music in the chimney; and saw the furniture of the room dancing about, as if moving to the infernal melody. In short, the fact was soon established, beyond the interposition of a doubt, that *the house was haunted.*

The days of faery are over. The tale of enchantment—the legend of ghostly power—of unearthly warning and supernatural visitation, have lost their hold on the minds of the great multitude. People sleep quietly where they are placed—no matter by what means they have reached the end of their journey—and there is an end to the church-yard rambles of discontented ghosts—

> ————"That creep
> From out the places where they sleep—
> To publish forth some hidden sin,
> Or drink the ghastly moonshine in,"—

And as for witches, the race is extinct—or, if a few yet remain, they are a miserable libel upon the diabolical reputation of those who figured in the

days of Paris and Mather. Haunted houses are getting to be novelties—
and corpse-lights and apparitions and unearthly noises, and signs and
omens and wonders, are no longer troublesome. Ours is a matter-of-fact
age—an age of steam and railway and McAdamization and labor-saving
machinery—the poetry of Time has gone by forever, and we have only the
sober prose left us.

Among the superstitions of our ancestors, that of Haunted Houses is
not the least remarkable. There is scarcely a town or village in New-
England which has not, at some period or other of its history, had one or
more of these ill-fated mansions. They were generally old, decayed buildings—untenanted, save by the imaginary demons, who there held their
midnight revels. But there are many instances of "prestigious spirits" who
were impudent enough to locate themselves in houses, where the hearth-
stone had not yet grown cold—where the big bible yet lay on the parlor-
table; and where, over Indian-pudding and pumpkin-pie, the good man of
the mansion always craved a blessing; where the big arm chair was always
officiously placed for the minister of the parish, whenever he favored the
family with the light of his countenance; and where the good lady taught
her children the Catechism every Saturday evening. This was indeed, a bold
act of effrontery on the part of the Powers of Evil, yet it was accounted
for on the ground, that good men and true were sometimes given over to
the buffetings of the enemy, of which fact, the case of Job was considered
ample proof.

The visitations to the house of McOrne became more frequent and
more terrific. The unfortunate Mary suffered severely. She fully believed in
the supernatural character of the sights and sounds which alarmed her;
and she looked upon old Alice Knight as the author: especially after hearing a whisper in her ear, in the darkness of midnight, that, unless she married Gilbert Knight she should be haunted as long as she lived. As for the
father, he battled long and manfully with the fears which were strengthened day by day—he laughed at the strange noises which filled his mansion, and ridiculed the fears of his daughter—but it was easy to see that
his strong mind was shaken by the controlling superstitions of the time;
and he yielded slowly to the belief, which had now extended itself through
the neighborhood, that his dwelling was under the immediate influence of
demoniac agency.

Many were the experiments tried throughout the neighborhood for the
discovery of the witch. The old, experienced grand-mothers gathered to-

gether almost every evening for consultation, and divers and multiform were the plans devised for counteracting the designs of Satan. All admitted that Alice Knight must be the witch, but unfortunately there was no positive proof of the fact. All the charms and forms of exorcism which were then believed to be potent weapons for the overthrowing of the powers of Wickedness having failed, it was finally settled among the good ladies that the minister of the parish could alone drive the evil spirits from the dwelling of their neighbor. But Adam McOrne was a sinful man; and his oaths had been louder than his prayers on this trying occasion: and, when it was proposed to him to invite the godly parson to his house, for the purpose of laying the spirits that troubled it, he swore fiercely, that rather than have his threshold darkened by the puritan priest, he would see his dwelling converted into the Devil's ball-room, and thronged with all the evil spirits on the face of the earth or beneath it. And, with shaking heads and prophetic visages, the good women left the perverse Scotchman to his fate.

Notwithstanding his bold exterior, the heart of Adam McOrne was daily failing within him. The wild, nursery tales of his childhood came back to him with painful distinctness—and the bogle and kelpie and dwarfish Brownie of his native land, rose fearfully before his imagination. His evenings were lonely and long; and he resolved to invite Gilbert Knight—the fierce sailor, who feared neither man nor fiend—to take up his residence with him: in the firm belief that no power, human or superhuman, could shake the nerves of a man, who had wrestled with the tempest upon every sea; and who had braved death in the red battle, when his shattered deck was slippery with blood and piled with human corses.

Gilbert obeyed the summons of McOrne with pleasure. He had heard the strange stories of the haunted mansion, which were upon every lip in the vicinity; and he felt perfectly convinced that his mother was employed in disturbing the domestic quiet of the Scotchman and his daughter—whether by natural means, or otherwise, he knew not. But he knew her revengeful disposition, and he feared, that unless her schemes were boldly interfered with, she would succeed in irreparably injuring the health and minds of her victims. Besides, he trusted that, should he succeed in accomplishing his purpose and laying the evil spirits of the mansion, he should effectually secure to himself the gratitude of both father and daughter.

Gilbert was received with much cordiality by Adam McOrne. "Ye may weel ken," said the old gentleman, "that I am no the least afeared o' a' this clishmaclaver, o' evil speerits, or deils or witch-hags; but my daughter, puir lassie, she's in an awsome way—a' the time shakin' wi' fear o' wraiths and witches and sic like ill-faured cattle." And Adam McOrne made an endeavor to look unconcerned and resolute in the presence of his guest, as he thus disclaimed any feeling of alarm on his own part. He could not bear that the bold sailor should look upon his weakness.

Even Mary McOrne welcomed the presence of her discarded lover. Yet, while she clung to him as to her only protector, she shuddered at the thought that Gilbert was the son of her evil tormentor—nay more, the horrible suspicion would at times steal over her that he had himself prompted his wicked parent to haunt her and terrify her into an acquiescence with his wishes. But, when she heard his frank and manly proposal to watch all night in a chamber, where the strange sights and sounds were most frequent, she could not but trust that her suspicion was ill-founded, and that in Gilbert Knight she should find a friend and a protector.

Adam McOrne, secretly overjoyed at the idea of having a sentinel in his dwelling, ordered a fire to be kindled in the suspected chamber; and placing a decanter of spirits on the table, he bade his guest good night, and left him to the loneliness of the haunted apartment.

It matters not now what thoughts passed through the mind of Gilbert, as he sat silent and alone, gazing on the glowing embers before him. That his mother was engaged in a strange and dark purpose, in regard to the family of McOrne, he was fully convinced—and he resolved to unravel the mystery of her midnight adventures, and relieve the feelings of the Scotchman and his daughter—even, although in so doing he should implicate his own mother, in guilty and malicious designs.

The old family clock struck one. At that moment a deep groan sounded fearfully through the room.—Gilbert rose to his feet and listened earnestly. It seemed to proceed from the room beneath him; and it was repeated several times, until it died away, like the last murmurs of one in the agonies of death. In a few moments he heard footsteps on the stair case ascending to a long, narrow passage at its head, which communicated with his apartment.

"I will know the cause of this," said Gilbert, mentally, as he threw open the door, and sprang into the passage. A figure attempted to glide past him, appareled in white, uttering, as it did so, a deep and hollow groan.

"Mortal or devil!" shouted Gilbert, springing forward and grasping the figure by the arm—"you go no further. Speak, witch, ghost, whatever you are—declare your errand!"

The figure struggled violently, but the iron grasp of Gilbert remained unshaken. At that moment the hurried voice of the old Scotchman sounded through the passage.

"Haud weel, haud weel, my braw lad; dinna let go your grip—in God's name haud weel!"

"Let me go," said the figure in a hoarse whisper—"Let me go, or you are a dead man!" Gilbert retained his hold, and endeavored to discover by the dim light which streamed from his apartment, the countenance of the speaker.

"Die, then, unnatural wretch!" shrieked the detected Alice, snatching a knife from her bosom, and aiming a furious stab at her son. Gilbert pressed his hand to his side, and staggered backward, exclaiming, as the features of his mother, now fully revealed, glared madly upon him—

"Woman, you have murdered your son!"

The knife dropped from the hand of Alice, and with a loud and almost demoniac shriek, she sprang down the stair case and vanished like a spectre.

Adam McOrne hurried forward, the moment he saw the white figure disappear, and followed Gilbert into his apartment. "Are ye hurt?—are ye wraith-smitten?" asked the Scotchman; and then, as his eye fell on the bloodied dress of Gilbert, he exclaimed—"Waes me—ye are a' streakit wi' bluid—ye are a dead man!"

Gilbert felt that his wound was severe, but with his usual presence of mind, he gave such directions to McOrne and his daughter, as to enable them to prevent the rapid effusion of blood, while a servant was despatched for the nearest physician. Mary McOrne seemed to forget the weakness of her sex, while she ministered to her wounded lover with a quick eye and a skillful hand. It is on occasions like this—when even the strong nerves of manhood are shaken—that the feeble hand of woman is often most efficient. In the hour of excitement and turmoil, the spirit of manly daring may blaze out, with sudden and terrible power—but in the deep trials of suffering humanity—in the watchings by the bed of affliction—then it is that the courage of woman predominates—the very excess of her sympathy sustains her.

The arrival of the physician dissipated in some degree the fears of

McOrne and his daughter. The wound of Gilbert was not considered as dangerous; and he was assured that a few days of confinement would be the only ill consequence resulting from it. The kind hearted Scotchman and his kinder hearted daughter watched by his bed until morning, at which time Gilbert was enabled to explain the singular circumstances of the night; and at the same time he expressed a wish that McOrne should visit the dwelling of his mother, who, he feared would resort to some violence upon herself, in the belief that she had, in her frantic passion, murdered her son.

Adam McOrne, convinced by the narration of Gilbert that human ingenuity and malice, instead of demoniac agency, had disturbed his dwelling, sallied out early in the morning to the rude and crazy dwelling of his tormentor.

He found the door open—and on entering, the first object that met his view was the form of Alice Knight, lying on the floor, insensible and motionless. He spoke to her, but she answered not—he lifted her arm, and it fell back with a dead weight upon her side.—She was dead—whether by terror or suicide, he knew not. "Ugh!" said Adam McOrne, in relating the discovery—"there she was—an ill-faured creature—a' cauld and ghaistly, lookin' for a' the world as if she wad hae thankit any Christian soul to hae gie'n her a decent burial."

She was buried the next day in the small garden adjoining her dwelling, for the good people of the neighborhood could not endure the idea of her reposing in their own quiet grave-yard. The minister of the parish indeed attended her funeral, and made a few general remarks upon the enormity of witchcraft and the exceeding craftiness of the great necromancer and magician, who had ensnared the soul of the ill-fated Alice—but when he ventured to pray for the repose of the unhappy woman, more than one of his hearers shook their heads, in the belief that even their own goodly minister had no right to interfere with the acknowledged property of the Enemy.

It is said that Alice did not sleep peaceably, nathless the prayers of the minister. Her house was often lighted up in the dead of the night, until

"Through ilka bore the flames were glancing,"

and the wild and unearthly figure of the old woman herself, crossed more than once the paths of the good people of the neighborhood. At least, such is the story, and it is not our present purpose to dispute it.

The manner in which old Alice contrived to perplex the Scotchman and his daughter, was at length revealed by the disclosures of the servants of the family. They had been persuaded by the old woman to aid her in the strange transactions—partly from an innate love of mischief, and partly from a pique against the worthy Scotchman, whose irritable temperament had more than once discovered itself in the unceremonious collision of his cane with the heads and shoulders of his domestics.

Gilbert recovered rapidly of his wound: and a few months after, the house, which had been given over to the evil powers, as the revelling-place of demons, was brilliantly illuminated for a merry bridal. And the rough, bold sailor, as the husband of Mary McOrne, settled down into a quiet, industrious and sober-minded citizen. Adam McOrne lived to a good old age, stoutly denying to the last that he had ever admitted the idea of witchcraft, and laughing, heartily as before, at the superstitions and credulity of his neighbors.

THREE NIGHTS
IN A HAUNTED HOUSE

J. Warren Newcomb, Jr.

I do not pretend to give, in my rendering of the following strange story, either the manner or the language in which my friend related it as we sat through the long night, he speaking and I listening. I cannot reproduce his manner. I have forgotten his words. I tell the tale in the first person, because that form of narrative gives more effect to its horrible features, and the horror that is in it constitutes, to my mind, its chief value and interest. As for its truth, I can only vouch for my friend's ordinary and usual accuracy of statement. Here is his story:

Several years since, just after Death had been fearfully busy in our family, sundering tie after tie, and leaving this world almost too dismal for existence, my only remaining sister and I resolved to leave New-York for a time, and to seek in the far country that peace of which familiar sights and sounds deprived us. We sought neither fashionable watering-place nor crowded mountain-tops, but rather some secluded village, where there were none to know or disturb us, and where we might possibly gather our shattered lives together again and prepare for the work of the world that still lay in the long track of the life-pilgrimage before us.

With this intent I went to Vermont, and pursuing my search with little other purpose than a vague longing for retirement, selected as our abiding-place a small village, hemmed in by mountains, and silent, save what babble was made by a stream that ran darkly and furiously down between rocky borders. On every hand, beyond the narrow valley, a giant growth of pines frowned upon the place, and above the pines there stood up against the sky rugged and gray rocks, around which in times of tempest the lightnings seemed to play as by right. It was a dreary place, that seemed to have been overlooked and forgotten by the great world without.

'This,' I said, 'is the place we seek. In its strange apathy and silence we will sleep away the sorrow that possesses us!' The very air and spirit of the spot were akin to my feelings and my grief.

I learned that there was a house to let a short distance from the long street that formed the village. This house had been some time without a tenant, and was to be had at a low rent. Finding the agent for the property, I learned that the owner resided in a distant State, and that the building, though somewhat out of repair, could readily be put in a habitable condition. With the agent I walked up the avenue leading to the mansion, to ascertain by personal examination whether his tale were all exaggeration. I found a high, square, red brick building of two and a half stories, standing in the midst of a waste of overgrown, neglected lawn and garden, with a few shambling out-houses in the rear. The fences had fallen to decay; there were no blinds to the tall and narrow windows; no cornice to relieve the bare and blank aspect of the walls. The chimneys stood up stiff and straight, with no warmth of homely smoke rising from their black throats; all was desolate, dreary and uninviting. Still, the house had an air of faded respectability, and seemed to wear even its thread-bare decay with a certain pride. It was like some men we see—poor fellows in mouldy and ragged clothing who 'have seen better days.' 'It cost more to build it,' the agent said, 'than any two houses in town.'

'It is just the place,' I thought: 'my soul is in unison with its desolation and decay.' As we stood gazing up at its exterior, a solitary crow flapped slowly overhead, and turning its eyes down upon us, gave one cracked and doleful croak, and then passed on.

We entered the building, and passed through it from cellar to garret. It had once been a fine house. The rooms were high, the hall broad, the stairs of easy ascent. In the kitchen was a wide and deep fireplace, in which hung an old-fashioned iron 'crane.' The last occupants had left behind them a broad, high-backed settle, upon which doubtless, in years gone by, there had been no little tender love-making. The hearth-stone was a large slab of white marble. I noticed it particularly on account of an unsightly crack across its centre.

Beside the kitchen, there were, on the lower floor, a large dining-room, two parlors with folding-doors, and a room opening into both kitchen and hall, in the rear of the dining-room, which, though small, would accommodate my desk, a study-table, and the few books I should bring with me. This room opened into the hall directly at the foot of the broad stair-way.

Through the centre of the house, from front to rear, ran the hall, and the solid stair-case, with a heavy mahogany balustrade, rose evenly and gently to the second story. The rooms on the second floor corresponded in size and position to those below, and there was over all a large and lofty garret, lighted by half-windows. One portion of this space was partitioned off, and it struck me that my guide slightly shuddered as he turned the key in the lock to the chamber thus formed. Indeed he had made a feeble attempt to ignore its existence, but I insisted upon seeing the entire house. There was nothing remarkable about the room, excepting a portrait in oil of a thin, dark-featured old man, that hung upon the wall. It was poorly done, and yet it had a certain life about it difficult to describe. You have met just such old men in the streets hundreds of times, I dare say, and passed them with an involuntary feeling of dislike and dread; some faces, after many years, gather so much of the Satanic in their expression.

'Who was that?' I asked.

'An old man who lived here years ago,' the agent said.

'Was he not insane?'

'I believe so,' the man said shortly, and then he rather hastily closed the door, and we descended to the ground floor.

The house was damp and mouldy from long disease. Dust was piled every where, and there was a silence not known to human habitations. We seemed, indeed, to be the only living things that had disturbed this deathly silence for long years. Even the spiders had died from want of prey, and their forsaken webs fluttered tenantless in the corners, or hung from the ceilings in dingy and useless festoons.

Before we parted, I had hired this dismal house for a year. Several weeks were occupied in getting it into a habitable state, a feat finally accomplished by the agent, aided by half the old women in the village. Then we brought up such furniture as we needed for the kitchen, dining-room and study, and for three bed-rooms on the second floor, our maid-servant positively refusing to sleep in 'that lonesome garret.'

I consider it somewhat remarkable, that in all the time from my hiring the place to our finally moving into it, no one in the village had even so much as hinted that it was haunted, or given us a single clue to the awful mystery that hung around it. Some knowledge they had, I know, of the terrible tragedy long ago enacted there, although they were not acquainted with its entirety as I so fearfully became.

Do you believe in clairvoyance? in spiritualism? or in the power of the soul during sleep to receive intelligence denied to it while awake? Can you tell what sleep is; what dreams are, or in how much a life separate from the body is permitted to the soul, under certain circumstances, before death? Or how far disembodied spirits have the power to haunt old scenes and reproduce old actions, so that living men, influenced by the dead, shall say: 'The place is haunted'? The speculation is extensive, never-ending. Every man has read and heard of ghosts, witches and hobgoblins. Listen and you shall hear what befell me, living, breathing, sober and sceptical.

We entered our new home on a cold and gloomy Friday in November. The rain fell in torrents from the leaden clouds, and the wind soughed and moaned through the dreary pine forest. Naught was to be seen from the windows but dark mountains and dull sky, and within was little to cheer us by its contrast. Fires had been lighted in all the rooms. On the kitchen-hearth a great pile of logs roared defiance to the blast, and yet there was a certain cheerlessness and chilliness about the place that no artificial warmth seemed able to dispel. My sister Alice trembled and shivered as we entered, and when we sat together after tea, soberly discussing our simple plans for the year's life before us, she pressed close to my side, glancing timidly now and again about the room.

After she had placed a lamp upon my study-table and kindly taken down one or two old favorites from the book-case for my possible necessities, she turned to kiss me 'good night,' and placing a hand upon my shoulder, said in a low and fearful voice: 'Henry, what if the place is haunted!'

I had not thought of that before. What if it were? Well, we had no reason to fear the power of evil; of all others, my sister had least cause, and so I told her as cheerfully as I could. But still, after she was gone, the thought clung to me: 'What if the house *were* haunted!'

I banished the thought, and taking up a book, was soon lost in the quiet past. Thus I read until the kitchen clock had struck eleven, when I closed the volume, and passing up the stairs to my bed-room, was soon asleep.

        ✻   ✻   ✻   ✻   ✻   ✻

It was singular that in my dream I should know that old man so well: a hard-featured, mean-spirited, and thoroughly selfish wretch, with more intellect than feeling, and not too much of either. It was strange that I should so thoroughly, and yet so briefly, have knowledge of all his past life, all his petty meannesses, his lusts, his sordid selfishness. It was passing strange that I should become so incorporated into the very essence of his soul that I discerned even the minute gradations by which he changed from an innocent child to the evil thing I saw him. It will be fearful if, at the Day of Judgment, men's souls shall be so laid bare to the souls of other men!

This old man, in my dream, had saved and scraped together money, little by little, till at length his sole labor was to increase by usury and careful speculation the wealth he had amassed. He had a certain pride, too, and he built this gaunt, brick house and buried himself in it—buried himself with an ancient house-keeper as miserly as himself. From day to day this pair vegetated, unwholesome human fungi, dry and useless excrescences on life.

Vegetated thus, till there came one day a letter, edged with black, informing the miser that a very wealthy kinsman, dying a widower, had designated him as guardian to his only child and heiress. Thus it came that a dark-haired beauty glided, calm and self-possessed, into the mazes of my dream. She was haughty, and of a commanding presence, with large hands and feet, great length of limb and an imperial bust. Fond of dress, of rich food, and, I fear, of wine. Not particularly given to lovers, too self-reliant and too proud for that.

They were an odd family, and it will seem strange to you that she should have desired to remain under her guardian's roof during even the few months that were wanting to her majority. It was not strange to me, though, who saw the pleasure she took in making the old man cringe before her haughtiness, and in humbling the pride of the ancient house-keeper.

I saw in my dream all the ward's scorn for the guardian; all the guardian's hatred of the ward. I saw, also, the glitter of his wicked eyes when her lovely arms wore bracelets heavier than common, or jewels of rare brilliancy flashed in her hair or heaved upon her bosom. As for the house-keeper, she loved and hated with her master. It was a pleasant household during those few months—a lovely household and cheerful to contemplate! So much so, that in the contemplation—with all the varying emotions of its members laid bare before me—I grew quite weary, and longed to recover the individuality I seemed to have strangely lost.

The months glided swiftly on, and the time for her final departure drew nigh. As it came nearer, I saw that the old man's eyes glittered more and more as he gazed at her, and that within his soul a dark and terrible purpose was beginning to be formed. I followed its growth, day by day, as in the French models one follows the chick, as, change after change, it progresses during incubation from the formless germ to the young bird that finally chips the shell. Thus there was growing in the miser's soul a dreadful form of evil. It took no step backward, but ever increased in outline and strength, until it grew ready for the hatching.

Presently the day came preceding that fixed upon for her departure. There was a strange and unusual gayety upon her that day. She laughed and sang bits of songs as she tramped about the house. She had the step of a grenadier, this full blown beauty, and never tripped daintily as slighter and more fairy-like women do.

As for the miser, he was a smouldering passion all the day. The chick in his breast was pecking at the shell, vigorous and ripe for the hatching. And the house-keeper, with a strange intuition of her master's purpose, hovered near him all day long, her face working with an agitation she strove in vain to control, and her nerves strung to the highest pitch of human endurance.

So the day passed. At dinner, and at the supper-table, the heiress was in the fullest flow of spirits. She took a whim, too, to wear some of her most brilliant ornaments on this last day, and the rings on her fingers, the pendants in her ears, the broach upon her bosom, shone with more than usual lustre. Fastened artfully in her hair, so that they only here and there peeped out from among the dark braids, was a string of large and perfect pearls. At all these things, and at the lovely woman who adorned them, the miser gazed with evil in his eyes, and the house-keeper silently nerved herself for what was to come.

So the day passed, and at night the maiden stood within her chamber completing her preparations for the morrow's journey. On the toilet-table beside her reposed the silver-bound casket in which she kept her jewelry. What she had worn that day lay with the rest, save only the pearls which still swam in the waves of her dark hair.

Thus far I dreamed, when a terrible night-mare took possession of me. I fancied two figures creeping through the night. From his chamber in the garret crawled the miser in stocking-footed stillness. He carried no light, but in one hand gleamed a long and cruel knife. From the cellar, where she had all the evening crouched like a venomous reptile, came the house-keeper. Beneath her apron she held fast to some heavy object. I knew that the steps of both were bent toward the chamber of the beautiful and un-conscious girl.

My personal identity was now so far restored that I longed to fly to her and warn her of the danger, but I was bound by the horrible bonds of night-mare, and could stir neither hand nor foot. I felt, now, that this was all a dream, yet the cruel agony of witnessing that murderous approach upon innocence and beauty, without the power to avert the coming blow, drove me nearly frantic. I strained and tugged at the bonds of the demon who held me, and at length, with a cry that must have sounded far beyond the house, I awoke!

The damp, gray dawn was peering in at the windows. Dimly and half-awake—as I lay for a second or two motionless on my bed, the fearful passages of my last night's dream still fresh in my aching brain—I gazed with an unquiet apprehension about the chamber, half-expecting to see the tall and voluptuous beauty disrobing before the mirror. Then I remembered it was only a dream, and blessed God that it was so.

These emotions passed rapidly away, and I was soon aware of quick footsteps hurrying toward my chamber. Arising hastily, I slipped on my pantaloons and hastened to the door. My sister Alice stood there, her face very white and her hands crossed flutteringly on her bosom.

'Oh! what a shriek!' whispered she. 'Did you hear it, Henry? It sounded so fearfully through the house. Oh! I know it's haunted! I am *sure* it's haunted!'

'It was only I,' I said; 'I was troubled with an awful dream, and in break-ing from it I cried out!'

'Oh! Dear,' the poor girl whimpered, 'I am so afraid to stay here, I am indeed! It is so lonely and so gloomy. Hear how it rains; I don't believe the sun ever shines here. Listen! what is that?'

'Nothing,' I said; 'I hear nothing.'

'Ah! well, but I heard it in the night. I lay awake and I heard something creeping, and creeping down the stair-way from the garret—I *know* I did! And then I felt that it was passing my door toward your chamber, and then came that horrid scream!'

What could I say but that the poor child, rendered nervous by her late griefs, was grown full of woman's fancies? What could I say but that it was nothing? This I said, but still Alice was not convinced. She was certain she had heard *something*, and that was sufficient to drive her half-crazy for the day.

After an early breakfast, for no one thought of sleep again that day, Bridget favored us with a lengthy address, on the subject of a banshee hereditary in her family. She concluded by stating that she was a poor orphan, with an old mother in Ireland, and that she could n't think of bringing trouble upon us along with the family ghost. After which she brought her trunk down to the lower hall and departed for the village.

I believed no more in ghosts before I entered that house than I did in a personal and substantial Devil, going up and down the world like a roaring lion; but this testimony, in addition to my strange dream, somewhat staggered me, and I caught myself repeating: 'What if the place *is* haunted!'

It made me nervous and unstable for a time; I could neither read, write, think nor converse. Bridget's sudden departure, entirely aside from our house-keeping and domestic arrangements, rendered the loneliness of the place yet more appalling.

Outside, the rain still fell with a heavy slant against the windows, and the sky was of the color of lead; within, the great fires still waged an unequal combat with the dampness and desolation of the rooms. Unable to bear up against the dreary influences of the scene, my sister Alice at length sat down in mute despair and gave herself up to a fit of silent weeping.

Fortunately, just when our spirits were at the lowest, a lumbering stage-coach drove up to the door, and my kind-hearted aunt Cherrystone clambered heavily out. Here was really and truly an acquisition. She had come, she said, to help set things to rights at our commencement at house-keeping, and she meant to stay with us a week, at least. That we were glad to see her, I need not say, and we quickly made her as comfortable as circumstances would permit.

She was a companionable and lively person usually, but even on her the blight of this cursed house seemed to fall as she crossed its threshold. Even her elasticity of spirit was not proof against the drip of the dreary rain and the soughing of the east wind in the pines.

It was a cold, damp house, she said; not a home-like place at all. Very lonesome and dismal, she thought, to live in. Did we believe that houses were ever haunted?

Haunted! Alice had said the same thing when we first entered it. That was not so strange, but that this aunt of ours, generally so free from thoughts of fearful things, should be filled with the same idea. Still I had little faith in either ghosts or dreams.

The day passed very slowly and rather sadly, the rain never ceasing, the fires never warming the damp house, the dreariness never lifting from off it. The day passed slowly and cheerlessly, and night came on again—night and sleep.

*   *   *   *   *   *

The proud girl, disrobing slowly in her chamber, laid off her outer garments and stepped before the mirror for a moment to admire the gloss and heaviness of the dark hair ere she loosened its fastenings and let down its raven beauty to the night. One large, plump hand, white and lovely as ever was kissed, she plunged into the maze of braided locks, and turning this way and that, regarded the black and white contrast in the glass. Black hair, lustrous and beautiful, and soft, milky-white hand, half-hidden in the blackness, she stood gazing upon for an instant. Then she raised the other hand toward her head, and suddenly stood petrified with a momentary and terrible fear!

She saw in the mirror the figure of an old man standing in the doorway! It was her guardian, with an unholy and baleful light in his devilish eyes, pausing at the entrance to her chamber!

I cannot describe the majesty of her slow turning toward the door. No words can fitly tell with what stern grandeur she swept her round, white arm in one great gesture of rebuke, contempt and command. Standing with heaving breast and pointing finger, slowly bidding the beast begone, no language of mine can tell how queenly she was, nor how much a beast was the intruder.

But what if he will not go? She does not think of that. She feels the force of her own strong nature, and proudly and fiercely casts on him an imperious rebuke. But with the man at the door her rebuffs go but a little way. He clutches more firmly the knife that he has thrust into his sleeve, and advances a step into the chamber. She feels, with a sickness almost too terrible to be borne, that his nature is as hard as her own, and tougher by all the difference of age and sex. Then for a brief second of time she sinks into a great faintness, but rallies bravely, clutching at the toilet-table beside her.

Is there no weapon in the room? Eagerly examining the apartment, she can discern no implement ready to her hand. Ah! how she longs for one of those handy stilettoes with which jealous Spanish dames are said sometimes to meet their lovers or their rivals! How she longs for any thing with which to repel this hideous old man, whose purpose shines in his eyes.

Robbery, beyond a doubt! Are there not jewels here rare enough to tempt the miser, who loses his ward to-morrow?

He has brooded over it day after day, till his poor and greedy soul has become filled with this single idea. Why did she so bedeck herself, so flaunt in her precious gems, each one setting off those yet more priceless, yet more to be coveted charms. Ah! why, in very wantonness did she tempt the old man with a wealth of which he could never honestly become the possessor?

Day after day he has brooded over it, and the fell purpose, slowly growing beneath the heat of his withered breast, has hatched the foulest of mid-night birds this night.

So he strides another step into the room.

She stood for an instant like one frozen, and then her great womanly fear—now that the man had shown his carelessness for her commands—overcoming her, she whispered with whitening lips: 'What do you seek here?'

He could not answer for a moment, and when he did, his voice was thick and uneven, and he shook from head to foot. It is no matter what he said. The queenly woman stood now in queenly wrath, and gave him back scorn for his insults, daring him with rash anger to lay his hand upon her.

And all this time, crouching just outside the door, like a cat watching for prey, the house-keeper, who had crept there from her hole in the cellar, lay in wait.

Then the old man advanced another step into the room—and another—and another, till he stood directly in front of the woman, his purpose glittering yet more fiercely in his eyes and illuminating every feature.

Then, in my dream, I heard her beg him, by his old love for her dead father, by his respect for what was holy and of good repute, to spare her. Yet he stood with a hard smile on his thin lips, trembling but cruelly determined, and would not hearken to her prayer.

It had not as yet occurred to her to use any physical strength against the man. She, who could have throttled him with that firm, white hand of hers, as easily almost as a cat chokes a mouse, had not yet arrived at the thought to do it. But when he approached in his mad folly close to her, she spurned him with a quick, vigorous blow that sent him reeling to the floor.

The knife dropped from his grasp as he fell, and the ring of it awoke in his heart that last, most cruel thought of murder. Gathering himself up, he seized the weapon and rushed upon the defenceless girl.

She was alone, with that fiend hacking at her with the knife! Would no one come to aid her? God give her strength for this most fearful and unequal contest!

He struck her at length, cutting a long, deep gash in her left arm.

Then the tiger in the woman was aroused, and with the look and snarl of a beast of prey, she threw herself upon him. Threw herself upon him with a fury that overbore all resistance, carrying him backward to the floor and sending his knife flying far across the room. Then kneeling upon him, she instinctively closed her white fingers about his throat till I could see the face growing purple and the tongue protruding.

Just at the instant when, in my dream, I savagely exulted over the terrible triumph of the girl, the figure outside the door stole swiftly in and swung aloft a heavy axe—

      *   *   *   *   *   *

Loud knocking, and my sister's voice at the door: 'For goodness' sake get up quickly, Henry, there is some one in the house!'

I arose hastily and opened the door. There stood my sister and aunt, trembling with affright.

'O Henry!' my sister said, 'we have heard such fearful noises in the house. Such woful sounds! I am sure some one has broken in upon us. There are burglars here, you may depend!'

Said my aunt: 'The house is haunted!'

Dressing ourselves as speedily as possible, we descended to the dining-room, where we lighted the lamps, and whence I made a careful search over the building. Windows and doors were all fast, and the only sound I heard was the dreary pelting of the rain and the perpetual murmur and sobbing of the wind in the pines. There was surely no one in the house.

Looking at my watch, I found the time to be about six o'clock, corresponding with my awaking the previous morning. I remembered my fearful visions distinctly, but forebore adding to the evident terror of the women by relating them. Sufficient unto them was the evil whereof they knew.

We ate no breakfast that morning, the uneasiness even of my aunt having deprived her of her usually good appetite. As for me, I was constantly repeating my two nights again, and dreaming those terrible dreams of Beauty and the Beast. We drew our chairs together near the kitchen hearth, and I piled great logs upon the glowing fire. The flames roared fiercely up the chimney and flashed a deep red lustre out into the room, but still the apartment wore a doleful look, and still the dreary and uncomfortable dampness hung about the house.

At length said my aunt: 'How much like a grave-stone this white marble hearth is; it should wear "In memory of" upon its surface.'

'Look!' my sister cried, 'the ashes have formed a Death's head near its centre, and an ugly crack divides it there!'

Surely a whimsical fancy might trace some likeness to the outlines of a skull in a little collection of ashes, whisked together by the draughts that wandered uncertainly about this strange house.

We left the kitchen and established ourselves in the dining-room. Toward noon my aunt brewed a dish of strong coffee, and I fetched a bottle of old Madeira from the cellar. Sipping the coffee and the wine, our spirits rose to that extent that we ventured to partake of a slender and cold dinner—the remains of our yesterday's provision. Shortly after the sun came forth, the clouds rolled away, and outside the house, at least, a certain cheerfulness began to prevail. The sun-shine was soon followed by my friend the agent, who knocked at the kitchen-door and then entered without a bidding. He came in quietly, but with a certain concern visible upon his face, and seated himself without a word. Then he looked about him with the air of one who has come expecting to hear complaints of some sort, and is prepared to answer them, but who hesitates to open the subject. No one volunteering any thing save the common salutations and a word or two upon the weather, he at length ventured to remark that he hoped we had found the house sufficiently commodious. Quite so, we assured him.

'Not so lively, perhaps,' he queried, 'as we had been accustomed to?'

'Not *quite*,' my aunt remarked, 'and yet not altogether free from *noise*.'

The agent looked disturbed. 'The wind *does* make an awful moaning through the pine-trees of windy nights,' he said, 'but then we shall not have such nights as the last two, long, I hope.'

'*I* shall not, for one,' quoth my aunt, with great firmness of manner; 'I shall leave the house this day.'

'Then I shall go, too,' said my sister; 'I would not pass such another night for any thing in the world.'

The agent did not seem so much surprised at these rather startling announcements as I should have anticipated. 'Heard any noises, ma'am?' said he to my aunt.

'Most fearful ones,' she said. 'The house is haunted!'

'Just so!' quoth the agent with imperturbable gravity; then turning to me: 'No mention was made in our agreement concerning any abatement in rent on account of a ghost, I believe?'

'None at all, Sir,' I said.

'I've heard talk,' he continued, 'of there being noises here, but I never put much faith in the stories. There has n't been a family in since I had charge of the property, and I had an idea the noises were all child's play. I did n't want to lose the chance of a tenant, so I did n't mention the nonsense to you. Any how, I reckon my principal will want his cash for the year, whether you stay or go.'

'Alice and I must leave this fearful place to-day,' said my aunt, 'and I hope and pray *you* will not think of remaining in the house, Henry.'

'I think I shall try the ghosts one night more, Aunt Mary,' I said.

In fact, I had become interested exceedingly in the tragedy that haunted my slumbers, and I wished, if possible, to see it played out. My scepticism was still so strong that I felt no fear in connection with our nocturnal visitations, being inclined to believe that I could yet explain them by other than supernatural causes, and to hope that they would cease to return if I faced them boldly. So I said: 'I think I shall try the ghosts one night more, Aunt Mary.'

It was vain for the women to endeavor to deter me from my purpose, I had become too earnestly determined to see the end of the business, and they finally relinquished the attempt as useless. Then came the question as to where they should go for the night, for it was as vain for me to urge them to sleep again in the house, as it was for them to argue me into flying from it. The agent said his wife had expressly commissioned him to say that she would be happy to accommodate any or all of us. Possibly I would go, too, 'just to humor the ladies!'

'You knew 't was haunted,' cried Alice, 'and you had no business to let us come here without telling us.'

'That was just my business,' he replied; 'I was acting under instructions from the owner.'

Presently the agent drove away, promising to return at nine o'clock in the evening to drive the ladies to his residence in the village. We passed rather a dismal afternoon and evening, even the hot tea and biscuit, produced in my aunt's well-known style, failing to cheer us, and I felt somewhat relieved when nine o'clock brought the agent, and ten minutes past nine carried him and the ladies off to the village.

I had determined not to go to bed this night, but rather to keep myself awake in my study, and so take the ghosts at an advantage. As a preliminary to my watch, I lighted a lantern, and beginning at the garret—where the old man of my dreams mocked me from the canvas on the wall—made a thorough exploration of the house. Every thing was in perfect order, all doors and windows fast, and so far as bolts and bars could protect me, I felt safe from harm. It was only when I reached the cellar that I recollected that I had no sort of weapon in case of an attack from mortal foes. As this thought struck me, I noticed an old and rusty iron bar standing in one corner of the cellar, which I appropriated and conveyed to my study. It was a somewhat clumsy weapon, but still formidable enough to repel any ordinary attack. Placing it at a convenient distance from my seat, and taking down a volume of 'Percy's Reliques,' I lighted a cigar and resigned myself to my watching.

I watched long and wearily, consuming cigar after cigar. It must have been past mid-night when sleep at length overcame me, and my head sank forward upon my arms, folded before me on the table, in which position I found myself on finally awaking from my third horrible night-mare in this house.

* * * * * *

It appeared to me that I sat in my study-chair, smoking and taking occasional sips of brandy-and-water, until the kitchen clock had struck twelve, one, two, three, four and five. The little bronze receptacle for cigar-ashes had long since risen to a gray mound upon the table, from the summit of which appeared the Cupid's head that formed the handle, peering out from the midst of dust and ashes. The bottle was half-emptied; the book was stale, and the loves of King Cophetua and the Beggar Maid had no charms. Still I sat there, and it was now past five o'clock when I heard a singular sound, as of something unwieldy and unhuman stumbling slowly down the broad stair-way. It certainly was not the step of one person, nor did it sound exactly like the steps of two. I listened, holding my breath, and then arose and stole quietly to my study-door, which opened directly at the stair-case foot. There they came, surely. A most horrible spectacle, too. She, old, ugly and shaking with terror, bore upon her shoulders something bulky and limp, that trailed behind her—white, red and black. He followed, holding aloft a candle. A cloth bound about his head rendered yet more conspicuous the ferocity of his face, while the terrible fear that possessed him added to his evil aspect.

But what is it borne slowly and painfully by the woman, one end upon her shoulders, the other striking flabbily and dully from step to step as she descends? See the white night-robe and the long, black hair dripping blood down the stair-way as the toilsome descent continues; and observe in the masses of the hair those pearls, unsought and uncared for, now that lust has brought forth death!

'Hurry! hurry!' whispers the phantom with the light, 'the day dawns and men will be stirring!'

'How can I hurry,' hisses the grizzly phantom tottering below him, 'with this cursed body on my shoulders? Why couldn't you let the girl go in peace?'

'I didn't kill her!' cries the other; ''t was none of my doing!'

'Ha! but she would have killed you but for me; she would have killed you in one minute more!'

'Well! well! Hurry! hurry! For day-light is coming, and men will be stirring!'

'What will you tell them,' cries the phantom with the burden; 'what will you say when they ask you where your ward is?'

'Let us bury her first with dispatch, and hide her clothes and her cursed jewels, and then we will consider what we shall say.'

'Murder will out, though—murder will out. Why weren't you satisfied with me, without bringing us to this, through your cursed fancy for a pair of white arms and a round shoulder!'

''T was the jewels, I tell you, the jewels! Who ever saw before such diamonds, such opals, such pearls! I never intended to kill the girl.'

'No, but she meant to kill you! She'd have done it but for me.'

'I wish she had!' groaned the man; 'on my soul, I wish she had! But why do you stop at the foot of the stairs? We must get her out of sight before the day-light!'

'Get her out of sight!' sneered the hag, 'get her out of sight! I tell you she will be found if you sink her a thousand feet!'

With her back to the other, the woman could not see as I could, how dark his brow grew at these words, and what a dangerous light glowed in his eyes as he looked down upon her. Still he only said: 'Hurry! hurry! for day-light comes and men will be stirring.'

Then the phantoms raised the body between them, bore it slowly past me, without heeding my presence, and passed with it into the kitchen.

Drawn by an impulse perfectly irresistible, I followed softly.

They bore it toward the door leading to the cellar-stairs, and in doing so passed the fire-place. Here the old man paused and uttered a low ejaculation, which caused the other to drop her end of the burden to the floor. As it fell, the pearls knotted in the hair clashed together, but the twain took no heed of the sound.

The old man pointed with a grim glee to the marble hearth-stone. 'There is a hollow beneath that stone,' he said, 'that I provided long ago for the concealment of precious things. We can place it there without fear of detection. Quick-lime will keep our secret for us. Only hurry! But wait till I get the bar.'

Hastily the figure with the light glided through the cellar-door, leaving its companion with darkness and the body. He soon returned, bearing a bar so like the one I knew to be in my study, that only the keenest longing to see the dreadful end restrained me from returning to ascertain if it were still in its place. He inserted one end of the bar between the stone and the flooring, and with an almost supernatural strength turned the slab over. I saw beneath it a dark and empty space, more than sufficient to contain the body.

They lifted it and placed it within. Then the old man made as though he would replace the stone.

'Wait,' cried the woman, 'I must have those pearls!' and she stooped over the vault.

As she did so, he swung upward the bar and brought it down full upon her head, into which it sank with a dull crash!

'Dead men tell no tales!' he whispered, as he turned the stone back to its place. It fell with a loud reverberation, and lay as before, save that it was cracked directly across the centre.

*   *   *   *   *   *

I was broad awake, raising my head from my folded arms. My lamp had burned out, but a cold, clear dawn breaking through the windows showed me the otherwise unchanged aspect of my study. Before me on the table lay a pile of cigar-ashes. At my elbow stood the half-filled bottle. Within easy reach was the bar I had fetched from the cellar. Grasping this, with my nerves strung to the very highest pitch, I hurried to the kitchen. With some labor I pried up the hearth-stone.

In the shallow pit before me lay some bits of rags, two piles of bones, and a mass of night-black hair, from which peeped out, here and there, fair pearls.

I dropped the stone, and threw down the bar, and through the cold, gray dawn I fled the house, nor looked behind me as I fled.

A NIGHT IN MONK-HALL*

(from *The Quaker City*)

George Lippard

Six years ago, in 1836, on a foggy night in spring, at the hour of one o'clock, I found myself reposing in one of the chambers of this mansion, on an old-fashioned bed, side by side with a girl, who, before her seduction, had resided in my native village. It was one o'clock when I was aroused by a hushed sound, like the noise of a distant struggle. I awoke, started up in bed, and looked round. The room was entirely without light, save from the fire-place, where a few pieces of half-burned wood, emitted a dim and uncertain flame. Now it flashed up brightly, giving a strange lustre to the old furniture of the room, the high-backed mahogany chairs, the antiquated bureau, and the low ceiling, with heavy cornices around the walls. Again the flame died away and all was darkness. I listened intently. I could hear no sound, save the breathing of the girl who slept by my side. And as I listened, a sudden awe came over me. True, I heard no noise, but that my sleep had been broken by a most appalling sound, I could not doubt. And the stories I had heard of Monk-hall came over me. Years before, in my native village, a wild rollicking fellow, Paul Western, Cashier of the County Bank, had indulged my fancy with strange stories of a brothel, situated in the outskirts of Philadelphia. Paul was a wild fellow, rather good looking, and went often to the city on business. He spoke of

---

*[Author's Note] The reader will remember, that Merivale entered Monk-Hall *for no licentious object, but with the distinct purpose of discovering the retreat of Western.* This story, told in Merivale's own words, is strictly true.

Monk-hall as a place hard to find, abounding in mysteries, and darkened by hideous crimes committed within its walls. It had three stories of chambers beneath the earth, as well as above. Each of these chambers was supplied with trap-doors, through the which the unsuspecting man might be flung by his murderer, without a moment's warning. There was but one range of rooms above the ground, where these trap-doors existed. From the garret to the first story, all in the same line, like the hatchways in a storehouse, sank this range of trap-doors, all carefully concealed by the manner in which the carpets were fixed. A secret spring in the wall of any one of these chambers, communicated with the spring hidden beneath the carpet. The spring in the wall might be so arranged, that a single footstep pressed on the spring, under the carpet, would open the trap-door, and plunge the victim headlong through the aperture. In such cases no man could stride across the floor without peril of his life. Beneath the ground another range of trap-doors were placed in the same manner, in the floors of three stories of the subterranean chambers. They plunged the victim— God knows where! With such arrangements for murder above and beneath the earth, might there not exist hideous pits or deep wells, far below the third story under ground, where the body of the victim would rot in darkness forever? As I remembered these details, the connection between Paul Western, the cheerful bachelor, and Emily Walraven, the woman who was sleeping at my side, flashed over my mind. The child of one of the first men of B———, educated without regard to expense by the doating father, with a mind singularly masculine, and a tall queenly form, a face distinguished for its beauty and a manner remarkable for its ladylike elegance, poor Emily had been seduced, some three years before, and soon after disappeared from the town. Her seducer no one knew, though from some hints dropped casually by my friend Paul, I judged that he at least could tell. Rumors came to the place, from time to time in relation to the beautiful but fallen girl. One rumor stated that she was now living as the mistress of a wealthy planter, who made his residence at times in Philadelphia. Another declared that she had become a common creature of the town, and this—great God, how terrible!—killed her poor father. The rumor flew round the village to-day—next Sunday old Walraven was dead and buried. They say that in his dying hour he charged Paul Western with his daughter's shame, and shrieked a father's curse upon his head. He left no property, for his troubles had preyed on his mind until he neglected his affairs, and he died insolvent.

Well two years passed on, and no one heard a word more of poor Emily. Suddenly in the spring of 1836, when this town as well as the whole Union was convulsed with the fever of speculation, Paul Western, after a visit to Philadelphia, with some funds of the Bank, amounting to near thirty thousand dollars, in his possession, suddenly disappeared, no one knew whither. My father was largely interested in the bank. He despatched me to town, in order that I might make a desperate effort to track up the footsteps of Western. Some items in the papers stated that the Cashier had fled to Texas, others that he had been drowned by accident, others that he had been spirited away. I alone possessed a clue to the place of his conceal-ment—thus ran my thoughts at all events—and that clue was locked in the bosom of Emily Walraven, the betrayed and deeply-injured girl. Sometime before his disappearance, and after the death of old Walraven, Paul dis-closed to me, under a solemn pledge of secrecy, the fact that Emily was liv-ing in Philadelphia, under his protection, supported by his money. He stated that he had furnished rooms at the brothel called Monk-hall. With this fact resting on my mind, I had hurried to Philadelphia. For days my search for Emily Walraven was in vain. One night, when about giving up the chase as hopeless, I strolled to the Chesnut Street Theatre. Forrest was playing Richelieu—there was a row in the third tier—a bully had offered violence to one of the ladies of the town. Attracted by the noise, I joined the throng rushing up stairs, and beheld the girl who had been stricken, standing pale and erect, a small poignard in her upraised hand, while her eyes flashed with rage as she dared the drunken 'buffer' to strike her again. I stood thunderstruck as I recognized Emily Walraven in the degraded yet beautiful woman who stood before me. Springing forward, with one blow I felled the bully to the floor, and in another moment, seizing Emily by the arm, I hurried down stairs, evaded the constables, who were about to arrest her, and gained the street. It was yet early in the evening—there were no cabs in the street—so I had to walk home with her.

All this I remembered well, as I sat listening in the lonely room.

I remembered the big tears that started from her eyes when she recog-nized me, her wild exclamations when I spoke of her course of life. "Don't talk to me—" she had almost shrieked as we hurried along the street—"it's too late for me to change now. For God's sake let me be happy in my degradation."

I remembered the warm flush of indignation that reddened over her face, as pointing carelessly to a figure which I observed through the fog, some distance ahead, I exclaimed—"Is not that Paul Western yonder?" Her voice was very deep and not at all natural in its tone as she replied, with assumed unconcern—"I know nothing about the man." At last, after threading a labyrinth of streets, compared to which the puzzling-garden was a mere frolic, we had gained Monk-hall, the place celebrated by the wonderful stories of my friend Western. Egad! As we neared the door I could have sworn that I beheld Western himself disappear in the door but this doubtless, I reasoned, had been a mere fancy.

Silence still prevailed in the room, still I heard but the sound of Emily breathing in her sleep, and yet my mind grew more and more heavy, with some unknown feeling of awe. I remembered with painful distinctness the hang-dog aspect of the door-keeper who had let us in, and the cut-throat visages of his two attendants seemed staring me visibly in the face. I grew quite nervous. Dark ideas of murder and the devil knows what, began to chill my very soul. I bitterly remembered that I had no arms. The only thing I carried with me was a slight cane, which had been lent me by the Landlord of the —— Hotel. It was a mere switch of a thing.

As these things came stealing over me, the strange connexion between the fate of Western and that of the beautiful woman who lay beside me, the sudden disappearance of the former, the mysterious character of Monk-hall, the startling sounds which had aroused me, the lonely appearance of the room, fitfully lighted by the glare on the hearth, all combined, deepened the impression of awe, which had gradually gained possession of my faculties. I feared to stir. You may have felt this feeling—this strange and incomprehensible feeling—but if you have not, just imagine a man seized with the night-mare when wide awake.

I was sitting upright in bed, chilled to the very heart, afraid to move an inch, almost afraid to breathe, when, far, far down through the chambers of the old mansion, I heard a faint hushed sound, like a man endeavouring to cry out when attacked by night-mare, and then—great God how distinct!—I heard the cry of 'Murder, murder, murder!' far, far, far below me.

The cry aroused Emily from her sleep. She started up in the bed and whispered, in a voice without tremor—"What is the matter Boyd—"

"Listen—" I cried with chattering teeth, and again, up from the depths of the mansion welled that awful sound, *Murder!* Murder! Murder! growing louder every time. Then far, far, far down I could hear a gurgling sound. It grew fainter every moment. Fainter, fainter, fainter. All was still as death.

"What does this mean?" I whispered almost fiercely, turning to Emily by my side—"What does this mean?" And a dark suspicion flashed over my mind.

The flame shot upward in the fire-place, and revealed every line of her intellectual countenance.

Her dark eyes looked firmly in my face as she answered, "In God's name I know not!"

The manner of the answer satisfied me as to her firmness, if it did not convince me of her innocence. I sat silent and sullen, conjuring over the incidents of the night.

"Come, Boyd—" she cried, as she arose from the bed—"You must leave the house. I never entertain visitors after this hour. It is my custom. I thank you for your protection at the theatre, but you must go home—"

Her manner was calm and self-possessed. I turned to her in perfect amazement.

"I will not leave the house—" I said, as a dim vision of being attacked by assassins on the stairway, arose to my mind.

"There is Devil-Bug and his cut-throat negroes—" thought I—"nothing so easy as to give me a 'cliff' with a knife from some dark corner; nothing so secret as my burial-place in some dark hole in the cellar—"

"I won't go home—" said I, aloud.

Emily looked at me in perfect wonder. It may have been affected, and it may have been real.

"Well then, I must go down stairs to get something to eat—" she said, in the most natural manner in the world—"I usually eat something about this hour—"

"You may eat old Devil-Bug and his niggers, if you like—" I replied laughing—"But out of this house my father's son don't stir till broad daylight."

With a careless laugh, she wound her night-gown round her, opened the door, and disappeared in the dark. Down, down, down, I could hear her go, her footsteps echoing along the stairway of the old mansion, down, down, down. In a few moments all was still.

Here I was, in a pretty 'fix.' In a lonely room at midnight, ignorant of the passages of the wizard's den, without arms, and with the pleasant prospect of the young lady coming back with Devil-Bug and his niggers to despatch me. I had heard the cry of 'Murder'—so ran my reasoning—they, that is the murderers—would suspect that I was a witness to their guilt, and, of course, would send me down some d——d trap-door on an especial message to the devil.

This was decidedly a bad case. I began to look around the room for some chance of escape, some arms to defend myself, or, perhaps from a motive of laudible curiosity, to know something more about the place where my death was to happen.

One moment, regular as the ticking of a clock, the room would be illuminated by a flash of red light from the fire-place, the next it would be dark as a grave. Seizing the opportunity afforded by the flash, I observed some of the details of the room. On the right side of the fire-place there was a closet: the door fastened to the post by a very singular button, shaped like a diamond; about as long as your little finger and twice as thick. On the other side of the fire-place, near the ceiling, was a small oblong window, about as large as two half sheets of writing paper, pasted together at the ends. Here let me explain the use of this window. The back part of Monk-hall is utterly destitute of windows. Light, faint and dim you may be sure, is admitted from the front by small windows, placed in the wall of each room. How many rooms there are on a floor, I know not, but, be they five or ten, or twenty, they are all lighted in this way.

Well, as I looked at this window, I perceived one corner of the curtain on the other side was turned up. This gave me very unpleasant ideas. I almost fancied I beheld a human face pressed against the glass, looking at me. Then the flash on the hearth died away, and all was dark. I heard a faint creaking noise—the light from the hearth again lighted the place—could I believe my eyes—the button on the closet-door turned slowly round!

Slowly—slowly—slowly it turned, making a slight grating noise. This circumstance, slight as it may appear to you, filled me with horror. What could turn the button, but a human hand? Slowly, slowly it turned, and the door sprung open with a whizzing sound. All was dark again. The cold sweat stood out on my forehead. Was my armed murderer waiting to spring at my throat? I passed a moment of intense horror. At last, springing hastily forward, I swung the door shut, and fastened the button. I can swear that I fastened it as tight as ever button was fastened. Regaining the bed I silently awaited the result. Another flash of light—Great God!—I could swear there was a face pressed against the oblong window! Another moment and it is darkness—creak, creak, creak—is that the sound of the button again? It was light again, and there, before my very eyes, the button moved slowly round! Slowly, slowly, slowly!

The door flew open again. I sat still as a statue. I felt it difficult to breathe. Was my enemy playing with me, like the cat ere she destroys her game!

I absently extended my hand. It touched the small black stick given me by the Landlord of the —— Hotel in the beginning of the evening. I drew it to me, like a friend. Grasping it with both hands, I calculated the amount of service it might do me. And as I grasped it, the top seemed parting from the lower portion of the cane. Great God! It was a sword cane! Ha-ha! I could at least strike *one* blow! My murderers should not despatch me without an effort of resistance. You see my arm is none of the puniest in the world; I may say that there are worse men than Boyd Merivale for a fight.

Clutching the sword-cane, I rushed forward, and standing on the threshold of the opened door, I made a lunge with all my strength through the darkness of the recess. Though I extended my arm to its full length, and the sword was not less than eighteen inches long, yet to my utter astonishment, I struck but the empty air! Another lunge and the same result!

Things began to grow rather queer. I was decidedly beat out as they say. I shut the closet door again, retreated to the bed, sword in hand, and awaited the result. I heard a sound, but it was the footstep of poor Emily, who that moment returned with a bed-lamp in one hand, and a small waiter, supplied with a boiled chicken and a bottle of wine in the other. There was nothing remarkable in her look, her face was calm, and her boiled chicken and bottle of wine, decidedly common place.

"Great God——" she cried as she gazed in my countenance—"What is the matter with you? Your face is quite livid—and your eyes are fairly starting from their sockets——"

"Good reason——" said I, as I *felt* that my lips were clammy and white—"That d—d button has been going round ever since you left, and that d—d door has been springing open every time it was shut——"

"Ha-ha-ha——" she laughed—"Would it have sprung open if you had not shut it?"

This was a very clear question and easy to answer; but——

"Mark you, my lady——" said I—"Here am I in a lonely house, under peculiar circumstances. I am waked up by the cry of 'Murder'—a door springs open without a hand being visible—a face peers at me through a window. As a matter of course I suspect there has been foul work done here to-night. And through every room of this house, Emily you must lead the way, while I follow, this good sword in hand. If the light goes out, or if you blow it out, you are to be pitied, for in either case, I swear by Living God, I will run you through with this sword—"

"Ha-ha-ha—" she fairly screamed with laughter as she sprung to the closet door—"Behold the mystery—"

And with her fair fingers she pointed to the socket of the button, and to the centre of the door. The door had been 'sprung,' as it is termed, by the weather. That is, the centre bulged inward, leaving the edge toward the door-post to press the contrary direction. The socket of the button, by continual wear, had been increased to twice its original size. Whenever the door was first buttoned, the head of the screw pressed against one of the edges of the socket. In a moment the pressure of the edge of the door, which you will remember was directed outward, dislodged the head of the screw and it sank, well-nigh half an inch into the worn socket of the button. Then the button, removed *farther* from the door than at first, would slowly turn, and the door spring open. All this was plain enough, and I smiled at my recent fright.

"Very good, Emily—" I laughed—"But the mystery of this sword— what of that? I made a lunge in the closet and it touched nothing—"

"You are suspicious, Boyd—" she answered with a laugh—"But the fact is, the closet is rather a deep one—"

"Rather—" said I—"and so are you, my dear—"

There may have been something very meaning in my manner, but certainly, although her full black eyes looked fixedly on me, yet I thought her face grew a shade paler as I spoke.

"And my dear—" I continued—"What do you make of the face peeping through the window:—"

"All fancy—all fancy—" she replied, but as she spoke I saw her eye glance hurriedly toward the very window. Did she *too* fear that she might behold the face?

"We will search the closet—" I remarked, throwing open the door— "What have we here? Nothing but an old cloak hanging to a hook—let's try it with my sword!"

Again I made a lunge with my sword: again I thrust at the empty air.

"Emily, there is a room beyond this cloak—you will enter first if you please. Remember my warning about the light if you please—"

"Oh now that I remember, this closet *does* open into the next room—" she said gaily, although her cheek—so it struck me—grew a little paler and her lip trembled slightly—"I had quite forgotten the circumstance—"

"Enter Emily, and don't forget the light—"

She flung the door aside and passed on with the light in her hand. I followed her. We stood in a small room, lighted like the other by an oblong window. There was no other window, no door, no outlet of any sort. Even a chimney-place was wanting. In one corner stood a massive bed—the quilt was unruffled. Two or three old fashioned chairs were scattered round the room, and from the spot where I stood looking over the foot of the bed, I could see the top of another chair, and nothing more, between the bed and the wall.

A trifling fact in Emily's behaviour may be remarked. The moment the light of the lamp which she held in her hand flashed round the room, she turned to me with a smile, and leading the way round the corner of the foot of the bed, asked me in a pleasant voice "Did I see any thing remarkable there?"

She shaded her eyes from the lamp as she spoke, and toyed me playfully under the chin. You will bear in mind that at this moment, I had turned my face toward the closet by which we had entered. My back was therefore toward the part of the room most remote from the closet. It was a trifling fact, but I may as well tell you, that the manner in which Emily held the light, threw that portion of the room, between the foot of the bed and the wall in complete shadow, while the rest of the chamber was bright as day.

Smilingly Emily toyed me under the chin, and at that moment I thought she looked extremely beautiful.

By Jove! I wish you could have seen her eyes shine, and her cheek—Lord bless you—a full blown rose wasn't a circumstance to it. She looked so beautiful, in fact, as she came sideling up to me, that I stepped backward in order to have a full view of her before I pressed a kiss on her pouting lips. I did step back, and did kiss her. It wasn't singular, perhaps, but her lips were hot as a coal. Again she advanced to me, again chucked me under the chin. Again I stepped back to look at her, again I wished to taste her lips so pouting, but rather warm, when—

To tell you the truth, stranger, even at this late day the remembrance makes my blood run cold!

—When I heard a sound like the sweeping of a tree-limb against a closed shutter, it was so faint and distant, and a stream of cold air came rushing up my back.

I turned around carelessly to ascertain the cause. I took but a single glance, and then—by G—d—I sprung at least ten feet from the place. There, at my very back, between the bed and the wall, opposite its foot, I beheld a carpeted space some three feet square, sinking slowly down, and separating itself from the floor. I had stepped my foot upon the spring—made ready for me, to be sure—and the trap-door sank below me.

You may suppose my feelings were somewhat excited. In truth, my heart, for a moment, felt as though it was turning to a ball of ice. First I looked at the trap-door and then at Emily. Her face was pale as ashes, and she leaned, trembling, against the bedpost. Advancing, sword in hand, I gazed down the trap-door. Great God! how dark and gloomy the pit looked! From room to room, from floor to floor, a succession of traps had fallen—far below—it looked like a mile, although that was but an exaggeration natural to a highly excited mind—far, far below gleamed a light, and a buzzing murmur came up this hatchway of death.

Stooping slowly down, sword in hand, my eye on the alert for Miss Emily, I disengaged a piece of linen, from a nail, near the edge of the trap-door. Where the linen—it was a shirt wristband—had been fastened, the carpet was slightly torn, as though a man in falling had grasped it with his finger ends.

The wristband was, in more correct language, a ruffle for the wrist. It came to my mind, in this moment, that I had often ridiculed Paul Western for his queer old bachelor ways. Among other odd notions, he had worn ruffles at his wrist. As I gathered this little piece of linen in my grasp, the trap-door slowly rose. I turned to look for Miss Emily, she had changed her position, and stood pressing her hand against the opposite wall.

"Now, Miss Emily, my dear—" I cried, advancing toward her—"Give me a plain answer to a plain question—and tell me—what in the devil do you think of yourself?"

Perfectly white in the face, she glided across the room and stood at the foot of the bed, in her former position, leaning against the post for support. You will observe that her form concealed the chair, whose top I had only seen across the bed.

"Step aside, Miss Emily, my dear—" I said, in as quiet a tone as I could command—"Or you see, my lady, I'll have to use a little necessary force—"

Instead of stepping aside, as a peaceable woman would have done, she sits right down in the chair, fixing those full black eyes of hers on my face, with a glance that looked very much like madness.

Extending my hand, I raised her from the seat. She rested like a dead weight in my arms. She had fainted. Wrapped in her night-gown, I laid her on the bed, and then examined the chair in the corner. Something about this chair attracted my attention. A coat hung over the round—a blue coat with metal buttons. A buff vest hung under this coat; and a high stock, with a shirt collar.

I knew these things at once. They belonged to my friend, Paul Western.

"And so, my lady—" I cried, forgetting that she had fainted; "Mr. Western came home, from the theatre, to his rooms, arrived just before us, took off his coat and vest, and stock and collar—maybe was just about to take off his boots—when he stepped on the spring and in a moment was in— in h—ll—"

Taking the light in one hand, I dragged or carried her, into the other room and laid her on the bed. After half an hour or so, she came to her senses.

"You see—you see—" were her first words uttered, with her eyes flashing like live-coals, and her lips white as marble—"You see, I could not help it, for my father's curse was upon him!"

She laughed wildly, and lay in my arms a maniac.

Stranger, I'll make a short story of the thing now. How I watched her all night till broad day, how I escaped from the house—for Mr. Devil-Bug, it seems, didn't suspect I knew anything—how I returned home without any news of Paul Western, are matters as easy to conceive as tell.

Why didn't I institute a search? Fiddle-faddle! Blazon my name to the world as a visitor to a Bagnio? Sensible thing, that! And then, although I was sure in my own soul, that the clothes which I had discovered belonged to Paul Western, it would have been most difficult to establish this fact in Court. One word more and I have done.

Never since that night has Paul Western been heard of by living man. Never since that night has Emily Walraven been seen in this breathing world. You start. Let me whisper a word in your ear. Suppose Emily joined in Western's murder from motives of revenge, what then were Devil-Bug's? (*He* of course was the real murderer.) Why the money to be sure. Why be troubled with Emily as a witness of his guilt, or a sharer of his money?

This is rather a—a *dark house,* and it's my opinion, stranger, that *he murdered her too!*

Ha-ha—why here's all the room to ourselves! All the club have either disappeared, or lie drunk on the floor! I saw Fitz-Cowles—I know him— sneak off a few moments since—I could tell by his eye that he is after some devils-trick! The parson has gone, and the judge has gone, the lawyer has fallen among the slain, and so, wishing you good night, stranger, I'll vanish! Beware of the Monks of Monk-hall!

A STORY OF THE WHITE MOUNTAIN NOTCH

E. P. King

Close by the road which crept between the hills, side by side with the noisy river that showed the way, there stood some five and sixty years ago the half farmhouse, half tavern, low and unpainted, among the trees. In front, across the narrow valley, brown rock and the varying green of hemlock, birch, and maple rose two thousand feet above it, giving varied lights and shadows in the afternoon sun. Behind, sloping and forest-covered, the huge mass of the hill at whose foot the tavern rested reared itself still higher. At the north a screen of sheer precipice, purple, brown, and red, barred the view. Only at the south did there seem any way of escape; while even there the mountains, ranged one behind the other in apparently endless phalanx, threatened to lose the traveller in the maze. But the little river ran confidently on. Already it had overcome its greatest difficulty and, but a hand-breadth wide, had stolen into the valley at the almost rock-bound north. When once through this Gate of the Notch, cascades came tumbling down the mountain-sides to greet it; and it spattered and splashed on, deftly sidled this way and that, in the long labyrinth of hills; and, at last, did find the sea and, a calm and dignified stream, lovingly lost itself in the greatness it had sought so long. And the road, spying the rivulet, had crept beside, crowding its way without an inch to spare at the head of the valley. Then it wandered more at will, here on the hillside, and there in the very depth of the cleft, sometimes rather arrogantly fording or bridging its companion, which bore all patiently, and cheerily led the way.

There was a city down by the sea. Now and then the birds and beasts of the forest fled into the deeper woods, startled by the approaching voices, the creaking and the rumble of the long caravans of farmers that came down through the Notch, laden with produce and making the long journey to the city together, for companionship's sake, to return with their frugal purchases. These could safely camp by the way; but a welcome tarrying-place to the solitary traveller was the weather-stained inn, and a necessary shelter in many a wild night.

It had even required some determination on the part of the innkeeper's family to live shut in this narrow defile. True, when they came to their new home, last autumn, the glories of the burning forests which were not consumed had welcomed them with a mass of gaudy loveliness. But before the snow fell, there had been grander exhibitions of nature. Through the beating rain the lightning would show, across the river, the torrents leaping from the crags; and in the darkness loosened bowlders, with crashing loud as thunder and with meteor-like trains, hurled themselves down the cliffs into the valley.

"It is well for us that we haven't that hill behind us," said the innkeeper. The sloping, verdure-clad mountain at whose base they were, seemed indeed a much safer companion.

If any family could endure the solitude of the winter among the hills, surely it was that of Samuel Willey and Polly, his wife, who had made this their home. David, an adopted son, had just attained his majority and was quite a companion for the older people. Eliza, of thirteen years, Jerry, of eleven, and Martha, nine, were old enough to be useful, as children were trained in those days. Not much but childish prattle was expected from Elbridge, a timid boy of seven years, and Sally, two years younger; yet nothing was more welcome in that lonely place, where the mother, when she would see the companionable smoke curling from a chimney-top, must cross the narrow road and watch that from her own hearthstone. Last of the household there was Allen, the hired man, almost like another father in his care for the children and his interest in all the work of the place. Yet it was a lonely winter. When spring came, it is no wonder there was talk of their removing to some one of the settlements.

A certain discovery helped persuade them to stay. It may be that dwellers among the hills are more imaginative than their kin that live on the monotonously level plains. It is certain, too, that the innkeeper came of a race that claimed the gift of second sight, some of whom, even then, doubtless held communication with the invisible world. Such people are often affected by slight incidents that might multiply unnoticed by their more prosaic brethren. Polly was no believer in these supernatural gifts, and the eldest daughter inherited her disposition; but Jerry was like his father, and it was he who had filled the willing ears of the smaller children with the few fairy tales he knew.

One bright morning in the spring, Jerry was at work in front of the house, now and then gazing wonderingly over the hills which had come to seem as almost living companions. The sun had melted the snow on the bare mountain-tops. Suddenly he called his mother with a joyful cry.

"Mother, mother, come and see the face!"

Polly left her work and, coming to the door, followed with her eyes her son's excited pointing.

"See the face, mother, in the rock!"

And even Polly, not at all given to seeing imaginary figures in the cliffs and trees, perceived plainly that the topmost crag of the hill that seemed to dominate the valley at the southeast shaped an upturned human face, calm and peaceful. By nightfall it had been shown to all the members of the household.

"It's a good sign, wife," said the husband.

"Ah, Samuel!" answered she, "thy faith in signs and spirits will get thee more trouble than good, I fear."

"Can't it be the spirit that rules this valley," said Jerry, "as they say other stone faces guard the other roads that lead from these once enchanted hills?"

"There's a young magician for ye!" laughed his mother.

"Don't make fun of the lad," said the father. "Thee'll take all belief away from him."

"I've no faith in thy signs, Samuel; but it's a comfort to feel we've a human face in sight, though it is in stone," said Polly.

Indeed, this discovery made them all more cheerful, and helped their decision to stay in their mountain home. All felt that they had gained a companion in the face on the mountain-top. Soon the innkeeper had repaired the house and put all in order for the summer travellers. The face was especially a source of wonder to the children, and they named it, from a favorite character in one of their few books, "Faithful." Often Jerry and Martha and Sally sat side by side watching it and wondering if it really cared for them; but timid little Elbridge feared more than loved it, and after sitting with the others awhile, would run to his mother, nervously crying, and bury his face in the folds of her dress.

"The ghosts shall not harm thee!" she would say; and the other children would try to reassure him.

And now it was the early part of June. The white patches of snow had disappeared from the mountains. The leaves at last, almost in one warm day, had burst from their enwrapping bud-scales, where they had lain all curled together, as for warmth, waiting for the soft touch of summer to call them. Summer was come. The road through the valley must be repaired; and the inn was the nightly shelter of the band of woodmen who day by day cleared away fallen trees, dragged off the bowlders that had rolled down the mountain-side, and put all in order for the summer travel, which would soon begin. Wonderful nights these were for the children. How their eyes opened, as some rough-bearded man told his story of adventure in the woods! Or they heard again the tale of the Indian sachem taken to the clouds in a chariot of fire, and from the top of one of their own mountains, too. They had seen that very peak when they had been beyond the cascades and through the Gate of the Notch, with their father; and again when they had wandered off with "Bruin," their dog companion, and were nearly lost, when Allen found them. Yes, that was the very mountain. Then there were the logging songs that the men sang. Not so soft and sweet, to be sure, as their mother's songs; but such grand, rich music the rude harmony seemed. Oh! these were glorious times, and the children heard with little satisfaction that they were soon to end; that to-morrow Nicholas, the cobbler, was coming; for the road-men must be going farther on, and their boots, well worn by this, the hardest section of their work, must be mended before they went.

With the morrow young Nicholas came. He had the latest news of the neighborhood, which was far too wide to be neighborly; and no pearls from the lips of the enchanted maid of old were more welcome than the bits of gossip he would tell now and then as he patched, or when his mouth was not full of his own hand-made pegs. To-day his news was especially welcome; for hour after hour the rain fell, and no out-of-door work could be done. The dull thumping on the lapstone became a cheery sound, and all were about the young cobbler, watching his work and listening to his tales.

It was in the latter part of the afternoon that Sally, who had been sitting in her father's lap, pressing her face against the window-pane and looking out into the storm, exclaimed delightedly,—

"O papa! The trees are walking, the trees are walking down the hill!"

At the same instant, there was a roar outside.

"A slide! A slide!" cried the father.

All leaped to the windows and doors. Indeed, but a short distance north of the house, the trees did move; some standing upright for six or seven rods, then slowly toppling over, and, prostrate, writhing along. The mountain-side had given way; and a mass of mingled timber, earth, and bowlders, shaking the very house with its motion, swept down the hill, and spread over the road, and along the river-bank. The poor people, helplessly imprisoned in the valley, saw the frightful destruction only a few yards from them, and stood silent in their terror. Then the little children, too young to appreciate the danger at first, from sheer sympathy began a wailing cry, the first sound that came from the group.

"There's fifty rod of road for us to clear," said one of the men.

"And it's well we're here to clear it," said another. "It would have taken house and all away, if it had been aimed at us."

Until the storm abated, the group, utterly powerless against such an avalanche, would turn pale at each roar of the wind without. At last the rain ceased and the clouds began to break away. By sunset the inmates of the tavern had somewhat regained their composure. The slide had been visited and plans laid for the attack upon it the next day.

"Thee can rest easy, Samuel," said Nicholas cheerfully, "for the lightning never strikes twice, thee knows."

"Mamma," whispered Sally, "don't you think our Faithful kept us?"

"Hush, child!" was the only answer. And again the songs were sung, and the stories passed from one to another. At last the house was quiet, though later than usual; for the cobbler sat up to finish his work, so as to be gone on the morrow. It was toward twelve o'clock when tired Polly went to close the door for the night. The swollen river was yet roaring below, but the sky was clear. Off in the east, the bright glow showed that the waning moon was just rising. Turning her eyes to the crag, she was half startled, so calm against the golden background stood the upturned face, as if it said, "I am Faithful." Stealing to Sally's bedside, she kissed the little trusting one, and then lay down to a calm night's rest.

With the morning, all was activity. Nicholas went on his way, with a new tale to tell. The road was partly cleared and partly remade atop the slide; and in a few days the road-menders departed. And the summer slipped away: a hot, dry summer; for it seemed that the cool wind would never blow from the sea, up the valley. So many visitors from the towns "down below" came through the pass that the days passed cheerfully; for, covered with the powdery dust of the road, each traveller was glad to rest awhile, before going further. The story of the landslide was to these ever an interesting topic of conversation; and many a look was cast at the dark mountain, whose top seemed to the excited listener almost to overhang and start downward at the instant. At last, the innkeeper determined to build a kind of cave or "camp," as he called it, down nearer the river. If another slide should come, it would at most, he reasoned, spread over the little meadow between the house and the stream. If the family started at the first warning of the avalanche, the camp could be reached; and, though the house might be destroyed, their lives at least would be saved.

It was late one afternoon that David and Jerry, returning from work, found the younger brother and sisters a few feet back of the house, gathered about a rock that Sally had taken as her especial dominion. Eliza, seated in the doorway, was reading aloud. Her audience was feasting on the red raspberries from out a child-made set of birch-bark cups and plates; and Sally, nestling in a cleft that opened back toward the hillside, was very red fingered and rosy lipped, as she listened wondering, and tasted with critical satisfaction. Her place, besides being that of her choice, was a matter of convenience; for when the story became unintelligible to her five years, she could safely yield to the soothing quality in Eliza's voice, and as she nodded and fell asleep the sides of the cleft would hold her like an arm-chair. More than once the mother had laughingly said that Sally had two friends in stone—the face on the mountain and this half-buried bowlder that held her so easily in its arms.

There came a pause in the story.

"The camp is finished," said Jerry; "and father thinks that we are safe now, even if there come another slide."

"O Jerry," cried Martha, "don't let us go into that cold, dark place! Didn't our Faithful keep us safe before?"

"Papa and mamma may go, and we'll stay behind," said Sally.

"Wicked Sally!" cried Eliza. "Thee'd soon get frightened; and try to follow us. Then thee'd sure get lost."

"Then I'd go straight on till I got to our Faithful," answered she.

"I'm afraid even a face as faithful as ours couldn't feed us," said David. "There may never be another slide; but if there ever is one, or if father ever calls us to go with him, we must all go together."

"We won't," whispered Sally to Martha.

Their mother's voice just then called them to supper, and more words were prevented. That night the completed camp was the subject of the family talk.

"And if the time ever does come," said the father, "Allen, thee must look after my wife.—Thee can help Eliza, David; and Jerry and I will take care of the smaller children."

"I'll go with thee, mamma," cried Elbridge, clinging to his mother's dress.

Little Sally, away from the candle-light, shook her head decidedly.

"May the time never come!" said the mother.

"If it does come, Sally wants to stay here. She says Faithful will keep us," said Martha.

"Poor little trusting ones!" said their father, kissing them both. "The goblin stories have turned your heads, I fear."

He stepped to the door. The moon, near its full, was just rising over the crag that made the face. He saw the profile, dark against the brilliant nimbus, and almost believed; but reason came to his rescue. Yet the sight was beautiful; and he called the household, who watched while the golden disc rolled by and above till it threw a flood of light on the upturned features. Then all retired for the night; and Martha and Sally climbed to the loft, and into their bed by a window, and watched the face in the moonlight until they fell into quiet slumber.

Not many days after, the wind blew from the south, and there were the first signs of rain after the drouth. On a Sunday, the last in August, the clouds began to gather, and the welcome rain pattered on the leaves as it advanced up the valley. The next day it was still raining; and all day long the clouds followed each other like the ranks of an army, crowding as they came to the narrow pass, and getting denser and blacker. The rain continually increased. When night shut in, such a tempest burst over that doomed intervale that the river, swollen to a mighty torrent, swept resistless, high above its usual banks; while the avalanches tore down the mountain-sides, and left what were before green-crowned summits only bare, ragged rock. Then, as if beckoned by some unseen hand, the clouds rose and dissipated, and the moonless, starlit night looked down on the desolate valley.

The events at the Willey House no one knows. The next night an urgent traveller, who had toiled over the road from the north, and through the narrow Gate of the Notch, came to the house at dusk expecting to find the usual hospitality. The house, indeed, was standing, but what destruction around! Great trees were strewn about like straws. Huge bowlders were scattered in endless and appalling confusion. The house was open, but deserted, and evidently had been left in haste. "They are safe at the next neighbor's," thought he, and lay down to troubled sleep on one of the tumbled beds. At daybreak he rose and looked more about him. A groaning coming from the barn proved to be from animals crushed under the partial ruin, and he released them; but there were no signs of human inhabitants. He looked around to see by what wonder the house had been preserved in the midst of so much ruin. The chaos was terrifying, though it was at rest. It was easy to see what had saved the building. A slide had come tearing directly toward it, a confused mass of earth and water, trees and rocks, until a huge spruce, that must have been upright in the van, wedged itself in the cleft of the rock where Sally used to sit. Held there like the wand of command in the hand of a giant, trees and earth had piled against it, until a barrier was made that turned the mass of the slide right and left, to unite below the house and continue its work of destruction. Like a huge sea-wave, the avalanche reared itself until its crest almost overhung the little dwelling, and but a narrow passage-way intervened between its foot and the walls; but the wave had not broken—not a timber of the house was marred.

Continuing his journey down the notch, all along he saw the devastation that told of the violence of the storm. But at the next neighbor's there was no news of the innkeeper's family; nor at the nearest village when he reached it, five and twenty miles away. There the dog "Bruin" had been seen, running from house to house and barking excitedly. Then he had gone off again towards the mountains; that was all they knew. A search was immediately begun; and, sure that they must have been overtaken by the slide in their attempt to escape, a troop of neighbors was soon digging about the house and the overwhelmed camp.

And they found, first, the body of Allen, the hired man, and next, with her hand almost clasped in his, the mother, and little Elbridge close behind her. Then they discovered the bodies of David and Eliza and the father, separated from one another, the two latter under the water of the swollen river. Close by the side of their old home they buried them. Then the neighbors departed; the road was rebuilt; the tavern was soon reoccupied, the sun shone bright as ever; the shrunken rivulet caught the cascades in its bosom and babbled on as innocently as before; and little trace of the tragedy was left in the valley.

The little unpainted inn still stands brown among the green of the trees which have grown around it, but one may yet see where the encircling slide parted, and may walk among the bowlders brought down from the mountain-top that dreadful night. The bodies of Jerry and Martha and Sally were never found. "Bruin" was seen for awhile, darting back and forth over the road, and then he too disappeared. Some people thought the children might have escaped and lost themselves in the woods; but search failed to reveal a trace of them—unless one may believe the tales of imaginative travellers that stay a night in the forests toward the southeast, that they hear voices, as of children climbing the slopes of the hill. Of course it is only the creaking of the trees that they hear. But the face may yet be seen from the door of the tavern, still calmly and peacefully upturned; and, by those that know the tale, it is still called as the children named it, "Faithful."

Part II

BLURRED
VISIONS

DÉSIRÉE'S BABY

Kate Chopin

As the day was pleasant, Madame Valmondé drove over to L'Abri to see Désirée and the baby.

It made her laugh to think of Désirée with a baby. Why, it seemed but yesterday that Désirée was little more than a baby herself; when Monsieur in riding through the gateway of Valmondé had found her lying asleep in the shadow of the big stone pillar.

The little one awoke in his arms and began to cry for "Dada." That was as much as she could do or say. Some people thought she might have strayed there of her own accord, for she was of the toddling age. The prevailing belief was that she had been purposely left by a party of Texans, whose canvas-covered wagon, late in the day, had crossed the ferry that Coton-Maïs kept, just below the plantation. In time Madame Valmondé abandoned every speculation but the one that Désirée had been sent to her by a beneficent Providence to be the child of her affection, seeing that she was without child of the flesh. For the girl grew to be beautiful and gentle, affectionate and sincere; the idol of Valmondé.

It was no wonder, when she stood one day against the stone pillar in whose shadow she had lain asleep, eighteen years before, that Armand Aubigny riding by and seeing her there, had fallen in love with her. That was the way all the Aubignys fell in love, as if struck by a pistol shot. The wonder was, that he had not loved her before; for he had known her since his father brought him home from Paris, a boy of eight, after his mother died there. The passion that awoke in him that day, when he saw her at the gate, swept along like an avalanche, or like a prairie fire, or like anything that drives headlong over all obstacles.

Monsieur Valmondé grew practical and wanted things well considered: that is, the girl's obscure origin. Armand looked into her eyes and did not care. He was reminded that she was nameless. What did it matter about a name when he could give her one of the oldest and proudest in Louisiana? He ordered the *corbeille* from Paris, and contained himself with what patience he could until it arrived, then they were married.

Madame Valmondé had not seen Désirée and the baby for four weeks. When she reached L'Abri she shuddered at the first sight of it, as she always did. It was a sad looking place, which for many years had not known the gentle presence of a mistress. Old Monsieur Aubigny having married and buried his wife in France, and she having loved her own land too well ever to leave it. The roof came down steep and black like a cowl reaching out beyond the wide galleries that encircled the yellow stuccoed house. Big, solemn oaks grew close to it, and their thick-leaved, far-reaching branches shadowed it like a pall. Young Aubigny's rule was a strict one, too, and under it his negroes had forgotten how to be gay, as they had been during the old master's easy-going and indulgent lifetime.

The young mother was recovering slowly, and lay full length, in her soft white muslins and laces, upon a couch. The baby was beside her, upon her arm, where he had fallen asleep at her breast. The yellow nurse woman sat beside a window fanning herself.

Madame Valmondé bent her portly figure over Désirée and kissed her, holding her an instant tenderly in her arms. Then she turned to the child.

"This is not the baby!" she exclaimed, in startled tones. French was the language spoken at Valmondé in those days.

"I knew you would be astonished," laughed Désirée, "at the way he has grown. The little *cochon de lait!* Look at his legs, mamma, and his hands and finger-nails—real finger-nails. Zandrine had to cut them this morning. Isn't it so, Zandrine?"

The woman bowed her turbaned head majestically, "*Mais si,* Madame."

"And the way he cries," went on Désirée, "is deafening. Armand heard him the other day as far away as La Blanche's cabin."

Madame Valmondé had never removed her eyes from the child. She picked it up and walked with it over to the window that was lightest. She scanned it narrowly, then looked as searchingly at Zandrine, whose face was turned to gaze across the fields.

"Yes, the child has grown, has changed;" said Madame Valmondé, slowly, as she replaced it beside its mother. "What does Armand say?"

Désirée's face became suffused with a glow that was happiness itself.

"Oh, Armand is the proudest father in the parish, I believe, chiefly because it is a boy, to bear his name; though he says not—that he would have loved a girl as well. But I know it isn't true. I know he says that to please me. And mamma," she added, drawing Madame Valmondé's head down to her, and speaking in a whisper, "he hasn't punished one of them—not one of them—since baby is born. Even Négrillon, who pretended to have burnt his leg that he might rest from work—he only laughed, and said Négrillon was a great scamp. Oh, mamma, I'm so happy; it frightens me."

What Désirée said was true. Marriage, and later the birth of his son, had softened Armand Aubigny's imperious and exacting nature greatly. This was what made the gentle Désirée so happy, for she loved him desperately. When he frowned she trembled, but loved him. When he smiled, she asked no greater blessing of God. But Armand's dark, handsome face had not often been disfigured by frowns since the day he fell in love with her.

When the baby was about three months old, Désirée awoke one day to the conviction that there was something in the air menacing her peace. It was at first too subtle to grasp. It had only been a disquieting suggestion; an air of mystery among the blacks; unexpected visits from far-off neighbors who could hardly account for their coming. Then a strange, an awful change in her husband's manner, which she dared not ask him to explain. When he spoke to her, it was with averted eyes, from which the old love-light seemed to have gone out. He absented himself from home; and when there, avoided her presence and that of her child, without excuse. And the very spirit of Satan seemed suddenly to take hold of him in his dealings with the slaves. Désirée was miserable enough to die.

She sat in her room, one hot afternoon, in her peignoir, listlessly drawing through her fingers the strands of her long, silky brown hair that hung about her shoulders. The baby, half naked, lay asleep upon her own great mahogany bed, that was like a sumptuous throne, with its satin-lined half-canopy. One of La Blanche's little quadroon boys—half naked too—stood fanning the child slowly with a fan of peacock feathers. Désirée's eyes had been fixed absently and sadly upon the baby, while she was striving to penetrate the threatening mist that she felt closing about her. She looked from her child to the boy who stood beside him, and back again; over and over. "Ah!" It was a cry that she could not help; which she was not conscious of having uttered. The blood turned like ice in her veins, and a clammy moisture gathered upon her face.

She tried to speak to the little quadroon boy; but no sound would come, at first. When he heard his name uttered, he looked up, and his mistress was pointing to the door. He laid aside the great, soft fan, and obediently stole away, over the polished floor, on his bare tiptoes.

She stayed motionless, with gaze riveted upon her child, and her face the picture of fright.

Presently her husband entered the room, and without noticing her, went to a table and began to search among some papers which covered it.

"Armand," she called to him, in a voice which must have stabbed him, if he was human. But he did not notice. "Armand," she said again. Then she rose and tottered towards him. "Armand," she panted once more, clutching his arm, "look at our child. What does it mean? tell me."

He coldly but gently loosened her fingers from about his arm and thrust the hand away from him. "Tell me what it means!" she cried despairingly.

"It means," he answered lightly, "that the child is not white; it means that you are not white."

A quick conception of all that this accusation meant for her, nerved her with unwonted courage to deny it. "It is a lie—it is not true, I am white! Look at my hair, it is brown; and my eyes are gray, Armand, you know they are gray. And my skin is fair," seizing his wrist. "Look at my hand—whiter than yours, Armand," she laughed hysterically.

"As white as La Blanche's," he said cruelly; and went away leaving her alone with their child.

When she could hold a pen in her hand, she sent a despairing letter to Madame Valmondé.

"My mother, they tell me I am not white. Armand has told me I am not white. For God's sake tell them it is not true. You must know it is not true. I shall die. I must die. I cannot be so unhappy, and live."

The answer that came was as brief:

"My own Désirée: Come home to Valmondé—back to your mother who loves you. Come with your child."

When the letter reached Désirée she went with it to her husband's study, and laid it open upon the desk before which he sat. She was like a stone image: silent, white, motionless after she placed it there.

In silence he ran his cold eyes over the written words. He said nothing. "Shall I go, Armand?" she asked in tones sharp with agonized suspense.

"Yes, go."

"Do you want me to go?"

"Yes, I want you to go."

He thought Almighty God had dealt cruelly and unjustly with him; and felt, somehow, that he was paying Him back in kind when he stabbed thus into his wife's soul. Moreover he no longer loved her, because of the unconscious injury she had brought upon his home and his name.

She turned away like one stunned by a blow, and walked slowly towards the door, hoping he would call her back.

"Good-bye, Armand," she moaned.

He did not answer her. That was his last blow at fate. After it was dealt he felt like a remorseless murderer.

Désirée went in search of her child. Zandrine was pacing the sombre gallery with it. She took the little one from the nurse's arms with no word of explanation, and descending the steps, walked away, under the live oak branches.

It was an October afternoon. Out in the still fields the negroes were picking cotton, and the sun was just sinking.

Désirée had not changed the thin white garment nor the slippers which she wore. Her head was uncovered and the sun's rays brought a golden gleam from its brown meshes. She did not take the broad, beaten road which led to the far-off plantation of Valmondé. She walked across a deserted field, where the stubble bruised her tender feet, so delicately shod, and tore her thin gown to shreds.

She disappeared among the reeds and willows that grew thick along the banks of the deep, sluggish bayou; and she did not come back again.

*   *   *   *   *   *

Some weeks later there was a curious scene enacted at L'Abri. In the centre of the smoothly swept back-yard was a great bonfire. Armand Aubigny sat in the wide hallway that commanded a view of the spectacle; and it was he who dealt out to a half-dozen negroes the material which kept this fire ablaze.

A graceful cradle of willow, with all its dainty furbishings, was laid upon the pyre, which had already been fed with the richness of a priceless *layette*. Then there were silk gowns, and velvet and satin ones added to these; laces, too, and embroideries; bonnets and gloves—for the *corbeille* had been of rare quality.

The last thing to go was a tiny bundle of letters; innocent little scribblings that Désirée had sent to him during the days of their espousal. There was the remnant of one back in the drawer from which he took them. But it was not Désirée's. It was part of an old letter from his mother to his father. He read it. She was thanking God for the blessing of her husband's love;

"But, above all," she wrote, "night and day, I thank the good God for having so arranged our lives that our dear Armand will never know that his mother, who adores him, belongs to the race that is cursed with the brand of slavery."

YOUNG GOODMAN BROWN

Nathaniel Hawthorne

Young Goodman Brown came forth at sunset into the street at Salem village; but put his head back, after crossing the threshold, to exchange a parting kiss with his young wife. And Faith, as the wife was aptly named, thrust her own pretty head into the street, letting the wind play with the pink ribbons of her cap while she called to Goodman Brown.

"Dearest heart," whispered she, softly and rather sadly, when her lips were close to his ear, "prithee put off your journey until sunrise and sleep in your own bed to-night. A lone woman is troubled with such dreams and such thoughts that she's afeard of herself sometimes. Pray tarry with me this night, dear husband, of all nights in the year."

"My love and my Faith," replied young Goodman Brown, "of all nights in the year, this one night must I tarry away from thee. My journey, as thou callest it, forth and back again, must needs be done 'twixt now and sunrise. What, my sweet, pretty wife, dost thou doubt me already, and we but three months married?"

"Then God bless you!" said Faith, with the pink ribbons; "and may you find all well when you come back."

"Amen!" cried Goodman Brown. "Say thy prayers, dear Faith, and go to bed at dusk, and no harm will come to thee."

So they parted; and the young man pursued his way until, being about to turn the corner by the meeting-house, he looked back and saw the head of Faith still peeping after him with a melancholy air, in spite of her pink ribbons.

"Poor little Faith!" thought he, for his heart smote him. "What a wretch am I to leave her on such an errand! She talks of dreams, too. Methought as she spoke there was trouble in her face, as if a dream had warned her what work is to be done to-night. But no, no; 't would kill her to think it. Well, she's a blessed angel on earth; and after this one night I'll cling to her skirts and follow her to heaven."

With this excellent resolve for the future, Goodman Brown felt himself justified in making more haste on his present evil purpose. He had taken a dreary road, darkened by all the gloomiest trees of the forest, which barely stood aside to let the narrow path creep through, and closed immediately behind. It was all as lonely as could be; and there is this peculiarity in such a solitude, that the traveller knows not who may be concealed by the innumerable trunks and the thick boughs overhead; so that with lonely footsteps he may yet be passing through an unseen multitude.

"There may be a devilish Indian behind every tree," said Goodman Brown to himself; and he glanced fearfully behind him as he added, "What if the devil himself should be at my very elbow!"

His head being turned back, he passed a crook of the road, and, looking forward again, beheld the figure of a man, in grave and decent attire, seated at the foot of an old tree. He arose at Goodman Brown's approach and walked onward side by side with him.

"You are late, Goodman Brown," said he. "The clock of the Old South was striking as I came through Boston, and that is full fifteen minutes agone."

"Faith kept me back a while," replied the young man, with a tremor in his voice, caused by the sudden appearance of his companion, though not wholly unexpected.

It was now deep dusk in the forest, and deepest in that part of it where these two were journeying. As nearly as could be discerned, the second traveller was about fifty years old, apparently in the same rank of life as Goodman Brown, and bearing a considerable resemblance to him, though perhaps more in expression than features. Still they might have been taken for father and son. And yet, though the elder person was as simply clad as the younger, and as simple in manner too, he had an indescribable air of one who knew the world, and who would not have felt abashed at the governor's dinner table or in King William's court, were it possible that his affairs should call him thither. But the only thing about him that could be fixed upon as remarkable was his staff, which bore the likeness of a great black snake, so curiously wrought that it might almost be seen to twist and wriggle itself like a living serpent. This, of course, must have been an ocular deception, assisted by the uncertain light.

"Come, Goodman Brown," cried his fellow-traveller, "this is a dull pace for the beginning of a journey. Take my staff, if you are so soon weary."

"Friend," said the other, exchanging his slow pace for a full stop, "having kept covenant by meeting thee here, it is my purpose now to return whence I came. I have scruples touching the matter thou wot'st of."

"Sayest thou so?" replied he of the serpent, smiling apart. "Let us walk on, nevertheless, reasoning as we go; and if I convince thee not thou shalt turn back. We are but a little way in the forest yet."

"Too far! too far!" exclaimed the goodman, unconsciously resuming his walk. "My father never went into the woods on such an errand, nor his father before him. We have been a race of honest men and good Christians since the days of the martyrs; and shall I be the first of the name of Brown that ever took this path and kept"—

"Such company, thou wouldst say," observed the elder person, interpreting his pause. "Well said, Goodman Brown! I have been as well acquainted with your family as with ever a one among the Puritans; and that's no trifle to say. I helped your grandfather, the constable, when he lashed the Quaker woman so smartly through the streets of Salem; and it was I that brought your father a pitch-pine knot, kindled at my own hearth, to set fire to an Indian village, in King Philip's war. They were my good friends, both; and many a pleasant walk have we had along this path, and returned merrily after midnight. I would fain be friends with you for their sake."

"If it be as thou sayest," replied Goodman Brown, "I marvel they never spoke of these matters; or, verily, I marvel not, seeing that the least rumor of the sort would have driven them from New England. We are a people of prayer, and good works to boot, and abide no such wickedness."

"Wickedness or not," said the traveller with the twisted staff, "I have a very general acquaintance here in New England. The deacons of many a church have drunk the communion wine with me; the selectmen of divers towns make me their chairman; and a majority of the Great and General Court are firm supporters of my interest. The governor and I, too—But these are state secrets."

"Can this be so?" cried Goodman Brown, with a stare of amazement at his undisturbed companion. "Howbeit, I have nothing to do with the governor and council; they have their own ways, and are no rule for a simple husbandman like me. But, were I to go on with thee, how should I meet the eye of that good old man, our minister, at Salem village? Oh, his voice would make me tremble both Sabbath day and lecture day."

Thus far the elder traveller had listened with due gravity; but now burst into a fit of irrepressible mirth, shaking himself so violently that his snake-like staff actually seemed to wriggle in sympathy.

"Ha! ha! ha!" shouted he again and again; then composing himself, "Well, go on, Goodman Brown, go on; but, prithee, don't kill me with laughing."

"Well, then, to end the matter at once," said Goodman Brown, considerably nettled, "there is my wife, Faith. It would break her dear little heart; and I'd rather break my own."

"Nay, if that be the case," answered the other, "e'en go thy ways, Goodman Brown. I would not for twenty old women like the one hobbling before us that Faith should come to any harm."

As he spoke he pointed his staff at a female figure on the path, in whom Goodman Brown recognized a very pious and exemplary dame, who had taught him his catechism in youth, and was still his moral and spiritual adviser, jointly with the minister and Deacon Gookin.

"A marvel, truly, that Goody Cloyse should be so far in the wilderness at nightfall," said he. "But with your leave, friend, I shall take a cut through the woods until we have left this Christian woman behind. Being a stranger to you, she might ask whom I was consorting with and whither I was going."

"Be it so," said his fellow-traveller. "Betake you to the woods, and let me keep the path."

Accordingly the young man turned aside, but took care to watch his companion, who advanced softly along the road until he had come within a staff's length of the old dame. She, meanwhile, was making the best of her way, with singular speed for so aged a woman, and mumbling some indistinct words—a prayer, doubtless—as she went. The traveller put forth his staff and touched her withered neck with what seemed the serpent's tail.

"The devil!" screamed the pious old lady.

"Then Goody Cloyse knows her old friend?" observed the traveller, confronting her and leaning on his writhing stick.

"Ah, forsooth, and is it your worship indeed?" cried the good dame. "Yea, truly is it, and in the very image of my old gossip, Goodman Brown, the grandfather of the silly fellow that now is. But—would your worship believe it?—my broomstick hath strangely disappeared, stolen, as I suspect, by that unhanged witch, Goody Cory, and that, too, when I was all anointed with the juice of smallage, and cinquefoil, and wolf's bane"—

"Mingled with fine wheat and the fat of a new-born babe," said the shape of old Goodman Brown.

"Ah, your worship knows the recipe," cried the old lady, cackling aloud. "So, as I was saying, being all ready for the meeting, and no horse to ride on, I made up my mind to foot it; for they tell me there is a nice young man to be taken into communion to-night. But now your good worship will lend me your arm, and we shall be there in a twinkling."

"That can hardly be," answered her friend. "I may not spare you my arm, Goody Cloyse; but here is my staff, if you will."

So saying, he threw it down at her feet, where, perhaps, it assumed life, being one of the rods which its owner had formerly lent to the Egyptian magi. Of this fact, however, Goodman Brown could not take cognizance. He had cast up his eyes in astonishment, and, looking down again, beheld neither Goody Cloyse nor the serpentine staff, but his fellow-traveller alone, who waited for him as calmly as if nothing had happened.

"That old woman taught me my catechism," said the young man; and there was a world of meaning in this simple comment.

They continued to walk onward, while the elder traveller exhorted his companion to make good speed and persevere in the path, discoursing so aptly that his arguments seemed rather to spring up in the bosom of his auditor than to be suggested by himself. As they went, he plucked a branch of maple to serve for a walking stick, and began to strip it of the twigs and little boughs, which were wet with evening dew. The moment his fingers touched them they became strangely withered and dried up as with a week's sunshine. Thus the pair proceeded, at a good free pace, until suddenly, in a gloomy hollow of the road, Goodman Brown sat himself down on the stump of a tree and refused to go any farther.

"Friend," said he, stubbornly, "my mind is made up. Not another step will I budge on this errand. What if a wretched old woman do choose to go to the devil when I thought she was going to heaven: is that any reason why I should quit my dear Faith and go after her?"

"You will think better of this by and by," said his acquaintance, composedly. "Sit here and rest yourself a while; and when you feel like moving again, there is my staff to help you along."

Without more words, he threw his companion the maple stick, and was as speedily out of sight as if he had vanished into the deepening gloom. The young man sat a few moments by the roadside, applauding himself greatly, and thinking with how clear a conscience he should meet the minister in his morning walk, nor shrink from the eye of good old Deacon Gookin. And what calm sleep would be his that very night, which was to have been spent so wickedly, but so purely and sweetly now, in the arms of Faith! Amidst these pleasant and praiseworthy meditations, Goodman Brown heard the tramp of horses along the road, and deemed it advisable to conceal himself within the verge of the forest, conscious of the guilty purpose that had brought him thither, though now so happily turned from it.

On came the hoof tramps and the voices of the riders, two grave old voices, conversing soberly as they drew near. These mingled sounds appeared to pass along the road, within a few yards of the young man's hiding-place; but, owing doubtless to the depth of the gloom at that particular spot, neither the travellers nor their steeds were visible. Though their figures brushed the small boughs by the wayside, it could not be seen that they intercepted, even for a moment, the faint gleam from the strip of bright sky athwart which they must have passed. Goodman Brown alternately crouched and stood on tiptoe, pulling aside the branches and thrusting forth his head as far as he durst without discerning so much as a shadow. It vexed him the more, because he could have sworn, were such a thing possible, that he recognized the voices of the minister and Deacon Gookin, jogging along quietly, as they were wont to do, when bound to some ordination or ecclesiastical council. While yet within hearing, one of the riders stopped to pluck a switch.

"Of the two, reverend sir," said the voice like the deacon's, "I had rather miss an ordination dinner than to-night's meeting. They tell me that some of our community are to be here from Falmouth and beyond, and others from Connecticut and Rhode Island, besides several of the Indian pow-wows, who, after their fashion, know almost as much deviltry as the best of us. Moreover, there is a goodly young woman to be taken into communion."

"Mighty well, Deacon Gookin!" replied the solemn old tones of the minister. "Spur up, or we shall be late. Nothing can be done, you know, until I get on the ground."

The hoofs clattered again; and the voices, talking so strangely in the empty air, passed on through the forest, where no church had ever been gathered or solitary Christian prayed. Whither, then, could these holy men be journeying so deep into the heathen wilderness? Young Goodman Brown caught hold of a tree for support, being ready to sink down on the ground, faint and overburdened with the heavy sickness of his heart. He looked up to the sky, doubting whether there really was a heaven above him. Yet there was the blue arch, and the stars brightening in it.

"With heaven above and Faith below, I will yet stand firm against the devil!" cried Goodman Brown.

While he still gazed upward into the deep arch of the firmament and had lifted his hands to pray, a cloud, though no wind was stirring, hurried across the zenith and hid the brightening stars. The blue sky was still visible, except directly overhead, where this black mass of cloud was sweeping swiftly northward. Aloft in the air, as if from the depths of the cloud, came a confused and doubtful sound of voices. Once the listener fancied that he could distinguish the accents of towns-people of his own, men and women, both pious and ungodly, many of whom he had met at the communion table, and had seen others rioting at the tavern. The next moment, so indistinct were the sounds, he doubted whether he had heard aught but the murmur of the old forest, whispering without a wind. Then came a stronger swell of those familiar tones, heard daily in the sunshine at Salem village, but never until now from a cloud of night. There was one voice, of a young woman, uttering lamentations, yet with an uncertain sorrow, and entreating for some favor, which, perhaps, it would grieve her to obtain; and all the unseen multitude, both saints and sinners, seemed to encourage her onward.

"Faith!" shouted Goodman Brown, in a voice of agony and desperation; and the echoes of the forest mocked him, crying, "Faith! Faith!" as if bewildered wretches were seeking her all through the wilderness.

The cry of grief, rage, and terror was yet piercing the night, when the unhappy husband held his breath for a response. There was a scream, drowned immediately in a louder murmur of voices, fading into far-off laughter, as the dark cloud swept away, leaving the clear and silent sky above Goodman Brown. But something fluttered lightly down through the air and caught on the branch of a tree. The young man seized it, and beheld a pink ribbon.

"My Faith is gone!" cried he, after one stupefied moment. "There is no good on earth; and sin is but a name. Come, devil; for to thee is this world given."

And, maddened with despair, so that he laughed loud and long, did Goodman Brown grasp his staff and set forth again, at such a rate that he seemed to fly along the forest path rather than to walk or run. The road grew wilder and drearier and more faintly traced, and vanished at length, leaving him in the heart of the dark wilderness, still rushing onward with the instinct that guides mortal man to evil. The whole forest was peopled with frightful sounds—the creaking of the trees, the howling of wild beasts, and the yell of Indians; while sometimes the wind tolled like a distant church bell, and sometimes gave a broad roar around the traveller, as if all Nature were laughing him to scorn. But he was himself the chief horror of the scene, and shrank not from its other horrors.

"Ha! ha! ha!" roared Goodman Brown when the wind laughed at him. "Let us hear which will laugh loudest. Think not to frighten me with your deviltry. Come witch, come wizard, come Indian powwow, come devil himself, and here comes Goodman Brown. You may as well fear him as he fear you."

In truth, all through the haunted forest there could be nothing more frightful than the figure of Goodman Brown. On he flew among the black pines, brandishing his staff with frenzied gestures, now giving vent to an inspiration of horrid blasphemy, and now shouting forth such laughter as set all the echoes of the forest laughing like demons around him. The fiend in his own shape is less hideous than when he rages in the breast of man. Thus sped the demoniac on his course, until, quivering among the trees, he saw a red light before him, as when the felled trunks and branches of a clearing have been set on fire, and throw up their lurid blaze against the sky, at the hour of midnight. He paused, in a lull of the tempest that had driven him onward, and heard the swell of what seemed a hymn, rolling solemnly from a distance with the weight of many voices. He knew the tune; it was a familiar one in the choir of the village meeting-house. The verse died heavily away, and was lengthened by a chorus, not of human voices, but of all the sounds of the benighted wilderness pealing in awful harmony together. Goodman Brown cried out, and his cry was lost to his own ear by its unison with the cry of the desert.

In the interval of silence he stole forward until the light glared full upon his eyes. At one extremity of an open space, hemmed in by the dark wall of the forest, arose a rock, bearing some rude, natural resemblance either to an altar or a pulpit, and surrounded by four blazing pines, their tops aflame, their stems untouched, like candles at an evening meeting. The mass of foliage that had overgrown the summit of the rock was all on fire, blazing high into the night and fitfully illuminating the whole field. Each pendent twig and leafy festoon was in a blaze. As the red light arose and fell, a numerous congregation alternately shone forth, then disappeared in shadow, and again grew, as it were, out of the darkness, peopling the heart of the solitary woods at once.

"A grave and dark-clad company," quoth Goodman Brown.

In truth they were such. Among them, quivering to and fro between gloom and splendor, appeared faces that would be seen next day at the council board of the province, and others which, Sabbath after Sabbath, looked devoutly heavenward, and benignantly over the crowded pews, from the holiest pulpits in the land. Some affirm that the lady of the governor was there. At least there were high dames well known to her, and wives of honored husbands, and widows, a great multitude, and ancient maidens, all of excellent repute, and fair young girls, who trembled lest their mothers should espy them. Either the sudden gleams of light flashing over the ob- scure field bedazzled Goodman Brown, or he recognized a score of the church members of Salem village famous for their especial sanctity. Good old Deacon Gookin had arrived, and waited at the skirts of that venerable saint, his revered pastor. But, irreverently consorting with these grave, rep- utable, and pious people, these elders of the church, these chaste dames and dewy virgins, there were men of dissolute lives and women of spotted fame, wretches given over to all mean and filthy vice, and suspected even of horrid crimes. It was strange to see that the good shrank not from the wicked, nor were the sinners abashed by the saints. Scattered also among their pale-faced enemies were the Indian priests, or powwows, who had of- ten scared their native forest with more hideous incantations than any known to English witchcraft.

"But where is Faith?" thought Goodman Brown; and, as hope came into his heart, he trembled.

Another verse of the hymn arose, a slow and mournful strain, such as the pious love, but joined to words which expressed all that our nature can conceive of sin, and darkly hinted at far more. Unfathomable to mere mortals is the lore of fiends. Verse after verse was sung; and still the chorus of the desert swelled between like the deepest tone of a mighty organ; and with the final peal of that dreadful anthem there came a sound, as if the roaring wind, the rushing streams, the howling beasts, and every other voice of the unconcerted wilderness were mingling and according with the voice of guilty man in homage to the prince of all. The four blazing pines threw up a loftier flame, and obscurely discovered shapes and visages of horror on the smoke wreaths above the impious assembly. At the same moment the fire on the rock shot redly forth and formed a glowing arch above its base, where now appeared a figure. With reverence be it spoken, the figure bore no slight similitude, both in garb and manner, to some grave divine of the New England churches.

"Bring forth the converts!" cried a voice that echoed through the field and rolled into the forest.

At the word, Goodman Brown stepped forth from the shadow of the trees and approached the congregation, with whom he felt a loathful brotherhood by the sympathy of all that was wicked in his heart. He could have well-nigh sworn that the shape of his own dead father beckoned him to advance, looking downward from a smoke wreath, while a woman, with dim features of despair, threw out her hand to warn him back. Was it his mother? But he had no power to retreat one step, nor to resist, even in thought, when the minister and good old Deacon Gookin seized his arms and led him to the blazing rock. Thither came also the slender form of a veiled female, led between Goody Cloyse, that pious teacher of the catechism, and Martha Carrier, who had received the devil's promise to be queen of hell. A rampant hag was she. And there stood the proselytes beneath the canopy of fire.

"Welcome, my children," said the dark figure, "to the communion of your race. Ye have found thus young your nature and your destiny. My children, look behind you!"

They turned; and flashing forth, as it were, in a sheet of flame, the fiend worshippers were seen; the smile of welcome gleamed darkly on every visage.

"There," resumed the sable form, "are all whom ye have reverenced from youth. Ye deemed them holier than yourselves, and shrank from your own sin, contrasting it with their lives of righteousness and prayerful aspirations heavenward. Yet here are they all in my worshipping assembly. This night it shall be granted you to know their secret deeds: how hoary-bearded elders of the church have whispered wanton words to the young maids of their households; how many a woman, eager for widows' weeds, has given her husband a drink at bedtime and let him sleep his last sleep in her bosom; how beardless youths have made haste to inherit their fathers' wealth; and how fair damsels—blush not, sweet ones—have dug little graves in the garden, and bidden me, the sole guest, to an infant's funeral. By the sympathy of your human hearts for sin ye shall scent out all the places—whether in church, bed-chamber, street, field, or forest—where crime has been committed, and shall exult to behold the whole earth one stain of guilt, one mighty blood spot. Far more than this. It shall be yours to penetrate, in every bosom, the deep mystery of sin, the fountain of all wicked arts, and which inexhaustibly supplies more evil impulses than human power—than my power at its utmost—can make manifest in deeds. And now, my children, look upon each other."

They did so; and, by the blaze of the hell-kindled torches, the wretched man beheld his Faith, and the wife her husband, trembling before that unhallowed altar.

"Lo, there ye stand, my children," said the figure, in a deep and solemn tone, almost sad with its despairing awfulness, as if his once angelic nature could yet mourn for our miserable race. "Depending upon one another's hearts, ye had still hoped that virtue were not all a dream. Now are ye undeceived. Evil is the nature of mankind. Evil must be your only happiness. Welcome again, my children, to the communion of your race."

"Welcome," repeated the fiend worshippers, in one cry of despair and triumph.

And there they stood, the only pair, as it seemed, who were yet hesitating on the verge of wickedness in this dark world. A basin was hollowed, naturally, in the rock. Did it contain water, reddened by the lurid light? or was it blood? or, perchance, a liquid flame? Herein did the shape of evil dip his hand and prepare to lay the mark of baptism upon their foreheads, that they might be partakers of the mystery of sin, more conscious of the secret guilt of others, both in deed and thought, than they could now be of their own. The husband cast one look at his pale wife, and Faith at him. What polluted wretches would the next glance show them to each other, shuddering alike at what they disclosed and what they saw!

"Faith! Faith!" cried the husband, "look up to heaven, and resist the wicked one."

Whether Faith obeyed he knew not. Hardly had he spoken when he found himself amid calm night and solitude, listening to a roar of the wind which died heavily away through the forest. He staggered against the rock, and felt it chill and damp; while a hanging twig, that had been all on fire, besprinkled his cheek with the coldest dew.

The next morning young Goodman Brown came slowly into the street of Salem village, staring around him like a bewildered man. The good old minister was taking a walk along the graveyard to get an appetite for breakfast and meditate his sermon, and bestowed a blessing, as he passed, on Goodman Brown. He shrank from the venerable saint as if to avoid an anathema. Old Deacon Gookin was at domestic worship, and the holy words of his prayer were heard through the open window. "What God doth the wizard pray to?" quoth Goodman Brown. Goody Cloyse, that excellent old Christian, stood in the early sunshine at her own lattice, catechizing a little girl who had brought her a pint of morning's milk. Goodman Brown snatched away the child as from the grasp of the fiend himself. Turning the corner by the meeting-house, he spied the head of Faith, with the pink ribbons, gazing anxiously forth, and bursting into such joy at sight of him that she skipped along the street and almost kissed her husband before the whole village. But Goodman Brown looked sternly and sadly into her face, and passed on without a greeting.

Had Goodman Brown fallen asleep in the forest and only dreamed a wild dream of a witch-meeting?

Be it so if you will; but, alas! it was a dream of evil omen for young Goodman Brown. A stern, a sad, a darkly meditative, a distrustful, if not a desperate man did he become from the night of that fearful dream. On the Sabbath day, when the congregation were singing a holy psalm, he could not listen because an anthem of sin rushed loudly upon his ear and drowned all the blessed strain. When the minister spoke from the pulpit with power and fervid eloquence, and, with his hand on the open Bible, of the sacred truths of our religion, and of saint-like lives and triumphant deaths, and of future bliss or misery unutterable, then did Goodman Brown turn pale, dreading lest the roof should thunder down upon the gray blasphemer and his hearers. Often, awaking suddenly at midnight, he shrank from the bosom of Faith; and at morning or eventide, when the family knelt down at prayer, he scowled and muttered to himself, and gazed sternly at his wife, and turned away. And when he had lived long, and was borne to his grave a hoary corpse, followed by Faith, an aged woman, and children and grandchildren, a goodly procession, besides neighbors not a few, they carved no hopeful verse upon his tombstone, for his dying hour was gloom.

AN ILLUSION IN RED AND WHITE

Stephen Crane

Nights on the Cuban blockade were long, at times exciting, often dull. The men on the small leaping dispatch-boats became as intimate as if they had all been buried in the same coffin. Correspondents, who in New York, had passed as fairly good fellows sometimes turned out to be perfect rogues of vanity and selfishness, but still more often the conceited chumps of Park Row became the kindly and thoughtful men of the Cuban blockade. Also each correspondent told all he knew, and sometimes more. For this gentle tale I am indebted to one of the brightening stars of New York journalism.

"Now, this is how I imagine it happened. I don't say it happened this way, but this is how I imagine it happened. And it always struck me as being a very interesting story. I hadn't been on the paper very long, but just about long enough to get a good show, when the city editor suddenly gave me this sparkling murder assignment.

"It seems that up in one of the back counties of New York State a farmer had taken a dislike to his wife; and so he went into the kitchen with an axe, and in the presence of their four little children he just casually rapped his wife on the nape of the neck with the head of this axe. It was early in the morning, but he told the children they had better go to bed. Then he took his wife's body out in the woods and buried it.

"This farmer's name was Jones. The widower's eldest child was named Freddy. A week after the murder, one of the long-distance neighbours was rattling past the house in his buckboard when he saw Freddy playing in

105

the road. He pulled up, and asked the boy about the welfare of the Jones family.

"'Oh, we're all right,' said Freddy, 'only ma—she ain't—she's dead.'

"'Why, when did she die?' cried the startled farmer. 'What did she die of?'

"'Oh,' answered Freddy, 'last week a man with red hair and big white teeth and real white hands came into the kitchen, and killed ma with an axe.'

"The farmer was indignant with the boy for telling him this strange childish nonsense, and drove off much disgruntled. But he recited the incident at a tavern that evening, and when people began to miss the familiar figure of Mrs. Jones at the Methodist Church on Sunday mornings, they ended by having an investigation. The calm Jones was arrested for murder, and his wife's body was lifted from its grave in the woods and buried by her own family.

"The chief interest now centred upon the children. All four declared that they were in the kitchen at the time of the crime, and that the murderer had red hair. The hair of the virtuous Jones was grey. They said that the murderer's teeth were large and white. Jones only had about eight teeth, and these were small and brown. They said the murderer's hands were white. Jones's hands were the colour of black walnuts. They lifted their dazed, innocent faces, and crying, simply because the mysterious excitement and their new quarters frightened them, they repeated their heroic legend without important deviation, and without the parroty sameness which would excite suspicion.

"Women came to the jail and wept over them, and made little frocks for the girls, and little breeches for the boys, and idiotic detectives questioned them at length. Always they upheld the theory of the murderer with red hair, big white teeth, and white hands. Jones sat in his cell, his chin sullenly on his first vest button. He knew nothing about any murder, he said. He thought his wife had gone on a visit to some relatives. He had had a quarrel with her, and she had said that she was going to leave him for a time, so that he might have proper opportunities for cooling down. Had he seen the blood on the floor? Yes, he had seen the blood on the floor. But he had been cleaning and skinning a rabbit at that spot on the day of his wife's disappearance. He had thought nothing of it. What had his children said when he returned from the fields? They had told him that their mother had been killed by an axe in the hands of a man with red hair, big white teeth, and white hands. To questions as to why he had not informed the police of the county, he answered that he had not thought it a matter of sufficient importance. He had cordially hated his wife, anyhow, and he was glad to be rid of her. He decided afterward that she had run off; and he had never credited the fantastic tale of the children.

"Of course, there was very little doubt in the minds of the majority that Jones was guilty, but there was a fairly strong following who insisted that Jones was a coarse and brutal man, and perhaps weak in his head— yes—but not a murderer. They pointed to the children and declared that children could never lie, and these kids, when asked, said that the murder had been committed by a man with red hair, large white teeth, and white hands. I myself had a number of interviews with the children, and I was amazed at the convincing power of their little story. Shining in the depths of the limpid up-turned eyes, one could fairly see tiny mirrored images of men with red hair, big white teeth, and white hands.

"Now, I'll tell you how it happened—how I imagine it was done. Some time after burying his wife in the woods Jones strolled back into the house. Seeing nobody, he called out in the familiar fashion, 'Mother!' Then the kids came out whimpering. 'Where is your mother?' said Jones. The children looked at him blankly. 'Why, pa,' said Freddy, 'you came in here, and hit ma with the axe; and then you sent us to bed.' 'Me?' cried Jones. 'I haven't been near the house since breakfast-time.'

"The children did not know how to reply. Their meagre little sense informed them that their father had been the man with the axe, but he denied it, and to their minds everything was a mere great puzzle with no meaning whatever, save that it was mysteriously sad and made them cry.

"'What kind of a looking man was it?' said Jones.

"Freddy hesitated. 'Now—he looked a good deal like you, pa.'

"'Like me?' said Jones. 'Why, I thought you said he had red hair?'

"'No, I didn't,' replied Freddy. 'I thought he had grey hair, like yours.'

"'Well,' said Jones, 'I saw a man with kind of red hair going along the road up yonder, and I thought maybe that might have been him.'

"Little Lucy, the second child, here piped up with intense conviction. 'His hair was a little teeny bit red. I saw it.'

"'No,' said Jones. 'The man I saw had very red hair. And what did his teeth look like? Were they big and white?'

"'Yes,' answered Lucy, 'they were.'

"Even Freddy seemed to incline to think it.

"'His teeth may have been big and white.'

"Jones said little more at that time. Later he intimated to the children that their mother had gone off on a visit, and although they were full of wonder, and sometimes wept because of the oppression of an incomprehensible feeling in the air, they said nothing. Jones did his chores. Everything was smooth.

"The morning after the day of the murder, Jones and his children had a breakfast of hominy and milk.

"'Well, this man with red hair and big white teeth, Lucy,' said Jones. 'Did you notice anything else about him?'

"Lucy straightened in her chair, and showed the childish desire to come out with brilliant information which would gain her father's approval. 'He had white hands—hands all white—'

"'How about you, Freddy?'

"'I didn't look at them much, but I think they were white,' answered the boy.

"'And what did little Martha notice?' cried the tender parent. 'Did she see the big bad man?'

"Martha, aged four, replied solemnly, 'His hair was all yed, and his hand was white—all white.'

"'That's the man I saw up the road,' said Jones to Freddy.

"'Yes, sir, it seems like it must have been him,' said the boy, his brain now completely muddled.

"Again Jones allowed the subject of his wife's murder to lapse. The children did not know that it was a murder, of course. Adults were always performing in a way to make children's heads swim. For instance, what could be more incomprehensible than that a man with two horses, dragging a queer thing, should walk all day, making the grass turn down and the earth turn up? And why did they cut the long grass and put it in a barn? And what was a cow for? Did the water in the well like to be there? All these actions and things were grand, because they were associated with the high estate of grown-up people, but they were deeply mysterious. If, then, a man with red hair, big white teeth, and white hands should hit their mother on the nape of the neck with an axe, it was merely a phenomenon of grown-up life. Little Henry, the baby, when he had a want, howled and pounded the table with his spoon. That was all of life to him. He was not concerned with the fact that his mother had been murdered.

"One day Jones said to his children suddenly, 'Look here: I wonder if you could have made a mistake. Are you absolutely sure that the man you saw had red hair, big white teeth, and white hands?'

"The children were indignant with their father. 'Why, of course, pa, we ain't made no mistake. We saw him as plain as day.'

"Later young Freddy's mind began to work like ketchup. His nights were haunted with terrible memories of the man with the red hair, big white teeth, and white hands, and the prolonged absence of his mother made him wonder and wonder. Presently he quite gratuitously developed the theory that his mother was dead. He knew about death. He had once seen a dead dog; also dead chickens, rabbits, and mice. One day he asked his father, 'Pa, is ma ever coming back?'

"Jones said: 'Well, no; I don't think she is.' This answer confirmed the boy in his theory. He knew that dead people did not come back.

"The attitude of Jones toward this descriptive legend of the man with the axe was very peculiar. He came to be in opposition to it. He protested against the convictions of the children, but he could not move them. It was the one thing in their lives of which they were stonily and absolutely positive.

"Now that really ends the story. But I will continue for your amusement. The jury hung Jones as high as they could, and they were quite right: because Jones confessed before he died. Freddy is now a highly respected driver of a grocery wagon in Ogdensburg. When I was up there a good many years afterward people told me that when he ever spoke of the tragedy at all he was certain to denounce the alleged confession as a lie. He considered his father a victim to the stupidity of juries, and some day he hopes to meet the man with the red hair, big white teeth, and white hands, whose image still remains so distinct in his memory that he could pick him out in a crowd of ten thousand."

LOST

Philander Deming

H e was lost in the edge of the Adirondack Wilderness. It must have been the sound of the flail. "Thud, thud, thud," came the beat of the dull, thumping strokes through the thick, opaque, gray fog. Willie was hardly four years old; and when once he was a few rods away from the barn, off on the plain of monotonous yellow stubble, he could not tell where he was, and could not detect the deceptive nature of the sound and its echo. He could see nothing: whichever way he looked, wherever he walked, there were the same reverberations; and the same narrow dome of watery gray was everywhere shutting close down around him. As he followed the muffled sound, in his efforts to get back to the barn, it seemed to retreat from him, and he ran faster to overtake it. He ran on and on, and so was lost.

That night and the next day a few neighbors, gathered from the adjoining farms, searched for Willie. They wandered about the fields and the margin of the woods, but found no trace of the lost child. It became apparent that a general search must be made.

The fog had cleared away on the second morning after Willie was lost, as about a hundred woodsmen and farmers and hunters, gathered from the farms and forest and settlement nearby, called Whiskey Hollow, stood and sat in grotesque groups around the little farmhouse and barn, waiting the grand organization into line, preparatory to sweeping the woods, and finding Willie.

During all the hours of the two previous nights the lanterns and torches had been flashing in and out behind the logs and brush of the fallows; and the patches of snow that lingered in spite of the April rains gave evidence that every foot of the adjacent clearing had been trampled over in the search. But the men were not yet satisfied that the search about the farm had been thorough. Standing by the house, they could see the field of the night's work—the level stubble of the grain-lot, and the broad, irregular hollow used as pasture, and filled with stumps and logs and brush. Here and there could be seen men still busy poking sticks under the logs, and working around bog holes in the low ground. "You see it stands to reason," said Jim, addressing a group by the house, "that a little chap less than four years old could not get out of this clearing into the woods."

A white-haired patriarch remarked, with great confidence and solemnity, "The boy is within half a mile of the house; and, if I can have command of six men, I will find him." The patriarch continued to press his suggestion until he secured his company and started off, feeling that he carried a great weight of responsibility. He joined the log-pokers and bog-explorers; but nothing came of his search.

The morning was wearing away; the men, gathered from a great distance, were impatient of the delay to organize the line.

Willie had been out nearly forty-eight hours. Could it be that he had passed beyond the stubble-field into the forest, nearly half a mile from the house? If he had managed to cross the brook at the edge of the woods, he had the vast Adirondack Wilderness before him. It was time to search thoroughly and upon a large scale, if the boy was to be found alive.

But a reason for delay was whispered around—the fortune-woman was coming. Soon a rough farm-wagon came up the road and through the yard-gate, and stopped in front of the door of the farmhouse. There was a hush of voices, and a reverent look upon the part of some of the men, and a snicker and digging of their neighbors' ribs upon the part of others, as a large, coarse-featured woman was helped out of the wagon by the driver of the team.

This female was the famous fortune-woman. Some of these dwellers on the edge of the wilderness were no better than the classic Greek and noble Roman of ancient times; for they believed in divination.

The fortune-woman went into the house where the mother of Willie sat, crying. The men crowded the room and windows and door. Some of the men looked solemn; some jeered. Out at the door Josh explained apologetically to the unbelievers, that, "inasmuch as some thinks as how she can tell, and some thinks as how she can't, so it were thought better for to go and fetch her, so as that all might satisfactory themselves, and no fault found, and every thing done for the little boy."

After a brief *séance* with the teacup in the house, the fortune-woman, urged by the men, went "out of doors" and walked up along the hollow with her teacup, experimenting to find the child. About half of the men straggled after her. Jim declared to the group who lingered at the house that he would sell out and leave, if the entire crowd disgraced the town by following after that "old she-devil."

To a stranger coming upon the field at this time, the scene was curious and picturesque, and some of it unaccountable. In the background was a vast descending plain of evergreen forest, sloping away from the Adirondack highlands to the dim distance of the St. Lawrence Valley, where could be seen the white, thread-like line of the great river; and still beyond the Canada woods, melting away to a measureless distance of airy blue. In the foreground was a vulgar old woman waddling along, and snatching here and there a teacupful of water from the puddles formed by the melting snow; and fifty vigorous men in awe-struck attitudes were gazing at her, and, when she moved, they followed her.

Odd as this grotesque performance seemed, it had in it a touch of the old heathenish grandeur belonging to the ancient superstitions. The same strange light that through all time has shone from human faces as souls reach after the great infinite unknown shone from the faces of some of these men. There were fine visages among them. Burly Josh and a hunter with dark, poetic eyes would have been a match for handsome, pious Æneas or the heroes of Hellas, who watched the flight of birds, and believed in a fortune-woman at Delphos.

But the simple faith of these modern worshippers was not rewarded: after the Greek pattern, the oracle gave ambiguous responses. The old woman proclaimed, with her eyes snapping venomously, that there was "a big black baste a-standin' over the swate child." She announced, with a swing of her right arm extending around half a circle, that "the dear, innocent darlin' was somewhere about off that way from the house." She scolded the men sharply for their laziness, telling them they had not looked for the lost child, but were waiting around the house, "while the blessed baby starved, and the big black baste stood over him."

Dan caught at this, and declared that the "old hypocrite" was no fool.

She knew enough to understand that "it was no way to find a lost boy to shell out a whole township of able-bodied men, and set them to chase an old woman around a lot."

The fortune-woman came back to the house, held a final grand *séance* with the teacup divinity, and declared that the "swate child" was within half a mile of the place, and if they would only look they would find him, and that, if they did not look, within two days "the big black baste would devour the poor, neglected darlin'." After this the fortune-woman was put into the wagon again, and Josh drove her home. It was fully in accordance with the known perversity of human nature, that the faith of the believers in her infallibility was not in the slightest degree shaken.

The company, having been increased by fresh arrivals to more than one hundred men, organized for the search. The colonel ranged the men in line about twenty feet apart, extending across the wide stubble-field and the pasture. The men were directed by the colonel to "dress to the left;" that is, as he explained it, for each to watch the man at the left, and keep twenty feet from him, and observe all the ground in marching.

The word was given, and the line, more than half a mile long, began to move sidewise or platoon fashion, sweeping from the road by the house across the clearing to the woods. It was a grand charge upon the great wilderness. The long platoon, under the instruction of their commander, swept the woods bordering the clearing, and then, doubling back, made semicircular curves, going deeper and deeper at each return into the primeval forest. The limit of their marching and counter-marching in one direction was a river too broad to be crossed by fallen trees: it was sure that Willie could not have crossed the river. The termination of the marches in the other direction was controlled by the judgment of the colonel. It was a magnificent tramp through the wild, wet woods, under the giant trees, each eye strained, and expectant of the lost boy. Here and there, in advance of the line as it progressed, a partridge, aroused by the voices of the men, would start from the undergrowth, and trip along a few steps with her sharp, coquettish *"quit, quit, quit,"* and then whir away to some adjacent hollow, to be soon again aroused by the advancing line.

The afternoon was wearing away. The woods had been thoroughly explored for about two miles from the clearing,—far beyond what it seemed possible for an infant less than four years old to penetrate.

The colonel said he could think of nothing more to be done. The men returned in struggling groups to the farmhouse, tired, sad, hungry, and dispirited. There were many speculations whether Willie could be still alive, and, if alive, whether he could get through another night. "You see," said Josh, "such a *little* feller, and three days and two nights a-wettin' and a-freezin' and a-thawin', and no grub: why, he couldn't, don't you see?"

It was never found out, not even in Whiskey Hollow, where the men unveiled all their iniquities, who the wretch was that first started the dark suggestion about the *murder* of little Willie. Dan became very angry when the men, fatigued and famished, straggling back to the farmhouse from the disorganized line, as above narrated, began to hint that "things was tremendous queer," and that "them as lost could find," and that John, Willie's father, was a perfect hyena when he was "mad."

Dan, for the only time that day, became profane as he denounced the sneak, whoever it might be, who had started such a suggestion. He expressed the conviction that the fortune-woman had her foot in it some way. Superstitious fools, he said, were likely to be suspicious.

But Dan's anathemas did not stay the rising tide. As the searchers came back, suspicious glances were turned upon the father, who sat with his afflicted family at the house. Some of the searchers stealthily examined under the barn, believing that Willie had been "knocked on the head" with a flail, and concealed under the floor.

But John the father was no coward, and he had neighbors and friends who believed in him. They told him of the suspicions arising against him. On the instant he called a meeting at the little hovel of a schoolhouse, a few rods down the road. The hundred searchers gathered there, and filled the room, sitting, lolling, and lying upon the benches. The father of the lost child, almost a stranger to most of the searchers, took his place at the teacher's desk, and confronted his accusers.

It was plain, direct work. Here were a hundred men who had exhausted all known means of finding the lost boy; and more than fifty of them had said in effect to the man before them, "We think you killed him." All were looking at John: he rose up, and, facing the crowd with a dauntless eye, he made a speech.

If this were a story told by Homer or Herodotus, I suppose John's speech would figure as a wonderful piece of eloquence; for a man never had a grander opportunity to try his strength in persuading others than John had. But in fact there was nothing grand about the matter, except that here was a straightforward man with nerves of steel, who had been "hard hit," as Dan said, by the loss of his boy, and was now repelling with courage, and almost scorn, a thrust that might have killed a weaker man.

His speech was grammatically correct, cool, deliberate, and dignified. He said he had no knowledge of the black-hearted man who had originated so cruel a suspicion at such a time, and he did not wish to know who he was. He asked his hearers to consider how entirely without support in the known facts of the case the accusations were that had been suggested against him. It was a purely gratuitous assumption, with not a particle of evidence of any kind to establish it. He had understood that he was supposed to have killed his child in anger, and then concealed the body. Such a thing could not have happened with him as killing his own child or any other child in that way; and, if it had so happened, he would not have concealed it. He only wished to brand this creation of some vile man, there present probably, as a lie. That was all he had to say upon that point.

In continuing his speech, when he alluded to what he had suffered in losing the boy he loved the best of any thing on earth, there was a twitching of the muscles of his face, which, however he instantly controlled as unworthy of him. He closed his speech by appealing to his friends, who had known him long and well, to come forward at this time, and testify to his integrity.

As he ceased, the men rose up from the benches, and conversed together freely of the probabilities about John. A group of three or four gathered around him, and, placing their hands upon his shoulders, told the crowd that they had known John for twenty years, and that he was incapable of murder, or perfidy, or deceit, and as honest a man as could be found in the county.

It was decided not to search any farther that day, as there was no prospect now that Willie would be found alive. The men went home, agreeing to come again after three days, by which time the sleet and light snow that had fallen would have melted, and search for the body might be successfully made.

John went to his house. As he met his afflicted family, and realized that little Willie was now gone, that the search was given up, and his child was dead, his Spartan firmness yielded, and he wept such tears as strong, proud men weep when broken on the wheel of life. The last cruel stab at his moral nature and integrity hurt hard. He was a pure, upright man, a church-member, and without reproach.

As the three days were passing away that were to elapse before the search for the body should begin, it became apparent in the community that John's Homeric speech had done no good. The wise heads of Whiskey Hollow declared, that at the next search there would be, first of all, a thorough overhauling about the immediate premises. Their suspicions found some favor in the community. Some were discussing indignantly and some with tolerance, the probability of John's guilt. Even good Deacon Beezman, a magistrate who "lived out on the main road," and who was supposed to carry in his own person at least half of the integrity and intelligence of his neighborhood, declared that he would not spend more of his precious time in searching for the boy. He made it the chief point in the case that John "acted guilty." He had noticed that this rustic Spartan sat in his house, and read his newspaper with apparent interest, as in ordinary times, on the day of the last search; and this indifference was evidence of his guilt. It was apparent that any color of proof, if there had been any such thing, might have served as a pretence for an arrest of the afflicted father.

The morning appointed as the time to seek for the body came. The excitement was high; and men came from great distances to join in the exploration.

Eight miles away, up across the river that flowed through the forest, dwelt Logan Bill, a hunter. At an early hour he left his cabin, and took his course down the stream toward the gathering-point. There was an April sun shining; but in the wilderness solitudes it was cold and dreary. He kept along the margin of the stream to avoid the tangle of brush and fallen trees.

At nine o'clock, Logan was still three miles from John's clearing. He was passing through a hollow where the black spruce and pine made the forest gloomy. He came upon a bundle of clothing; he turned it over: it was Willie!

And thus alone in the wilderness Logan solved the mystery. Through three miles of trackless forest, under the sombre, sighing trees of the great woods, through the fog and falling rain and snow, the child had struggled on, feeling its way in the night along the margin of the river, until it grew weak and sick, and fell and died.

There was a choking in Logan's throat as he lifted the cold little body, and carried it onward down the stream, and noted the places where the infant must have climbed and scrambled in its little battle for life. It was a strange two hours to him as he bore the pure, beautiful, frozen corpse toward the settlement.

At eleven o'clock he reached the clearing. He saw the scattered groups of men gathered about John's house and barn. Some of the men seemed to be searching the barn to find the body of the boy they believed to be murdered. Logan felt his frame tremble, and his temples throb, realizing as he did the weight of life and death wrapped in the burden that he bore. He spoke no word, and made no gesture, but, holding the dead child in his arms, marched directly past the barn to the door-yard, and up in front of the house. There he stopped, and stood and looked with agitated face at the farmhouse door.

The shock of Logan's sudden coming was so great that no one said, "The body is found;" but all the men stopped talking, and some, pale and agitated, gathered in a close huddle around Logan, and looked at the little, white, frosted face, and in hushed tones asked where Logan had found the body.

A blanket was brought, and spread upon a dry place in the yard, and Logan laid his little burden upon it.

John came out, and approached the spot where his little Willie was lying. There was a deeper hush as the crowd made way for the father; and the rough men, some of whom were now crying, looked hard at John "to see how he would take it." John stood and gazed, unmoved and lion-like: not a muscle of his strong face quivered as he saw his boy. He called in a tone of authority for his family to come, and said to his wife in a clear, calm voice, as she came trembling, weeping, fainting, "Mother, look upon your son."

He turned, and surveyed the crowd with the same dauntless eye he had shown in making his Homeric speech at the schoolhouse. To some of the company that eye was now a dagger.

John was cool, calm, and polite. He uttered no reproach, and was kind in his words to all. A half-hour passed. The crowd went away in groups, discussing the amazing wonder, "how ever it could be that such a little feller as Willie could have got so far away from the house."

The next day religious services were held, and in the afternoon little Willie was laid to rest upon a sunny knoll. John wept at the grave. A poisoned arrow was drawn from the strong man's heart, and a great grief was there in its stead.

JEAN-AH POQUELIN

George Washington Cable

In the first decade of the present century, when the newly established American Government was the most hateful thing in Louisiana—when the Creoles were still kicking at such vile innovations as the trial by jury, American dances, anti-smuggling laws, and the printing of the Governor's proclamation in English—when the Anglo-American flood that was presently to burst in a crevasse of immigration upon the delta had thus far been felt only as slippery seepage which made the Creole tremble for his footing—there stood, a short distance above what is now Canal Street, and considerably back from the line of villas which fringed the river-bank on Tchoupitoulas Road, an old colonial plantation-house half in ruin.

It stood aloof from civilization, the tracts that had once been its indigo fields given over to their first noxious wildness, and grown up into one of the horridest marshes within a circuit of fifty miles.

The house was of heavy cypress, lifted up on pillars, grim, solid, and spiritless, its massive build a strong reminder of days still earlier, when every man had been his own peace officer and the insurrection of the blacks a daily contingency. Its dark, weather-beaten roof and sides were hoisted up above the jungly plain in a distracted way, like a gigantic ammunition-wagon stuck in the mud and abandoned by some retreating army. Around it was a dense growth of low water willows, with half a hundred sorts of thorny or fetid bushes, savage strangers alike to the "language of flowers" and to the botanist's Greek. They were hung with countless strands of discolored and prickly smilax, and the impassable mud below bristled with *chevaux de frise* of the dwarf palmetto. Two lone forest-trees, dead cypresses, stood in the centre of the marsh, dotted with roosting vultures.

The shallow strips of water were hid by myriads of aquatic plants, under whose coarse and spiritless flowers, could one have seen it, was a harbor of reptiles, great and small, to make one shudder to the end of his days.

The house was on a slightly raised spot, the levee of a draining canal. The waters of this canal did not run; they crawled, and were full of big, ravening fish and alligators, that held it against all comers.

Such was the home of old Jean Marie Poquelin, once an opulent indigo planter, standing high in the esteem of his small, proud circle of exclusively male acquaintances in the old city; now a hermit, alike shunned by and shunning all who had ever known him. "The last of his line," said the gossips. His father lies under the floor of the St. Louis Cathedral, with the wife of his youth on one side, and the wife of his old age on the other. Old Jean visits the spot daily. His half-brother—alas! there was a mystery; no one knew what had become of the gentle, young half-brother, more than thirty years his junior, whom once he seemed so fondly to love, but who, seven years ago, had disappeared suddenly, once for all, and left no clew of his fate.

They had seemed to live so happily in each other's love. No father, mother, wife to either, no kindred upon earth. The elder a bold, frank, impetuous, chivalric adventurer; the younger a gentle, studious, book-loving recluse; they lived upon the ancestral estate like mated birds, one always on the wing, the other always in the nest.

There was no trait in Jean Marie Poquelin, said the old gossips, for which he was so well known among his few friends as his apparent fondness for his "little brother." "Jacques said this," and "Jacques said that;" he "would leave this or that, or any thing to Jacques," for "Jacques was a scholar," and "Jacques was good," or "wise," or "just," or "far-sighted," as the nature of the case required; and "he should ask Jacques as soon as he got home," since Jacques was never elsewhere to be seen.

It was between the roving character of the one brother, and the bookishness of the other, that the estate fell into decay. Jean Marie, generous gentleman, gambled the slaves away one by one, until none was left, man or woman, but one old African mute.

The indigo-fields and vats of Louisiana had been generally abandoned as unremunerative. Certain enterprising men had substituted the culture of sugar; but while the recluse was too apathetic to take as so active a course, the other saw larger, and, at that time, equally respectable profits, first in smuggling, and later in the African slave-trade. What harm could he see in it? The whole people said it was vitally necessary, and to minister to a vital public necessity,—good enough, certainly, and so he laid up many a doubloon, that made him none the worse in the public regard.

One day old Jean Marie was about to start upon a voyage that was to be longer, much longer, than any that he had yet made. Jacques had begged him hard for many days not to go, but he laughed him off, and finally said, kissing him:

"*Adieu, 'tit frère.*"

"No," said Jacques, "I shall go with you."

They left the old hulk of a house in the sole care of the African mute, and went away to the Guinea coast together.

Two years after, old Poquelin came home without his vessel. He must have arrived at his house by night. No one saw him come. No one saw "his little brother;" rumor whispered that he, too, had returned, but he had never been seen again.

A dark suspicion fell upon the old slave-trader. No matter that the few kept the many reminded of the tenderness that had ever marked his bearing to the missing man. The many shook their heads. "You know he has a quick and fearful temper;" and "why does he cover his loss with mystery?" "Grief would out with the truth."

"But," said the charitable few, "look in his face; see that expression of true humanity." The many did look in his face, and, as he looked in theirs, he read the silent question: "Where is thy brother Abel?" The few were silenced, his former friends died off, and the name of Jean Marie Poquelin became a symbol of witchery, devilish crime, and hideous nursery fictions.

The man and his house were alike shunned. The snipe and duck hunters forsook the marsh, and the woodcutters abandoned the canal. Sometimes the hardier boys who ventured out there snake-shooting heard a slow thumping of oar-locks on the canal. They would look at each other for a moment half in consternation, half in glee, then rush from their sport in wanton haste to assail with their gibes the unoffending, withered old man who, in rusty attire, sat in the stern of a skiff, rowed homeward by his white-headed African mute.

"O Jean-ah Poquelin! O Jean-ah! Jean-ah Poquelin!"

It was not necessary to utter more than that. No hint of wickedness, deformity, or any physical or moral demerit; merely the name and tone of mockery: "Oh, Jean-ah Poquelin!" and while they tumbled one over another in their needless haste to fly, he would rise carefully from his seat, while the aged mute, with downcast face, went on rowing, and rolling up his brown fist and extending it toward the urchins, would pour forth such an unholy broadside of French imprecation and invective as would all but craze them with delight.

Among both blacks and whites the house was the object of a thousand superstitions. Every midnight, they affirmed, the *feu follet* came out of the marsh and ran in and out of the rooms, flashing from window to window. The story of some lads, whose words in ordinary statements were worthless, was generally credited, that the night they camped in the woods, rather than pass the place after dark, they saw, about sunset, every window blood-red, and on each of the four chimneys an owl sitting, which turned his head three times round, and moaned and laughed with a human voice. There was a bottomless well, everybody professed to know, beneath the sill of the big front door under the rotten veranda; whoever set his foot upon that threshold disappeared forever in the depth below.

What wonder the marsh grew as wild as Africa! Take all the Faubourg Ste. Marie, and half the ancient city, you would not find one graceless dare-devil reckless enough to pass within a hundred yards of the house after nightfall.

The alien races pouring into old New Orleans began to find the few streets named for the Bourbon princes too strait for them. The wheel of fortune, beginning to whirl, threw them off beyond the ancient corporation lines, and sowed civilization and even trade upon the lands of the Graviers and Girods. Fields became roads, roads streets. Everywhere the leveller was peering through his glass, rodsmen were whacking their way through willow-brakes and rose-hedges, and the sweating Irishmen tossed the blue clay up with their long-handled shovels.

"Ha! that is all very well," quoth the Jean-Baptistes, feeling the reproach of an enterprise that asked neither co-operation nor advice of them, "but wait till they come yonder to Jean Poquelin's marsh; ha! ha! ha!" The supposed predicament so delighted them, that they put on a mock terror and whirled about in an assumed stampede, then caught their clasped hands between their knees in excess of mirth, and laughed till the tears ran; for whether the street-makers mired in the marsh, or contrived to cut through old "Jean-ah's" property, either event would be joyful. Meantime a line of tiny rods, with bits of white paper in their split tops, gradually extended its way straight through the haunted ground, and across the canal diagonally.

"We shall fill that ditch," said the men in mud-boots, and brushed close along the chained and padlocked gate of the haunted mansion. Ah, Jean-ah Poquelin, those were not Creole boys, to be stampeded with a little hard swearing.

He went to the Governor. That official scanned the odd figure with no slight interest. Jean Poquelin was of short, broad frame, with a bronzed leonine face. His brow was ample and deeply furrowed. His eye, large and black, was bold and open like that of a war-horse, and his jaws shut together with the firmness of iron. He was dressed in a suit of Attakapas cottonade, and his shirt unbuttoned and thrown back from the throat and bosom, sailor-wise, showed a herculean breast, hard and grizzled. There was no fierceness or defiance in his look, no harsh ungentleness, no symptom of his unlawful life or violent temper; but rather a peaceful and peaceable fearlessness. Across the whole face, not marked in one or another feature, but as it were laid softly upon the countenance like an almost imperceptible veil, was the imprint of some great grief. A careless eye might easily overlook it, but, once seen, there it hung—faint, but unmistakable.

The Governor bowed.

"*Parlez-vous français?*" asked the figure.

"I would rather talk English, if you can do so," said the Governor.

"My name, Jean Poquelin."

"How can I serve you, Mr. Poquelin?"

"My 'ouse is yond'; *dans le marais là-bas.*"

The Governor bowed.

"Dat *marais* billong to me."

"Yes, sir."

"To me; Jean Poquelin; I hown 'im meself."

"Well, sir?"

"He don't billong to you; I get him from me father."

"That is perfectly true, Mr. Poquelin, as far as I am aware."

"You want to make strit pass yond'?"

"I do not know, sir; it is quite probable; but the city will indemnify you for any loss you may suffer—you will get paid, you understand."

"Strit can't pass dare."

"You will have to see the municipal authorities about that, Mr. Poquelin."

A bitter smile came upon the old man's face:

"*Pardon, Monsieur,* you is not *le Gouverneur?*"

"Yes."

"*Mais,* yes. You har *le Gouverneur*—yes. Veh-well. I come to you. I tell you, strit can't pass at me 'ouse."

"But you will have to see"—

"I come to you. You is *le Gouverneur.* I know not the new laws. I ham a Fr-r-rench-a-man! Fr-rench-a-man have something *aller au contraire*—he come at his *Gouverneur.* I come at you. If me not had been bought from me king like *bossals* in the hold time, ze king gof—France would-a-show *Monsieur le Gouverneur* to take care his men to make strit in right places. *Mais,* I know; we billong to *Monsieur le Président.* I want you do somesin for me, eh?"

"What is it?" asked the patient Governor.

"I want you tell *Monsieur le Président,* strit—can't—pass—at—me—'ouse."

"Have a chair, Mr. Poquelin;" but the old man did not stir. The Governor took a quill and wrote a line to a city official, introducing Mr. Poquelin, and asking for him every possible courtesy. He handed it to him, instructing him where to present it.

"Mr. Poquelin," he said with a conciliatory smile, "tell me, is it your house that our Creole citizens tell such odd stories about?"

The old man glared sternly upon the speaker, and with immovable features said:

"You don't see me trade some Guinea nigga'?"

"Oh, no."

"You don't see me make some smugglin'?"

"No, sir; not at all."

"But, I am Jean Marie Poquelin. I mine me hown bizniss. Dat all right? Adieu."

He put his hat on and withdrew. By and by he stood, letter in hand, before the person to whom it was addressed. This person employed an interpreter.

"He says," said the interpreter to the officer, "he come to make you the fair warning how you muz not make the street pas' at his 'ouse."

The officer remarked that "such impudence was refreshing;" but the experienced interpreter translated freely.

"He says: 'Why you don't want?'" said the interpreter.

The old slave-trader answered at some length.

"He says," said the interpreter, again turning to the officer, "the marass is a too unhealth' for peopl' to live."

"But we expect to drain his old marsh; it's not going to be a marsh."

"*Il dit*"—The interpreter explained in French.

The old man answered tersely.

"He says the canal is a private," said the interpreter.

"Oh! *that* old ditch; that's to be filled up. Tell the old man we're going to fix him up nicely."

Translation being duly made, the man in power was amused to see a thunder-cloud gathering on the old man's face.

"Tell him," he added, "by the time we finish, there'll not be a ghost left in his shanty."

The interpreter began to translate, but—

"*J' comprends, J' comprends*," said the old man, with an impatient gesture, and burst forth, pouring curses upon the United States, the President, the Territory of Orleans, Congress, the Governor and all his subordinates, striding out of the apartment as he cursed, while the object of his maledictions roared with merriment and rammed the floor with his foot.

"Why, it will make his old place worth ten dollars to one," said the official to the interpreter.

"'Tis not for de worse of de property," said the interpreter.

"I should guess not," said the other, whittling his chair,—"seems to me as if some of these old Creoles would liever live in a crawfish hole than to have a neighbor."

"You know what make old Jean Poquelin make like that? I will tell you. You know"—

The interpreter was rolling a cigarette, and paused to light his tinder; then, as the smoke poured in a thick double stream from his nostrils, he said, in a solemn whisper:

"He is a witch."

"Ho, ho, ho!" laughed the other.

"You don't believe it? What you want to bet?" cried the interpreter, jerking himself half up and thrusting out one arm while he bared it of its coat-sleeve with the hand of the other. "What you want to bet?"

"How do you know?" asked the official.

"Dass what I goin' to tell you. You know, one evening I was shooting some *grosbec.* I killed three; but I had trouble to fine them, it was becoming so dark. When I have them I start' to come home; then I got to pas' at Jean Poquelin's house."

"Ho, ho, ho!" laughed the other, throwing his leg over the arm of his chair.

"Wait," said the interpreter. "I come along slow, not making some noises; still, still"—

"And scared," said the smiling one.

"*Mais,* wait. I get all pas' the 'ouse. 'Ah!' I say; 'all right!' Then I see two thing' before! Hah! I get as cold and humide, and shake like a leaf. You think it was nothing? There I see, so plain as can be (though it was making nearly dark), I see Jean—Marie—Po-que-lin walkin' right in front, and right there beside of him was something like a man—but not a man—white like paint!—I dropp' on the grass from scared—they pass'; so sure as I live 'twas the ghos' of Jacques Poquelin, his brother!"

"Pooh!" said the listener.

"I'll put my han' in the fire," said the interpreter.

"But did you never think," asked the other, "that that might be Jack Poquelin, as you call him, alive and well, and for some cause hid away by his brother?"

"But there har' no cause!" said the other, and the entrance of third parties changed the subject.

Some months passed and the street was opened. A canal was first dug through the marsh, the small one which passed so close to Jean Poquelin's house was filled, and the street, or rather a sunny road, just touched a corner of the old mansion's dooryard. The morass ran dry. Its venomous denizens slipped away through the bulrushes; the cattle roaming freely upon its hardened surface trampled the superabundant undergrowth. The bellowing frogs croaked to westward. Lilies and the flower-de-luce sprang up in the place of reeds; a smilax and poison-oak gave way to the purple-plumed iron-weed and pink spiderwort; the bindweeds ran everywhere blooming as they ran, and on one of the dead cypresses a giant creeper hung its green burden of foliage and lifted its scarlet trumpets. Sparrows and red-birds flitted through the bushes, and dewberries grew ripe beneath. Over all these came a sweet, dry smell of salubrity which the place had not known since the sediments of the Mississippi first lifted it from the sea.

But its owner did not build. Over the willow-brakes, and down the vista of the open street, bright new houses, some singly, some by ranks, were prying in upon the old man's privacy. They even settled down toward his southern side. First a wood-cutter's hut or two, then a market gardener's shanty, then a painted cottage, and all at once the faubourg had flanked and half surrounded him and his dried-up marsh.

Ah! then the common people began to hate him. "The old tyrant!" "You don't mean an old *tyrant?*" "Well, then, why don't he build when the public need demands it? What does he live in that unneighborly way for?" "The old pirate!" "The old kidnapper!" How easily even the most ultra Louisianians put on the imported virtues of the North when they could be brought to bear against the hermit. "There he goes, with the boys after him! Ah! ha! ha! Jean-ah Poquelin! Ah! Jean-ah! Aha! aha! Jean-ah Marie! Jean-ah Poquelin! The old villain!" How merrily the swarming Américains echo the spirit of persecution! "The old fraud," they say—"pretends to live in a haunted house, does he? We'll tar and feather him some day. Guess we can fix him."

He cannot be rowed home along the old canal now; he walks. He has broken sadly of late, and the street urchins are ever at his heels. It is like the days when they cried: "Go up, thou bald-head," and the old man now and then turns and delivers ineffectual curses.

To the Creoles—to the incoming lower class of superstitious Germans, Irish, Sicilians, and others—he became an omen and embodiment of public and private ill-fortune. Upon him all the vagaries of their superstitions gathered and grew. If a house caught fire, it was imputed to his machinations. Did a woman go off in a fit, he had bewitched her. Did a child stray off for an hour, the mother shivered with the apprehension that Jean Poquelin had offered him to strange gods. The house was the subject of every bad boy's invention who loved to contrive ghostly lies. "As long as that house stands we shall have bad luck. Do you not see our pease and beans dying, our cabbages and lettuce going to seed, and our gardens turning to dust, while every day you can see it raining in the woods? The rain will never pass old Poquelin's house. He keeps a fetich. He has conjured the whole Faubourg St. Marie. And why, the old wretch? Simply because our playful and innocent children call after him as he passes."

A "Building and Improvement Company," which had not yet got its charter, "but was going to," and which had not, indeed, any tangible capital yet, but "was going to have some," joined the "Jean-ah Poquelin" war. The haunted property would be such a capital site for a market-house! They sent a deputation to the old mansion to ask its occupant to sell. The deputation never got beyond the chained gate and a very barren interview with the African mute. The President of the Board was then empowered (for he had studied French in Pennsylvania and was considered qualified) to call and persuade M. Poquelin to subscribe to the company's stock; but—

"Fact is, gentlemen," he said at the next meeting, "it would take us at least twelve months to make Mr. Pokaleen understand the rather original features of our system, and he wouldn't subscribe when we'd done; besides, the only way to see him is to stop him on the street."

There was a great laugh from the Board; they couldn't help it. "Better meet a bear robbed of her whelps," said one.

"You're mistaken as to that," said the President. "I did meet him, and stopped him, and found him quite polite. But I could get no satisfaction from him; the fellow wouldn't talk in French, and when I spoke in English he hoisted his old shoulders up, and gave the same answer to every thing I said."

"And that was—?" asked one or two, impatient of the pause.

"That it 'don't worse w'ile?'"

One of the Board said: "Mr. President, this market-house project, as I take it, is not altogether a selfish one; the community is to be benefited by it. We may feel that we are working in the public interest [the Board smiled knowingly], if we employ all possible means to oust this old nuisance from among us. You may know that at the time the street was cut through, this old Poquelann did all he could to prevent it. It was owing to a certain connection which I had with that affair that I heard a ghost story [smiles, followed by a sudden dignified check]—ghost story, which, of course, I am not going to relate; but I *may* say that my profound conviction, arising from a prolonged study of that story, is, that this old villain, John Poquelann, has his brother locked up in that old house. Now, if this is so, and we can fix it on him, I merely *suggest* that we can make the matter highly useful. I don't know," he added, beginning to sit down, "but that it is an action we owe to the community—hem!"

"How do you propose to handle the subject?" asked the President.

"I was thinking," said the speaker, "that, as a Board of Directors, it would be unadvisable for us to authorize any action involving trespass; but if you, for instance, Mr. President, should, as it were, for mere curiosity, *request* some one, as, for instance, our excellent Secretary, simply as a personal favor, to look into the matter—this is merely a suggestion."

The Secretary smiled sufficiently to be understood that, while he certainly did not consider such preposterous service a part of his duties as secretary, he might, notwithstanding, accede to the President's request; and the Board adjourned.

Little White, as the Secretary was called, was a mild, kind-hearted little man, who, nevertheless, had no fear of any thing, unless it was the fear of being unkind.

"I tell you frankly," he privately said to the President, "I go into this purely for reasons of my own."

The next day, a little after nightfall, one might have descried this little man slipping along the rear fence of the Poquelin place, preparatory to vaulting over into the rank, grass-grown yard, and bearing himself altogether more after the manner of a collector of rare chickens than according to the usage of secretaries.

The picture presented to his eye was not calculated to enliven his mind. The old mansion stood out against the western sky, black and silent. One long, lurid pencil-stroke along a sky of slate was all that was left of daylight. No sign of life was apparent; no light at any window, unless it might have been on the side of the house hidden from view. No owls were on the chimneys, no dogs were in the yard.

He entered the place, and ventured up behind a small cabin which stood apart from the house. Through one of its many crannies he easily detected the African mute crouched before a flickering pine-knot, his head on his knees, fast asleep.

He concluded to enter the mansion, and, with that view, stood and scanned it. The broad rear steps of the veranda would not serve him; he might meet some one midway. He was measuring, with his eye, the proportions of one of the pillars which supported it, and estimating the practicability of climbing it, when he heard a footstep. Some one dragged a chair out toward the railing, then seemed to change his mind and began to pace the veranda, his footfalls resounding on the dry boards with singular loudness. Little White drew a step backward, got the figure between himself and the sky, and at once recognized the short, broad-shouldered form of old Jean Poquelin.

He sat down upon a billet of wood, and, to escape the stings of a whining cloud of mosquitoes, shrouded his face and neck in his handkerchief, leaving his eyes uncovered.

He had sat there but a moment when he noticed a strange, sickening odor, faint, as if coming from a distance, but loathsome and horrid.

Whence could it come? Not from the cabin; not from the marsh, for it was as dry as powder. It was not in the air; it seemed to come from the ground.

Rising up, he noticed, for the first time, a few steps before him a narrow footpath leading toward the house. He glanced down it—ha! right there was some one coming—ghostly white!

Quick as thought, and as noiselessly, he lay down at full length against the cabin. It was bold strategy, and yet, there was no denying it, little White felt that he was frightened. "It is not a ghost," he said to himself. "I *know* it cannot be a ghost;" but the perspiration burst out at every pore, and the air seemed to thicken with heat. "It is a living man," he said in his thoughts. "I hear his footstep, and I hear old Poquelin's footsteps, too, separately, over on the veranda. I am not discovered; the thing has passed; there is that odor again; what a smell of death! Is it coming back? Yes. It stops at the door of the cabin. Is it peering in at the sleeping mute? It moves away. It is in the path again. Now it is gone." He shuddered. "Now, if I dare venture, the mystery is solved." He rose cautiously, close against the cabin, and peered along the path.

The figure of a man, a presence if not a body—but whether clad in some white stuff or naked the darkness would not allow him to determine—had turned, and now, with a seeming painful gait, moved slowly from him. "Great Heaven! can it be that the dead do walk?" He withdrew again the hands which had gone to his eyes. The dreadful object passed between two pillars and under the house. He listened. There was a faint sound as of feet upon a staircase; then all was still except the measured tread of Jean Poquelin walking on the veranda, and the heavy respirations of the mute slumbering in the cabin.

The little Secretary was about to retreat; but as he looked once more toward the haunted house a dim light appeared in the crack of a closed window, and presently old Jean Poquelin came, dragging his chair, and sat down close against the shining cranny. He spoke in a low, tender tone in the French tongue, making some inquiry. An answer came from within. Was it the voice of a human? So unnatural was it—so hollow, so discordant, so unearthly—that the stealthy listener shuddered again from head to foot, and when something stirred in some bushes near by—though it may have been nothing more than a rat—and came scuttling through the grass, the little Secretary actually turned and fled. As he left the enclosure he moved with bolder leisure through the bushes; yet now and then he spoke aloud: "Oh, oh! I see, I understand!" and shut his eyes in his hands.

How strange that henceforth little White was the champion of Jean Poquelin! In season and out of season—wherever a word was uttered against him—the Secretary, with a quiet, aggressive force that instantly arrested gossip, demanded upon what authority the statement or conjecture was made; but as he did not condescend to explain his own remarkable attitude, it was not long before the disrelish and suspicion which had followed Jean Poquelin so many years fell also upon him.

It was only the next evening but one after his adventure that he made himself a source of sullen amazement to one hundred and fifty boys, by ordering them to desist from their wanton hallooing. Old Jean Poquelin, standing and shaking his cane, rolling out his long-drawn maledictions, paused and stared, then gave the Secretary a courteous bow and started on. The boys, save one, from pure astonishment, ceased; but a ruffianly little Irish lad, more daring than any had yet been, threw a big hurtling clod, that struck old Poquelin between the shoulders and burst like a shell. The enraged old man wheeled with uplifted staff to give chase to the scampering vagabond; and—he may have tripped, or he may not, but he fell full length. Little White hastened to help him up, but he waved him off with a fierce imprecation and staggering to his feet resumed his way homeward. His lips were reddened with blood.

Little White was on his way to the meeting of the Board. He would have given all he dared to spend to have staid away, for he felt both too fierce and too tremulous to brook the criticisms that were likely to be made.

"I can't help it, gentlemen; I can't help you to make a case against the old man, and I'm not going to."

"We did not expect this disappointment, Mr. White."

"I can't help that, sir. No, sir; you had better not appoint any more investigations. Somebody'll investigate himself into trouble. No, sir; it isn't a threat, it is only my advice, but I warn you that whoever takes the task in hand will rue it to his dying day—which may be hastened, too."

The President expressed himself "surprised."

"I don't care a rush," answered little White, wildly and foolishly. "I don't care a rush if you are, sir. No, my nerves are not disordered; my head's as clear as a bell. No, I'm *not* excited."

A Director remarked that the Secretary looked as though he had waked from a nightmare.

"Well, sir, if you want to know the fact, I have; and if you choose to cultivate old Poquelin's society you can have one, too."

"White," called a facetious member, but White did not notice. "White," he called again.

"What?" demanded White, with a scowl.

"Did you see the ghost?"

"Yes, sir; I did," cried White, hitting the table, and handing the President a paper which brought the Board to other business.

The story got among the gossips that somebody (they were afraid to say little White) had been to the Poquelin mansion by night and beheld something appalling. The rumor was but a shadow of the truth, magnified and distorted as is the manner of shadows. He had seen skeletons walking, and had barely escaped the clutches of one by making the sign of the cross.

Some madcap boys with an appetite for the horrible plucked up courage to venture through the dried marsh by the cattle-path, and come before the house at a spectral hour when the air was full of bats. Something which they but half saw—half a sight was enough—sent them tearing back through the willow-brakes and acacia bushes to their homes, where they fairly dropped down, and cried:

"Was it white?" "No—yes—nearly so—we can't tell—but we saw it." And one could hardly doubt, to look at their ashen faces, that they had, whatever it was.

"If that old rascal lived in the country we come from," said certain Américains, "he'd have been tarred and feathered before now, wouldn't he, Sanders?"

"Well, now he just would."

"And we'd have rid him on a rail, wouldn't we?"

"That's what I allow."

"Tell you what you *could* do." They were talking to some rollicking Creoles who had assumed an absolute necessity for doing *something*. "What is it you call this thing where an old man marries a young girl, and you come out with horns and"—

"*Charivari?*" asked the Creoles.

"Yes, that's it. Why don't you shivaree him?" Felicitous suggestion.

Little White, with his wife beside him, was sitting on their doorsteps on the sidewalk, as Creole custom had taught them, looking toward the sunset. They had moved into the lately-opened street. The view was not attractive on the score of beauty. The houses were small and scattered, and across the flat commons, spite of the lofty tangle of weeds and bushes, and spite of the thickets of acacia, they needs must see the dismal old Poquelin mansion, tilted awry and shutting out the declining sun. The moon, white and slender, was hanging the tip of its horn over one of the chimneys.

"And you say," said the Secretary, "the old black man has been going by here alone? Patty, suppose old Poquelin should be concocting some mischief; he don't lack provocation; the way that clod hit him the other day was enough to have killed him. Why, Patty, he dropped as quick as *that!* No wonder you haven't seen him. I wonder if they haven't heard something about him up at the drug-store. Suppose I go and see."

"Do," said his wife.

She sat alone for half an hour, watching that sudden going out of the day peculiar to the latitude.

"That moon is ghost enough for one house," she said, as her husband returned. "It has gone right down the chimney."

"Patty," said little White, "the drug-clerk says the boys are going to shivaree old Poquelin to-night. I'm going to try to stop it."

"Why, White," said his wife, "you'd better not. You'll get hurt."

"No, I'll not."

"Yes, you will."

"I'm going to sit out here until they come along. They're compelled to pass right by here."

"Why, White, it may be midnight before they start; you're not going to sit out here till then."

"Yes, I am."

"Well, you're very foolish," said Mrs. White in an undertone, looking anxious, and tapping one of the steps with her foot.

They sat a very long time talking over little family matters.

"What's that?" at last said Mrs. White.

"That's the nine-o'clock gun," said White, and they relapsed into a long-sustained, drowsy silence.

"Patty, you'd better go in and go to bed," said he at last.

"I'm not sleepy."

"Well, you're very foolish," quietly remarked little White, and again silence fell upon them.

"Patty, suppose I walk out to the old house and see if I can find out any thing."

"Suppose," said she, "you don't do any such—listen!"

Down the street arose a great hubbub. Dogs and boys were howling and barking; men were laughing, shouting, groaning, and blowing horns, whooping, and clanking cow-bells, whinnying, and howling, and rattling pots and pans.

"They are coming this way," said little White. "You had better go into the house, Patty."

"So had you."

"No. I'm going to see if I can't stop them."

"Why, White!"

"I'll be back in a minute," said White, and went toward the noise.

In a few moments the little Secretary met the mob. The pen hesitates on the word, for there is a respectable difference, measurable only on the scale of the half century, between a mob and a *charivari*. Little White lifted his ineffectual voice. He faced the head of the disorderly column, and cast himself about as if he were made of wood and moved by the jerk of a string. He rushed to one who seemed, from the size and clatter of his tin pan, to be a leader. *"Stop these fellows, Bienvenu, stop them just a minute, till I tell them something."* Bienvenu turned and brandished his instruments of discord in an imploring way to the crowd. They slackened their pace, two or three hushed their horns and joined the prayer of little White and Bienvenu for silence. The throng halted. The hush was delicious.

"Bienvenu," said little White, "don't shivaree old Poquelin to-night; he's"—

"My fwang," said the swaying Bienvenu, "who tail you I goin' to chahivahi somebody, eh? You sink bickause I make a little playfool wiz zis tin pan zat I am *dhonk?*"

"Oh, no, Bienvenu, old fellow, you're all right. I was afraid you might not know that old Poquelin was sick, you know, but you're not going there, are you?"

"My fwang, I vay soy to tail you zat you ah dhonk as de dev'. I am *shem* of you. I ham ze servan' of ze *publique*. Zese *citoyens* goin' to wickwest Jean Poquelin to give to the Ursuline' two hondred fifty dolla'"—

"*Hé quoi!*" cried a listener, "*Cinq cent piastres, oui!*"

"*Oui!*" said Bienvenu, "and if he wiffuse we make him some lit' *musique;* tar-ra ta!" He hoisted a merry hand and foot, then frowning, added: "Old Poquelin got no bizniz dhink s'much w'isky."

"But, gentlemen," said little White, around whom a circle had gathered, "the old man is very sick."

"My faith!" cried a tiny Creole, "we did not make him to be sick. W'en we have say we going make *le charivari,* do you want that we hall tell a lie? My faith! 'sfools!"

"But you can shivaree somebody else," said desperate little White.

"*Oui!*" cried Bienvenu, "*et chahivahi* Jean-ah Poquelin tomo'w!"

"Let us go to Madame Schneider!" cried two or three, and amid huzzas and confused cries, among which was heard a stentorian Celtic call for drinks, the crowd again began to move.

"*Cent piastres pour l'hôpital de charité!*"

"Hurrah!"

"One hougred dolla' for Charity Hospital!"

"Hurrah!"

"Whang!" went a tin pan, the crowd yelled, and Pandemonium gaped again. They were off at a right angle.

Nodding, Mrs. White looked at the mantle-clock.

"Well, if it isn't away after midnight."

The hideous noise down street was passing beyond earshot. She raised a sash and listened. For a moment there was silence. Some one came to the door.

"Is that you, White?"

"Yes." He entered. "I succeeded, Patty."

"Did you?" said Patty, joyfully.

"Yes. They've gone down to shivaree the old Dutchwoman who married her step-daughter's sweetheart. They say she has got to pay a hundred dollars to the hospital before they stop."

The couple retired, and Mrs. White slumbered. She was awakened by her husband snapping the lid of his watch.

"What time?" she asked.

"Half-past three. Patty, I haven't slept a wink. Those fellows are out yet. Don't you hear them?"

"Why, White, they're coming this way!"

"I know they are," said White, sliding out of bed and drawing on his clothes, "and they're coming fast. You'd better go away from that window, Patty. My! what a clatter!"

"Here they are," said Mrs. White, but her husband was gone. Two or three hundred men and boys passed the place at a rapid walk straight down the broad, new street, toward the hated house of ghosts. The din was terrific. She saw little White at the head of the rabble brandishing his arms and trying in vain to make himself heard; but they only shook their heads laughing and hooting the louder, and so passed, bearing him on before them.

Swiftly they pass out from among the houses, away from the dim oil lamps of the street, out into the broad starlit commons, and enter the willowy jungles of the haunted ground. Some hearts fail and their owners lag behind and turn back, suddenly remembering how near morning it is. But the most part push on, tearing the air with their clamor.

Down ahead of them in the long, thicket-darkened way there is—singularly enough—a faint, dancing light. It must be very near the old house; it is. It has stopped now. It is a lantern, and is under a well-known sapling which has grown up on the wayside since the canal was filled. Now it swings mysteriously to and fro. A goodly number of the more ghost-fearing give up the sport; but a full hundred move forward at a run, doubling their devilish howling and banging.

Yes; it is a lantern, and there are two persons under the tree. The crowd draws near—drops into a walk; one of the two is the old African mute; he lifts the lantern up so that it shines on the other; the crowd recoils; there is a hush of all clangor, and all at once, with a cry of mingled fright and horror from every throat, the whole throng rushes back, dropping every thing, sweeping past little White and hurrying on, never stopping until the jungle is left behind, and then to find that not one in ten has seen the cause of the stampede, and not one of the tenth is certain what it was.

There is one huge fellow among them who looks capable of any villany. He finds something to mount on, and, in the Creole *patois*, calls a general halt. Bienvenu sinks down, and, vainly trying to recline gracefully, resigns the leadership. The herd gather round the speaker; he assures them that they have been outraged. Their right peaceably to traverse the public streets has been trampled upon. Shall such encroachments be endured? It is now daybreak. Let them go now by the open light of day and force a free passage of the public highway!

A scattering consent was the response, and the crowd, thinned now and drowsy, straggled quietly down toward the old house. Some drifted ahead, others sauntered behind, but every one, as he again neared the tree, came to a stand-still. Little White sat upon a bank of turf on the opposite side of the way looking very stern and sad. To each new-comer he put the same question:

"Did you come here to go to old Poquelin's?"

"Yes."

"He's dead." And if the shocked hearer started away he would say: "Don't go away."

"Why not?"

"I want you to go to the funeral presently."

If some Louisianian, too loyal to dear France or Spain to understand English, looked bewildered, some one would interpret for him; and presently they went. Little White led the van, the crowd trooping after him down the middle of the way. The gate, that had never been seen before unchained, was open. Stern little White stopped a short distance from it; the rabble stopped behind him. Something was moving out from under the veranda. The many whisperers stretched upward to see. The African mute came very slowly toward the gate, leading by a cord in the nose a small brown bull, which was harnessed to a rude cart. On the flat body of the cart, under a black cloth, were seen the outlines of a long box.

"Hats off, gentlemen," said little White, as the box came in view, and the crowd silently uncovered.

"Gentlemen," said little White, "here come the last remains of Jean Marie Poquelin, a better man, I'm afraid, with all his sins,—yes a better— a kinder man to his blood—a man of more self-forgetful goodness—than all of you put together will ever dare to be."

There was a profound hush as the vehicle came creaking through the gate; but when it turned away from them toward the forest, those in front started suddenly. There was a backward rush, then all stood still again staring one way; for there, behind the bier, with eyes cast down and labored step, walked the living remains—all that was left—of little Jacques Poquelin, the long-hidden brother—a leper, as white as snow.

Dumb with horror, the cringing crowd gazed upon the walking death. They watched, in silent awe, the slow *cortège* creep down the long, straight road and lessen on the view, until by and by it stopped where a wild, unfrequented path branched off into the undergrowth toward the rear of the ancient city.

"They are going to the *Terre aux Lépreux*," said one in the crowd. The rest watched them in silence.

The little bull was set free; the mute, with the strength of an ape, lifted the long box to his shoulder. For a moment more the mute and the leper stood in sight, while the former adjusted his heavy burden; then, without one backward glance upon the unkind human world, turning their faces toward the ridge in the depths of the swamp known as the Leper's Land, they stepped into the jungle, disappeared, and were never seen again.

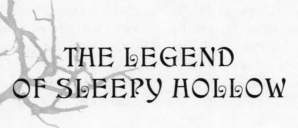

THE LEGEND
OF SLEEPY HOLLOW

Washington Irving

(FOUND AMONG THE PAPERS OF THE
LATE DIEDRICH KNICKERBOCKER)

A pleasing land of drowsy head it was,
Of dreams that wave before the half-shut eye;
And of gay castles in the clouds that pass,
Forever flushing round a summer sky.
Castle of Indolence

In the bosom of one of those spacious coves which indent the eastern shore of the Hudson, at that broad expansion of the river denominated by the ancient Dutch navigators the Tappaan Zee, and where they always prudently shortened sail, and implored the protection of St. Nicholas when they crossed, there lies a small market town or rural port, which by some is called Greensburgh, but which is more generally and properly known by the name of Tarry Town. This name was given, we are told, in former days, by the good housewives of the adjacent country, from the inveterate propensity of their husbands to linger about the village tavern on market days. Be that as it may, I do not vouch for the fact, but merely advert to it, for the sake of being precise and authentic. Not far from this village, perhaps about two miles, there is a little valley, or rather lap of land among high hills, which is one of the quietest places in the whole world. A small brook glides through it, with just murmur enough to lull one to repose; and the occasional whistle of a quail, or tapping of a woodpecker, is almost the only sound that ever breaks in upon the uniform tranquillity.

I recollect that, when a stripling, my first exploit in squirrel shooting was in a grove of tall walnut trees that shades one side of the valley. I had wandered into it at noon time, when all nature is peculiarly quiet, and was startled by the roar of my own gun, as it broke the sabbath stillness around, and was prolonged and reverberated by the angry echoes. If ever I should wish for a retreat, whither I might steal from the world and its distractions, and dream quietly away the remnant of a troubled life, I know of none more promising than this little valley.

From the listless repose of the place, and the peculiar character of its inhabitants, who are descendants from the original Dutch settlers, this sequestered glen has long been known by the name of SLEEPY HOLLOW, and its rustic lads are called the Sleepy Hollow Boys throughout all the neighboring country. A drowsy dreamy influence seems to hang over the land, and to pervade the very atmosphere. Some say that the place was bewitched by a high German doctor during the early days of the settlement; others, that an old Indian chief, the prophet or wizard of his tribe, held his pow-wows there before the country was discovered by Master Hendrick Hudson. Certain it is, the place still continues under the sway of some witching power, that holds a spell over the minds of the good people, causing them to walk in a continual reverie. They are given to all kinds of marvellous beliefs; are subject to trances and visions and frequently see strange sights, and hear music and voices in the air. The whole neighborhood abounds with local tales, haunted spots, and twilight superstitions; stars shoot and meteors glare oftener across the valley than in any other part of the country, and the nightmare, with her whole nine fold, seems to make it the favorite scene of her gambols.

The dominant spirit, however, that haunts this enchanted region, and seems to be commander-in-chief of all the powers of the air, is the apparition of a figure on horseback without a head. It is said by some to be the ghost of a Hessian trooper, whose head had been carried away by a cannon ball, in some nameless battle during the revolutionary war, and who is ever and anon seen by the country folk, hurrying along in the gloom of night, as if on the wings of the wind. His haunts are not confined to the valley, but extend at times to the adjacent roads, and especially to the vicinity of a church at no great distance. Indeed, certain of the most authentic historians of those parts, who have been careful in collecting and collating the floating facts concerning this spectre, allege that the body of the trooper, having been buried in the church yard, the ghost rides forth to the scene of battle in nightly quest of his head; and that the rushing speed with which he sometimes passes along the Hollow, like a midnight blast, is owing to his being belated, and in a hurry to get back to the church yard before day-break.

Such is the general purport of this legendary superstition, which has furnished materials for many a wild story in that region of shadows; and the spectre is known, at all the country firesides, by the name of The Headless Horseman of Sleepy Hollow.

It is remarkable that the visionary propensity I have mentioned is not confined to the native inhabitants of the valley, but is unconsciously im-bibed by every one who resides there for a time. However wide awake they may have been before they entered that sleepy region, they are sure, in a lit-tle time to inhale the witching influence of the air, and begin to grow imaginative—to dream dreams, and see apparitions.

I mention this peaceful spot with all possible laud; for it is in such little retired Dutch valleys, found here and there embosomed in the great state of New York, that population, manners, and customs, remain fixed, while the great torrent of migration and improvement, which is making such in-cessant changes in other parts of this restless country, sweeps by them un-observed. They are like those little nooks of still water, which border a rapid stream, where we may see the straw and bubble riding quietly at an-chor, or slowly revolving in their mimic harbor, undisturbed by the rush of the passing current. Though many years have elapsed since I trod the drowsy shades of Sleepy Hollow, yet I question whether I should not still find the same trees and the same families vegetating in its sheltered bosom.

In this by place of nature there abode, in a remote period of American history, that is to say, some thirty years since, a worthy wight of the name of Ichabod Crane, who sojourned, or, as he expressed it, "tarried," in Sleepy Hollow, for the purpose of instructing the children of the vicinity. He was a native of Connecticut, a state which supplies the Union with pi-oneers for the mind as well as for the forest, and sends forth yearly its le-gions of frontier woodmen and country schoolmasters. The cognomen of Crane was not inapplicable to his person. He was tall, but exceedingly lank, with narrow shoulders, long arms and legs, hands that dangled a mile out of his sleeves, feet that might have served for shovels, and his whole frame most loosely hung together. His head was small, and flat at top, with huge ears, large green glassy eyes, and a long snipe nose, so that it looked like a weathercock perched upon his spindle neck, to tell which way the wind blew. To see him striding along the profile of a hill on a windy day, with his clothes bagging and fluttering about him, one might have mistaken him for the genius of famine descending upon the earth, or some scarecrow eloped from a cornfield.

His school-house was a low building of one large room, rudely constructed of logs; the windows partly glazed, and partly patched with leaves of old copy books. It was most ingeniously secured at vacant hours, by a withe twisted in the handle of the door, and stakes set against the window shutters; so that though a thief might get in with perfect ease, he would find some embarrassment in getting out; an idea most probably borrowed by the architect, Yost Van Houten, from the mystery of an eelpot. The school house stood in a rather lonely but pleasant situation, just at the foot of a woody hill, with a brook running close by, and a formidable birch tree growing at one end of it. From hence the low murmur of his pupils' voices conning over their lessons, might be heard of a drowsy summer's day, like the hum of a bee hive; interrupted now and then by the authoritative voice of the master, in the tone of menace or command, or peradventure, by the appalling sound of the birch, as he urged some tardy loiterer along the flowery path of knowledge. Truth to say, he was a conscientious man, and ever bore in mind the golden maxim, "spare the rod and spoil the child."—Ichabod Crane's scholars certainly were not spoiled.

I would not have it imagined, however, that he was one of those cruel potentates of the school, who joy in the smart of their subjects; on the contrary, he administered justice with discrimination rather than severity; taking the burthen off the backs of the weak, and laying it on those of the strong. Your mere puny stripling, that winced at the least flourish of the rod, was passed by with indulgence; but the claims of justice were satisfied, by inflicting a double portion on some little, tough, wrong headed, broad skirted Dutch urchin, who sulked and swelled and grew dogged and sullen beneath the birch. All this he called "doing his duty by their parents;" and he never inflicted a chastisement without following it by the assurance, so consolatory to the smarting urchin, that "he would remember it and thank him for it the longest day he had to live."

When school hours were over, he was even the companion and playmate of the larger boys; and on holiday afternoons would convoy some of the smaller ones home, who happened to have pretty sisters, or good house-wives for mothers, noted for the comforts of the cupboard. Indeed, it be-hooved him to keep on good terms with his pupils. The revenue arising from his school was small, and would have been scarcely sufficient to fur-nish him with daily bread, for he was a huge feeder, and though lank, had the dilating powers of an anaconda; but to help out his maintenance, he was, according to country custom in those parts, boarded and lodged at the houses of the farmers, whose children he instructed. With these he lived successively a week at a time; thus going the rounds of the neighbor-hood, with all his worldly effects tied up in a cotton handkerchief.

That all this might not be too onerous on the purses of his rustic pa-trons, who are apt to consider the costs of schooling a grievous burthen, and schoolmasters as mere drones, he had various ways of rendering him-self both useful and agreeable. He assisted the farmers occasionally in the lighter labors of their farms; helped to make hay; mended the fences; took the horses to water; drove the cows from pasture; and cut wood for the winter fire. He laid aside, too, all the dominant dignity and absolute sway, with which he lorded it in his little empire, the school, and became won-derfully gentle and ingratiating. He found favor in the eyes of the mothers, by petting the children, particularly the youngest; and like the lion bold, which whilom so magnanimously the lamb did hold, he would sit with a child on one knee, and rock a cradle with his foot, for whole hours to-gether.

In addition to his other vocations, he was the singing master of the neighborhood, and picked up many bright shillings by instructing the young folks in psalmody. It was a matter of no little vanity to him, on Sundays, to take his station in front of the church gallery, with a band of chosen singers; where, in his own mind, he completely carried away the palm from the parson. Certain it is, his voice resounded far above all the rest of the congregation; and there are peculiar quavers still to be heard in that church, and which may even be heard half a mile off, quite to the op-posite side of the mill-pond, on a still Sunday morning, which are said to be legitimately descended from the nose of Ichabod Crane. Thus, by divers little make-shifts, in that ingenious way which is commonly denominated "by hook and by crook," the worthy pedagogue got on tolerably enough, and was thought, by all who understood nothing of the labor of head-work, to have a wonderfully easy life of it.

The schoolmaster is generally a man of some importance in the female circle of a rural neighborhood; being considered a kind of idle gentleman like personage, of vastly superior taste and accomplishments to the rough country swains, and, indeed, inferior in learning only to the parson. His appearance, therefore, is apt to occasion some little stir at the tea-table of a farm-house, and the addition of a supernumerary dish of cakes or sweet-meats, or, peradventure, the parade of a silver tea-pot. Our man of letters, therefore, was peculiarly happy in the smiles of all the country damsels. How he would figure among them in the church-yard, between services on Sundays; gathering grapes for them from the wild vines that overrun the surrounding trees; reciting for their amusement all the epitaphs on the tombstones; or sauntering, with a whole bevy of them, along the banks of the adjacent mill-pond; while the more bashful country bumpkins hung sheepishly back, envying his superior elegance and address.

From his half itinerant life, also, he was a kind of travelling gazette, carrying the whole budget of local gossip from house to house; so that his appearance was always greeted with satisfaction. He was, moreover, esteemed by the women as a man of great erudition, for he had read several books quite through, and was a perfect master of Cotton Mather's History of New England Witchcraft, in which, by the way, he most firmly and potently believed.

He was, in fact, an odd mixture of small shrewdness and simple credulity. His appetite for the marvellous, and his powers of digesting it, were equally extraordinary; and both had been increased by his residence in this spell bound region. No tale was too gross or monstrous for his capacious swallow. It was often his delight, after his school was dismissed of an afternoon, to stretch himself on the rich bed of clover, bordering the little brook that whimpered by his school-house, and there con over old Mather's direful tales, until the gathering dusk of evening made the printed page a mere mist before his eyes.

Then, as he wended his way, by swamp and stream and awful woodland, to the farm-house where he happened to be quartered, every sound of nature, at that witching hour, fluttered his excited imagination: the moan of the whip-poor-will* from the hill-side; the boding cry of the tree-toad, that harbinger of storm; the dreary hooting of the screech-owl, or the sud-

---

*The whip-poor-will is a bird which is only heard at night. It receives its name from its note which is thought to resemble those words.

den rustling in the thicket, of birds frightened from their roost. The fire flies, too, which sparkled most vividly in the darkest places, now and then startled him, as one of uncommon brightness would stream across his path; and if, by chance, a huge blockhead of a beetle came winging his blundering flight against him, the poor varlet was ready to give up the ghost, with the idea that he was struck with a witch's token. His only resource on such occasions, either to drown thought, or drive away evil spirits, was to sing psalm tunes;—and the good people of Sleepy Hollow, as they sat by their doors of an evening, were often filled with awe, at hearing his nasal melody, "in linked sweetness long drawn out," floating from the distant hill, or along the dusky road.

Another of his sources of fearful pleasure was, to pass long winter evenings with the old Dutch wives, as they sat spinning by the fire, with a row of apples roasting and sputtering along the hearth, and listen to their marvellous tales of ghosts and goblins, and haunted fields and haunted brooks, and haunted bridges and haunted houses, and particularly of the headless horseman, or galloping Hessian of the Hollow, as they sometimes called him. He would delight them equally by his anecdotes of witchcraft, and of the direful omens and portentous sights and sounds in the air, which prevailed in the earlier times of Connecticut; and would frighten them wofully with speculations upon comets and shooting stars; and with the alarming fact that the world did absolutely turn round, and that they were half the time topsy-turvy!

But if there was a pleasure in all this, while snugly cuddling in the chimney corner of a chamber that was all of a ruddy glow from the crackling wood fire, and where, of course, no spectre dared to show its face, it was dearly purchased by the terrors of his subsequent walk homewards. What fearful shapes and shadows beset his path amidst the dim and ghastly glare of a snowy night!—With what wistful look did he eye every trembling ray of light streaming across the waste fields from some distant window!—How often was he appalled by some shrub covered with snow, which, like a sheeted spectre, beset his very path!—How often did he shrink with curdling awe at the sound of his own steps on the frosty crust beneath his feet; and dread to look over his shoulder, lest he should behold some uncouth being tramping close behind him!—and how often was he thrown into complete dismay by some rushing blast, howling among the trees, in the idea that it was the Gallopping Hessian on one of his nightly scourings.

All these, however, were mere terrors of the night, phantoms of the mind, that walk in darkness; and though he had seen many spectres in his time, and been more than once beset by Satan in divers shapes, in his lonely perambulations, yet daylight put an end to all these evils; and he would have passed a pleasant life of it, in despite of the Devil and all his works, if his path had not been crossed by a being that causes more perplexity to mortal man than ghosts, goblins, and the whole race of witches put together, and that was—a woman.

Among the musical disciples who assembled, one evening in each week, to receive his instructions in psalmody, was Katrina Van Tassel, the daughter and only child of a substantial Dutch farmer. She was a blooming lass of fresh eighteen; plump as a partridge; ripe and melting and rosy cheeked as one of her father's peaches, and universally famed, not merely for her beauty, but her vast expectations. She was withal a little of a coquette, as might be perceived even in her dress, which was a mixture of ancient and modern fashions, as most suited to set off her charms. She wore the ornaments of pure yellow gold, which her great-great-grandmother had brought over from Saardam; the tempting stomacher of the olden time; and withal a provokingly short petticoat, to display the prettiest foot and ankle in the country round.

Ichabod Crane had a soft and foolish heart toward the sex; and it is not to be wondered at, that so tempting a morsel soon found favor in his eyes; more especially after he had visited her in her paternal mansion. Old Baltus Van Tassel was a perfect picture of a thriving, contented, liberal-hearted farmer. He seldom, it is true, sent either his eyes or his thoughts beyond the boundaries of his own farm; but within those every thing was snug, happy, and well-conditioned. He was satisfied with his wealth, but not proud of it; and piqued himself upon the hearty abundance, rather than the style in which he lived. His strong hold was situated on the banks of the Hudson, in one of those green, sheltered, fertile nooks, in which the Dutch farmers are so fond of nestling. A great elm tree spread its broad branches over it; at the foot of which bubbled up a spring of the softest and sweetest water, in a little well, formed of a barrel; and then stole sparkling away through the grass, to a neighboring brook, that babbled along among elders and dwarf willows. Hard by the farm-house was a vast barn, that might have served for a church; every window and crevice of which seemed bursting forth with the treasures of the farm; the flail was busily resounding within it from morning to night; swallows and martins

skimmed twittering about the eaves; and rows of pigeons, some with one
eye turned up, as if watching the weather, some with their heads under
their wings, or buried in their bosoms, and others swelling, and cooing,
and bowing about their dames, were enjoying the sunshine on the roof.
Sleek unwieldy porkers were grunting in the repose and abundance of their
pens; whence sallied forth, now and then, troops of sucking pigs, as if to
snuff the air. A stately squadron of snowy geese were riding in an adjoining pond, convoying whole fleets of ducks; regiments of turkeys were gob-
bling through the farm yard, and guinea fowls fretting about it, like ill
tempered housewives, with their peevish discontented cry. Before the barn
door strutted the gallant cock, that pattern of a husband, a warrior, and a
fine gentleman, clapping his burnished wings, and crowing in the pride and
gladness of his heart—sometimes tearing up the earth with his feet, and
then generously calling his ever-hungry family of wives and children to enjoy the rich morsel which he had discovered.

The pedagogue's mouth watered, as he looked upon this sumptuous
promise of luxurious winter fare. In his devouring mind's eye, he pictured
to himself every roasting-pig running about with a pudding in his belly,
and an apple in his mouth; the pigeons were snugly put to bed in a comfortable pie, and tucked in with a coverlet of crust; the geese were swim-
ming in their own gravy; and the ducks pairing cosily in dishes, like snug
married couples, with a decent competency of onion sauce: In the porkers
he saw carved out the future sleek side of bacon, and juicy relishing ham;
not a turkey, but he beheld daintily trussed up, with its gizzard under its
wing, and, peradventure, a necklace of savory sausages; and even bright
chanticleer himself lay sprawling on his back, in a side dish, with uplifted
claws, as if craving that quarter, which his chivalrous spirit disdained to
ask while living.

As the enraptured Ichabod fancied all this, and as he rolled his great
green eyes over the fat meadow-lands, the rich fields of wheat, of rye, of
buckwheat, and Indian corn, and the orchards burthened with ruddy fruit,
which surrounded the warm tenement of Van Tassel, his heart yearned after the damsel who was to inherit these domains, and his imagination ex-
panded with the idea, how they might be readily turned into cash, and the
money invested in immense tracts of wild land, and shingle palaces in the
wilderness. Nay, his busy fancy already realized his hopes, and presented to
him the blooming Katrina, with a whole family of children, mounted on
the top of a wagon loaded with household trumpery, with pots and kettles

dangling beneath; and he beheld himself bestriding a pacing mare, with a colt at her heels, setting out for Kentucky, Tennessee, or the Lord knows where.

When he entered the house, the conquest of his heart was complete. It was one of those spacious farm-houses, with high-ridged, but lowly-sloping roofs, built in the style handed down from the first Dutch settlers; the low projecting eaves formed a piazza along the front, capable of being closed up in bad weather. Under this were hung flails, harness, various utensils of husbandry, and nets for fishing in the neighboring river. Benches were built along the sides for summer use; and a great spinning wheel at one end, and a churn at the other, showed the various uses to which this important porch might be devoted. From this piazza the wondering Ichabod entered the hall, which formed the centre of the mansion, and the place of usual residence. Here, rows of resplendent pewter, ranged on a long dresser, dazzled his eyes. In one corner stood a huge bag of wool ready to be spun; in another a quantity of linsey-woolsey just from the loom; ears of Indian corn, and strings of dried apples and peaches, hung in gay festoons along the walls, mingled with the gaud of red peppers; and a door left ajar, gave him a peep into the best parlor, where the claw footed chairs, and dark mahogany tables, shone like mirrors; andirons, with their accompanying shovel and tongs, glistened from their covert of asparagus tops; mock-oranges and conch-shells decorated the mantelpiece; strings of various colored birds' eggs were suspended above it: a great ostrich egg was hung from the centre of the room, and a corner cupboard, knowingly left open, displayed immense treasures of old silver and well-mended china.

From the moment Ichabod laid his eyes upon these regions of delight, the peace of his mind was at an end, and his only study was how to gain the affections of the peerless daughter of Van Tassel. In this enterprise, however, he had more real difficulties than generally fell to the lot of a knight-errant of yore, who seldom had any thing but giants, enchanters, fiery dragons, and such like easily-conquered adversaries, to contend with; and had to make his way merely through gates of iron and brass, and walls of adamant, to the castle keep, where the lady of his heart was confined; all which he achieved as easily as a man would carve his way to the centre of a Christmas pie, and then the lady gave him her hand as a matter of course. Ichabod, on the contrary, had to win his way to the heart of a country coquette, beset with a labyrinth of whims and caprices, which were for ever presenting new difficulties and impediments, and he had to encounter a host of fearful adversaries of real flesh and blood, the numerous rustic admirers, who beset every portal to her heart; keeping a watchful and angry eye upon each other, but ready to fly out in the common cause against any new competitor.

Among these, the most formidable, was a burly, roaring, roystering blade, of the name of Abraham, or, according to the Dutch abbreviation, Brom Van Brunt, the hero of the country round, which rang with his feats of strength and hardihood. He was broad-shouldered and double-jointed, with short curly black hair, and a bluff, but not unpleasant countenance, having a mingled air of fun and arrogance. From his Herculean frame and great powers of limb, he had received the nick name of BROM BONES, by which he was universally known. He was famed for great knowledge and skill in horsemanship, being as dexterous on horseback as a Tartar. He was foremost at all races and cock-fights, and with the ascendancy which bodily strength acquires in rustic life, was the umpire in all disputes, setting his hat on one side, and giving his decisions with an air and tone admitting of no gainsay or appeal. He was always ready for either a fight or a frolic; but had more mischief than ill-will in his composition; and with all his overbearing roughness, there was a strong dash of waggish good humor at bottom. He had three or four boon companions, who regarded him as their model, and at the head of whom he scoured the country, attending every scene of feud or merriment for miles round. In cold weather he was distinguished by a fur cap, surmounted with a flaunting fox's tail; and when the folks at a country gathering descried this well-known crest at a distance, whisking about among a squad of hard riders, they always stood by for a squall. Sometimes his crew would be heard dashing along past the farm houses at midnight, with whoop and halloo, like a troop of Don Cossacks; and the old dames, startled out of their sleep, would listen for a moment till the hurry-scurry had clattered by, and then exclaim, "Ay, there goes Brom Bones and his gang!" The neighbors looked upon him with a mixture of awe, admiration, and good will; and when any mad cap prank, or rustic brawl, occurred in the vicinity, always shook their heads, and warranted Brom Bones was at the bottom of it.

This rantipole hero had for some time singled out the blooming Katrina for the object of his uncouth gallantries, and though his amorous toyings were something like the gentle caresses and endearments of a bear, yet it was whispered that she did not altogether discourage his hopes. Certain

it is, his advances were signals for rival candidates to retire, who felt no inclination to cross a lion in his amours; insomuch, that when his horse was
seen tied to Van Tassel's paling, of a Sunday night, a sure sign that his master was courting, or, as it is termed, "sparking," within, all other suitors
passed by in despair, and carried the war into other quarters.

Such was the formidable rival with whom Ichabod Crane had to contend, and, considering all things, a stouter man than he would have shrunk
from the competition, and a wiser man would have despaired. He had,
however, a happy mixture of pliability and perseverance in his nature; he
was in form and spirit like a supple-jack—yielding, but tough; though he
bent, he never broke; and though he bowed beneath the slightest pressure,
yet, the moment it was away—jerk!—he was as erect, and carried his head
as high as ever.

To have taken the field openly against his rival would have been madness; for he was not a man to be thwarted in his amours, any more than
that stormy lover, Achilles. Ichabod, therefore, made his advances in a quiet
and gently-insinuating manner. Under cover of his character of singing-
master, he made frequent visits at the farm-house; not that he had any
thing to apprehend from the meddlesome interference of parents, which is
so often a stumbling block in the path of lovers. Balt Van Tassel was an
easy indulgent soul; he loved his daughter better even than his pipe, and
like a reasonable man, and an excellent father, let her have her way in every
thing. His notable little wife, too, had enough to do to attend to her
housekeeping and manage her poultry; for, as she sagely observed, ducks
and geese are foolish things, and must be looked after, but girls can take
care of themselves. Thus while the busy dame bustled about the house, or
plied her spinning-wheel at one end of the piazza, honest Balt would sit
smoking his evening pipe at the other, watching the achievements of a little
wooden warrior, who, armed with a sword in each hand, was most valiantly
fighting the wind on the pinnacle of the barn. In the mean time, Ichabod
would carry on his suit with the daughter by the side of the spring under
the great elm, or sauntering along in the twilight, that hour so favorable to
the lover's eloquence.

I profess not to know how women's hearts are wooed and won. To me
they have always been matters of riddle and admiration. Some seem to
have but one vulnerable point, or door of access; while others have a thousand avenues, and may be captured in a thousand different ways. It is a
great triumph of skill to gain the former, but a still greater proof of gen-

eralship to maintain possession of the latter, for a man must battle for his fortress at every door and window. He who wins a thousand common hearts, is therefore entitled to some renown; but he who keeps undisputed sway over the heart of a coquette, is indeed a hero. Certain it is, this was not the case with the redoubtable Brom Bones; and from the moment Ichabod Crane made his advances, the interests of the former evidently declined; his horse was no longer seen tied at the palings on Sunday nights, and a deadly feud gradually arose between him and the preceptor of Sleepy Hollow.

Brom, who had a degree of rough chivalry in his nature, would fain have carried matters to open warfare, and have settled their pretensions to the lady, according to the mode of those most concise and simple reasoners, the knights-errant of yore—by single combat; but Ichabod was too conscious of the superior might of his adversary to enter the lists against him: he had overheard a boast of Bones, that he would "double the schoolmaster up, and lay him on a shelf of his own school-house;" and he was too wary to give him an opportunity. There was something extremely provoking in this obstinately pacific system; it left Brom no alternative but to draw upon the funds of rustic waggery in his disposition, and to play off boorish practical jokes upon his rival. Ichabod became the object of whimsical persecution to Bones, and his gang of rough riders. They harried his hitherto peaceful domains; smoked out his singing school, by stopping up the chimney; broke into the school-house at night, in spite of its formidable fastenings of withe and window stakes, and turned everything topsyturvy: so that the poor schoolmaster began to think all the witches in the country held their meetings there. But what was still more annoying, Brom took all opportunities of turning him into ridicule in presence of his mistress, and had a scoundrel dog whom he taught to whine in the most ludicrous manner, and introduced as a rival of Ichabod's to instruct her in psalmody.

In this way matters went on for some time, without producing any material effect on the relative situations of the contending powers. On a fine autumnal afternoon, Ichabod, in pensive mood, sat enthroned on the lofty stool from whence he usually watched all the concerns of his little literary realm. In his hand he swayed a ferule, that sceptre of despotic power; the birch of justice reposed on three nails, behind the throne, a constant terror to evil doers; while on the desk before him might be seen sundry contraband articles and prohibited weapons, detected upon the persons of idle urchins; such as half munched apples, popguns, whirligigs, fly-cages, and whole legions of rampant little paper game-cocks. Apparently there had been some appalling act of justice recently inflicted, for his scholars were all busily intent upon their books, or slyly whispering behind them with one eye kept upon the master; and a kind of buzzing stillness reigned throughout the school-room. It was suddenly interrupted by the appearance of a negro, in tow-cloth jacket and trowsers, a round-crowned fragment of a hat, like the cap of Mercury, and mounted on the back of a ragged, wild, half-broken colt, which he managed with a rope by way of halter. He came clattering up to the school door with an invitation to Ichabod to attend a merry-making, or "quilting frolic," to be held that evening at Mynheer Van Tassel's; and having delivered his message with that air of importance, and effort at fine language, which a negro is apt to display on petty embassies of the kind, he dashed over the brook, and was seen scampering away up the hollow, full of the importance and hurry of his mission.

All was now bustle and hubbub in the late quiet school-room. The scholars were hurried through their lessons, without stopping at trifles; those who were nimble skipped over half with impunity, and those who were tardy, had a smart application now and then in the rear, to quicken their speed, or help them over a tall word. Books were flung aside without being put away on the shelves, inkstands were overturned, benches thrown down, and the whole school was turned loose an hour before the usual time, bursting forth like a legion of young imps, yelping and racketing about the green, in joy at their early emancipation.

The gallant Ichabod now spent at least an extra half hour at his toilet, brushing and furbishing up his best, and indeed only suit of rusty black, and arranging his looks by a bit of broken looking-glass, that hung up in the school-house. That he might make his appearance before his mistress in the true style of a cavalier, he borrowed a horse from the farmer with whom he was domiciliated, a choleric old Dutchman, of the name of Hans Van Ripper, and, thus gallantly mounted, issued forth like a knight-errant in quest of adventures. But it is meet I should, in the true spirit of romantic story, give some account of the looks and equipments of my hero and his steed. The animal he bestrode was a broken-down plough-horse, that had outlived almost every thing but his viciousness. He was gaunt and shagged, with a ewe neck and a head like a hammer; his rusty mane and tail were tangled and knotted with burrs; one eye had lost its

pupil, and was glaring and spectral; but the other had the gleam of a genuine devil in it. Still he must have had fire and mettle in his day, if we may
judge from the name he bore of Gunpowder. He had, in fact, been a favorite steed of his master's, the choleric Van Ripper, who was a furious
rider, and had infused, very probably, some of his own spirit into the animal; for, old and broken down as he looked, there was more of the lurking
devil in him than in any young filly in the country.

Ichabod was a suitable figure for such a steed. He rode with short stirrups, which brought his knees nearly up to the pommel of the saddle; his
sharp elbows stuck out like grasshoppers'; he carried his whip perpendicu-
larly in his hand, like a sceptre, and, as his horse jogged on, the motion of
his arms was not unlike the flapping of a pair of wings. A small wool hat
rested on the top of his nose, for so his scanty strip of forehead might be
called; and the skirts of his black coat fluttered out almost to the horse's
tail. Such was the appearance of Ichabod and his steed, as they shambled
out of the gate of Hans Van Ripper, and it was altogether such an apparition as is seldom to be met with in broad daylight.

It was, as I have said, a fine autumnal day, the sky was clear and serene,
and nature wore that rich and golden livery which we always associate with
the idea of abundance. The forests had put on their sober brown and yellow, while some trees of the tenderer kind had been nipped by the frosts
into brilliant dyes of orange, purple, and scarlet. Streaming files of wild
ducks began to make their appearance high in the air; the bark of the
squirrel might be heard from the groves of beech and hickory nuts, and the
pensive whistle of the quail at intervals from the neighboring stubble field.

The small birds were taking their farewell banquets. In the fulness of
their revelry, they fluttered, chirping and frolicking, from bush to bush, and
tree to tree, capricious from the very profusion and variety around them.
There was the honest cock-robin, the favorite game of stripling sportsmen,
with its loud querulous note; and the twittering blackbirds flying in sable
clouds; and the golden-winged-woodpecker, with his crimson crest, his
broad black gorget, and splendid plumage; and the cedar bird, with its red-
tipt wings and yellow-tipt tail, and its little monteiro cap of feathers; and
the blue-jay, that noisy coxcomb, in his gay light-blue coat and white un-
der-clothes; screaming and chattering, nodding, and bobbing, and bowing,
and pretending to be on good terms with every songster of the grove.

As Ichabod jogged slowly on his way, his eye, ever open to every symptom of culinary abundance, ranged with delight over the treasures of jolly autumn. On all sides he beheld vast store of apples; some hanging in oppressive opulence on the trees; some gathered into baskets and barrels for the market; others heaped up in rich piles for the cider-press. Further on he beheld great fields of Indian corn, with its golden ears peeping from their leafy coverts, and holding out the promise of cakes and hasty pudding; and the yellow pumpkins lying beneath them, turning up their fair round bellies to the sun, and giving ample prospects of the most luxurious of pies; and anon he passed the fragrant buckwheat fields, breathing the odor of the bee-hive, and as he beheld them, soft anticipations stole over his mind of dainty slap-jacks, well buttered, and garnished with honey or treacle, by the delicate little dimpled hand of Katrina Van Tassel.

Thus feeding his mind with many sweet thoughts and "sugared suppositions," he journeyed along the sides of a range of hills which look out upon some of the goodliest scenes of the mighty Hudson. The sun gradually wheeled his broad disk down into the west. The wide bosom of the Tappaan Zee lay motionless and glassy, excepting that here and there a gentle undulation waved and prolonged the blue shadow of the distant mountain. A few amber clouds floated in the sky, without a breath of air to move them. The horizon was of a fine golden tint, changing gradually into a pure apple green, and from that into the deep blue of the mid-heaven. A slanting ray lingered on the woody crests of the precipices that overhung some parts of the river, giving greater depth to the dark-gray and purple of their rocky sides. A sloop was loitering in the distance, dropping slowly down with the tide, her sail hanging uselessly against the mast; and as the reflection of the sky gleamed along the still water, it seemed as if the vessel was suspended in the air.

It was toward evening that Ichabod arrived at the castle of the Heer Van Tassel, which he found thronged with the pride and flower of the adjacent country. Old farmers, a spare, leathern-faced race, in homespun coats and breeches, blue stockings, huge shoes and magnificent pewter buckles. Their brisk withered little dames, in close crimped caps, long-waisted short-gowns, homespun petticoats, with scissors and pin-cushions, and gay calico pockets hanging on the outside. Buxom lasses, almost as antiquated as their mothers, excepting where a straw hat, a fine ribband, or perhaps a white frock, gave symptoms of city innovation. The sons, in short square-skirted coats with rows of stupendous brass buttons, and their hair generally queued in the fashion of the times, especially if they could procure an eel-skin for the purpose, it being esteemed throughout the country, as a potent nourisher and strengthener of the hair.

Brom Bones, however, was the hero of the scene, having come to the gathering on his favorite steed Daredevil, a creature, like himself, full of mettle and mischief, and which no one but himself could manage. He was, in fact, noted for preferring vicious animals, given to all kinds of tricks, which kept the rider in constant risk of his neck, for he held a tractable well-broken horse as unworthy of a lad of spirit.

Fain would I pause to dwell upon the world of charms that burst upon the enraptured gaze of my hero, as he entered the state parlor of Van Tassel's mansion. Not those of the bevy of buxom lasses, with their luxurious display of red and white; but the ample charms of a genuine Dutch country tea-table, in the sumptuous time of autumn. Such heaped up platters of cakes of various and almost indescribable kinds, known only to experienced Dutch housewives! There was the doughty dough-nut, the tenderer oly koek, and the crisp and crumbling cruller; sweet cakes and short cakes, ginger cakes and honey cakes, and the whole family of cakes. And then there were apple pies and peach pies and pumpkin pies; besides slices of ham and smoked beef; and moreover delectable dishes of preserved plums, and peaches, and pears, and quinces; not to mention broiled shad and roasted chickens; together with bowls of milk and cream, all mingled higgledy-piggledy, pretty much as I have enumerated them, with the motherly tea-pot sending up its clouds of vapor from the midst—Heaven bless the mark! I want breath and time to discuss this banquet as it deserves, and am too eager to get on with my story. Happily, Ichabod Crane was not in so great a hurry as his historian, but did ample justice to every dainty.

He was a kind and thankful creature, whose heart dilated in proportion as his skin was filled with good cheer; and whose spirits rose with eating, as some men's do with drink. He could not help, too, rolling his large eyes round him as he ate, and chuckling with the possibility that he might one day be lord of all this scene of almost unimaginable luxury and splendor. Then, he thought, how soon he'd turn his back upon the old school-house; snap his fingers in the face of Hans Van Ripper, and every other niggardly patron, and kick any itinerant pedagogue out of doors that should dare to call him comrade!

Old Baltus Van Tassel moved about among his guests with a face dilated with content and good humor, round and jolly as the harvest moon. His hospitable attentions were brief, but expressive, being confined to a shake of the hand, a slap on the shoulder, a loud laugh, and a pressing invitation to "fall to, and help themselves."

And now the sound of the music from the common room, or hall, summoned to the dance. The musician was an old grayheaded negro, who had been the itinerant orchestra of the neighborhood for more than half a century. His instrument was as old and battered as himself. The greater part of the time he scraped away on two or three strings, accompanying every movement of the bow with a motion of the head; bowing almost to the ground, and stamping with his foot whenever a fresh couple were to start.

Ichabod prided himself upon his dancing as much as upon his vocal powers. Not a limb, not a fibre about him was idle; and to have seen his loosely hung frame in full motion, and clattering about the room, you would have thought Saint Vitus himself, that blessed patron of the dance, was figuring before you in person. He was the admiration of all the negroes; who, having gathered, of all ages and sizes, from the farm and the neighborhood, stood forming a pyramid of shining black faces at every door and window, gazing with delight at the scene, rolling their white eye balls, and showing grinning rows of ivory from ear to ear. How could the flogger of urchins be otherwise than animated and joyous? The lady of his heart was his partner in the dance, and smiling graciously in reply to all his amorous oglings, while Brom Bones, sorely smitten with love and jealousy, sat brooding by himself in one corner.

When the dance was at an end, Ichabod was attracted to a knot of the sager folks, who, with old Van Tassel, sat smoking at one end of the piazza, gossiping over former times, and drawling out long stories about the war.

This neighborhood, at the time of which I am speaking, was one of those highly-favored places which abound with chronicle and great men. The British and American line had run near it during the war; it had, therefore, been the scene of marauding, and infested with refugees, cowboys, and all kinds of border chivalry. Just sufficient time had elapsed to enable each story-teller to dress up his tale with a little becoming fiction, and, in the indistinctness of his recollection, to make himself the hero of every exploit.

There was the story of Doffue Martling, a large, blue bearded Dutchman who had nearly taken a British frigate with an old iron nine-pounder from a mud breast-work, only that his gun burst at the sixth discharge. And there was an old gentleman who shall be nameless, being too rich a mynheer to be lightly mentioned, who, in the battle of Whiteplains, being an excellent master of defence, parried a musket ball with a small sword, insomuch that he absolutely felt it whiz round the blade, and glance off at the hilt: in proof of which, he was ready at any time to show the sword, with the hilt a little bent. There were several more who had been equally great in the field, not one of whom but was persuaded that he had a considerable hand in bringing the war to a happy termination.

But all these were nothing to the tales of ghosts and apparitions that succeeded. The neighborhood is rich in legendary treasures of the kind. Local tales and superstitions thrive best in these sheltered, long-settled retreats; but are trampled under foot by the shifting throng that forms the population of most of our country places. Besides there is no encouragement for ghosts in most of our villages, for they have scarce had time to finish their first nap, and turn themselves in their graves, before their surviving friends have travelled away from the neighborhood; so that when they turn out of a night to walk their rounds, they have no acquaintance left to call upon. This is perhaps the reason why we so seldom hear of ghosts except in our long-established Dutch communities.

The immediate cause, however, of the prevalence of supernatural stories in these parts, was doubtless owing to the vicinity of Sleepy Hollow. There was a contagion in the very air that blew from that haunted region; it breathed forth an atmosphere of dreams and fancies infecting all the land. Several of the Sleepy Hollow people were present at Van Tassel's, and, as usual, were doling out their wild and wonderful legends. Many dismal tales were told about funeral trains, and mourning cries and wailings heard and seen about the great tree where the unfortunate Major André was taken, and which stood in the neighborhood. Some mention was made also of the woman in white, that haunted the dark glen at Raven Rock, and was often heard to shriek on winter nights before a storm, having perished there in the snow. The chief part of the stories, however, turned upon the favorite spectre of Sleepy Hollow, the headless horseman, who had been heard several times of late, patrolling the country; and, it was said, tethered his horse nightly among the graves in the church-yard.

The sequestered situation of this church seems always to have made it a favorite haunt of troubled spirits. It stands on a knoll, surrounded by locust trees and lofty elms, from among which its decent whitewashed walls shine modestly forth, like Christian purity, beaming through the shades of retirement. A gentle slope descends from it to a silver sheet of water, bordered by high trees, between which, peeps may be caught at the blue hills of the Hudson. To look upon its grass-grown yard, where the sunbeams seem to sleep so quietly, one would think that there at least the dead might rest in peace. On one side of the church extends a wide woody dell, along which raves a large brook among broken rocks and trunks of fallen trees. Over a deep black part of the stream, not far from the church, was formerly thrown a wooden bridge; the road that led to it, and the bridge itself, were thickly shaded by overhanging trees, which cast a gloom about it, even in the day time; but occasioned a fearful darkness at night. This was one of the favorite haunts of the headless horseman; and the place where he was most frequently encountered. The tale was told of old Brouwer, a most heretical disbeliever in ghosts, how he met the horseman returning from his foray into Sleepy Hollow, and was obliged to get up behind him; how they galloped over bush and brake, over hill and swamp, until they reached the bridge; when the horseman suddenly turned into a skeleton, threw old Brouwer into the brook, and sprang away over the tree-tops with a clap of thunder.

This story was immediately matched by a thrice marvellous adventure of Brom Bones, who made light of the galloping Hessian as an arrant jockey. He affirmed that, on returning one night from the neighboring village of Sing Sing, he had been overtaken by this midnight trooper; that he had offered to race with him for a bowl of punch, and should have won it too, for Daredevil beat the goblin horse all hollow, but just as they came to the church bridge, the Hessian bolted, and vanished in a flash of fire.

All these tales, told in that drowsy under tone with which men talk in the dark, the countenances of the listeners only now and then receiving a casual gleam from the glare of a pipe, sank deep in the mind of Ichabod. He repaid them in kind with large extracts from his invaluable author, Cotton Mather, and added many very marvellous events that had taken place in his native State of Connecticut, and fearful sights which he had seen in his nightly walks about Sleepy Hollow.

The revel now gradually broke up. The old farmers gathered together their families in their wagons, and were heard for some time rattling along the hollow roads, and over the distant hills. Some of the damsels, mounted on pillions behind their favorite swains, and their light-hearted laughter, mingling with the clatter of hoofs, echoed along the silent woodlands, sounding fainter and fainter until they gradually died away—and the late scene of noise and frolic was all silent and deserted. Ichabod only lingered behind, according to the custom of country lovers, to have a tête-à-tête with the heiress, fully convinced that he was now on the high road to success. What passed at this interview I will not pretend to say, for in fact I do not know. Something, however, I fear me, must have gone wrong, for he certainly sallied forth, after no very great interval, with an air quite desolate and chop-fallen—Oh these women! these women! Could that girl have been playing off any of her coquettish tricks?—Was her encouragement of the poor pedagogue all a mere sham to secure her conquest of his rival?—Heaven only knows, not I!—Let it suffice to say, Ichabod stole forth with the air of one who had been sacking a hen-roost, rather than a fair lady's heart. Without looking to the right or left to notice the scene of rural wealth, on which he had so often gloated, he went straight to the stable, and with several hearty cuffs and kicks, roused his steed most uncourteously from the comfortable quarters in which he was soundly sleeping, dreaming of mountains of corn and oats, and whole valleys of timothy and clover.

It was the very witching time of night that Ichabod, heavy-hearted and crest-fallen, pursued his travel homewards, along the sides of the lofty hills which rise above Tarry Town, and which he had traversed so cheerily in the afternoon. The hour was as dismal as himself. Far below him, the Tappaan Zee spread its dusky and indistinct waste of waters, with here and there the tall mast of a sloop, riding quietly at anchor under the land. In the dead hush of midnight, he could even hear the barking of the watch dog from the opposite shore of the Hudson; but it was so vague and faint as only to give an idea of his distance from this faithful companion of man. Now and then, too, the long-drawn crowing of a cock, accidentally awakened, would sound far, far off, from some farm-house away among the hills—but it was like a dreaming sound in his ear. No signs of life occurred near him, but occasionally the melancholy chirp of a cricket, or perhaps the guttural twang of a bull-frog, from a neighboring marsh, as if sleeping uncomfortably, and turning suddenly in his bed.

All the stories of ghosts and goblins that he had heard in the afternoon, now came crowding upon his recollection. The night grew darker and darker; the stars seemed to sink deeper in the sky, and driving clouds occasionally hid them from his sight. He had never felt so lonely and dismal. He was, moreover, approaching the very place where many of the scenes of the ghost stories had been laid. In the centre of the road stood an enormous tulip tree, which towered like a giant above all the other trees of the neighborhood, and formed a kind of landmark. Its limbs were gnarled, and fantastic, large enough to form trunks for ordinary trees, twisting down almost to the earth, and rising again into the air. It was connected with the tragical story of the unfortunate André, who had been taken prisoner hard by; and was universally known by the name of Major André's tree. The common people regarded it with a mixture of respect and superstition, partly out of sympathy for the fate of its ill-starred namesake, and partly from the tales of strange sights and doleful lamentations told concerning it.

As Ichabod approached this fearful tree, he began to whistle; he thought his whistle was answered—it was but a blast sweeping sharply through the dry branches. As he approached a little nearer, he thought he saw something white, hanging in the midst of the tree: he paused and ceased whistling; but on looking more narrowly, perceived that it was a place where the tree had been scathed by lightning, and the white wood laid bare. Suddenly he heard a groan—his teeth chattered and his knees smote against the saddle: it was but the rubbing of one huge bough upon another, as they were swayed about by the breeze. He passed the tree in safety, but new perils lay before him.

About two hundred yards from the tree a small brook crossed the road, and ran into a marshy and thickly wooded glen, known by the name of Wiley's Swamp. A few rough logs, laid side by side, served for a bridge over this stream. On that side of the road where the brook entered the wood, a group of oaks and chestnuts, matted thick with wild grapevines, threw a cavernous gloom over it. To pass this bridge, was the severest trial. It was at this identical spot that the unfortunate André was captured, and under the covert of those chestnuts and vines were the sturdy yeomen concealed who surprised him. This has ever since been considered a haunted stream, and fearful are the feelings of the schoolboy who has to pass it alone after dark.

As he approached the stream his heart began to thump; he summoned up, however, all his resolution, gave his horse half a score of kicks in the ribs, and attempted to dash briskly across the bridge; but instead of starting forward, the perverse old animal made a lateral movement, and ran broadside against the fence. Ichabod, whose fears increased with the delay, jerked the reins on the other side, and kicked lustily with the contrary foot: it was all in vain; his steed started, it is true, but it was only to plunge to the opposite side of the road into a thicket of brambles and alder bushes. The schoolmaster now bestowed both whip and heel upon the starveling ribs of old Gunpowder, who dashed forward, snuffling and snorting, but

came to a stand just by the bridge, with a suddenness that had nearly sent
his rider sprawling over his head. Just at this moment a plashy tramp by the
side of the bridge caught the sensitive ear of Ichabod. In the dark shadow
of the grove, on the margin of the brook, he beheld something huge, misshapen, black and towering. It stirred not, but seemed gathered up in the
gloom, like some gigantic monster ready to spring upon the traveller.

The hair of the affrighted pedagogue rose upon his head with terror.
What was to be done? To turn and fly was now too late; and besides, what
chance was there of escaping ghost or goblin, if such it was, which could
ride upon the wings of the wind? Summoning up, therefore, a show of
courage, he demanded in stammering accents—"Who are you?" He received no reply. He repeated his demand in a still more agitated voice. Still
there was no answer. Once more he cudgelled the sides of the inflexible
Gunpowder, and shutting his eyes, broke forth with involuntary fervor into
a psalm tune. Just then the shadowy object of alarm put itself in motion,
and with a scramble and a bound, stood at once in the middle of the road.
Though the night was dark and dismal, yet the form of the unknown
might now in some degree be ascertained. He appeared to be a horseman
of large dimensions, and mounted on a black horse of powerful frame. He
made no offer of molestation or sociability, but kept aloof on one side of
the road, jogging along on the blind side of old Gunpowder, who had now
got over his fright and waywardness.

Ichabod, who had no relish for this strange midnight companion, and
bethought himself of the adventure of Brom Bones with the galloping
Hessian, now quickened his steed, in hopes of leaving him behind. The
stranger, however, quickened his horse to an equal pace. Ichabod pulled up,
and fell into a walk, thinking to lag behind—the other did the same. His
heart began to sink within him; he endeavored to resume his psalm tune,
but his parched tongue clove to the roof of his mouth, and he could not
utter a stave. There was something in the moody and dogged silence of
this pertinacious companion, that was mysterious and appalling. It was
soon fearfully accounted for. On mounting a rising ground, which brought
the figure of his fellow-traveller in relief against the sky, gigantic in height,
and muffled in a cloak, Ichabod was horror-struck, on perceiving that he
was headless!—but his horror was still more increased, on observing, that
the head, which should have rested on his shoulders, was carried before
him on the pommel of the saddle: his terror rose to desperation; he rained
a shower of kicks and blows upon Gunpowder, hoping, by a sudden move-

ment, to give his companion the slip—but the spectre started full jump with him. Away, then, they dashed, through thick and thin; stones flying, and sparks flashing at every bound. Ichabod's flimsy garments fluttered in the air, as he stretched his long lank body away over his horse's head, in the eagerness of his flight.

They had now reached the road which turns off to Sleepy Hollow; but Gunpowder, who seemed possessed with a demon, instead of keeping up it, made an opposite turn, and plunged headlong down hill to the left. This road leads through a sandy hollow, shaded by trees for about a quarter of a mile, where it crosses the bridge famous in goblin story, and just beyond swells the green knoll on which stands the whitewashed church.

As yet the panic of the steed had given his unskilful rider an apparent advantage in the chase; but just as he had got half way through the hollow, the girths of the saddle gave way, and he felt it slipping from under him. He seized it by the pommel, and endeavored to hold it firm, but in vain; and he had just time to save himself by clasping old Gunpowder round the neck, when the saddle fell to the earth, and he heard it trampled under foot by his pursuer. For a moment the terror of Hans Van Ripper's wrath passed across his mind—for it was his Sunday saddle; but this was no time for petty fears: the goblin was hard on his haunches; and (unskilful rider that he was!) he had much ado to maintain his seat; sometimes slipping on one side, sometimes on another, and sometimes jolted on the high ridge of his horse's back-bone, with a violence that he verily feared would cleave him asunder.

An opening in the trees now cheered him with the hopes that the church bridge was at hand. The wavering reflection of a silver star in the bosom of the brook told him that he was not mistaken. He saw the walls of the church dimly glaring under the trees beyond. He recollected the place where Brom Bones' ghostly competitor had disappeared. "If I can but reach that bridge," thought Ichabod, "I am safe." Just then he heard the black steed panting and blowing close behind him; he even fancied that he felt his hot breath. Another convulsive kick in the ribs, and old Gunpowder sprung upon the bridge; he thundered over the resounding planks; he gained the opposite side; and now Ichabod cast a look behind to see if his pursuer should vanish, according to rule, in a flash of fire and brimstone. Just then he saw the goblin rising in his stirrups, and in the very act of hurling his head at him. Ichabod endeavored to dodge the horrible missile, but too late. It encountered his cranium with a tremendous crash—he was tumbled headlong into the dust, and Gunpowder, the black steed, and the goblin rider, passed by like a whirlwind.

The next morning the old horse was found without his saddle, and with the bridle under his feet, soberly cropping the grass at his master's gate. Ichabod did not make his appearance at breakfast—dinner-hour came, but no Ichabod. The boys assembled at the school-house, and strolled idly about the banks of the brook; but no schoolmaster. Hans Van Ripper now began to feel some uneasiness about the fate of poor Ichabod, and his saddle. An inquiry was set on foot, and after diligent investigation they came upon his traces. In one part of the road leading to the church, was found the saddle trampled in the dirt; the tracks of horses' hoofs deeply dented in the road, and evidently at furious speed, were traced to the bridge, beyond which, on the bank of a broad part of the brook, where the water ran deep and black, was found the hat of the unfortunate Ichabod, and close beside it a shattered pumpkin.

The brook was searched, but the body of the schoolmaster was not to be discovered. Hans Van Ripper, as executor of his estate, examined the bundle which contained all his worldly effects. They consisted of two shirts and a half; two stocks for the neck; a pair or two of worsted stockings; an old pair of corduroy small-clothes; a rusty razor; a book of psalm tunes, full of dog's-ears; and a broken pitchpipe. As to the books and furniture of the school-house, they belonged to the community, excepting Cotton Mather's History of Witchcraft, a New England Almanack, and a book of dreams and fortune telling; in which last was a sheet of foolscap much scribbled and blotted in several fruitless attempts to make a copy of verses in honor of the heiress of Van Tassel. These magic books and the poetic scrawl were forthwith consigned to the flames by Hans Van Ripper; who from that time forward determined to send his children no more to school; observing, that he never knew any good come of this same reading and writing. Whatever money the schoolmaster possessed, and he had received his quarter's pay but a day or two before, he must have had about his person at the time of his disappearance.

The mysterious event caused much speculation at the church on the following Sunday. Knots of gazers and gossips were collected in the churchyard, at the bridge, and at the spot where the hat and pumpkin had been found. The stories of Brouwer, of Bones, and a whole budget of others, were called to mind; and when they had diligently considered them all, and compared them with the symptoms of the present case, they shook their heads, and came to the conclusion that Ichabod had been carried off by the galloping Hessian. As he was a bachelor, and in nobody's debt, nobody troubled his head any more about him. The school was removed to a different quarter of the hollow, and another pedagogue reigned in his stead.

It is true, an old farmer, who had been down to New York on a visit several years after, and from whom this account of the ghostly adventure was received, brought home the intelligence that Ichabod Crane was still alive; that he had left the neighborhood partly through fear of the goblin and Hans Van Ripper, and partly in mortification at having been suddenly dismissed by the heiress; that he had changed his quarters to a distant part of the country; had kept school and studied law at the same time; had been admitted to the bar, turned politician, electioneered, written for the newspapers, and finally had been made a Justice of the Ten Pound Court. Brom Bones too, who, shortly after his rival's disappearance conducted the blooming Katrina in triumph to the altar, was observed to look exceedingly knowing whenever the story of Ichabod was related, and always burst into a hearty laugh at the mention of the pumpkin; which led some to suspect that he knew more about the matter than he chose to tell.

The old country wives, however, who are the best judges of these matters, maintain to this day, that Ichabod was spirited away by supernatural means; and it is a favorite story often told about the neighborhood round the winter evening fire. The bridge became more than ever an object of superstitious awe, and that may be the reason why the road has been altered of late years, so as to approach the church by the border of the mill-pond. The school-house being deserted, soon fell to decay, and was reported to be haunted by the ghost of the unfortunate pedagogue; and the ploughboy, loitering homeward of a still summer evening, has often fancied his voice at a distance, chanting a melancholy psalm tune among the tranquil solitudes of Sleepy Hollow.

POSTSCRIPT

Found in the Handwriting of Mr. Knickerbocker

The preceding Tale is given, almost in the precise words in which I heard it related at a corporation meeting of the ancient city of Manhattoes, at which were present many of its sagest and most illustrious burghers. The narrator was a pleasant, shabby, gentlemanly old fellow, in pepper-and-salt clothes, with a sadly humorous face, and one whom I strongly suspected of being poor—he made such efforts to be entertaining. When his story was concluded, there was much laughter and approbation, particularly from two or three deputy aldermen, who had been asleep a greater part of the time. There was, however, one tall, dry-looking old gentleman, with beetling eye brows, who maintained a grave and rather severe face throughout; now and then folding his arms, inclining his head, and looking down upon the floor, as if turning a doubt over in his mind. He was one of your wary men, who never laugh, but upon good grounds—when they have reason and the law on their side. When the mirth of the rest of the company had subsided, and silence was restored, he leaned one arm on the elbow of his chair, and sticking the other akimbo, demanded, with a slight but exceedingly sage motion of the head, and contraction of the brow, what was the moral of the story, and what it went to prove?

The story teller, who was just putting a glass of wine to his lips, as a refreshment after his toils, paused for a moment, looked at his inquirer with an air of infinite deference, and lowering the glass slowly to the table, observed, that the story was intended most logically to prove:—

"That there is no situation in life but has its advantages and pleasures—provided we will but take a joke as we find it:

"That, therefore, he that runs races with goblin troopers is likely to have rough riding of it:

"Ergo, for a country schoolmaster to be refused the hand of a Dutch heiress, is a certain step to high preferment in the state."

The cautious old gentleman knit his brows tenfold closer after this explanation, being sorely puzzled by the ratiocination of the syllogism; while methought the one in pepper-and-salt eyed him with something of a triumphant leer. At length he observed, that all this was very well, but still he thought the story a little on the extravagant—there were one or two points on which he had his doubts.

"Faith, sir," replied the story teller, "as to that matter, I don't believe one-half of it myself."

D.K.

Part III

MIRROR
IMAGES

THE YELLOW SIGN

Robert Chambers

I

"Let the red dawn surmise
What we shall do,
When this blue starlight dies
And all is through."

There are so many things which are impossible to explain! Why should certain chords in music make me think of the brown and golden tints of autumn foliage? Why should the Mass of Sainte-Cécile send my thoughts wandering among caverns whose walls blaze with ragged masses of virgin silver? What was it in the roar and turmoil of Broadway at six o'clock that flashed before my eyes the picture of a still Breton forest where sunlight filtered through spring foliage, and Sylvia bent, half curiously, half tenderly, over a small, green lizard, murmuring, "To think that this also is a little ward of God?"

When I first saw the watchman his back was towards me. I looked at him indifferently, until he went into the church. I paid no more attention to him than I had to any other man who lounged through Washington Square that morning, and when I shut my window and turned back into my studio I had forgotten him. Late in the afternoon, the day being warm, I raised the window again and leaned out to get a sniff of air. A man was standing in the court-yard of the church, and I noticed him again with as little interest as I had that morning. I looked across the square to where the fountain was playing, and then, with my mind filled with vague impressions of trees, asphalt drives, and the moving groups of nursemaids and holiday-makers, I started to walk back to my easel. As I turned, my listless glance included the man below in the church-yard. His face was towards me now, and with a perfectly involuntary movement I bent to see it. At the same moment he raised his head and looked at me. Instantly I thought of a coffin-worm. Whatever it was about the man that repelled me, I did not know, but the impression of a plump, white grave-worm was so intense and nauseating that I must have shown it in my expression, for he turned his puffy face away with a movement which made me think of a disturbed grub in a chestnut.

I went back to my easel and motioned the model to resume her pose. After working awhile, I was satisfied that I was spoiling what I had done as rapidly as possible, and I took up a palette-knife and scraped the color out again. The flesh tones were sallow and unhealthy, and I did not understand how I could have painted such sickly color into a study which before that had glowed with healthy tones.

I looked at Tessie. She had not changed, and the clear flush of health dyed her neck and cheeks as I frowned.

"Is it something I've done?" she asked.

"No; I've made a mess of this arm, and for the life of me I can't see how I came to paint such mud as that into the canvas," I replied.

"Don't I pose well?" she insisted.

"Of course, perfectly."

"Then it's not my fault?"

"No. It's my own."

"I'm very sorry," she said.

I told her she could rest while I applied rag and turpentine to the plague-spot on my canvas, and she went off to smoke a cigarette and look over the illustrations in the *Courier Français*.

I did not know whether it was something in the turpentine or a defect in the canvas, but the more I scrubbed the more that gangrene seemed to spread. I worked like a beaver to get it out, and yet the disease appeared to creep from limb to limb of the study before me. Alarmed, I strove to arrest it, but now the color on the breast changed and the whole figure seemed to absorb the infection as a sponge soaks up water. Vigorously I plied palette-knife, turpentine, and scraper, thinking all the time what a séance I should hold with Duval, who had sold me the canvas; but soon I noticed that it was not the canvas which was defective, nor yet the colors of Edward. "It must be the turpentine," I thought, angrily, "or else my eyes have become so blurred and confused by the afternoon light that I can't see straight." I called Tessie, the model. She came and leaned over my chair, blowing rings of smoke into the air.

"What *have* you been doing to it?" she exclaimed.

"Nothing," I growled; "it must be this turpentine!"

"What a horrible color it is now," she continued. "Do you think my flesh resembles green cheese?"

"No, I don't," I said, angrily, "did you ever know me to paint like that before?"

"No, indeed!"

"Well, then!"

"It must be the turpentine, or something," she admitted.

She slipped on a Japanese robe and walked to the window. I scraped and rubbed until I was tired, and finally picked up my brushes and hurled them through the canvas with a forcible expression, the tone alone of which reached Tessie's ears.

Nevertheless she promptly began: "That's it! Swear and act silly and ruin your brushes! You have been three weeks on that study, and now look! What's the good of ripping the canvas? What creatures artists are!"

I felt about as much ashamed as I usually did after such an outbreak, and I turned the ruined canvas to the wall. Tessie helped me clean my brushes, and then danced away to dress. From the screen she regaled me with bits of advice concerning whole or partial loss of temper, until thinking perhaps I had been tormented sufficiently, she came out to implore me to button her waist where she could not reach it on the shoulder.

"Everything went wrong from the time you came back from the window and talked about that horrid-looking man you saw in the church-yard," she announced.

"Yes, he probably bewitched the picture," I said, yawning. I looked at my watch.

"It's after six, I know," said Tessie, adjusting her hat before the mirror.

"Yes," I replied, "I didn't mean to keep you so long." I leaned out of the window, but recoiled with disgust, for the young man with the pasty face stood below in the church-yard. Tessie saw my gesture of disapproval, and leaned from the window.

"Is that the man you don't like?" she whispered.

I nodded.

"I can't see his face, but he does look fat and soft. Someway or other," she continued, turning to look at me, "he reminds me of a dream—an awful dream—I once had. Or," she mused, looking down at her shapely shoes, "was it a dream after all?"

"How should I know?" I smiled.

Tessie smiled in reply.

"You were in it," she said, "so perhaps you might know something about it."

"Tessie! Tessie!" I protested, "don't you dare flatter by saying that you dream about me!"

"But I did," she insisted. "Shall I tell you about it?"

"Go ahead," I replied, lighting a cigarette.

Tessie leaned back on the open window-sill and began, very seriously:

"One night last winter I was lying in bed thinking about nothing at all in particular. I had been posing for you and I was tired out, yet it seemed impossible for me to sleep. I heard the bells in the city ring ten, eleven, and midnight. I must have fallen asleep about midnight, because I don't remember hearing the bells after that. It seemed to me that I had scarcely closed my eyes when I dreamed that something impelled me to go to the window. I rose, and, raising the sash, leaned out. Twenty-fifth Street was deserted as far as I could see. I began to be afraid; everything outside seemed so—so black and uncomfortable. Then the sound of wheels in the distance came to my ears, and it seemed to me as though that was what I must wait for. Very slowly the wheels approached, and, finally, I could make out a vehicle moving along the street. It came nearer and nearer, and when it passed beneath my window I saw it was a hearse. Then, as I trembled with fear, the driver turned and looked straight at me. When I awoke I was standing by the open window shivering with cold, but the black-plumed hearse and the driver were gone. I dreamed this dream again in March last, and again awoke beside the open window. Last night the dream came again. You remember how it was raining; when I awoke, standing at the open window, my night-dress was soaked."

"But where did I come into the dream?" I asked.

"You—you were in the coffin; but you were not dead."

"In the coffin?"

"Yes."

"How did you know? Could you see me?"

"No; I only knew you were there."

"Had you been eating Welsh rarebits, or lobster salad?" I began, laughing, but the girl interrupted me with a frightened cry.

"Hello! What's up?" I said, as she shrank into the embrasure by the window.

"The—the man below in the church-yard; he drove the hearse."

"Nonsense," I said; but Tessie's eyes were wide with terror. I went to the window and looked out. The man was gone. "Come, Tessie," I urged, "don't be foolish. You have posed too long; you are nervous."

"Do you think I could forget that face?" she murmured. "Three times I saw the hearse pass below my window, and every time the driver turned and looked up at me. Oh, his face was so white and—and soft! It looked dead—it looked as if it had been dead a long time."

I induced the girl to sit down and swallow a glass of Marsala. Then I sat down beside her and tried to give her some advice.

"Look here, Tessie," I said, "you go to the country for a week or two, and you'll have no more dreams about hearses. You pose all day, and when night comes your nerves are upset. You can't keep this up. Then again, instead of going to bed when your day's work is done, you run off to picnics at Sulzer's Park, or go to the Eldorado or Coney Island, and when you come down here next morning you are fagged out. There was no real hearse. That was a soft-shell-crab dream."

She smiled faintly.

"What about the man in the church-yard?"

"Oh, he's only an ordinary, unhealthy, every-day creature."

"As true as my name is Tessie Rearden, I swear to you, Mr. Scott, that the face of the man below in the church-yard is the face of the man who drove the hearse!"

"What of it?" I said. "It's an honest trade."

"Then you think I *did* see the hearse?"

"Oh," I said, diplomatically, "if you really did, it might not be unlikely that the man below drove it. There is nothing in that."

Tessie rose, unrolled her scented handkerchief, and, taking a bit of gum from a knot in the hem, placed it in her mouth. Then, drawing on her gloves, she offered me her hand with a frank "Good-night, Mr. Scott," and walked out.

II

The next morning, Thomas, the bell-boy, brought me the *Herald* and a bit of news. The church next door had been sold. I thanked Heaven for it, not that I, being a Catholic, had any repugnance for the congregation next door, but because my nerves were shattered by a blatant exhorter, whose every word echoed through the aisle of the church as if it had been my own rooms, and who insisted on his r's with a nasal persistence which revolted my every instinct. Then, too, there was a fiend in human shape, an organist, who reeled off some of the grand old hymns with an interpretation of his own, and I longed for the blood of a creature who could play the "Doxology" with an amendment of minor chords which one hears only in a quartet of very young undergraduates. I believe the minister was a good man, but when he bellowed, "And the Lorrrd said unto Moses, the Lorrrd is a man of war; the Lorrrd is his name. My wrath shall wax hot, and I will kill you with the sworrrd!" I wondered how many centuries of purgatory it would take to atone for such a sin.

"Who bought the property?" I asked Thomas.

"Nobody that I knows, sir. They do say the gent wot owns this 'ere 'Amilton flats was lookin' at it. 'E might be a bildin' more studios."

I walked to the window. The young man with the unhealthy face stood by the church-yard gate, and at the mere sight of him the same overwhelming repugnance took possession of me.

"By-the-way, Thomas," I said, "who is that fellow down there?"

Thomas sniffed. "That there worm, sir? 'E's night-watchman of the church, sir. 'E maikes me tired a-sittin' out all night on them steps and lookin' at you insultin' like. I'd 'a' punched 'is 'ed, sir—beg pardon, sir—"

"Go on, Thomas."

"One night a comin' 'ome with 'Arry, the other English boy, I sees 'im a sittin' there on them steps. We 'ad Molly and Jen with us, sir, the two girls on the tray service, an' 'e looks so insultin' at us that I up and sez, 'Wat you lookin' hat, you fat slug?'—beg pardon, sir, but that's 'ow I sez, sir. Then 'e don't say nothin', and I sez, 'Come out and I'll punch that puddin' 'ed.' Then I hopens the gate an' goes in, but 'e don't say nothin', only looks insultin' like. Then I 'its 'im one; but, ugh! 'is 'ed was that cold and mushy it ud sicken you to touch 'im."

"What did he do then?" I asked, curiously.

"'Im? Nawthin'."

"And you, Thomas?"

The young fellow flushed with embarrassment, and smiled uneasily.

"Mr. Scott, sir, I ain't no coward, an' I can't make it out at all why I run. I was in the Fifth Lawncers, sir, bugler at Tel-el-Kebir, an' was shot by the wells."

"You don't mean to say you ran away?"

"Yes, sir; I run."

"Why?"

"That's just what I want to know, sir. I grabbed Molly an' run, an' the rest was as frightened as I."

"But what were they frightened at?"

Thomas refused to answer for a while; but now my curiosity was aroused about the repulsive young man below, and I pressed him. Three years' sojourn in America had not only modified Thomas's cockney dialect, but had given him the American's fear of ridicule.

"You won't believe me, Mr. Scott, sir?"

"Yes, I will."

"You will lawf at me, sir?"

"Nonsense!"

He hesitated. "Well, sir, it's Gawd's truth, that when I 'it 'im, 'e grabbed me wrists, sir, and when I twisted 'is soft, mushy fist one of 'is fingers come off in me 'and."

The utter loathing and horror of Thomas's face must have been re-flected in my own, for he added:

"It's orful, an' now when I see 'im I just go away. 'E maikes me hill."

When Thomas had gone I went to the window. The man stood beside the church railing, with both hands on the gate; but I hastily retreated to my easel again, sickened and horrified, for I saw that the middle finger of his right hand was missing.

At nine o'clock Tessie appeared and vanished behind the screen, with a merry "Good-morning, Mr. Scott." When she had reappeared and taken her pose upon the model-stand I started a new canvas, much to her de-light. She remained silent as long as I was on the drawing, but as soon as the scrape of the charcoal ceased, and I took up my fixative, she began to chatter.

"Oh, I had such a lovely time last night. We went to Tony Pastor's."

"Who are 'we'?" I demanded.

"Oh, Maggie—you know, Mr. Whyte's model—and Pinkie Mc-

Cormick—we call her Pinkie because she's got that beautiful red hair you artists like so much—and Lizzie Burke."

I sent a shower of spray from the fixative over the canvas, and said, "Well, go on."

"We saw Kelly, and Baby Barnes, the skirt-dancer, and—and all the rest. I made a mash."

"Then you have gone back on me, Tessie?"

She laughed and shook her head.

"He's Lizzie Burke's brother, Ed. He's a perfect gen'l'man."

I felt constrained to give her some parental advice concerning mashing, which she took with a bright smile.

"Oh, I can take care of a strange mash," she said, examining her chewing-gum, "but Ed is different. Lizzie is my best friend."

Then she related how Ed had come back from the stocking-mill in Lowell, Massachusetts, to find her and Lizzie grown up—and what an accomplished young man he was—and how he thought nothing of squandering half a dollar for ice-cream and oysters to celebrate his entry as clerk into the woollen department of Macy's. Before she finished I began to paint, and she resumed the pose, smiling and chattering like a sparrow. By noon I had the study fairly well rubbed in and Tessie came to look at it.

"That's better," she said.

I thought so, too, and ate my lunch with a satisfied feeling that all was going well. Tessie spread her lunch on a drawing-table opposite me, and we drank our claret from the same bottle and lighted our cigarettes from the same match. I was very much attached to Tessie. I had watched her shoot up into a slender but exquisitely formed woman from a frail, awkward child. She had posed for me during the last three years, and among all my models she was my favorite. It would have troubled me very much indeed had she become "tough" or "fly," as the phrase goes; but I never noticed any deterioration of her manner, and felt at heart that she was all right. She and I never discussed morals at all, and I had no intention of doing so, partly because I had none myself, and partly because I knew she would do what she liked in spite of me. Still I did hope she would steer clear of complications, because I wished her well, and then also I had a selfish desire to retain the best model I had. I knew that mashing, as she termed it, had no significance with girls like Tessie, and that such things in America did not resemble in the least the same things in Paris. Yet, having lived with my eyes open, I also knew that somebody would take Tessie away some day, in one manner or another, and though I professed to myself that marriage was nonsense, I sincerely hoped that, in this case, there would be a priest at the end of the vista. I am a Catholic. When I listen to high mass, when I sign myself, I feel that everything, including myself, is more cheerful; and when I confess, it does me good. A man who lives as much alone as I do must confess to somebody. Then, again, Sylvia was Catholic, and it was reason enough for me. But I was speaking of Tessie, which is very different. Tessie also was Catholic, and much more devout than I, so, taking it all in all, I had little fear for my pretty model until she should fall in love. But *then* I knew that fate alone would decide her future for her, and I prayed inwardly that fate would keep her away from men like me and throw into her path nothing but Ed Burkes and Jimmy McCormicks, bless her sweet face!

Tessie sat blowing rings of smoke up to the ceiling and tinkling the ice in her tumbler.

"Do you know that I also had a dream last night?" I observed.

"Not about that man?" she asked, laughing.

"Exactly. A dream similar to yours, only much worse."

It was foolish and thoughtless of me to say this, but you know how little tact the average painter has.

"I must have fallen asleep about ten o'clock," I continued, "and after a while I dreamed that I awoke. So plainly did I hear the midnight bells, the wind in the tree-branches, and the whistle of steamers from the bay, that even now I can scarcely believe I was not awake. I seemed to be lying in a box which had a glass cover. Dimly I saw the street lamps as I passed, for I must tell you, Tessie, the box in which I reclined appeared to lie in a cushioned wagon which jolted me over a stony pavement. After a while I became impatient and tried to move, but the box was too narrow. My hands were crossed on my breast so I could not raise them to help myself. I listened and then tried to call. My voice was gone. I could hear the trample of the horses attached to the wagon, and even the breathing of the driver. Then another sound broke upon my ears like the raising of a window-sash. I managed to turn my head a little, and found I could look, not only through the glass cover of my box, but also through the glass panes in the side of the covered vehicle. I saw houses, empty and silent, with neither light nor life about any of them excepting one. In that house a window was open on the first floor and a figure all in white stood looking down into the street. It was you."

Tessie had turned her face away from me and leaned on the table with her elbow.

"I could see your face," I resumed, "and it seemed to me to be very sorrowful. Then we passed on and turned into a narrow, black lane. Presently the horses stopped. I waited and waited, closing my eyes with fear and impatience, but all was silent as the grave. After what seemed to me hours, I began to feel uncomfortable. A sense that somebody was close to me made me unclose my eyes. Then I saw the white face of the hearse-driver looking at me through the coffin-lid—"

A sob from Tessie interrupted me. She was trembling like a leaf. I saw I had made an ass of myself, and attempted to repair the damage.

"Why, Tess," I said, "I only told you this to show you what influence your story might have on another person's dreams. You don't suppose I really lay in a coffin, do you? What are you trembling for? Don't you see that your dream and my unreasonable dislike for that inoffensive watchman of the church simply set my brain working as soon as I fell asleep?"

She laid her head between her arms and sobbed as if her heart would break. What a precious triple donkey I had made of myself! But I was about to break my record. I went over and put my arm about her.

"Tessie, dear, forgive me," I said; "I had no business to frighten you with such nonsense. You are too sensible a girl, too good a Catholic to believe in dreams."

Her hand tightened on mine and her head fell back upon my shoulder, but she still trembled and I petted her and comforted her.

"Come, Tess, open your eyes and smile."

Her eyes opened with a slow, languid movement and met mine, but their expression was so queer that I hastened to reassure her again.

"It's all humbug, Tessie. You surely are not afraid that any harm will come to you because of that?"

"No," she said, but her scarlet lips quivered.

"Then what's the matter? Are you afraid?"

"Yes. Not for myself."

"For me, then?" I demanded, gayly.

"For you," she murmured, in a voice almost inaudible. "I—I care for you."

At first I started to laugh, but when I understood her a shock passed through me, and I sat like one turned to stone. This was the crowning bit of idiocy I had committed. During the moment which elapsed between her reply and my answer I thought of a thousand responses to that innocent confession. I could pass it by with a laugh, I could misunderstand her and reassure her as to my health, I could simply point out that it was impossible she could love me. But my reply was quicker than my thoughts, and I might think and think now when it was too late, for I had kissed her on the mouth.

That evening I took my usual walk in Washington Park, pondering over the occurrences of the day. I was thoroughly committed. There was no back-out now, and I stared the future straight in the face. I was not good, not even scrupulous, but I had no idea of deceiving either myself or Tessie. The one passion of my life lay buried in the sunlit forests of Brittany. Was it buried forever? Hope cried "No!" For three years I had been listening to the voice of Hope, and for three years I had waited for a footstep on my threshold. Had Sylvia forgotten? "No!" cried Hope.

I said that I was not good. That is true, but still I was not exactly a comic-opera villain. I had led an easy-going, reckless life, taking what invited me of pleasure, deploring and sometimes bitterly regretting consequences. In one thing alone, except my painting, was I serious, and that was something which lay hidden if not lost in the Breton forests.

It was too late now for me to regret what had occurred during the day. Whatever it had been, pity, a sudden tenderness for sorrow, or the more brutal instinct of gratified vanity, it was all the same now, and unless I wished to bruise an innocent heart my path lay marked before me. The fire and strength, the depth of passion of a love which I had never even suspected, with all my imagined experience in the world, left me no alternative but to respond or send her away. Whether because I am so cowardly about giving pain to others, or whether it was that I have little of the gloomy Puritan in me, I do not know, but I shrank from disclaiming responsibility for that thoughtless kiss, and, in fact, had no time to do so before the gates of her heart opened and the flood poured forth. Others who habitually do their duty and find a sullen satisfaction in making themselves and everybody else unhappy, might have withstood it. I did not. I dared not. After the storm had abated I did tell her that she might better have loved Ed Burke and worn a plain gold ring, but she would not hear of it, and I thought perhaps that as long as she had decided to love somebody she could not marry, it had better be me. I at least could treat her with an intelligent affection, and whenever she became tired of her infatuation she could go none the worse for it. For I was decided on that point, although I

knew how hard it would be. I remembered the usual termination of pla-
tonic *liaisons,* and thought how disgusted I had been whenever I heard of
one. I knew I was undertaking a great deal for so unscrupulous a man as I
was, and I dreaded the future, but never for one moment did I doubt that
she was safe with me. Had it been anybody but Tessie, I should not have
bothered my head about scruples. For it did not occur to me to sacrifice
Tessie as I would have sacrificed a woman of the world. I looked the future
squarely in the face, and saw the several probable endings to the affair. She
would either tire of the whole thing, or become so unhappy that I should
have either to marry her or go away. If I married her we would be unhappy,
I with a wife unsuited to me, and she with a husband unsuitable for any
woman. For my past life could scarcely entitle me to marry. If I went away
she might either fall ill, recover, and marry some Eddie Burke, or she might
recklessly or deliberately go and do something foolish. On the other hand,
if she tired of me, then her whole life would be before her with beautiful
vistas of Eddie Burkes and marriage rings, and twins, and Harlem flats,
and Heaven knows what. As I strolled along through the trees by the
Washington Arch, I decided that she should find a substantial friend in me
anyway, and the future could take care of itself. Then I went into the house
and put on my evening dress, for the little, faintly perfumed note on my
dresser said, "Have a cab at the stage door at eleven," and the note was
signed "Edith Carmichel, Metropolitan Theatre."

   I took supper that night, or, rather, we took supper, Miss Carmichel
and I, at Solari's, and the dawn was just beginning to gild the cross on the
Memorial Church as I entered Washington Square after leaving Edith at
the Brunswick. There was not a soul in the park as I passed among the
trees and took the walk which leads from the Garibaldi statue to the
Hamilton apartment house, but as I passed the church-yard I saw a figure
sitting on the stone steps. In spite of myself a chill crept over me at the
sight of the white, puffy face, and I hastened to pass. Then he said something which might have been addressed to me or might merely have been a
mutter to himself, but a sudden furious anger flamed up within me that
such a creature should address me. For an instant I felt like wheeling about
and smashing my stick over his head, but I walked on, and, entering the
Hamilton, went to my apartment. For some time I tossed about the bed
trying to get the sound of his voice out of my ears, but could not. It filled
my head, that muttering sound, like thick, oily smoke from a fat-rendering

vat or an odor of noisome decay. And as I lay and tossed about, the voice in my ears seemed more distinct, and I began to understand the words he had muttered. They came to me slowly, as if I had forgotten them, and at last I could make some sense out of the sounds. It was this:

"Have you found the Yellow Sign?"

"Have you found the Yellow Sign?"

"Have you found the Yellow Sign?"

I was furious. What did he mean by that? Then with a curse upon him and his I rolled over and went to sleep, but when I awoke later I looked pale and haggard, for I had dreamed the dream of the night before, and it troubled me more than I cared to think.

I dressed and went down into my studio. Tessie sat by the window, but as I came in she rose and put both arms around my neck for an innocent kiss. She looked so sweet and dainty that I kissed her again, and then sat down before the easel.

"Hello! Where's the study I began yesterday?" I asked.

Tessie looked conscious, but did not answer. I began to hunt among the piles of canvases, saying: "Hurry up, Tess, and get ready; we must take advantage of the morning light."

When at last I gave up the search among the other canvases and turned to look around the room for the missing study, I noticed Tessie standing by the screen with her clothes still on.

"What's the matter," I asked, "don't you feel well?"

"Yes."

"Then hurry."

"Do you want me to pose as—as I have always posed?"

Then I understood. Here was a new complication. I had lost, of course, the best nude model I had ever seen. I looked at Tessie. Her face was scarlet. Alas! Alas! We had eaten of the tree of knowledge, and Eden and native innocence were dreams of the past—I mean for her.

I suppose she noticed the disappointment on my face, for she said: "I will pose if you wish. The study is behind the screen here where I put it."

"No," I said, "we will begin something new"; and I went into my wardrobe and picked out a Moorish costume which fairly blazed with tinsel. It was a genuine costume, and Tessie retired to the screen with it enchanted. When she came forth again I was astonished. Her long, black hair was bound above her forehead with a circlet of turquoises, and the ends curled about her glittering girdle. Her feet were encased in the embroidered pointed slippers, and the skirt of her costume, curiously wrought with arabesques in silver, fell to her ankles. The deep metallic blue vest, embroidered with silver, and the short Mauresque jacket, spangled and sewn with turquoises, became her wonderfully. She came up to me and held up her face, smiling. I slipped my hand into my pocket, and, drawing out a gold chain with a cross attached, dropped it over her head.

"It's yours, Tessie."

"Mine?" she faltered.

"Yours. Now go and pose." Then with a radiant smile she ran behind the screen, and presently reappeared with a little box on which was written my name.

"I had intended to give it to you when I went home to-night," she said, "but I can't wait now."

I opened the box. On the pink cotton inside lay a clasp of black onyx, on which was inlaid a curious symbol or letter in gold. It was neither Arabic nor Chinese, nor, as I found afterwards, did it belong to any human script.

"It's all I had to give you for a keepsake," she said, timidly.

I was annoyed, but I told her how much I should prize it, and promised to wear it always. She fastened it on my coat beneath the lapel.

"How foolish, Tess, to go and buy me such a beautiful thing as this," I said.

"I did not buy it," she laughed.

"Where did you get it?"

Then she told me how she had found it one day while coming from the aquarium in the Battery, how she had advertised it and watched the papers, but at last gave up all hopes of finding the owner.

"That was last winter," she said, "the very day I had the first horrid dream about the hearse."

I remembered my dream of the previous night but said nothing, and presently my charcoal was flying over a new canvas, and Tessie stood motionless on the model-stand.

III

The day following was a disastrous one for me. While moving a framed canvas from one easel to another my foot slipped on the polished floor and I fell heavily on both wrists. They were so badly sprained that it was useless to attempt to hold a brush, and I was obliged to wander about the studio, glaring at unfinished drawings and sketches, until despair seized me and I sat down to smoke and twiddle my thumbs with rage. The rain blew against the windows and rattled on the roof of the church, driving me into a nervous fit with its interminable patter. Tessie sat sewing by the window, and every now and then raised her head and looked at me with such innocent compassion that I began to feel ashamed of my irritation and looked about for something to occupy me. I had read all the papers and all the books in the library, but for the sake of something to do I went to the bookcases and shoved them open with my elbow. I knew every volume by its color and examined them all, passing slowly around the library and whistling to keep up my spirits. I was turning to go into the dining-room when my eye fell upon a book bound in serpent-skin standing in a corner of the top shelf of the last bookcase. I did not remember it, and from the floor could not decipher the pale lettering on the back, so I went to the smoking-room and called Tessie. She came in from the studio and climbed up to reach the book.

"What is it?" I asked.

"'The King in Yellow.'"

I was dumfounded. Who had placed it there? How came it in my rooms? I had long ago decided that I should never open that book, and nothing on earth could have persuaded me to buy it. Fearful lest curiosity might tempt me to open it, I had never even looked at it in book-stores. If I ever had had any curiosity to read it, the awful tragedy of young Castaigne, whom I knew, prevented me from exploring its wicked pages. I had always refused to listen to any description of it, and, indeed, nobody ever ventured to discuss the second part aloud, so I had absolutely no knowledge of what those leaves might reveal. I stared at the poisonous, mottled binding as I would at a snake.

"Don't touch it, Tessie," I said; "come down."

Of course my admonition was enough to arouse her curiosity, and before I could prevent it she took the book, and, laughing, danced off into the studio with it. I called to her, but she slipped away with a tormenting smile at my helpless hands, and I followed her with some impatience.

"Tessie!" I cried, entering the library, "listen; I am serious. Put that book away. I do not wish you to open it!" The library was empty. I went into both drawing-rooms, then into the bedrooms, laundry, kitchen, and finally returned to the library and began a systematic search. She had hidden herself so well that it was half an hour later when I discovered her crouching white and silent by the latticed window in the store-room above. At the first glance I saw she had been punished for her foolishness. "The King in Yellow" lay at her feet; but the book was open at the second part. I looked at Tessie and saw it was too late. She had opened "The King in Yellow." Then I took her by the hand and led her into the studio. She seemed dazed, and when I told her to lie down on the sofa she obeyed me without a word. After a while she closed her eyes and her breathing became regular and deep; but I could not determine whether or not she slept. For a long while I sat silently beside her, but she neither stirred nor spoke, and at last I rose and, entering the unused store-room, took the book in my least injured hand. It seemed heavy as lead; but I carried it into the studio again, and, sitting down on the rug beside the sofa, opened it and read it through from beginning to end.

When, faint with the excess of my emotions, I dropped the volume and leaned wearily back against the sofa, Tessie opened her eyes and looked at me.

We had been speaking for some time in a dull, monotonous strain before I realized that we were discussing "The King in Yellow." Oh the sin of writing such words—words which are clear as crystal, limpid and musical as bubbling springs, words which sparkle and glow like the poisoned diamonds of the Medicis! Oh the wickedness, the hopeless damnation, of a soul who could fascinate and paralyze human creatures with such words— words understood by the ignorant and wise alike, words which are more precious than jewels, more soothing than music, more awful than death!

We talked on, unmindful of the gathering shadows, and she was begging me to throw away the clasp of black onyx quaintly inlaid with what we now knew to be the Yellow Sign. I never shall know why I refused, though even at this hour, here in my bedroom as I write this confession, I should be glad to know *what* it was that prevented me from tearing the Yellow Sign from my breast and casting it into the fire. I am sure I wished to do so, and yet Tessie pleaded with me in vain. Night fell, and the hours dragged on, but still we murmured to each other of the King and the Pallid Mask, and midnight sounded from the misty spires in the fog-wrapped city. We spoke of Hastur and of Cassilda, while outside the fog rolled against the blank window-panes as the cloud waves roll and break on the shores of Hali.

The house was very silent now, and not a sound came up from the misty streets. Tessie lay among the cushions, her face a gray blot in the gloom, but her hands were clasped in mine, and I knew that she knew and read my thoughts as I read hers, for we had understood the mystery of the Hyades, and the Phantom of Truth was laid. Then, as we answered each other, swiftly, silently, thought on thought, the shadows stirred in the gloom about us, and far in the distant streets we heard a sound. Nearer and nearer it came—the dull crunching of wheels, nearer and yet nearer, and now, outside, before the door, it ceased, and I dragged myself to the window and saw a black-plumed hearse. The gate below opened and shut, and I crept, shaking, to my door, and bolted it, but I knew no bolts, no locks, could keep that creature out who was coming for the Yellow Sign. And now I heard him moving very softly along the hall. Now he was at the door, and the bolts rotted at his touch. Now he had entered. With eyes starting from my head I peered into the darkness, but when he came into the room I did not see him. It was only when I felt him envelop me in his cold, soft grasp that I cried out and struggled with deadly fury, but my hands were useless, and he tore the onyx clasp from my coat and struck me full in the face. Then, as I fell, I heard Tessie's soft cry, and her spirit fled; and even while falling I longed to follow her, for I knew that the King in Yellow had opened his tattered mantle and there was only God to cry to now.

I could tell more, but I cannot see what help it will be to the world. As for me, I am past human help or hope. As I lie here, writing, careless even whether or not I die before I finish, I can see the doctor gathering up his powders and phials with a vague gesture to the good priest beside me, which I understand.

They will be very curious to know the tragedy—they of the outside world who write books and print millions of newspapers, but I shall write no more, and the father confessor will seal my last words with the seal of sanctity when his holy office is done. They of the outside world may send their creatures into wrecked homes and death-smitten firesides, and their newspapers will batten on blood and tears, but with me their spies must halt before the confessional. They know that Tessie is dead, and that I am dying. They know how the people in the house, aroused by an infernal scream, rushed into my room, and found one living and two dead, but they do not know what I shall tell them now; they do not know that the doctor said, as he pointed to a horrible, decomposed heap on the floor—the livid corpse of the watchman from the church: "I have no theory, no explanation. That man must have been dead for months!"

I think I am dying. I wish the priest would—

THE HOLLOW OF
THE THREE HILLS

Nathaniel Hawthorne

In those strange old times when fantastic dreams and madmen's reveries were realized among the actual circumstances of life, two persons met together at an appointed hour and place. One was a lady graceful in form and fair of feature, though pale and troubled and smitten with an untimely blight in what should have been the fullest bloom of her years; the other was an ancient and meanly-dressed woman of ill-favored aspect, and so withered, shrunken and decrepit that even the space since she began to decay must have exceeded the ordinary term of human existence. In the spot where they encountered no mortal could observe them. Three little hills stood near each other, and down in the midst of them sunk a hollow basin almost mathematically circular, two or three hundred feet in breadth and of such depth that a stately cedar might but just be visible above the sides. Dwarf pines were numerous upon the hills and partly fringed the outer verge of the intermediate hollow, within which there was nothing but the brown grass of October and here and there a tree-trunk that had fallen long ago and lay moldering with no green successor from its roots. One of these masses of decaying wood, formerly a majestic oak, rested close beside a pool of green and sluggish water at the bottom of the basin. Such scenes as this (so gray tradition tells) were once the resort of a power of evil and his plighted subjects, and here at midnight or on the dim verge of evening they were said to stand round the mantling pool disturbing its putrid waters in the performance of an impious baptismal rite. The chill beauty of an autumnal sunset was now gilding the three hilltops, whence a paler tint stole down their sides into the hollow.

"Here is our pleasant meeting come to pass," said the aged crone, "according as thou hast desired. Say quickly what thou wouldst have of me, for there is but a short hour that we may tarry here."

As the old withered woman spoke a smile glimmered on her countenance like lamplight on the wall of a sepulcher. The lady trembled and cast her eyes upward to the verge of the basin, as if meditating to return with her purpose unaccomplished. But it was not so ordained.

"I am stranger in this land, as you know," said she, at length. "Whence I come it matters not, but I have left those behind me with whom my fate was intimately bound, and from whom I am cut off forever. There is a weight in my bosom that I cannot away with, and I have come hither to inquire of their welfare."

"And who is there by this green pool that can bring thee news from the ends of the earth?" cried the old woman, peering into the lady's face. "Not from my lips mayst thou hear these tidings; yet be thou bold, and the daylight shall not pass away from yonder hilltop before thy wish be granted."

"I will do your bidding though I die," replied the lady, desperately.

The old woman seated herself on the trunk of the fallen tree, threw aside the hood that shrouded her gray locks and beckoned her companion to draw near.

"Kneel down," she said, "and lay your forehead on my knees."

She hesitated a moment, but the anxiety that had long been kindling burned fiercely up within her. As she knelt down the border of her garment was dipped into the pool; she laid her forehead on the old woman's knees, and the latter drew a cloak about the lady's face, so that she was in darkness. Then she heard the muttered words of prayer, in the midst of which she started and would have arisen.

"Let me flee! Let me flee and hide myself, that they may not look upon me!" she cried. But, with returning recollection, she hushed herself and was still as death, for it seemed as if other voices, familiar in infancy and unforgotten through many wanderings and in all the vicissitudes of her heart and fortune, were mingling with the accents of the prayer. At first the words were faint and indistinct—not rendered so by distance, but rather resembling the dim pages of a book which we strive to read by an imperfect and gradually brightening light. In such a manner, as the prayer proceeded, did those voices strengthen upon the ear, till at length the petition ended, and the conversation of an aged man and of a woman broken and decayed like himself became distinctly audible to the lady as she knelt. But those strangers appeared not to stand in the hollow depth between the three hills. Their voices were encompassed and re-echoed by the walls of a chamber the windows of which were rattling in the breeze; the regular vibration of a clock, the crackling of a fire and the tinkling of the embers as they fell among the ashes rendered the scene almost as vivid as if painted to the eye. By a melancholy hearth sat these two old people, the man calmly despondent, the woman querulous and tearful, and their words were all of sorrow. They spoke of a daughter, a wanderer they knew not where, bearing dishonor along with her and leaving shame and affliction to bring their gray heads to the grave. They alluded also to other and more recent woe, but in the midst of their talk their voices seemed to melt into the sound of the wind sweeping mournfully among the autumn leaves; and when the lady lifted her eyes, there was she kneeling in the hollow between three hills.

"A weary and lonesome time yonder old couple have of it," remarked the old woman, smiling in the lady's face.

"And did you also hear them?" exclaimed she, a sense of intolerable humiliation triumphing over her agony and fear.

"Yea, and we have yet more to hear," replied the old woman, "wherefore cover thy face quickly."

Again the withered hag poured forth the monotonous words of a prayer that was not meant to be acceptable in heaven, and soon in the pauses of her breath strange murmurings began to thicken, gradually increasing, so as to drown and overpower the charm by which they grew. Shrieks pierced through the obscurity of sound and were succeeded by the singing of sweet female voices, which in their turn gave way to a wild roar of laughter broken suddenly by groanings and sobs, forming altogether a ghastly confusion of terror and mourning and mirth. Chains were rattling, fierce and stern voices uttered threats and the scourge resounded at their command. All these noises deepened and became substantial to the listener's ear, till she could distinguish every soft and dreamy accent of the love-songs that died causelessly into funeral-hymns. She shuddered at the unprovoked wrath which blazed up like the spontaneous kindling of flame, and she grew faint at the fearful merriment raging miserably around her. In the midst of this wild scene, where unbound passions jostled each other in a drunken career, there was one solemn voice of a man, and a manly and melodious voice it might once have been. He went to and fro continually, and his feet sounded upon the floor. In each member of that frenzied company whose own burning thoughts had become their exclusive world he sought an auditor for the story of his individual wrong, and interpreted their laughter and tears as his reward of scorn or pity. He spoke of woman's perfidy, of a wife who had broken her holiest vows, of a home and heart made desolate. Even as he went on, the shout, the laugh, the shriek, the sob, rose up in unison, till they changed into the hollow, fitful and uneven sound of the wind as it fought among the pine trees on those three lonely hills.

The lady looked up, and there was the withered woman smiling in her face.

"Couldst thou have thought there were such merry times in a mad-house?" inquired the latter.

"True, true!" said the lady to herself; "there is mirth within its walls, but misery, misery without."

"Wouldst thou hear more?" demanded the old woman.

"There is one other voice I would fain listen to again," replied the lady, faintly.

"Then lay down thy head speedily upon my knees, that thou mayst get thee hence before the hour be past."

The golden skirts of day were yet lingering upon the hills, but deep shades obscured the hollow and the pool, as if somber night were rising thence to overspread the world. Again that evil woman began to weave her spell. Long did it proceed unanswered, till the knolling of a bell stole in among the intervals of her words like a clang that had traveled far over valley and rising ground and was just ready to die in the air. The lady shook upon her companion's knees as she heard that boding sound. Stronger it grew, and sadder, and deepened into the tone of a death-bell, knolling dolefully from some ivy-mantled tower and bearing tidings of mortality and woe to the cottage, to the hall and to the solitary wayfarer, that all might weep for the doom appointed in turn to them. Then came a measured tread, passing slowly, slowly on, as of mourners with a coffin, their garments trailing on the ground, so that the ear could measure the length of their melancholy array. Before them went the priest, reading the burial-service, while the leaves of his book were rustling in the breeze. And though no voice but his was heard to speak aloud, still there were revilings and anathemas, whispered but distinct, from women and from men, breathed against the daughter who had wrung the aged hearts of her parents, the wife who had betrayed the trusting fondness of her husband, the mother who had sinned against natural affection and left her child to die. The sweeping sound of the funeral train faded away like a thin vapor, and the wind, that just before had seemed to shake the coffin-pall, moaned sadly round the verge of the hollow between three hills. But when the old woman stirred the kneeling lady, she lifted not her head.

"Here has been a sweet hour's sport!" said the withered crone, chuckling to herself.

THOUGH ONE ROSE FROM THE DEAD

William Dean Howells

You are very welcome to the Alderling incident, my dear Acton, if you think you can do anything with it, and I will give it as circumstantially as possible. The thing has its limitations, I should think, for the fictionists, chiefly in a sort of roundedness which leaves little play to the imagination. It seems to me that it would be more to your purpose if it were less *pat,* in its catastrophe, but you are a better judge of all that than I am, and I will put the facts in your hands, and keep my own hands off, so far as any plastic use of the material is concerned.

The first I knew of the peculiar Alderling situation was shortly after William James's *Will to Believe* came out. I had been telling the Alderlings about it, for they had not seen it, and I noticed that from time to time they looked significantly at each other. When I had got through, he gave a little laugh, and she said, "Oh, you may laugh!" and then I made bold to ask, "What is it?"

"Marion can tell you," he said. He motioned towards the coffee-pot and asked, "More?" I shook my head, and he said, "Come out, and let us see what the maritime interests have been doing for us. Pipe or cigar?" I chose cigarettes, and he brought the box off the table, stopping on his way to the veranda, and taking his pipe and tobacco-pouch from the hall mantel.

Mrs. Alderling had got to the veranda before us, and done things to the chairs and cushions, and was leaning against one of the slender, fluted pine columns like some rich, blond caryatid just off duty, with the blue of her dress and the red of her hair showing deliciously against the background of white house-wall. He and she were an astonishing and satisfying contrast; in the midst of your amazement you felt the divine propriety of a woman like her wanting just such a wiry, smoky-complexioned, black-browed, black-bearded, bald-headed little man as he was.

Before he sat down where she was going to put him he stood stoopingly, and frowned at the waters of the cove lifting from the foot of the lawn that sloped to it before the house. "Three lumbermen, two goodish-sized yachts, a dozen sloop-rigged boats: not so bad. About the usual number that come loafing in to spend the night. You ought to see them when it threatens to breeze up. Then they're here in flocks. Go on, Marion."

He gave a soft groan of comfort as he settled in his chair and began pulling at his short black pipe, and she let her eyes dwell on him in a rapture that curiously interested me. People in love are rarely interesting—that is, flesh-and-blood people. Of course I know that lovers are the life of fiction, and that a story of any kind can scarcely hold the reader without them. Yet lovers in real life are, so far as I have observed them, bores. They are confessed to be disgusting before or after marriage when they let their fondness appear, but even when they try to hide it they are tiresome. Character goes down before passion in them; nature is reduced to propensity. Then, how is it that the novelist manages to keep these, and to give us nature and character while seeming to offer nothing but propensity and passion? Perhaps he does not give them. Perhaps what he does is to hypnotize us so that we each of us identify ourselves with the lovers, and add our own natures and characters to the single principle that animates them. But if we have them there before us in the tiresome reality they exclude us from their pleasure in each other and stop up the perspective of our happiness with their hulking personalities, bare of all the iridescence of potentiality which we could have cast about them. Something of this iridescence may cling to unmarried lovers, in spite of themselves, but wedded bliss is a sheer offense.

I do not know why it was not an offense in the case of the Alderlings unless it was because they both, in their different ways, saw the joke of the thing. At any rate, I found that in their charm for each other they had somehow not ceased to be amusing for me, and I waited confidently for the answer she would make to his whimsically abrupt bidding. But she did not answer very promptly even when he had added, "Wanhope, here, is scenting something psychological in the reason of my laughing at you."

Mrs. Alderling stood looking at him, not me, with a smile hovering about the corners of her mouth, which, when it decided not to alight anywhere, scarcely left her aspect graver for its flitting. She said at last in her slow, deep-throated voice, "I guess I will let you tell him."

"Oh, I'll tell him fast enough," said Alderling, nursing his knee, and bringing it well up toward his chin, between his clasped hands. "Marion has always had the notion that I should live again if I believed I should, and that as I don't believe I shall, I am not going to. The joke of it is," and he began to splutter laughter round the stem of his pipe, "she's as much of an agnostic as I am. She doesn't believe she is going to live again, either."

Mrs. Alderling said, "I don't care for it in my case."

That struck me as rather touching, but I had no right to enter uninvited into the intimacy of her meaning, and I said, looking as little at her as I need, "Aren't you both rather belated?"

"You mean that protoplasm has gone out?" he chuckled.

"Not exactly," I answered. "But you know that a great many things are allowed now that were once forbidden to the True Disbelievers."

"You mean that we may trust in the promises, as they used to be called, and still keep the Unfaith?"

"Something like that."

Alderling took his pipe out, apparently to give his whole face to the pleasure of teasing his wife. "That'll be a great comfort to Marion," he said, and he threw back his head and laughed.

She smiled faintly, vaguely, tolerantly, as if she enjoyed his pleasure in teasing her.

"Where have you been," I asked, "that you don't know the changed attitude in these matters?"

"Well, here for the last three years. We tried it the first winter after we came, and found it was not so bad, and we simply stayed on. But I haven't really looked into the question since I gave the conundrum up twenty years ago, on what was then the best authority. Marion doesn't complain. She knew what I was when she married me. She was another. We were neither of us very bigoted disbelievers. We should not have burned anybody at the stake for saying that we had souls."

Alderling put back his pipe and cackled round it, taking his knee between his hands again.

"You know," she explained, more in my direction than to me, "that I had none to begin with. But Alderling had. His people believed in the future life."

"That's what they said," Alderling crowed. "And Marion has always thought that if she had believed that way, she could have kept me up to it; and so when I died I should have lived again. It is perfectly logical, though it isn't capable of a practical demonstration. If Marion had come of a believing family, she could have brought me back into the fold. Her great mistake was in being brought up by an uncle who denied that he was living here, even. The poor girl could not do a thing when it came to the life hereafter."

The smile now came hovering back, and alighted at a corner of Mrs. Alderling's mouth, making it look, oddly enough, rather rueful. "It didn't matter about me. I thought it a pity that Alderling's talent should stop here."

"Did you ever know anything like that?" he cried. "Perfectly willing to thrust me out into a cold other-world, and leave me to struggle on without her, when I had got used to her looking after me. Now I'm not so selfish as that. I shouldn't want to have Marion living on through all eternity if I wasn't with her. It would be too lonely for her."

He looked up at her, with his dancing eyes, and she put her hand down over his shoulder into the hand that he lifted to meet it, in a way that would have made me sick in some people. But in her the action was so casual, so absent, that it did not affect me disagreeably.

"Do you mean that you haven't been away since you came here three years ago?" I asked.

"We ran up to the theater once in Boston last winter, but it bored us to the limit." Alderling poked his knife-blade into the bowl of his pipe as he spoke, having freed his hand for the purpose, while Mrs. Alderling leaned back against the slim column again. He said gravely: "It was a great thing for Marion, though. In view of the railroad accident that didn't happen, she convinced herself that her sole ambition was that we should die together. Then, whether we found ourselves alive or not, we should be company for each other. She's got it arranged with the thunderstorms, so that one bolt will do for us both, and she never lets me go out on the water alone, for fear I shall watch my chance, and get drowned without her."

I did not trouble myself to make out how much of this was mocking, and as there was no active participation in the joke expected of me, I kept on the safe side of laughing. "No wonder you've been able to do such a lot of pictures," I said. "But I should have thought you might have found it dull—I mean dull together—at odd times."

"Dull?" he shouted. "It's stupendously dull! Especially when our country neighbors come in to 'liven us up.' We've got neighbors here that can stay longer in half an hour than most people can in a week. We get tired of each other at times, but after a call from the people in the next house we return with rapture to our delusion that we are interesting."

"And you never," I ventured, making my jocosity as ironical as possible, "wear upon each other?"

"Horribly!" said Alderling, and his wife smiled contentedly, behind him. "We haven't a whole set of china in the house, from exchanging it across the table, and I haven't made a study of Marion—you must have noticed how many Marions there were—that she hasn't thrown at my head. Especially the Madonnas. She likes to throw the Madonnas at me."

I ventured still farther, addressing myself to Mrs. Alderling. "Does he keep it up all the time—this *blague?*"

"Pretty much," she answered passively, with entire acquiescence in the fact if it were the fact, or the joke if it were the joke.

"But I didn't see anything of yours, Mrs. Alderling," I said. She had had her talent, as a girl, and some people preferred it to her husband's—but there was no effect of it anywhere in the house.

"The housekeeping is enough," she answered, with her tranquil smile.

There was nothing in her smile that was leading, and I did not push my inquiry, especially as Alderling did not seem disposed to assist. "Well," I said, "I suppose you will forgive to science my feeling that your situation is most suggestive."

"Oh, don't mind *us!*" said Alderling.

"I won't, thank you," I answered. "Why, it's equal to being cast away together on an uninhabited island."

"Quite," he assented.

"There can't," I went on, "be a corner of your minds that you haven't mutually explored. You must know each other," I cast about for the word, and added abruptly, "by heart."

"I don't suppose he meant anything pretty?" said Alderling, with a look up over his shoulder at his wife; and then he said to me, "We do; and there are some very curious things I could tell you, if Marion would ever let me get in a word."

"Do let him, Mrs. Alderling," I entreated, humoring his joke at her silence.

She smiled, and softly shrugged, and then sighed.

"I could make your flesh creep," he went on, "or I could if you were not a psychologist. I assure you that we are quite weird at times."

"As how?"

"Oh, just knowing what the other is thinking, at a given moment, and saying it. There are times when Marion's thinking is such a nuisance to me that I have to yell down to her from my loft to stop it. The racket it makes breaks me all up. It's a relief to have her talk, and I try to make her, when she's posing, just to escape the din of her thinking. Then the willing! We experimented with it, after we had first noticed it, but we don't, any more. It's too dead easy."

"What do you mean by the willing?"

"Oh, just wishing one that the other was there, and there he or she is."

"Is he trying to work me, Mrs. Alderling?" I appealed to her, and she answered from her calm:

"It is very unaccountable."

"Then you really mean it! Why can't you give me an illustration?"

"Why, you know," said Alderling more seriously than he had yet spoken, "I don't believe those things, if they are real, can ever be got to show off. That's the reason why your *Quests in the Occult* are mainly such rubbish, as far as the evidences are concerned. If Marion and I tried to give you an illustration, as you call it, the occult would snub us. But *is* there anything so very strange about it? The wonder is that a man and wife ever fail of knowing each what the other is thinking. They pervade each other's minds, if they are really married, and they are so present with each other that the tacit wish should be the same as a call. Marion and I are only an intensified instance of what may be done by living together. There is something, though, that is rather queer, but it belongs to psychomancy rather than psychology, as I understand it."

"Ah!" I said. "What is that?"

"Being visibly present when absent. It has not happened often, but it has happened that I have seen Marion in my loft when she was really somewhere else, and not when I had willed her or wished her to be there."

"Now, really," I said, "I must ask you for an instance."

"You want to heap up facts, Lombroso fashion? Well, this is as good as most of Lombroso's facts, or better. I went up one morning, last winter, to work at a study of a Madonna from Marion, directly after breakfast, and left her below in the dining-room, putting away the breakfast things. She has to do that occasionally, between the local helps, who are all we can get in the winter. She professes to like it, but you never can tell, from what a woman says; she has to do it, anyway." It is hard to convey a notion of the serene, impersonal acquiescence of Mrs. Alderling in taking this talk of her. "I was banging away at it when I knew she was behind me looking over my shoulder rather more stormily than she usually does; usually, she is a dead calm. I glanced up, and saw the calm succeed the storm. Then I kept on, and after a while I was aware of hearing her step on the stairs."

Alderling stopped, and smoked definitively, as if that were the end.

"Well," I said, after waiting a while, "I don't exactly get the unique value of the incident."

"Oh," he said, as if he had accidentally forgotten the detail, "the steps were coming up."

"Yes?"

"She opened the door, which she had omitted to do before, and when she came in she denied having been there already. She owned that she had been hurrying through her work, and thinking of mine, so as to make me do something, or undo something, to it; and then all at once she lost her impatience, and came up at her leisure. I don't exactly like to tell what she wanted."

He began to laugh provokingly, and she said, tranquilly, "I don't mind your telling Mr. Wanhope."

"Well, then, strictly in the interest of psychomancy, I will confide that she had found some traces of a model that I used to paint my Madonnas from, before we were married, in that picture. She had slept on her suspicion, and then when she could not stand it any longer, she had come up in the spirit to say that she was not going to be mixed up in a Madonna with any such minx. The words are mine, but the meaning was Marion's. When she found me taking the minx out, she went quietly back to washing her dishes, and then returned in the body to give me a sitting."

We were silent a moment, till I asked, "Is this true, Mrs. Alderling?"

"About," she said. "I don't remember the storm, exactly."

"Well, I don't see why you bother to remain in the body at all," I remarked.

"We haven't arranged just how to leave it together," said Alderling. "Marion, here, if I managed to get off first, would have no means of knowing whether her theory of the effect of my unbelief on my future was right or not; and if *she* gave *me* the slip, she would always be sorry that she had not stayed here to convert me."

"Why don't you agree that if either of you lives again, he or she shall make some sign to let the other know?" I suggested.

"Well, that has been tried so often, and has it ever worked? It's open to the question whether the dead do not fail to show up because they are forbidden to communicate with the living; and you are just where you were, as to the main point. No, I don't see any way out of it."

Mrs. Alderling went into the house and came out with a book in her hand, and her fingers in it at two places. It was that impressive collection of Christ's words from the *New Testament* called *The Great Discourse*. She put the book before me first at one place and then at another, and I read at one, "He that believeth on me shall never die," and at the other, "Except ye believe in me ye shall all likewise perish." She did not say anything in showing me these passages, and I found something in her action touchingly childlike and elemental, as well as curiously heathenish. It was as if some poor pagan had brought me his fetish to test its effect upon me. "Yes," I said, "those are things that we hardly know what to do with in our philosophy. They seem to be said as with authority, and yet somehow we cannot admit their validity in a philosophical inquiry as to a future life. Aren't they generally taken to mean that we shall be unhappy or happy hereafter, rather than that we shall be or not be at all? And what is believing? Is it the mere act of acknowledgment, or is it something more vital, which expresses itself in conduct?"

She did not try to say. In fact, she did not answer at all. Whatever point was in her mind she did not or could not debate it. I perceived, in a manner, that her life was so largely subliminal that if she had tried she could not have met my question any more than if she had not had the gift of speech at all. But in her inarticulate fashion she had exposed to me a state of mind which I was hardly withheld by the decencies from exploring. "You know," I said, "that psychology almost begins by rejecting the authority of these sayings, and that while we no longer deny anything we cannot allow anything merely because it has been strongly affirmed. Supposing that there is a life after this, how can it be denied to one and bestowed upon another because one has assented to a certain supernatural claim and another has refused to do so? That does not seem reasonable, it does not seem right. Why should you base your conclusion as to that life upon a promise and a menace which may not really refer to it in the sense which they seem to have?"

"Isn't it all there is?" she asked, and Alderling burst into his laugh.

"I'm afraid she's got you there, Wanhope. When it comes to polemics there's nothing like the passive obstruction of Mrs. Alderling. Marion might never have been an early Christian herself—I think she's an inexpugnable pagan—but she would have gone round making it awfully uncomfortable for the other unbelievers."

"You know," she said to him, and I never could decide how much she was in earnest, "that I can't believe till you do. I couldn't take the risk of keeping on without you."

Alderling followed her indoors, where she now went to put the book away, with his mock addressed to me, "Did you ever know such a stubborn woman?"

II

One conclusion from my observation of the Alderlings during the week I spent with them was that it is bad for a husband and wife to be constantly and unreservedly together, not because they grow tired of each other, but because they grow more intensely interested in each other. Children, when they come, serve the purpose of separating the parents; they seem to unite them in one care, but they divide them in their employments, at least in the normally constituted family. If they are rich and can throw the care of the children upon servants then they cannot enjoy the relief from each other that children bring to the mother who nurtures and teaches them and to the father who must work for them harder than before. The Alderlings were not rich enough to have been freed from the wholesome responsibilities of parentage, but they were childless, and so they were not detached from the perpetual thought of each other. If they had only had different tastes, it might have been better, but they were both artists, she not less than he, though she no longer painted. When their common thoughts were not centered upon each other's being they were centered on his work, which, viciously enough, was the constant reproduction of her visible personality. I could always see them studying each other, he with an eye to her beauty, she with an eye to his power.

He was every now and then saying to her, "Hold on, Marion," and staying her in some pose or movement, while he made mental note of it, and I was conscious of her preying upon his inmost thoughts and following him into the recesses of his reveries, where it is best for a man to be alone, even if he is sometimes a beast there. Now and then I saw him get up and shake himself restively, but I am bound to say in her behalf that her pursuit of him seemed quite involuntary, and that she enjoyed it no more than he did. Twenty times I was on the point of asking, "Why don't you people go in for a good long separation? Is there nothing to call you to Europe, Alderling? Haven't you got a mother, or sister, or something that you could visit, Mrs. Alderling? It would do you both a world of good."

But it happened, oddly enough, that the Alderlings were as kinless as they were childless, and if he had gone to Europe he would have taken her with him, and prolonged their seclusion by the isolation in which people necessarily live in a foreign country. I found I was the only acquaintance who had visited them during the year of their retirement on the coast, where they had stayed, partly through his inertia, and partially from his superstition that he could paint better away from the ordinary associations and incentives; and they ceased, before I left, to get the good they might of my visit because they made me a part of their intimacy instead of making themselves part of my strangeness.

After a day or two their queer experiences began to resume themselves unabashed by my presence. These were mostly such as they had already more than hinted to me: the thought-transferences, and the unconscious hypnotic suggestions which they made to each other. There was more novelty in the last than the first. If I could trust them, and they did not seem to wish to exploit their mysteries for the effect on me, they were with each other because one or the other had willed it. She would say, if we were sitting together without him, "I think Rupert wants me; I'll be back in a moment," and he, if she were not by, for some time, would get up with, "Excuse me, I have got to go to Marion; she's calling me."

I had to take a great deal of this on faith; in fact, none of it was susceptible of proof; but I have not been able since to experience all the skepticism which usually replaces the impression left by sympathy with such supposed occurrences. The thing was not quite what we call uncanny; the people were so honest, both of them, that the morbid character of like situations was wanting. The events, if they could be called so, were not invited, I was quite sure, and they were varied by such diversions as we had in reach. I went blueberrying with Mrs. Alderling in the morning, after she

had got her breakfast dishes put away, in order that we might have something for dessert at our midday dinner; and I went fishing off the old
stone crib with Alderling in the afternoon, so that we might have cunners
for supper. The farmerfolks and fisherfolks seemed to know them and to
be on tolerant terms with them, though it was plain that they still considered them probational in their fellow-citizenship. I do not think they were
liked the less because they did not assume to be of the local sort, but let
their difference stand, if it would. There was nothing countrified in her
dress, which was frankly conventional; the short walking-skirt had as sharp
a slant in front as her dinner-gown would have had, and he wore his
knickerbockers—it was then the now-faded hour of knickerbockers—with
an air of going out golfing in the suburbs. She had stayed on with him
through the first winter in the place they had taken for the summer, because she wished to be with him, rather than because she wished to be
there, and he had stayed because he had not found just the moment to
break away, though afterwards he pretended a reason for staying. They had
no more voluntarily cultivated the natural than the supernatural; he kindled the fire for her, and she made the coffee for him, not because they
preferred, but because they must; and they had arrived at their common
ground in the occult by virtue of being alone together, and not by seeking
the solitude for the experiment which the solitude promoted. Mrs. Alderling did not talk less nor he more when either was alone with me than
when we were all together; perhaps he was more silent and she not quite so
much; she was making up for him in his absence as he was for her in her
presence. But they were always hospitable and attentive hosts, and though
under the peculiar circumstances of Mrs. Alderling's having to do the
housework herself I necessarily had to do a good many things for myself,
there were certain little graces which were never wanting from her hands:
my curtains were always carefully drawn, and my coverlet triangularly
opened, so that I did not have to pull it down myself. There was a freshly
trimmed lamp on the stand at my bed-head, and a book and paper-cutter
put there, with a decanter of whisky and a glass of water. I note these
things to you, because they are touches which help remove the sense of
anything intentional in the occultism of the Alderlings.

I do not know whether I shall be able to impart the feeling of an obscure pathos in the case of Mrs. Alderling, which I certainly did not experience in Alderling's. Temperamentally he was less fitted to undergo the
rigors of their seclusion than she was; in his liking to talk, he needed an

audience and a variety of listening, and she in her somewhat feline calm could not have been troubled by any such need. You can be silent to yourself, but you cannot very well be loquacious, without danger of having the devil for a listener, if the old saying is true. Yet still, I felt a keener poignancy in her sequestration. Her beauty had even greater claim to regard than his eloquence. She was a woman who could have commanded a whole roomful with it, and no one would have wanted a word from her.

I am not able to say now how much of all this is observation of previous facts and how much speculation based upon subsequent occurrences. At the best I can only let it stand for characterization. In the same interest I will add a fact in relation to Mrs. Alderling which ought to have its weight against any undue appeal I have been making in her behalf. Without in the least blaming her, I will say that I think Mrs. Alderling ate too much. She must have had naturally a strong appetite, which her active life sharpened, and its indulgence formed a sort of refuge from the pressure of the intense solitude in which she lived, and which was all the more a solitude because it was *solitude à deux*. I noticed that beyond the habit of cooks she partook of the dishes she had prepared, and that after Alderling and I had finished dinner, and he was impatient to get at his pipe, she remained prolonging her dessert.

At the risk of giving the effect of something sensuous, even sensual, in her, I find myself insisting upon this detail, which did not lessen her peculiar charm. As far as the mystical quality of the situation was concerned, I fancy your finding that rather heightened by her innocent *gourmandise*. You must have noticed how inextricably, for this life at least, the spiritual is trammeled in the material, how personal character and ancestral propensity seem to flow side by side in the same individual without necessarily affecting each other. On the moral side Mrs. Alderling was no more to be censured for the refuge which her nerves sought from the situation in overeating than Alderling for the smoking in which he escaped from the pressure they both felt from one another; and she was no less fitted than he for their joint experience.

III

I do not suppose it was with the notion of keeping her weight down that Mrs. Alderling rowed a good deal on the cove before the cottage; but she had a boat, which she managed very well, and which she was out in, pretty much the whole time when she was not cooking, or eating, or sleeping, or roaming the berry-pastures with me, or sitting to Alderling for his Madonnas. He did not care for the water himself; he said he knew every inch of that cove, and was tired of it; but he rather liked his wife's going, and they may both have had an unconscious relief from each other in the absences which her excursions promoted. She swam as well as she rowed, and often we saw her going down waterproofed to the shore, where we presently perceived her pulling off in her bathing-dress. Well out in the cove she had the habit of plunging overboard, and after a good swim she rowed back, and then, discreetly waterproofed again, she climbed the lawn back to the house. Now and then she took me out in her boat, but so far as I remember Alderling never went with her. Once I ventured to ask him if he never felt anxious about her. He said no, he should not have been afraid to go with her, and she could take better care of herself than he could. Besides, by means of their telepathy they were in constant communion, and he could make her feel at any sort of chance, that he did not wish her to take it, and she would not. This was the only occasion when he treated their peculiar psychomancy boastfully, and the only occasion when I felt a distinct misgiving of his sincerity.

The day before I left Mrs. Alderling went down about eleven in the morning to her boat, and rowed out into the cove. She rowed far toward the other shore, whither, following her with my eye from Alderling's window, I saw its ridge blotted out by a long low cloud. It was straight and level as a wall, and looked almost as dense, and I called Alderling.

"Oh, that fog won't come in before afternoon," he said. "We usually get it about four o'clock. But even if it does," he added dreamily, "Marion can manage. I'd trust her anywhere in this cove in any kind of weather."

He went back to his work, and painted away for five or six minutes. Then he asked me, still at the window, "What's the fog doing now?"

"Well, I don't know," I answered. "I should say it was making in."

"Do you see Marion?"

"Yes, she seems to be taking her bath."

Again he painted a while before he asked, "Has she had her dip?"

"She's getting back into her boat."

"All right," said Alderling, in a tone of relief. "She's good to beat any fog in these parts ashore. I wish you would come and look at this a minute."

I went, and we lost ourselves for a time in our criticism of the picture. He was harder on it than I was. He allowed, "*C'est un bon portrait*, as the French used to say of a faithful landscape, though I believe now the portrait can't be too good for them. I can't say about landscape. But in a Madonna I feel that there can be too much Marion, not for me, of course, but for the ideal, which I suppose we are bound to respect. Marion is not spiritual, but I would not have her less of the earth earthy, for all the angels that ever spread themselves 'in strong level flight'."

I recognized the words from *The Blessed Damozel*, and I made bold to be so personal as to say, "If her hair were a little redder than 'the color of ripe corn' one might almost feel that the Blessed Damozel had been painted from Mrs. Alderling. It's the lingering earthiness in her that makes the Damozel so divine."

"Yes, that was a great conception. I wonder none of the fellows do that kind of thing now."

I laughed, and said, "Well, so few of them have had the advantage of seeing Mrs. Alderling. And besides, Rossettis don't happen every day."

"It was the period, too. I always tell her that she belongs among the later eighteen-sixties. But she insists that she wasn't even born then. Marion is tremendously single-minded."

"She has her mind all on you."

He looked askance at me. "You've noticed—"

He suddenly flung his brush from him, and started up, with a loudly shouted, "Yes, yes! I'm coming," and hurled himself out of the garret which he used for his studio, and cleared the stairs with two bounds.

By the time I reached the outer door of the cottage he was a dark blur in the white blur of the fog which had swallowed up the cove, and was rising round the house-walls from the grass. I heard him shouting, "Marion!" and a faint mellow answer, far out in the cove, "Hello!" and then "Where are you?" and her answer, "Here!" I heard him jump into a boat, and the thump of the oars in the rowlocks, and then the rapid beat of the oars, while he shouted, "Keep calling!" and she answered, "I will!" and called, "Hello! Hello! Hello!"

I made my mental comment that this time their mystical means of communication was somehow not working. But after her last hello no sound broke the white silence of the fog except the throb of Alderling's oars. She was evidently resting on hers, lest she should baffle his attempts to find her by trying to find him. I suppose ten minutes or so passed, when the dense air brought me the sound of low laughing that was also like the sound of low sobbing, and then I knew that they had met somewhere in the blind space. I began to hear rowing again, but only as of one boat, and suddenly out of the mist, almost at my feet, Alderling's boat shot up on the shelving beach, and his wife leaped ashore and ran past me up the lawn, while he pulled her boat out on the gravel. She must have been trailing it from the stern of his.

IV

I was abroad when Mrs. Alderling died, but I heard that it was from a typhoid fever which she had contracted from the water in their well, as was supposed. The water-supply all along that coast is scanty, and that summer most of the wells were dry, and quite a plague of typhoid raged among the people drinking the dregs. The fever might have gone the worse with her because of her overfed robustness; at any rate it went badly enough. I first heard of her death from Minver at the club, and I heard with still greater astonishment that Alderling was down there alone where she had died. Minver said that somebody ought to go down and look after the poor old fellow, but nobody seemed to feel it exactly his office. Certainly I did not feel it mine, and I thought it rather a hardship when a few days after I found a letter from Alderling at the club quite piteously beseeching me to come to him. He had read of my arrival home in a stray New York paper, and he was firing his letter, he said, at the club with one chance in a thousand of hitting me with it. I hesitated a day out of self-respect, or self-assertion, and then, the weather coming on suddenly hot, in the beginning of September, I went.

Of course I had meant to go, all along, but I was not so glad when I arrived, as I might have been if Alderling had given me a little warmer welcome. His mood had changed since writing to me, and the strongest feeling he showed at seeing me was what affected me very like a cold surprise.

If I had broken in on a solitude in that place before, I was now the intruder upon a desolation. Alderling was living absolutely alone except for the occasional presence of a neighboring widow—all the middle-aged women there are widows, with dim or dimmer memories of husbands lost off the Banks, or elsewhere at sea—who came in to get his meals and make his bed, and then had instructions to leave. It was in one of her prevailing absences that I arrived with my bag, and I had to hammer a long time with the knocker on the open door before Alderling came clacking down the stairs in his slippers from the top of the house, and gave me his somewhat defiant greeting. I could almost have said that he did not recognize me at the first bleared glance, and his inability, when he realized who it was, to make me feel at home, encouraged me to take the affair into my own hands.

He looked frightfully altered, but perhaps it was the shaggy beard that he had let grow over his poor, lean muzzle that mainly made the difference. His clothes hung gauntly upon him, and he had a weak-kneed stoop. His coat sleeves were tattered at the wrists, and one of them showed the white lining at the elbow. I simply shuddered at his shirt.

"Will you smoke?" he asked huskily, almost at the first word, and with an effect of bewilderment in his hospitality that almost made me shed tears.

"Well, not just yet, Alderling," I said. "Shall I go to my old room?"

"Go anywhere," he answered, and he let me carry my bag to the chamber where I had slept before.

It was quite as his wife would have arranged it, even to the detail of a triangular portion of the bedding turned down as she used to do it for me. The place was well aired and dusted and gave me the sense of being as immaculately clean and fresh as Alderling was not. He sat down in a chair by the window, and he remained while I laid out my things, and made my brief toilet, unabashed by those incidents for which I did not feel it necessary to banish him, if he liked staying.

We had supper by-and-by, a very well-cooked meal of fried fresh cod and potatoes, with those belated blackberries which grow so sweet when they hang long on the canes into September. There was a third plate laid, and I expected that when the housekeeper had put the victuals on the table, and brought in the tea, she would sit down with us, country-fashion, but she did not reappear till she came with the dessert and coffee. Alderling ate hungrily, and much more than I had remembered his doing, but perhaps I formerly had the impression of Mrs. Alderling's fine appetite so strongly in mind that I had failed to note his. Certainly, however, there was a difference in one sort which I could not be mistaken in, and that was his not talking. Her mantle of silence had fallen upon him, and whereas he used hardly to give me a chance in the conversation, he now let me do all of it. He scarcely answered my questions, and he asked none of his own; but I saw that he liked being talked to, and I did my best, shying off from his sorrow, as people foolishly do, and speaking banalities about my trip to Europe, and the Psychological Congress in Geneva, and the fellows at the club, and heaven knows what rot else.

He listened, but I do not know whether he heard much of my clack, and I got very tired of it myself at last. When I had finished my blackberries, he asked mechanically, in an echo of my former visit, with a repetition of his gesture towards the coffee-pot, "More?" I shook my head, and he led the way out to the veranda, stopping to get his pipe and tobacco from the mantel. But when we sat down in the early falling September twilight outside, he did not light his pipe, letting me smoke my cigarette alone.

"Are you off your tobacco?" I asked.

"I don't smoke," he answered, but he did not explain why, and I did not feel authorized to ask.

The talk went on as lopsidedly as before, and I began to get sleepy. I made bold to yawn, but Alderling did not mind that, and then I made bold to say that I thought I would go to bed. He followed me indoors, saying that he would go to bed, too. The hall was lighted from a hanging-lamp and two clear-burning hand-lamps which the widow had put for us on a small table. She had evidently gone home, and left us to ourselves. He took one lamp and I the other, and he started upstairs before me. If he were not coming down again, he meant to let the hanging-lamp burn, and I had nothing to say about that; but I suggested concerning the wide-open door behind me, "Shall I close the door, Alderling?" and he answered without looking round, "I don't shut it."

He led the way into my room, and he sat down as when I had come, and absently watched my processes of getting into bed. There was something droll, and yet miserable, in his behavior. At first, I thought he might be staying merely for the comfort of a human presence, and again, I thought he might be afraid, for I felt a little creepy myself, for no assignable reason, except that Absence, which he must have been incomparably more sensible of than I. From certain ineffectual movements that he made, and from certain preliminary noises in his throat, which ended in nothing,

I decided that he wished to say something to me, tell me something, and could not. But I was selfishly sleepy, and it seemed to me that anything he had on his mind would keep there till morning, at least, and that if he got it off on mine now, it might give me a night of wakeful speculation. So when I got into bed and pulled the sheet up under my chin, I said, "Well, I don't want to turn you out, old fellow."

He started, and answered, "Oh!" and went without other words, carrying his lamp with him and moving with a weak-kneed shuffle, like a very old man.

He was going to leave the door open behind him, but I called out, "I wish you'd shut me in, Alderling," and after a hesitation he came back and closed the door.

V

We breakfasted as silently on his part as we had supped, but when we had finished, and I was wondering what he was going to let me do with myself, and on the whole what the deuce I had come for, he said in the longest speech I had yet had from him, "Wouldn't you like to come up and see what I've been doing?"

I said I should like it immensely, and he led the way upstairs, as far as his attic studio. The door of that, like the other doors in the house, stood open, and I got the emotion which the interior gave me, full force, at the first glance. The place was so startlingly alive with that dead woman on a score of canvases in the character in which he had always painted her that I could scarcely keep from calling out; but I went about, pretending to examine the several Madonnas, and speaking rubbish about them, while he stood stoopingly in the midst of them like the little withered old man he looked.

I glanced about for a seat, and was going to take that in which Mrs. Alderling used to pose for him, but he called out with sudden sharpness, "Not that!" and without appearing to notice I found a box, which I inverted, and sat down on.

"Tell me about your wife, Alderling," I said, and he answered with a sort of scream:

"I wanted you to ask me! Why didn't you ask me before? What did you suppose I got you here for?"

With that he shrank down, a miserable heap, in his own chair, and bowed his hapless head and cried. It was more affecting than any notion I can give you of it, and I could only wait patiently for his grief to wash itself out in one of those paroxysms which come to bereavement and leave it somehow a little comforted when they pass.

"I was waiting, for the stupid reasons you will imagine, to let you speak first," I said, "but here in her presence I couldn't hold in any longer."

He asked with strange eagerness, "You noticed that?"

I chose to feign that he meant in the pictures. "Over and over again," I answered.

He would not have my feint. "I don't mean in these wretched caricatures!"

"Well?" I assented provisionally.

"I mean her very self, listening, looking, living—waiting!"

Whether I had insanity or sorrow to deal with, I could not gainsay the unhappy man, and I only said what I really felt: "Yes, the place seems strangely full of her. I wish you would tell me about her."

He asked with a certain slyness, "Have you heard anything about her already? At the club? From that fool woman in the kitchen?"

"For heaven's sake, no, Alderling!"

"Or about me?"

"Nothing whatever!"

He seemed relieved of whatever suspicion he felt, but he said finally, and with an air of precaution, "I should like to know just how much you mean by the place seeming full of her."

"Oh, I suppose the association of her personality with the whole house, and especially this room. I didn't mean anything preternatural, I believe."

"Then you don't believe in a life after death?" he demanded with a kind of defiance.

I thought this rather droll, seeing what his own position had been, but that was not the moment for the expression of my amusement. "The tendency is to a greater tolerance of the notion," I said. "Men like James and Royce, among the psychologists, and Shaler, among the scientists, scarcely leave us at peace in our doubts, any more, much less our denials."

He said, as if he had forgotten the question, "They called it a very light case, and they thought she was getting well. In fact, she did get well, and then—there was a relapse. They laid it to her eating some fruit which they allowed her."

Alderling spoke with a kind of bitter patience, but in my own mind I was not able to put all the blame on the doctors. Neither did I blame that innocently earthy creature, who was of no more harm in her strong appetite than any other creature which gluts its craving as simply as it feels it. The sense of her presence was deepened by the fact of those childlike self-indulgences which Alderling's words recalled to me. I made no comment, however, and he asked gloomily, as if with a return of his suspicion, "And you haven't heard of anything happening afterwards?"

"I don't know what you refer to," I told him, "but I can safely say I haven't, for I haven't heard anything at all."

"They contended that it *didn't* happen," he resumed indignantly. "She died, they said, and by all the tests she had been dead a whole day. She died with her hand in mine. I was not trying to hold her back; she had a kind of majestic preoccupation in her going, so that I would not have dared to detain her if I could. You've seen them go, and how they seem to draw those last, long, deep breaths as if they had no thought in the world but of the work of getting out of it. When her breathing stopped I expected it to go on, but it did not go on, and that was all. Nothing startling, nothing dramatic, just simple, natural, *like her!* I gave her hand back, I put it on her breast myself, and crossed the other on it. She looked as if she were sleeping, with that faint color hovering in her face, which was not wasted, but I did not make-believe about it; I accepted the fact of her death. In your *Quests in the Occult*," Alderling broke off, with a kind of superiority that was of almost the quality of contempt, "I believe you don't allow yourself to be daunted by a diametrical difference of opinion among the witnesses of an occurrence, as to its nature, or as to its reality, even?"

"Not exactly that," I said. "I think I argued that the passive negation of one witness ought not to invalidate the testimony of another as to this experience. One might hear and see things, and strongly affirm them, and another absorbed in something else, or in a mere suspense of the observant faculties, might quite as honestly declare that so far as his own knowledge was concerned, nothing of the kind happened. I held that in such a case counter-testimony should not be allowed to invalidate the testimony for the fact."

"Yes, that is what I meant," said Alderling. "You say it more clearly in the book, though."

"Oh, of course."

He began again, more remotely from the affair in hand than he had left

off, as if he wanted to give himself room for parley with my possible in-
credulity. "You know how it was with Marion about my not believing that
I should live again. Her notion was a sort of joke between us, especially
when others were by, but it was a serious thing with her, in her heart. Perhaps it had originally come to her as a mere fancy, and from entertaining it
playfully she found herself with a mental inmate that finally dispossessed
her judgment. You remember how literally she brought those Scripture
texts to bear on it?"

"Yes. May I say that it was very affecting?"

"Affecting!" Alderling repeated in a tone of amaze at the inadequacy of
my epithet. "She was always finding things that bore upon the point. After
a while she got to concealing them, as if she thought they annoyed me.
They never did; they amused me; and when I saw that she had something
of the sort on her mind, I would say, 'Well, out with it, Marion!' She
would always begin, 'Well, you may laugh!'" and as he repeated her words
Alderling did laugh, forlornly, and as I must say, rather blood-curdlingly.

I could not prompt him to go on, but he presently did so himself, deso-
lately enough. "I suppose, if I was in her mind at all in that supreme moment, when she seemed to be leaving this life behind with such a solemn
effect of rating it at nothing, it may have been a pang to her that I was not
following her into the dark, with any ray of hope for either of us. She
could not have returned from it with the expectation of convincing me, for
I used to tell her that if one came back from the dead I should merely
know that he had been mistaken about being dead, and was giving me a
dream from his trance. She once asked me if I thought Lazarus was not
really dead, with a curious, childlike interest in the miracle, and she was
disheartened when I reminded her that Lazarus had not testified of any
life hereafter, and it did not matter whether he had been really dead or not
when he was resuscitated, as far as that was concerned. Last year, we read
the *Bible* a good deal together here, and to tease her I pretended to be convinced of the contrary by the very passages that persuaded her. As she told
you, she did not care for herself. You remember that?"

"Distinctly," I said.

"It was always so. She never cared. I was perfectly aware that if she
could have assured life hereafter to me she would have given her life here to
do it. You know how some women, when they are married, absolutely give
themselves up, try to lose themselves in the behoof of their husbands? I

don't say it rightly; there are no words that will express the utterness of their abdication."

"I know what you mean," I said, "and it was one of the facts which most interested me in Mrs. Alderling."

He took up the affair at a quite different point, and as though that were the question in hand.

"That gift, or knack, or trick, or whatever it was, of one compelling the presence of the other by thinking or willing it was as much mine as hers, and she tried sometimes to get me to say that I would use it with her if she died before I did; and if she were where the conditions were opposed to her coming to me, my will would help her overcome the hindrance: our united wills would form a current of volition that she could travel back on against all obstacles. I don't know whether I make myself clear?" he appealed.

"Yes, perfectly," I said. "It is very curious."

He said in a kind of muse, "I don't know just where I was." Then he began again, "Oh, yes! It was at the ceremony—down there in the library. Some of the country people came in; I suppose they thought they ought, and I suppose they wanted to; it didn't matter to me. I had sent for Doctor Norrey, as soon as the relapse came, and he was there with me. Of course there was the minister, conducting the services. He made a prayer full of helpless repetitions, which I helplessly noticed, and some scrambling remarks, mostly misdirected at me, affirming and reaffirming that the sister they had lost was only gone before, and that she was now in a happier world.

"The singing and the praying and the preaching came to an end, and then there was that soul-sickening hush, that exanimate silence, of which the noise of rustling clothes and scraping feet formed a part, as the people rose in the hall, where chairs had been put for them, leaving me and Norrey alone with Marion. Every fiber of my frame recognized the moment of parting and protested. A tremendous wave of will swept through me and from me, a resistless demand for her presence, and it had power upon her. I heard her speak, and say, as distinctly as I repeat the words, 'I will come for you!' and the youth and the beauty that had been growing more and more wonderful in her face, ever since she died, shone like a kind of light from it. I answered her, 'I am ready now!' and then Norrey scuffled to his feet, with a conventional face of sympathy, and said, 'No hurry, my dear Alderling,' and I knew he had not heard or seen anything, as well as I did afterwards when I questioned him. He thought I was giving them notice that they could take her away. What do you think?"

"How what do I think?" I asked.

"Do you think that it happened?"

There was something in Alderling's tone and manner that made me, instead of answering directly that I did not, temporize and ask, "Why?"

"Because—because," and Alderling caught his breath like a child that is trying to keep itself from crying, "because *I* don't." He broke into a sobbing that seemed to wrench and tear his poor little body, and if I had thought of anything to say I could not have said it to his headlong grief with any hope of assuaging it. "I am satisfied now," he said, at last wiping his wet face, and striving for some composure of its trembling features, "that it was all a delusion, the effect of my exaltation, of my momentary aberration, perhaps. Don't be afraid of saying what you really think," he added scornfully, "with the notion of sparing me. You couldn't doubt it or deny it more completely than I do."

I confess this unexpected turn struck me dumb. I did not try to say anything, and Alderling went on.

"I don't deny that she is living, but I can't believe that I shall ever live to see her again; or, if you prefer, die to see her. There is the play of the poor animal instinct, or the mechanical persistence of expectation in me, so that I can't shut the doors without the sense of shutting her out, or put out the lights without feeling that I am leaving her in the dark. But I know it is all foolishness, as well as you do, all craziness. If she is alive it is because she believed she should live, and I shall perish because I didn't believe. I should like to believe, now, if only to see her again, but it is too late. If you disuse any member of your body, or any faculty of your mind it withers away, and if you deny your soul your soul ceases to be."

I found myself saying, "That is very interesting," from a certain force of habit, which you have noted in me, when confronted with a novel instance of any kind. "But," I suggested, "why not act upon the reverse of that principle, and create the fact by affirmation which you think your denial destroys?"

"Because," he repeated wearily, "it is too late. You might as well ask the fakir who has held his arm upright for twenty years, till it has stiffened there, to restore the dry stock by exercise. It is too late, I tell you."

"But, look here, Alderling," I pursued, beginning to taste the joy of argument. "You say that your will had such power upon her after you knew her to be dead that you made her speak to you?"

"No, I don't say that now," he returned. "I know now that it was a delusion."

"But if you once had that power of summoning her to you, by strongly wishing for her presence, when you were both living here, why doesn't it stand to reason that you could do it still, if she is living there and you here?"

"I never had any such power," he replied, with the calm of absolute tragedy. "That was a delusion too. I leave the door open, night and day, because I must, but if she came I should know it was not she."

Of course you know your own business, my dear Acton, but if you think of using the story of the Alderlings—and there is no reason why you should not, for they are both dead, without kith or kin surviving, so far as I know, unless he has some relatives in Germany, who would never penetrate the disguise you could give the case—it seems to me that here is your climax. However, you shall be the judge of what it is best for you to do, when you have the whole story, and I will give it you without more ado, merely premising that I have a sort of shame for the aptness of the catastrophe.

I stayed with Alderling nearly a week, and I will own that I bored myself. In fact, I am not sure but we bored each other. At any rate when I told him, the night before I intended going, that I meant to leave him in the morning, he seemed resigned or indifferent, or perhaps merely inattentive. From time to time we had recurred to the matter of his experience, or his delusion, but with apparently increasing impatience on his part, and certainly decreasing interest on mine; so that at last I think he was willing to have me go. But in the morning he seemed reluctant, and pleaded with me to stay a few days longer with him. I alleged engagements, more or less unreal, for I was never on such terms with Alderling that I felt I need make any special sacrifice to him. He gave way, suspiciously, rather, and when I came down from my room, after having put the last touches to my packing, I found him on the veranda looking out to seaward, where a heavy fogbank hung.

You will sense here the sort of patness which I feel cheapens the catastrophe; and yet as I consider it, again, the fact is not without its curious importance, and its bearing upon what went before. I do not know but it gives the whole affair a relief which it would not otherwise have.

He was to have driven me to the station, some miles away, before noon, and I supposed we should sit down together, and try to have some sort of talk before I went. But Alderling appeared to have forgotten about my going, and after a while took himself off to his studio, and left me alone to watch the inroads of the fog. It came on over the harbor rapidly, as on that morning when Mrs. Alderling had been so nearly lost in it, and presently the masts and shrouds of the shipping at anchor were sticking up out of it as if they were sunk into a body as dense as the sea under them.

I amused myself watching it blot out one detail of the prospect after another, while the fog-horn lowed through it, and the bell-buoy, far out beyond the light-house ledge, tolled mournfully. The milk-white mass moved landward, and soon the air was blind with the mist which hid the grass twenty yards away. There was an awfulness in the silence, which nothing broke but the lowing of the horn, and the tolling of the bell, except when now and then the voice of a sailor came through it, like that of some drowned man sending up his hail from the bottom of the bay.

Suddenly I heard a joyful shout from the attic overhead. "I am coming! I am coming!" Alderling called out through his window, and then a cry came from over the water, which seemed to answer him, but which there is no reason in the world to believe was not a girlish shout from one of the yachts, swallowed up in the fog. His lunging descent of the successive stairways followed, and he burst through the doorway beside me, and ran bareheaded down the sloping lawn.

I followed, with what notion of help or hindrance I should not find it easy to say, but before I reached the water's edge—in fact I never did reach it, and had some difficulty making my way back to the house—I heard the rapid throb of the oars in the rowlocks as he pulled through the white opacity.

You know the rest, for it was the common property of our enterprising press at the time, when the incident was fully reported, with my ineffectual efforts to be satisfactorily interviewed as to the nothing I knew. The oarless boat was found floating far out to sea after the fog lifted.

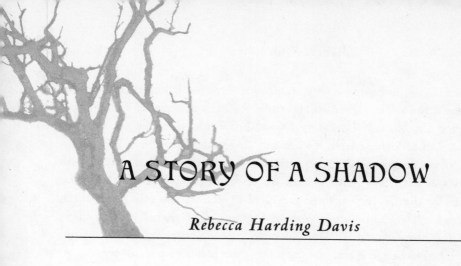

A STORY OF A SHADOW

Rebecca Harding Davis

The house stands in a quiet by-street in Philadelphia. After being vacant for many years it was bought by C. W. Knapp, a widower, and teacher of quiz-classes in one of the medical colleges, who took his mother and child there to live. A few months later his cousin, a Miss Demar, from Ohio, came to visit him, and soon perceived the singular hold the house had upon him.

"There are inexplicable passages in the Bible," she said, speaking of the matter afterward, "which refer to certain buildings as possessing life of their own. They had human diseases, and were blessed and cursed like men by the priesthood. This house reminded me of those Jewish buildings. It affected me from the day I entered it as an inferior grade of life would do; an animal's—a dog's, for instance. Of course, looking at it rationally, the impression became the merest absurdity; but it always came back, do what I would. It was not a disagreeable impression in itself."

She said nothing of this fancy to Mr. Knapp, accounting for his interest in his new possession on more rational grounds.

"To ordinary eyes it's an ordinary house enough," he used to say as they came home together in the evening twilight. "There it is: dull red brick, based and capped with brown stone; shutters dark and heavy; high stoop. Yet the moment my eye rested on it I said, 'There's a house could tell a story if it would.' I was on tenter-hooks until I found whether mother would like it. I think she's very comfortable in it, Mary, eh?"—anxiously.

"Very comfortable, Charley."

Knapp scans it complacently as they come up the street. The yellow sunset flames up behind it in the cold sky, throwing it into bold relief; in front the row of maples rustle cheerfully their few red, ragged leaves in the nipping air. Nobody but Mary Demar knew how that pile of dull red bricks had suddenly barred his life and absorbed all his hopes and plans. She looks curiously at the stout little man beside her, with his jaunty black dress and felt hat set on the back of his head, the broad rim making a frame for the fat, high-colored face, and twinkling blue eyes under their spectacles. They had been intimate as brothers all of their lives. She knew how the money had been saved, penny by penny, since he was a boy, on which he married. For since he was a boy there had been but one woman in the world for Charley Knapp, and when she was gone, even his most casual acquaintance knew that it was impossible he would ever marry again. Miss Demar had come to him a year ago, when she heard his wife was dead. She found him quiet and silent. "I am stifling here," he said to her. "I'll take what money I have and go out of the country with the boy. My only chance is to get away out of doors." Yet she had scarcely reached home when she heard that he had put all his savings into this house, and settled down for life.

"You changed your mind about going abroad, Charley?" she said now, gently.

He did not answer for a moment. "Yes. Well, mother was alone, and fancied I would be out of temptation if she had me in charge. Cain vagabondizing over the world was the only idea my journey suggested to her, so I gave it up."

His sorrow, then, was to be a sealed subject even to her. Mary was re-buffed, but the rebuff pleased her. She leaned more heavily upon his arm. Knapp's thinking, as usual, went on in his face, to be seen of all men, while he kept time to it by whistling under his breath and rattling his cane on the tree-boxes. He always carried a noise with him, like any other over-grown boy.

"It's curious, though," he broke out at last, "how that journey I did not take clings to me. Sometimes now, when I go into the halls, I think that here the sea was lost, and the nights on deck, the moon whitening the rim of water; and when we are at breakfast in the pretty dining-room I think how it swallowed up China and her wall and pagodas, and California cañons, Yosemite, and all. It's damnably selfish in me, but it makes me like the house. There are bits of the whole world built into the walls for me. Then," energetically, "it's such a home for her and Tom! When it's time for the boy to rough it at school, there's the garden to bring him back to Nature. Why, the smell of those bean-pods and grass after a rain would make the worst man choke in his wickedness! I've been thinking, too, as soon as he's old enough to want his friends about him, I'd run those side rooms into one, for dancing. He'll be a social fellow, Tom. I see that in his eye. When the dog marries there'll be plenty of room for him to bring his wife home—and their children, if God sends them any. Here we are, '130!'" glancing up over the door. "To think it's nothing but a pile of bricks and a number to people. Hey, Mary?"

"It would certainly be very inconsistent if the house were *not* numbered," said his mother, who was waiting inside. "The mat, Charles, my dear! Have some care for the carpets." Charley caught her in his arms and whisked her round. She began to laugh, but choked it off with a sigh. She was her son duplicated in caps and petticoats. Nature meant her to be dumpy and good-tempered, but her face had been twisted by some bastard notion of godliness into a perpetual penitence and woful looking-for of judgment. She also protested against the sins of the world by a nasal twang—the ghost of a bagpipe. It was in play now. "Some of your boon companions are here for supper, as usual, Charles."

Knapp peeped through the open parlor door at a couple of half-fledged medical students guiltily conscious of their neckties and best coats. "All right, boys! I'll bring Tom and be with you in a moment!" He met Mary a moment afterward, with Tom astride of his shoulders. "They'll bore you horribly," anxiously. "But you'll not mind. There's such a lot of fellows like that in the college—strangers—got no mother here, nor friends, d'ye see—no place open for them but the theatres or rum-shops. I try to make it like home here. They're a little heavy, to be sure. But you'll like the boys, even the flashiest and most priggish among them."

"I'll come down and give you some music, Charley."

"All right."

Mrs. Knapp came into Mary's room and dumped herself with a wretched thud on a chair. "So it goes! Billiards, chess, pipes, night after night. They've not got to drinking yet, but what is tobacco but a mean makeshift for liquor? You'll say why don't I talk to Charles? But what does Charles care for *my* opinion? He has these men roystering with him for breakfast, dinner, and supper. He's introduced them to young girls, and says he hopes love affairs will come of it. Love affairs! Yes; and even with that the half's not told. Why, he has brought actors here. They wore their street clothes, to be sure, and did not play any of their fantastic tricks before me, I assure you. But to think it is not fifteen months since poor Sophy was laid to rest! Ah, child, now you see what man's love is worth!"

Miss Demar nodded, twisting her long hair about her head.

"Up from the ear, Mary—there. Not that Charles wasn't a sincere mourner at first. But I did hope Sophy's death would have been a call to his Master's service. I intended him always for a missionary, you know."

"Yes."

"Yes, Charles has been my cross. The Lord knows wherewith to try us," wiping her eyes. Miss Demar turned to speak, but changing her mind put on her collar. "Not but that he's a good son, Mary; but when I think of him as unregenerate, all his kindness to the poor but filthy rags—Now there's your aunt Johns. She gave up her son to carry the banner of the Cross to Africa. But when Charles wanted to leave me, it was to go gaping about at hills and sunsets and Papistical pictures—"

It was at this moment that Miss Demar, who had been standing motionless for a few seconds, turned on her with a startled face. "What is it that is in this house?" she said.

"You saw it?" Mrs. Knapp started up, looking from side to side. "I'm sure I don't know what you mean," petulantly. "There's a story that a child was killed here, or a bride—some ridiculous report that has hung about the house for years. You've heard the story and fancied you saw something."

"No, I never heard it; and I really saw nothing." Miss Demar, ashamed of having betrayed herself, tried to go on with her dressing, but her fingers shook and the blood burned in them.

Like most American women, Mary Demar's nerves lay on the surface, charged like the wires of an electric battery; but she had steady eyes and a broad chest, and usually managed to keep them in order. As soon as the dribble of talk behind her stopped, and she was left alone, she sat down to reason with herself. She had literally seen and heard nothing. In the midst of her annoyance with Charley's mother there had come upon her the sudden consciousness of a something present in the house, which was apart from its bricks and mortar and from its human inmates—some strength, vehement and kindly, which, as if for a whim, had turned her face to face with the poor old woman, showed her gray hairs, the honest love for her boy under her bigotry, the grave not far from her. It might have been Charley's self taking part with his mother.

"It certainly was not *I*," said Miss Demar with a shrug. "Such charity is not in me."

She began after that to ask questions carelessly about the house and its history, wondering herself at the hold the matter had taken upon her. Mary Demar had been betrothed for years to a man whom she loved with her whole heart. It was but a few days ago that she had discovered a fact in his early life which made him unfit to be her husband. It was not natural that idle vagaries about an old house should interest her now. Yet she could not shake them off; there was, too, an unaccountable feeling that this mystery concerned her personally.

"What do you know of this house?" she asked of Charley one evening as they were watching the sunset from the garden.

"Nothing. When the searches were made to establish a clear title, oddly enough it was impossible to find out when it was built or by whom. People had a vague dislike to living in it; it lay vacant for years in this crowded neighborhood. Old Seth—Kenyon's protégé, you know—"

Miss Demar's countenance changed suddenly. "Yes, I know Seth."

"He has some ancient ghost story about it. The vaguest nonsense! To my notion it's the most cheerful place I was ever in. This garden, for instance—"

Now the garden was a straight, long strip of ground, enclosed by a high, solid fence, which shaded the trim parterres of their neighbors—a strange, solitary place, which seemed to have brought its alien air into the city. The damp grass yielding to their feet was brown with the field clover; wild honeysuckles and grapes, such as tangle the hedges in unused lanes, grew along the borders; rows of hollyhocks stood like sentinels, turning their watchful faces toward the house; the common June roses, which all summer long sweeten and redden forgotten graves in country churchyards, sent their perfume up to it. Even the flowers had a friendly message for Knapp's home. The lighted windows shone coldly from garret to basement on one end of the dusky garden; beyond the other end a little way, the Schuylkill rolled, laden with craft, down to the bay; the tall masts of the clustered ships struck fine black lines up into the yellow evening sky. The air was damp but quiet; even the floating white ball of dandelion seed scarcely moved in it over their heads.

"I wish I could hear that ghost story," said Miss Demar.

"Very well. We'll go down to Seth," glancing at a little brick house beyond the garden. "By the by, Kenyon will be surprised to find us so near the old man."

Miss Demar stopped. "You don't mean—Is Mr. Kenyon coming here?"

"Now don't be vexed, Mary. 'Pon my soul, I never said come. I only wrote on business yesterday, and mentioned that you were here. Why not? One always thinks of you two as so nearly husband and wife that these petty formalities seem out of place to my notion. It's half a year to the wedding, and the poor devil's there, working night and day to be ready for it. Why shouldn't he have a glimpse of you to keep his heart up?"

"It was a kind thought of you, Charley," said Miss Demar after a pause. Her coldness irritated Knapp. He always had doubted whether she was quite competent to appreciate a man like Kenyon. Charley was very fond of Mary, but she was only a younger brother to him. He had knuckled with her at marbles and talked over his business to her ever since they were grown. Coming too close, he had grown blind to the beauty in her thin, singular face, and to the indescribable sway which she held over other men.

"Here she is, with her admirable sense, downright as a sledge-hammer," he thought, as they walked over the grass, "and Kenyon full of subtle delicate fancies. He'll be dashed to pieces against her admirable sense. It's the old story of the clay and porcelain pitcher again." The next minute, full of remorse at his own harsh judgment of her, he caught her hand and drew it affectionately through his arm.

"What is it, Moll?" He fancied she looked worn and tired.

"I was thinking of Seth." She stopped, hesitated. Knapp's instincts were keen; whatever question she was about to ask, he said, for some reason imported much to her. "What do you know of him, Charley?"

"Very little. Less than I ought, for Kenyon put him in a manner under my care, years ago. But the old fellow heeds no charity and keeps his affairs to himself. Scotch-Irish, you know. I used to look in on him now and then, until we moved into this house. Now of course I see him every day."

"You do not know then what—what connection there was between him and Mr. Kenyon? Would he be likely to know anything of John's early life?"

"No, certainly not. Kenyon, as you know, is from Carolina; his family dies out with him. High-blooded, high-handed old race, the Kenyons, I've heard. I've often told John both his virtues and his faults were those of civilization pushed too far. It's odd, isn't it, that American families won't bear high culture for several generations? The physical stock gives out unless inferior blood is brought in." Knapp began to stammer, remembering suddenly that Miss Demar could hardly claim to belong to her lover's Brahmin caste. "What could Seth know about him?" he added hurriedly. "Lived all his life in that shanty. Kenyon and I met him accidentally on the street here one day, and John mentioned him as a person who had done him a kindness." Miss Demar stopped at this, coming into the path before him in her breathless eagerness to hear. "A kindness—where was I? What the deuce can this matter to you Mary? He said, if I remember rightly, something about an annuity he paid him, and asked me to have an oversight of the old fellow, and if he were in want to send him word."

"Mr. Kenyon is charitable," she said bitterly.

"Why do you use that tone about him? What possible sinister motive could he have in his kindness to the old man?"

Miss Demar was silent. But Knapp noticed the glitter in her half-shut eye, and an unusual steadiness in her walk. With all her sense she had a temper of which Charley stood in wholesome awe. He quickened his pace, and began to talk with a sudden gust of cheerfulness. "Now I do suppose Kenyon did not dwell on the subject because it was a matter of charity, and for the same reason I never mentioned it to Seth. There he goes. Hello, Seth!"

"You need not call him. I've changed my mind. I'm going into the house."

"God bless me, these women! Don't hurt the old fellow's feelings, Moll."

Miss Demar turned at that and came back. She was miserable, and in a passion that she was miserable. Charley, man-like, only thought how lack of temper improved her looks. No doubt Kenyon would think her delicate face lovely with the hair rumpled about it, and her dark eyes full of unshed tears. The old sailmaker, meanwhile, came hobbling up with a broad smile, carrying a bucket of coals in either hand. He was generally watching the garden for Knapp in the evening, to "have a conference on the political sitooation," in which Seth doled out the views of his oracle, the "Review," of which he chewed the cud perpetually.

"We came to find you, Seth. I want you to raise the best ghost you can out of the house yonder for this young lady."

Seth bowed, but his mouth suddenly dropped at the corners. "You ben't afeard of sperrits then, Mr. Knapp?"

"Not much. But—what is it, Mary!"

Miss Demar drew up her shawl and stood erect. She, stooping forward, looking at Seth as he leaned on the gate, the low light bringing his short heavy body and square head into full relief, as if she would have dragged the secret of his life out. He nodded to her, smiling.

"Miss Demar were in my house the other evening, and we discussed different matters. But not sperrits."

She laughed and said "No," with a sudden light-heartedness. Now that she was face to face with the old man, the dread that haunted her appeared utterly fantastic and impossible. He was just at home from his day's work, and, instead of going to bed as the other workmen did, had washed and brushed himself. A scuffed black suit of Knapp's was stretched over his broad, rawboned body, the big wrists and ankles grinning bare with a grim sort of protest. A thin fringe of white hair and whisker was brushed with a soldierly air about his high-featured face, red and rasped with soap, on the top of which an old beaver hat of Charley's was set jauntily. At every turn the body and brain of the old man betrayed, she fancied, the lifelong, dreadful drainage of poverty—betrayed it in nothing so much as in his aping the habits and gestures of gentlemen, and in the pitiful swagger with which he wore his begged clothes.

And this man she had believed to be John Kenyon's father.

Until Knapp told it to her a few moments ago, she had never heard this story of the family to which Kenyon belonged. But without it she recognized the absurdity of any connection between her lover and the sailmaker. Kenyon was a quiet homely man, thorough-bred as no other whom she had ever met. His enemies might question his intellect or kindliness; but whatever else he might be, that he was the product of generations of affluence and culture was a fact so patent that no one could doubt it—not the stranger who passed him on the street. His extravagance, his domineering temper, his morbid fastidiousness of taste, were all diseased outgrowths from that one cause, as Knapp had shrewdly noted.

Miss Demar forgot the proof which half an hour ago had seemed so inexorably sure to her. When she was in Seth's house the other evening a small photograph had fallen from one of his books into her lap. It was undoubtedly that of Kenyon as a much younger man. On the back a few lines were scrawled signed "Your son." There could be no question of the writing. She knew it better than her own. There was, too, the odd subtle likeness in the old man's face to the younger one, which came at times in an uneasy dropping of the eye or pose of the head. It was not there now. Miss

Demar, when she missed it, blushed and trembled as though her lover had kissed her, and was unbelieving and happy.

When she turned to Charley and the old man she found them fully launched on the ghost story.

"You see, Miss Demar," said Seth, "it's an old neighborhood on the bank here, and them sort of stories hang around old houses like spiders' webs agen the wall. Yon's the room," pointing to a chamber on whose windows the rising moon began to glitter. "There's no figger seen there, howsoever, nor sound heard." So intent was he on his story that he spat deliberately on each of his palms as if he were moistening his thread, and rubbed them, while slowly eying his hearers.

"What is there, then?"

"A shadder, sir," solemnly. "To them as is left alone in that room there comes a shadder on the wall. Nothing more."

"The murdered man, I suppose," said Mary cheerfully. Seth did not relish her cheerfulness. "I've no knowledge of my own what it is, ma'am. But I've heerd say that every man has a ghost that follers him—the shadder of them that he has wronged. It comes into sight to him on that wall."

"By George!" laughed Knapp. "I'll put Kenyon there to sleep when he comes, Mary. He shall have a fair tug with his ghost."

"Kenyon?" said Seth, and then was quickly silent. Miss Demar watched him.

"You have no more to tell us of the ghost, then?" she said, to try him. He turned a countenance to her which might have been cut out of wood, it was so vacant.

"Miss Demar spoke to you, Seth."

"I beg your pardon ma'am. My wits was wool-gatherin'. Regardin' the ghost? No, I know nothin' more. I believe I'll be goin' now," taking up his bucket. But he lingered, fingering the gate-latch.

"I'll send you the morning's paper over, Seth."

"Much obleeged, sir. You said," in a forced deliberate tone, "that a gentleman was to sleep in that room—Mr. Kenyon. Is he with you now? You'll excuse me for askin'," he added hastily, "but I—I had some acquaintance with him fifteen years ago."

"To be sure you had! Why, you've no idea how kindly Mr. Kenyon spoke of you to me, Seth—charged me to have an oversight over you, and so on. You were able to oblige him once in some way, I think he mentioned?"

"Did he put it in that way?" with a queer flickering smile. "No, it was no obligation."

"Well, Mr. Kenyon is a warm-hearted man, and very likely to exaggerate any little service. You couldn't have a more generous friend in your old age. And you're well on to seventy now, Seth."

The old man straightened his back, and put his hand mechanically to his hips. "I'm quite able to work for the little I eat," he said quietly. "I'll not be likely to need money from Mr. Kenyon. I'd be sorry if you gave him that impression. But when he comes, if you'll mention to him——" He stopped for a full minute. "If you'll mention to him that Seth Barnes is livin' yet, in the house where he used to know him, I'll be obleeged to you. You'll leave it to his own free will to come or not——if you please, sir?"

"Certainly, Seth, certainly. But Kenyon's the last man in the world to be uncivil to an old friend because he has not prospered like himself. You mistake him, Barnes."

Seth nodded gravely and, buckets in hand, limped away. "Well, really," said Knapp, "I thought Kenyon paid the old fellow an annuity. There must have been a mistake about it; I did not tell him John was coming to-night. I had a telegram from him; he'll be here in an hour. I thought I'd surprise you"——feeling with a certain pleasure that Miss Demar trembled and that her hand was cold. Her common sense was not so invincible, after all.

"We'll sit here and wait for him." He drew her to a bench, and remained silent. But Miss Demar was restless and impatient. She must keep off the one fact that filled the future for her. Tomorrow would prove whether Kenyon was a true man or the basest of frauds. She had but him in the world; she was an orphan, without kinsfolk.

Knapp sat smoking, nursing one foot on his knee, and glancing, she noticed, now and then, up at the two windows on which the moon cast a mysterious glitter.

"Confess that there is some reality in Seth's ghost story to you, after all, Charley," touching his arm.

"Nonsense! I never heard that story of the shadow. I did not even know it was to that room they had fastened the ghost. There is a curious fact about that room——a coincidence. Not that I believe in such rubbish as spirits, you know——"

"Of course not. But tell me the story."

"Two or three months after we moved into the house, I brought Russell Sands home one night. You remember him, don't you?"

"Very well. A slight fair-haired boy, with an innocent face, like a girl's?"

"Yes, that was Russell. Thorough mother's boy. Not a prig, or goodish either—as manly, spirited a little fellow as lived. That was four or five years ago. His mother was a widow, and she had but him." Knapp shifted his foot to the other knee, stroking it for a minute or two. "Well," hurriedly, "I lost sight of him for years, until I found him one night, as I was coming home, lying drunk on a market-house stall. He had grown out of all likeness to himself into a swollen bloated animal. He did not know me; I was glad of that. I brought him home and put him in that room to bed, and I went down below to smoke. About one o'clock (I was sitting quite quiet, somehow I couldn't sleep) I heard a noise overhead, a sudden gasp, as of fright or horror, and then there was a long silence. Presently the door of his chamber opened and Russell came down the stairs. He was perfectly sober, to my astonishment—quite master of himself. I shook hands with him and brought him in. He did not ask how he came there; sat down and talked in his usual self-possessed way on politics and the news of the day; but he was terribly shaken, and I saw there was some under-thought kept down, which now and then threatened to master him. I went down to the kitchen and broiled a bit of steak and made a strong cup of coffee for him, but he couldn't eat. He said, 'You'll sit up with me until morning, Uncle Charley? I would prefer not to be alone.' That was the only reference either of us made to his condition. The college boys have fallen into the way of calling me that, you see, and I like it; it makes them somehow free to ask help when they need it. But Russell is a man to whom you could not offer help. When the first streak of dawn came, he got up. I had brushed the mud off his overcoat without his knowledge. We stood in the front door together. The morning wind was keen. 'It will be a pleasant day,' he said, trying to be careless and easy. 'I thank you sincerely, Mr. Knapp, for your—your hospitality. I looked up at the great broad-shouldered fellow, and thought how death was dragging him down, and not a soul to stretch a hand to him. But I had to be guarded. I took hold of one of the lapels of his coat. 'Can I do anything for you—in any way, Russell?' I said, 'I'm an old friend of your father's, you know, my lad.' 'No I thank you,' he said dryly; but he stood looking abstractedly down the street, and turned presently. 'A curious thing happened to me last night,' trying to bluff it off with a careless laugh, but I saw the poor boy wanted to open his heart to me if he knew how. 'Did you ever hear that that room of yours was an uncanny sort of place? I woke suddenly with my eyes on the blank wall, and do you know the picture that hangs there I could have sworn was myself? As I used to be five years ago—not *this,*' with a gesture of terrible meaning over his face and bloated figure—'the Russell Sands now dead.' 'He's not dead,' I broke out, for I could keep quiet no longer. 'You can go back to your old self, dear boy, if you will.' 'O God! if I could believe that!' he cried, with a sort of sob. But in a moment or two he was cool and quiet again, buttoned up his coat, and talked of the weather until he bade me good-by. He held my hand a minute. 'There is no use talking of these things,' he said, 'but if ever I can go back to the boy I once was, I'll come to you, Uncle Charley.'"

"Well, and then?" said Mary.

"He went away with that. For a long time I could find no trace of him; but I heard of him finally out West. Kenyon had secured a place for him where he could free himself from his old associates, and had seen him last July. He reported the poor boy as hard at work; thin as a rail, his jaws sunken like death's, but his eyes clear and steady. It had been a long battle, but Kenyon thought he had won it. 'See Mr. Knapp when you go back,' he said; 'tell him I'm not ready to meet him yet, but I mean to come. I'll come!' wrenching his hand with a nervous laugh."

"Don't put him in the haunted chamber when he comes. Don't let him see the picture again and find that his fancy was only a fancy."

Knapp laughed uneasily. "Now there is where the curious part of the story comes in. The wall is a blank wall. *There was no picture there.*"

"Then it was the shadow of the man he had wronged the most that he saw." Miss Demar rose.

"Tut, tut! Now, Molly, you don't pretend to believe that folly of Seth's?" She took a turn up the long path for lack of argument. But to Miss Demar the point of the story lay in the part Kenyon had taken in it. She thought she had looked at him on every side, as journalist, treasurer, clerk, *homme de société*, and lover; but doing good? a philanthropist? The *rôle* was a new one. She sat down to think it over.

"He went to John?" she said when Knapp came back.

"Yes. Men are very apt to go to Kenyon who are in scrapes. Especially lately. He was the first mover in that scheme for aiding discharged convicts, you know?"

Of course he was! Of course he was the one to whom all men would turn for aid. A gush of tears choked her throat and eyes. The idea of

Kenyon's benevolence was new to her a minute ago, but it had sprouted up already, like Jack's scarlet beans, as high as heaven.

"No man," began Knapp, vehemently, "has a tenderer heart than— There he is!"

There he was: a sallow, thin man, carefully dressed in white linen, picking his steps down the walk to avoid the dust. Miss Demar tried to rise, but her knees shook under her, and a gusty heat went through her limbs. Charley was off like a flash, leading him down, wrenching his hand, watching him with any amount of inarticulate clucks and chuckles. How underbred and unmanly he always was beside Kenyon! Miss Demar also thought of the porcelain pitcher and the clay jug.

"Here she is! here she is! It's dark here, and your eyes are dulled coming out of the glare of the gas."

He brought Kenyon up to Miss Demar, and then was bolting off with a mumbled apology, when a second glance made him stay. He felt somehow that they would rather not be left alone. "A lover's quarrel, eh?" to himself. "There's a seat, Kenyon. Cursedly hot to-day, travelling, wasn't it? You're just off the cars?"

"No. I came in the afternoon train. I waited to shake off a little of the dust before I came up."

This was not the fiery, impulsive lover of a year ago. Knapp's face burned with the slight to Mary. There was, too, a certain uneasy guardedness about Kenyon which was utterly new in his usual simple, unaffected manner. Knapp, to cover it, rushed into the first subject that came to him.

"I was just giving Mary the account of Russell Sands. You think his reformation is complete?"

"I trust so. Sands can be of great use to our party in that part of Iowa. Just the magnetic sort of power about him that collects and leads weaker young men. I mean to make a lever of him out there as soon as I am sure he can be relied upon. I had that in view in sending him there."

"Politics is a bad field to put a man in who is trying to save himself from the devil of drink," said Knapp hastily.

"Yes. I suppose it is," carelessly. "But what would you do? Clever young fellows who choose that most disgusting mode of suicide are so common this winter in Washington that one grows hardened to them and their fate; while as to the importance of this next election there can be but one opinion."

"By the way, I hear, Kenyon, that if our party go in you are sure of an office here that pays—pays—'pon my soul I forget what, but something stu-pendous. What's in it, eh?"

Kenyon, who had leaned forward and kept his eyes on Miss Demar's face, dimly seen through the darkness, during this speech, waited with a curious anxiety for her to speak. But when she did not, he replied in a dry business tone: "Some such offer was made to me, but I rejected it. I'm in a condition to set my own terms. They must give me an appointment abroad—one that pays equally well, too."

There was that malignant influence astir among them which sometimes makes each pause in the conversation appear significant and oppressive.

Knapp broke the silence each time with a more awkward effort.

"You did not use to care for the loaves and fishes, John," forcing a laugh.

"I've altered, then," dryly. "At my age one grows tired of giving the whole of life to grubbing for the means to sustain it. What a curious place you have *here*," changing his tone. "There's something unnatural in it; something—I hardly know what it is," looking about him. "The dust and dampness, probably. But this house always affected me strangely."

"Why, my dear fellow, I lived in Germantown when you were here last. You never saw this house before."

"I think I have," said Kenyon quietly, though cursing himself inwardly for his mistake; for he had come fully prepared to face and escape the danger of detection. Knapp's house he knew was near to his father's. What more likely than that Miss Demar should meet the old man and discover his secret?

Kenyon had thrown up all his engagements this morning, and started at a half-hour's notice, though it was the last day of Congress and the culmination of all his plots and wire-pulling for the year was at hand. What was success if this chance robbed him of her? What did she know? He was on guard as never before in his life—eye, ear, every nerve under control, and watching. He could see her face but indistinctly; she had spoken but once to him.

His ready tongue failed him; he sat silent.

"By the way," began Knapp again desperately, "I was talking to Mary just now of your winter's work—discharged convicts, you know."

"Pray do not induce Miss Demar to mistake me for a philanthropist, Charley."

"You did not mean to use them for 'levers,' eh?"

"Not precisely. But I went into the work to strengthen my popularity."

"I don't believe it! You shall not so wrong yourself!"

Miss Demar rose in a heat and walked hastily away. Kenyon rose also, and sat down again. The words thrilled him as with an electric fire.

"She knows nothing. She is safe," he thought. He gave a short, uncadenced laugh. "But, it is true for all that," turning to Knapp. "I loathe demagogueism, but I am a demagogue. I hate work, yet I drudge harder than any man in Washington. I used to be *honest*, as men go, but now I cringe and fawn and lie—all for money."

Knapp looked at him in dismay.

"You did not use to care for it."

"I care for her. I care to earn a few years in which to sit down with her, with money and ease to enjoy the world before I go out of it. I mean to wash my hands in innocency as soon as I have the appointment and sit down, as I said, to take 'mine ease in mine inn.'"

Knapp coughed uneasily, jerking at his waistcoat as if it did not fit him. He had keenness enough to see that Kenyon's life had been a fierce, breathless race for one end, and that some obstacle to-night was about to balk him. He knew him to be always a gusty, uncertain fellow, with a temperament either at high tide or dead low ebb, as anybody could see, but he was not used to talk about it to other people. The mental pang must have been extreme that wrenched this vehement egotism from him.

"What in God's name can I do for him?" Knapp repeated blankly to himself.

For ordinary men whose troubles grew out of broken bones or empty pockets he had cures enough, but he looked upon Kenyon as of a different order of being from himself. It was Pegasus, he thought, coming to a cow-doctor for help.

He stood rattling some pennies in his pockets, looking at Kenyon's thin face under the broad Panama hat, turned toward Miss Demar with a cynical, sad smile.

"We'd better join Molly, eh?"

"One minute. There's an old man, Barnes, lives hereabouts somewhere?"

"In the alley—not ten steps from the gate. I told them you'd not forget him—I told him and Mary both. I'm deucedly glad you asked for Seth, do you know, Kenyon?"

"Miss Demar has seen him, then?"

"Oh, of course. He comes to the gate every night for the 'Review.' He has just gone."

"Reads the 'Review' yet, does he?"

Kenyon stopped. For the moment he forgot Knapp, Miss Demar, himself. He only remembered how the old man used to sit waiting at night until he had learned his lesson for school from the "dog-eared" spelling-book, to take his turn at it while the boy played teacher. There was the little kitchen, ship-shape and neat as a man-of-war's deck, the crackling coal fire, the pot of mush simmering on one side for supper when they had finished. How anxious and red the old man's face was as he stammered dully over the unconquerable three syllables. How dull he always was! Kenyon remembered how his boy's heart used to ache and sicken when he first began to understand that his father was dull and poor, and all that it meant to be either. He had dashed the book down one day and caught the old man about the neck, crying out in his impotent rage:

"Why should other men be what they are, and you this, dad? How could God be so unjust as to make such a difference between men?"

"I don't see as He does," the sailmaker said gently. "However, you are to go beyond them all, Jack, and as soon as I can read I mean to take the paper and go through it reg'lar. I'll keep posted that way, so as I'll not shame you."

That was twenty long years ago. The old man was poring over it yet! Did he hope that his boy would come back to him, late as it was? He had sent back the money again and again without a word. He was waiting for something better than money. Kenyon glanced down to the low house, the red roof of which was just seen above the fence. If he ever went back it must be now. If he married under a false name, so it must stand; the old man must remain thrust aside until the end. What if he went now? What if he crossed the alley and went to the old man sitting alone by his fire? Although he had put this thing away from him for twenty years, so whimsical and perverse was the man, that his heart throbbed and his eyes were wet at the thought; the next, they had reached Miss Demar.

"I found them in the dark for you." She held out a branch of wet, fragrant roses toward him.

The night almost hid her from him. She seemed to belong to and to crown its passionate warmth, its strength, its solemn beauty. So set apart did she seem from all other women, that he thought how, if the whole world was lost in the night, he could straightway find her, as she had found the roses for him. He took her hand in his.

Charley sauntered up to the porch and smoked a cigar while the lovers passed slowly down the dusky alleys of the garden. A night-moth flapped its wet wings in Kenyon's face; the damp air was heavy with the scent of the roses she had given him; from one of the ships on the river came broken snatches of music which the distance softened into sweetness and sadness.

When they came back to the house and into the light of the gas, the politician's sallow face, which had warped lately into a shrewd cunning, glowed with a finer beauty than Miss Demar's. A word from the woman he loved caused his legs to tremble like a sensitive boy's; there was a fiery impatience in his eye which reminded Charley of a racer that is stayed within a stride of his goal.

"If you get this appointment, you can marry at once?" he said as he led Kenyon to his room.

"Yes. Nothing shall come between us now."

Charley wrung his hand, and bade him a hasty good-night. The next moment he was back. "I say, Kenyon, pardon me, but you never looked into this matter of spiritualism, did you?"

"I? No; it was always a repugnant subject to me. But did it never occur to you, old fellow, that your habit of hurling new ideas at a man was confusing?"

"I don't know," absently. "Repugnant? Now that's just what it is to me. But—you don't think it possible that disembodied spirits could manifest themselves in a room—in any way—by means of matter, then? Yet there are some things—things which those who are pure, you know, John, have worn or touched, which seem to me to be alive with their presence. Yet—"

He stopped, turned to the window, his double chin quivering. "Well, it's all a puzzle," turning presently and looking wistfully about the room. "When I think about the different lives in men and horses and vegetables, I get perplexed. How can I say, into this matter a soul has gone, and in that there is none? Why should not a human spirit linger in a house, for instance, and affect the matter in it, as it affected the matter in his body? Now, why not?" again looking about the dim chamber with the same curious hesitation.

"I can't tell you why not. I only know it never does."

Kenyon laughed good-humoredly, impatient as he was to be left alone.

"Of course it never does. Bless me, I forgot what a bore this must all be to you. I only thought I'd warn you—but no matter. It's all trumpery gossip, no doubt." And still muttering to himself he burst out of the room and went stumbling down the stairs. Kenyon threw a quick glance about the room, as he threw off his coat and boots and sat down by the window. He had a vague impression when he came into it that there was some one in it besides Knapp and himself. He saw his mistake. It was a small, cheerful chamber, with no fireplace, its windows opening to the west. The walls were a pale green; a well-darned carpet on the floor, and a half-worn cottage suit of furniture of the same color ranged against the walls. Just the room one might look for in Knapp's house—commonplace, cheery, with the stamp of poverty on every part of it. Knapp knocked at the door that instant and dashed in with a fresh pitcher of water, went out with a final good-night, came back again to thrust his hand into the bed and punch the pillows. "There. All right. I was afraid they hadn't put on the new mattress. Good night. God bless you."

Knapp's whole life and nature, with all their cheerfulness, Kenyon thought, were commonplace—bore the poverty stamp. For himself—it would be different! Another step, and he would have turned his back on poverty and self-denial forever. God, who made the man, only knew how he loathed them both; with what panting, breathless delight, as he sat there, he looked into the world he was about to enter, where love was the first blessing and money almost its equal; the world to which he had been climbing since he was a ragged boy in yonder alley; full of luxurious houses, art, music, delicate viands, rare wines, beautiful women delicately dressed. "There is no reason why she should not consent to an immediate marriage," he thought. "My appointment is sure: then for France or Italy. I'll shake the dust of the country off my feet forever."

What made him spring up suddenly and, going to the window, turn to the house in the alley where the old man's light still burned? Leaning with his knuckles on the sill, he looked down into it steadily. Men who knew him in the office of the "Age," or in caucus, would not have recognized this face that he wore. He recovered himself presently.

"Bah! It can never be. If she guessed the truth, she would spurn me under her feet." Yet he could not put away the fancy that the old man was sitting there, watching the windows of this room—waiting—waiting; that he would watch there all night believing that his boy would come to him.

"If a man sets himself a high aim in life, he must put all obstacles out of his way; it is unavoidable"—as he began to prepare for bed. But when he caught sight of his ghastly face in the glass, he started back, and did not go near it again. He did not care to know how much it cost him to put this obstacle out of his way.

The sounds on the streets had died into silence. In some room below he heard Knapp's mother grumbling and scolding, and Charley's unwearied, cheerful little cackle in reply; then Tom woke with the colic, and Charley trotted to and fro—to and fro, carrying him for hours, until all the house was asleep and quiet. Long afterward, Kenyon, standing by the darkened window, saw Knapp go out into the garden for a moment's coolness and rest before he slept. He walked up and down slowly. The stars had come out, and threw faintly the lines of the bushy paths out from the darkness, massing into unbroken shadow the houses to the right. Beyond, a lamp at a mast-head here and there showed where the water flowed. The little man, thinking himself quite alone in the night, began to sing some old tune softly in his thin, chirrupy voice:

> "Here in the body pent,
>   Absent from thee I roam,
> And nightly pitch my moving tent
>   A day's march nearer home."

There was a slight pause, and he went on:

> "I want a true regard,
>   A single steady aim,
> Unmoved by suffering and reward,
>   To Thee and Thy great name."

Kenyon drew back. What dreadful Presence was this so near to commonplace Knapp, with his little body and little soul, of which he knew nothing? Kenyon's brain was feverish and strained. A new, vague idea entered readily among the thoughts that racked him: the something above the night—above him, his struggle, or his love—the infinite life before which his world of rare books, aesthetic dressing, and good eating sank into nothingness.

Knapp went into the house, and the night sank back into silence.

In the door of the little house in the alley an old man stood looking up to the darkened windows of his son's room. "It is too late; he will never come now," he said.

Kenyon lay upon the bed, his eyes covered with his hand. But he did not sleep.

The sun was not up. There was no sign of morning beyond the cold wind that shook the wet trees to and fro, and a gray lightening of the banked clouds over the river. Of all his unhealthy, unquiet life, this night had been to Kenyon the most unhealthy and the fiercest in its struggle. That first cold wind of dawn came with a wholesome freshness. He sat up, rubbed his aching eyes. It was time to be done with shadows and to go down into the real world. He wiped the hot sweat from his forehead and looked about as a man does after a sleepless night, his eyes falling at last by chance on the opposite wall to his bed. He had not thought the light strong enough to throw a shadow, but the reflection of the drifting clouds made strange shimmering figures on the blank surface. The clouds—what else could they be? The shadows slowly moved, approached each other, grew compact. Kenyon leaned forward; one could almost fancy that they took human forms. The strange illusion annoyed him; he drew down the curtains over the windows; the wind waved them fitfully. It was their shadows that he saw now; or was it—Good God! what was this that faced him, beckoning to him with strange and solemn gestures, showing him—

The blood ebbed back to his heart; he stood stiffly erect, his hands behind him, as he was used to stand when he faced an enemy in debate whom he recognized as stronger than himself. There was silence over all the city in that last hour of the night. The silence was nowhere more profound than in this little chamber through which the strange wind blew violently, yet without sound.

What Kenyon saw in that room he never told. Whether his old boy's life came back to him, or the life yet to come, what truth was pressed home to his calloused scheming brain, no man ever knew.

Death and disaster meet a man sometimes on his journey, and bring him for a brief moment face to face with himself, his friend, and God. When Kenyon left his chamber at dawn his face wore the look of one who voluntarily had met them and wrenched their secret from them.

He went down the garden and crossed the alley. Seth was stooping over the fire warming his chilled hands. He was going to his work, and did not mean to come back until Kenyon was gone. "He'd have come last night if he meant ever to own me," he told himself again and again. "I'll think of the boy as dead now. Better we'd both died when he was a boy."

A shadow struck across the doorway. The next moment a man stood before him, put his hands on his shoulders.

"Father! It's I, father."

Seth was not strong. He staggered under the first touch of his boy. "Jack?" he cried—"Jack?"

His son led him to a bench. The old man covered his face with his hands, but in a little while he looked up and motioned Kenyon to a chair. "It's your old seat, my lad. I'm glad to see you in it agen," he said, quietly untying his gingham cravat. His high-featured face had strangely lost its color.

Kenyon sat cowed, humiliated. This twenty years of neglect rose before him; the more inexorably as Seth neither by word nor look recalled them. The delicacy which kept the old man silent from showing even the reproach of joy had different birth from his own fine taste in books and music and wine. He felt that with all the old man's passionate love for the boy he had lost, he would weigh and measure the man who had come back to him. He knew, too, having finer intuitions than Miss Demar, that the man who thus measured him was weightier than he, stood on firmer ground, was built up of larger, more liberal elements.

In the heat of his passionate contrition and old, awakened love, he felt all the sacrifices he must make for his father could be borne. "You will come to Washington to me at once," he said. "We will have our home alone together. Nothing shall part us again."

"I think you're wrong there, Jack," Seth said gently. "My ways are not your ways. You shall come to me when you will, but I'll live out my life as I've begun. Old trees grow best on their own rooting."

Kenyon was silent. He was not sure of his own rooting; he was not sure of himself, of the work he had done or the work he had planned to do. Was it all a sham? Had he grasped only shadows, while Knapp, with his mediocre brain, and this ignorant laborer, had laid hold on reality?

To-day he would be done with shams, though it would cost all he had worked or cared for in life.

"Will you come with me a moment, father?" He led him quickly over to the garden, where Miss Demar stood gathering flowers for the breakfast table. He gave one passionate glance at the rare beauty in her face, at the fine soul that looked smiling from her eyes to welcome him, before he let the bar fall between them which could not be raised.

"Miss Demar, this is my father."

The smile deepened. She put out her hand cordially but calmly. "I knew he was your father long ago, Mr. Kenyon. Have you told him who I am?"

"Mary?"

"Will you welcome a daughter as well as a son?" she said, all flushed and glowing. When the old man laid his hand on her head she, too, had a glimpse beneath the beggar's clothes and vulgar words.

They lingered long in the solitary garden. Apart from the morning light and dewy freshness there was a curious calm in it. The house had, as it still has, a strange trick of falling into silence in the midst of the busiest summer's day.

"What unaccountable stories hang about this old place," said Miss Demar to her lover. She could not restrain her curiosity as to his experiences of the night before.

But his face was inscrutable. "Where such a man as that lives," he said, glancing at Knapp, "no morbid shadows would linger long, I fancy. Yet I can believe that under his roof stronger men than he would be haunted by the ghosts of what they might have been. Their best selves would come to meet them."

But he never told her more than that.

A TALE OF THE RAGGED MOUNTAINS

Edgar Allan Poe

During the fall of the year 1827, while residing near Charlottesville, Virginia, I casually made the acquaintance of Mr. Augustus Bedloe. This young gentleman was remarkable in every respect, and excited in me a profound interest and curiosity. I found it impossible to comprehend him either in his moral or his physical relations. Of his family I could obtain no satisfactory account. Whence he came, I never ascertained. Even about his age—although I call him a young gentleman—there was something which perplexed me in no little degree. He certainly *seemed* young—and he made a point of speaking about his youth—yet there were moments when I should have had little trouble in imagining him a hundred years of age. But in no regard was he more peculiar than in his personal appearance. He was singularly tall and thin. He stooped much. His limbs were exceedingly long and emaciated. His forehead was broad and low. His complexion was absolutely bloodless. His mouth was large and flexible, and his teeth were more wildly uneven, although sound, than I had ever before seen teeth in a human head. The expression of his smile, however, was by no means unpleasing, as might be supposed; but it had no variation whatever. It was one of profound melancholy—of a phaseless and unceasing gloom. His eyes were abnormally large, and round like those of a cat. The pupils, too, upon any accession or diminution of light, underwent contraction or dilation, just such as is observed in the feline tribe. In moments of excitement the orbs grew bright to a degree almost inconceivable; seeming to emit luminous rays, not of a reflected but of an intrinsic lustre, as does a candle or the sun; yet their ordinary condition was so totally vapid, filmy, and dull, as to convey the idea of the eyes of a long-interred corpse.

These peculiarities of person appeared to cause him much annoyance, and he was continually alluding to them in a sort of half-explanatory, half-apologetic strain, which, when I first heard it, impressed me very painfully. I soon, however, grew accustomed to it, and my uneasiness wore off. It seemed to be his design rather to insinuate than directly to assert that, physically, he had not always been what he was—that a long series of neuralgic attacks had reduced him from a condition of more than usual personal beauty, to that which I saw. For many years past he had been attended by a physician, named Templeton—an old gentleman, perhaps seventy years of age—whom he had first encountered at Saratoga, and from whose attention, while there, he either received, or fancied that he received, great benefit. The result was that Bedloe, who was wealthy, had made an arrangement with Dr. Templeton, by which the latter, in consideration of a liberal annual allowance, had consented to devote his time and medical experience exclusively to the care of the invalid.

Doctor Templeton had been a traveller in his younger days, and at Paris had become a convert, in great measure, to the doctrines of Mesmer. It was altogether by means of magnetic remedies that he had succeeded in alleviating the acute pains of his patient; and this success had very naturally inspired the latter with a certain degree of confidence in the opinions from which the remedies had been educed. The Doctor, however, like all enthusiasts, had struggled hard to make a thorough convert of his pupil, and finally so far gained his point as to induce the sufferer to submit to numerous experiments. By a frequent repetition of these, a result had arisen, which of late days has become so common as to attract little or no attention, but which, at the period of which I write, had very rarely been known in America. I mean to say, that between Doctor Templeton and Bedloe there had grown up, little by little, a very distinct and strongly marked *rapport*, or magnetic relation. I am not prepared to assert, however, that this *rapport* extended beyond the limits of the simple sleep-producing power; but this power itself had attained great intensity. At the first attempt to induce the magnetic somnolency, the mesmerist entirely failed. In the fifth or sixth he succeeded very partially, and after long continued effort. Only at the twelfth was the triumph complete. After this the will of the patient succumbed rapidly to that of the physician, so that, when I first

became acquainted with the two, sleep was brought about almost instantaneously by the mere volition of the operator, even when the invalid was
unaware of his presence. It is only now, in the year 1845, when similar miracles are witnessed daily by thousands, that I dare venture to record this apparent impossibility as a matter of serious fact.

The temperature of Bedloe was, in the highest degree sensitive, ex-
citable, enthusiastic. His imagination was singularly vigorous and creative;
and no doubt it derived additional force from the habitual use of morphine, which he swallowed in great quantity, and without which he would
have found it impossible to exist. It was his practice to take a very large
dose of it immediately after breakfast each morning—or, rather, immediately after a cup of strong coffee, for he ate nothing in the forenoon—and
then set forth alone, or attended only by a dog, upon a long ramble among
the chain of wild and dreary hills that lie westward and southward of
Charlottesville, and are there dignified by the title of the Ragged Mountains.

Upon a dim, warm, misty day, toward the close of November, and during the strange *interregnum* of the seasons which in America is termed the
Indian Summer, Mr. Bedloe departed as usual for the hills. The day passed,
and still he did not return.

About eight o'clock at night, having become seriously alarmed at his
protracted absence, we were about setting out in search of him, when he
unexpectedly made his appearance, in health no worse than usual, and in
rather more than ordinary spirits. The account which he gave of his expe-
dition, and of the events which had detained him, was a singular one indeed.

"You will remember," said he, "that it was about nine in the morning
when I left Charlottesville. I bent my steps immediately to the mountains,
and, about ten, entered a gorge which was entirely new to me. I followed
the windings of this pass with much interest. The scenery which presented
itself on all sides, although scarcely entitled to be called grand, had about
it an indescribable and to me a delicious aspect of dreary desolation. The
solitude seemed absolutely virgin. I could not help believing that the green
sods and the gray rocks upon which I trod had been trodden never before
by the foot of a human being. So entirely secluded, and in fact inaccessible,
except through a series of accidents, is the entrance of the ravine, that it is
by no means impossible that I was indeed the first adventurer—the very
first and sole adventurer who had ever penetrated its recesses.

"The thick and peculiar mist, or smoke, which distinguishes the Indian Summer, and which now hung heavily over all objects, served, no doubt, to deepen the vague impressions which these objects created. So dense was this pleasant fog that I could at no time see more than a dozen yards of the path before me. This path was excessively sinuous, and as the sun could not be seen, I soon lost all idea of the direction in which I journeyed. In the meantime the morphine had its customary effect—that of enduing all the external world with an intensity of interest. In the quivering of a leaf—in the hue of a blade of grass—in the shape of a trefoil—in the humming of a bee—in the gleaming of a dew-drop—in the breathing of the wind—in the faint odors that came from the forest—there came a whole universe of suggestion—a gay and motley train of rhapsodical and immethodical thought.

"Busied in this, I walked on for several hours, during which the mist deepened around me to so great an extent that at length I was reduced to an absolute groping of the way. And now an indescribable uneasiness possessed me—a species of nervous hesitation and tremor. I feared to tread, lest I should be precipitated into some abyss. I remembered, too, strange stories told about these Ragged Hills, and of the uncouth and fierce races of men who tenanted their groves and caverns. A thousand vague fancies oppressed and disconcerted me—fancies the more distressing because vague. Very suddenly my attention was arrested by the loud beating of a drum.

"My amazement was, of course, extreme. A drum in these hills was a thing unknown. I could not have been more surprised at the sound of the trump of the Archangel. But a new and still more astounding source of interest and perplexity arose. There came a wild rattling or jingling sound, as if of a bunch of large keys, and upon the instant a dusky-visaged and half-naked man rushed past me with a shriek. He came so close to my person that I felt his hot breath upon my face. He bore in one hand an instrument composed of an assemblage of steel rings, and shook them vigorously as he ran. Scarcely had he disappeared in the mist before, panting after him, with open mouth and glaring eyes, there darted a huge beast. I could not be mistaken in its character. It was a hyena.

"The sight of this monster rather relieved than heightened my terrors—for I now made sure that I dreamed, and endeavored to arouse myself to waking consciousness. I stepped boldly and briskly forward. I rubbed my eyes. I called aloud. I pinched my limbs. A small spring of water presented itself to my view, and here, stooping, I bathed my hands and my head and neck. This seemed to dissipate the equivocal sensations which had hitherto annoyed me. I arose, as I thought, a new man, and proceeded steadily and complacently on my unknown way.

"At length, quite overcome by exertion, and by a certain oppressive closeness of the atmosphere, I seated myself beneath a tree. Presently there came a feeble gleam of sunshine, and the shadow of the leaves of the tree fell faintly but definitely upon the grass. At this shadow I gazed wonderingly for many minutes. Its character stupefied me with astonishment. I looked upward. The tree was a palm.

"I now arose hurriedly, and in a state of fearful agitation—for the fancy that I dreamed would serve me no longer. I saw—I felt that I had perfect command of my senses—and these senses now brought to my soul a world of novel and singular sensation. The heat became all at once intolerable. A strange odor loaded the breeze. A low, continuous murmur, like that arising from a full, but gently flowing river, came to my ears, intermingled with the peculiar hum of multitudinous human voices.

"While I listened in an extremity of astonishment which I need not attempt to describe, a strong and brief gust of wind bore off the incumbent fog as if by the wand of an enchanter.

"I found myself at the foot of a high mountain, and looking down into a vast plain, through which wound a majestic river. On the margin of this river stood an Eastern-looking city, such as we read of in the Arabian Tales, but of a character even more singular than any there described. From my position, which was far above the level of the town, I could perceive its every nook and corner, as if delineated on a map. The streets seemed innumerable, and crossed each other irregularly in all directions, but were rather long winding alleys than streets, and absolutely swarmed with inhabitants. The houses were wildly picturesque. On every hand was a wilderness of balconies, of verandas, of minarets, of shrines, and fantastically carved oriels. Bazaars abounded; and in these were displayed rich wares in infinite variety and profusion—silks, muslins, the most dazzling cutlery, the most magnificent jewels and gems. Besides these things, were seen, on all sides, banners and palanquins, litters with stately dames close veiled, elephants gorgeously caparisoned, idols grotesquely hewn, drums, banners, and gongs, spears, silver and gilded maces. And amid the crowd, and the clamor, and the general intricacy and confusion—amid the million of black and yellow men, turbaned and robed, and of flowing beard, there

roamed a countless multitude of holy filleted bulls, while vast legions of
the filthy but sacred ape clambered, chattering and shrieking, about the
cornices of the mosques, or clung to the minarets and oriels. From the
swarming streets to the banks of the river, there descended innumerable
flights of steps leading to bathing places, while the river itself seemed to
force a passage with difficulty through the vast fleets of deeply-burthened
ships that far and wide encountered its surface. Beyond the limits of the
city arose, in frequent majestic groups, the palm and the cocoa, with other
gigantic and weird trees of vast age; and here and there might be seen a
field of rice, the thatched hut of a peasant, a tank, a stray temple, a gypsy
camp, or a solitary graceful maiden taking her way, with a pitcher upon her
head, to the banks of the magnificent river.

"You will say now, of course, that I dreamed; but not so. What I saw—
what I heard—what I felt—what I thought—had about it nothing of the
unmistakable idiosyncrasy of the dream. All was rigorously self-consistent.
At first, doubting that I was really awake, I entered into a series of tests,
which soon convinced me that I really was. Now, when one dreams, and, in
the dream, suspects that he dreams, the suspicion *never fails to confirm* itself,
and the sleeper is almost immediately aroused. Thus Novalis errs not in
saying that 'we are near waking when we dream that we dream.' Had the vision occurred to me as I describe it, without my suspecting it as a dream,
then a dream it might absolutely have been, but, occurring as it did, and
suspected and tested as it was, I am forced to class it among other phe-
nomena."

"In this I am not sure that you are wrong," observed Dr. Templeton,
"but proceed. You arose and descended into the city."

"I arose," continued Bedloe, regarding the Doctor with an air of profound astonishment, "I arose, as you say, and descended into the city. On
my way I fell in with an immense populace, crowding through every avenue, all in the same direction, and exhibiting in every action the wildest
excitement. Very suddenly, and by some inconceivable impulse, I became
intensely imbued with personal interest in what was going on. I seemed to
feel that I had an important part to play, without exactly understanding
what it was. Against the crowd which environed me, however, I experienced
a deep sentiment of animosity. I shrank from amid them, and, swiftly, by a
circuitous path, reached and entered the city. Here all was the wildest tumult and contention. A small party of men, clad in garments half-Indian,
half-European, and officered by gentlemen in a uniform partly British,

were engaged, at great odds, with the swarming rabble of the alleys. I joined the weaker party, arming myself with the weapons of a fallen officer, and fighting I knew not whom with the nervous ferocity of despair. We were soon overpowered by numbers, and driven to seek refuge in a species of kiosk. Here we barricaded ourselves, and, for the present, were secure. From a loop-hole near the summit of the kiosk, I perceived a vast crowd, in furious agitation, surrounding and assaulting a gay palace that overhung the river. Presently, from an upper window of this place, there descended an effeminate-looking person, by means of a string made of the turbans of his attendants. A boat was at hand, in which he escaped to the opposite bank of the river.

"And now a new object took possession of my soul. I spoke a few hurried but energetic words to my companions, and, having succeeded in gaining over a few of them to my purpose made a frantic sally from the kiosk. We rushed amid the crowd that surrounded it. They retreated, at first, before us. They rallied, fought madly, and retreated again. In the mean time we were borne far from the kiosk, and became bewildered and entangled among the narrow streets of tall, overhanging houses, into the recesses of which the sun had never been able to shine. The rabble pressed impetuously upon us, harrassing us with their spears, and overwhelming us with flights of arrows. These latter were very remarkable, and resembled in some respects the writhing creese of the Malay. They were made to imitate the body of a creeping serpent, and were long and black, with a poisoned barb. One of them struck me upon the right temple. I reeled and fell. An instantaneous and dreadful sickness seized me. I struggled—I gasped—I died."

"You will hardly persist *now*," said I smiling, "that the whole of your adventure was not a dream. You are not prepared to maintain that you are dead?"

When I said these words, I of course expected some lively sally from Bedloe in reply; but, to my astonishment, he hesitated, trembled, became fearfully pallid, and remained silent. I looked toward Templeton. He sat erect and rigid in his chair—his teeth chattered, and his eyes were starting from their sockets. "Proceed!" he at length said hoarsely to Bedloe.

"For many minutes," continued the latter, "my sole sentiment—my sole feeling—was that of darkness and nonentity, with the consciousness of death. At length there seemed to pass a violent and sudden shock through my soul, as if of electricity. With it came the sense of elasticity and of light. This latter I felt—not saw. In an instant I seemed to rise from the ground. But I had no bodily, no visible, audible, or palpable presence. The crowd had departed. The tumult had ceased. The city was in comparative repose. Beneath me lay my corpse, with the arrow in my temple, the whole head greatly swollen and disfigured. But all these things I felt—not saw. I took interest in nothing. Even the corpse seemed a matter in which I had no concern. Volition I had none, but appeared to be impelled into motion, and flitted buoyantly out of the city, retracing the circuitous path by which I had entered it. When I had attained that point of the ravine in the mountains at which I had encountered the hyena, I again experienced a shock as of a galvanic battery; the sense of weight, of volition, of substance, returned. I became my original self, and bent my steps eagerly homeward—but the past had not lost the vividness of the real—and not now, even for an instant, can I compel my understanding to regard it as a dream."

"Nor was it," said Templeton, with an air of deep solemnity, "yet it would be difficult to say how otherwise it should be termed. Let us suppose only, that the soul of the man of to-day is upon the verge of some stupendous psychal discoveries. Let us content ourselves with this supposition. For the rest I have some explanation to make. Here is a watercolor drawing, which I should have shown you before, but which an unaccountable sentiment of horror has hitherto prevented me from showing."

We looked at the picture which he presented. I saw nothing in it of an extraordinary character; but its effect upon Bedloe was prodigious. He nearly fainted as he gazed. And yet it was but a miniature portrait—a miraculously accurate one, to be sure—of his own very remarkable features. At least this was my thought as I regarded it.

"You will perceive," said Templeton, "the date of this picture—it is here, scarcely visible, in this corner—1780. In this year was the portrait taken. It is the likeness of a dead friend—a Mr. Oldeb—to whom I became much attached at Calcutta, during the administration of Warren Hastings. I was then only twenty years old. When I first saw you, Mr. Bedloe, at Saratoga, it was the miraculous similarity which existed between yourself and the painting which induced me to accost you, to seek your friendship, and to bring about those arrangements which resulted in my becoming your constant companion. In accomplishing this point, I was urged partly, and perhaps principally, by a regretful memory of the deceased, but also, in part, by an uneasy, and not altogether horrorless curiosity respecting yourself.

"In your detail of the vision which presented itself to you amid the hills, you have described, with the minutest accuracy, the Indian city of Benares, upon the Holy River. The riots, the combat, the massacre, were the actual events of the insurrection of Cheyte Sing, which took place in 1780, when Hastings was put in imminent peril of his life. The man escaping by the string of turbans was Cheyte Sing himself. The party in the kiosk were sepoys and British officers, headed by Hastings. Of this party I was one, and did all I could to prevent the rash and fatal sally of the officer who fell, in the crowded alleys, by the poisoned arrow of a Bengalee. That officer was my dearest friend. It was Oldeb. You will perceive by these manuscripts" (here the speaker produced a note-book in which several pages appeared to have been freshly written) "that at the very period in which you fancied these things amid the hills, I was engaged in detailing them upon paper here at home."

In about a week after this conversation, the following paragraphs appeared in a Charlottesville paper:

"We have the painful duty of announcing the death of Mr. Augustus Bedlo, a gentleman whose amiable manners and many virtues have long endeared him to the citizens of Charlottesville.

"Mr. B., for some years past, has been subject to neuralgia, which has often threatened to terminate fatally; but this can be regarded only as the mediate cause of his decease. The proximate cause was one of especial singularity. In an excursion to the Ragged Mountains, a few days since, a slight cold and fever were contracted, attended with great determination of blood to the head. To relieve this, Dr. Templeton resorted to topical bleeding. Leeches were applied to the temples. In a fearfully brief period the patient died, when it appeared that in the jar containing the leeches, had been introduced, by accident, one of the venomous vermicular sangsues which are now and then found in the neighboring ponds. This creature fastened itself upon a small artery in the right temple. Its close resemblance to the medicinal leech caused the mistake to be overlooked until too late.

"N. B. The poisonous sangsue of Charlottesville may always be distinguished from the medicinal leech by its blackness, and especially by its writhing or vermicular motions, which very nearly resemble those of a snake."

I was speaking with the editor of the paper in question, upon the topic of this remarkable accident, when it occurred to me to ask how it happened that the name of the deceased had been given as Bedlo.

"I presume," I said, "you have authority for this spelling, but I have always supposed the name to be written with an *e* at the end."

"Authority?—no," he replied. "It is a mere typographical error. The name is Bedlo with an *e*, all the world over, and I never knew it to be spelt otherwise in my life."

"Then," said I mutteringly, as I turned upon my heel, "then indeed has it come to pass that one truth is stranger than any fiction—for Bedloe, without the *e*, what is it but Oldeb conversed! And this man tells me that it is a typographical error."

Part IV

THE
INWARD
GAZE

MRS. MANSTEY'S VIEW

Edith Wharton

The view from Mrs. Manstey's window was not a striking one, but to her at least it was full of interest and beauty. Mrs. Manstey occupied the back room on the third floor of a New York boarding-house, in a street where the ash-barrels lingered late on the sidewalk and the gaps in the pavement would have staggered a Quintus Curtius. She was the widow of a clerk in a large wholesale house, and his death had left her alone, for her only daughter had married in California, and could not afford the long journey to New York to see her mother. Mrs. Manstey, perhaps, might have joined her daughter in the West, but they had now been so many years apart that they had ceased to feel any need of each other's society, and their intercourse had long been limited to the exchange of a few perfunctory letters, written with indifference by the daughter, and with difficulty by Mrs. Manstey, whose right hand was growing stiff with gout. Even had she felt a stronger desire for her daughter's companionship, Mrs. Manstey's increasing infirmity, which caused her to dread the three flights of stairs between her room and the street, would have given her pause on the eve of undertaking so long a journey; and without perhaps, formulating these reasons she had long since accepted as a matter of course her solitary life in New York.

She was, indeed, not quite lonely, for a few friends still toiled up now and then to her room; but their visits grew rare as the years went by. Mrs. Manstey had never been a sociable woman, and during her husband's lifetime his companionship had been all-sufficient to her. For many years she had cherished a desire to live in the country, to have a hen-house and a garden; but this longing had faded with age, leaving only in the breast of the

249

uncommunicative old woman a vague tenderness for plants and animals. It was, perhaps, this tenderness which made her cling so fervently to her view from her window, a view in which the most optimistic eye would at first have failed to discover anything admirable.

Mrs. Manstey, from her coign of vantage (a slightly projecting bow-window where she nursed an ivy and a succession of unwholesome-looking bulbs), looked out first upon the yard of her own dwelling, of which, however, she could get but a restricted glimpse. Still, her gaze took in the top-most boughs of the ailanthus below her window, and she knew how early each year the clump of dicentra strung its bending stalk with hearts of pink.

But of greater interest were the yards beyond. Being for the most part attached to boarding-houses they were in a state of chronic untidiness and fluttering, on certain days of the week, with miscellaneous garments and frayed table-cloths. In spite of this Mrs. Manstey found much to admire in the long vista which she commanded. Some of the yards were, indeed, but stony wastes, with grass in the cracks of the pavement and no shade in spring save that afforded by the intermittent leafage of the clothes-lines. These yards Mrs. Manstey disapproved of, but the others, the green ones, she loved. She had grown used to their disorder; the broken barrels, the empty bottles and paths unswept no longer annoyed her; hers was the happy faculty of dwelling on the pleasanter side of the prospect before her.

In the very next enclosure did not a magnolia open its hard white flowers against the watery blue of April? And was there not, a little way down the line, a fence foamed over every May by lilac waves of wistaria? Farther still, a horse-chestnut lifted its candelabra of buff and pink blossoms above broad fans of foliage; while in the opposite yard June was sweet with the breath of a neglected syringa, which persisted in growing in spite of the countless obstacles opposed to its welfare.

But if nature occupied the front rank in Mrs. Manstey's view, there was much of a more personal character to interest her in the aspect of the houses and their inmates. She deeply disapproved of the mustard-colored curtains which had lately been hung in the doctor's window opposite; but she glowed with pleasure when the house farther down had its old bricks washed with a coat of paint. The occupants of the houses did not often show themselves at the back windows, but the servants were always in sight. Noisy slatterns, Mrs. Manstey pronounced the greater number; she knew their ways and hated them. But to the quiet cook in the newly painted house, whose mistress bullied her, and who secretly fed the stray cats at nightfall, Mrs. Manstey's warmest sympathies were given. On one occasion her feelings were racked by the neglect of a housemaid, who for two days forgot to feed the parrot committed to her care. On the third day, Mrs. Manstey, in spite of her gouty hand, had just penned a letter, beginning: "Madam, it is now three days since your parrot has been fed," when the forgetful maid appeared at the window with a cup of seed in her hand.

But in Mrs. Manstey's more meditative moods it was the narrowing perspective of far-off yards which pleased her best. She loved, at twilight, when the distant brown-stone spire seemed melting in the fluid yellow of the west, to lose herself in vague memories of a trip to Europe, made years ago, and now reduced in her mind's eye to a pale phantasmagoria of indistinct steeples and dreamy skies. Perhaps at heart Mrs. Manstey was an artist; at all events she was sensible of many changes of color unnoticed by the average eye, and dear to her as the green of early spring was the black lattice of branches against a cold sulphur sky at the close of a snowy day. She enjoyed, also, the sunny thaws of March, when patches of earth showed through the snow, like ink-spots spreading on a sheet of white blotting-paper; and, better still, the haze of boughs, leafless but swollen, which replaced the clear-cut tracery of winter. She even watched with a certain interest the trail of smoke from a far-off factory chimney, and missed a detail in the landscape when the factory was closed and the smoke disappeared.

Mrs. Manstey, in the long hours which she spent at her window, was not idle. She read a little, and knitted numberless stockings; but the view surrounded and shaped her life as the sea does a lonely island. When her rare callers came it was difficult for her to detach herself from the contemplation of the opposite window-washing, or the scrutiny of certain green points in a neighboring flowerbed which might, or might not, turn into hyacinths, while she feigned an interest in her visitor's anecdotes about some unknown grandchild. Mrs. Manstey's real friends were the denizens of the yards, the hyacinths, the magnolia, the green parrot, the maid who fed the cats, the doctor who studied late behind his mustard-colored curtains; and the confidant of her tenderer musings was the church-spire floating in the sunset.

One April day, as she sat in her usual place, with knitting cast aside and eyes fixed on the blue sky mottled with round clouds, a knock at the door announced the entrance of her landlady. Mrs. Manstey did not care for her landlady, but she submitted to her visits with ladylike resignation. To-day, however, it seemed harder than usual to turn from the blue sky and the blossoming magnolia to Mrs. Sampson's unsuggestive face, and Mrs. Manstey was conscious of a distinct effort as she did so.

"The magnolia is out earlier than usual this year, Mrs. Sampson," she remarked, yielding to a rare impulse, for she seldom alluded to the absorbing interest of her life. In the first place it was a topic not likely to appeal to her visitors and, besides, she lacked the power of expression and could not have given utterance to her feelings had she wished to.

"The what, Mrs. Manstey?" inquired the landlady, glancing about the room as if to find there the explanation of Mrs. Manstey's statement.

"The magnolia in the next yard—in Mrs. Black's yard," Mrs. Manstey repeated.

"Is it, indeed? I didn't know there was a magnolia there," said Mrs. Sampson, carelessly. Mrs. Manstey looked at her; she did not know that there was a magnolia in the next yard!

"By the way," Mrs. Sampson continued, "speaking of Mrs. Black reminds me that the work on the extension is to begin next week."

"The what?" it was Mrs. Manstey's turn to ask.

"The extension," said Mrs. Sampson, nodding her head in the direction of the ignored magnolia. "You knew, of course, that Mrs. Black was going to build an extension to her house? Yes, ma'am. I hear it is to run right back to the end of the yard. How she can afford to build an extension in these hard times I don't see; but she always was crazy about building. She used to keep a boarding-house in Seventeenth Street, and she nearly ruined herself then by sticking out bow-windows and what not; I should have thought that would have cured her of building, but I guess it's a disease, like drink. Anyhow, the work is to begin on Monday."

Mrs. Manstey had grown pale. She always spoke slowly, so the landlady did not heed the long pause which followed. At last Mrs. Manstey said: "Do you know how high the extension will be?"

"That's the most absurd part of it. The extension is to be built right up to the roof of the main building; now, did you ever?"

Mrs. Manstey paused again. "Won't it be a great annoyance to you, Mrs. Sampson?" she asked.

"I should say it would. But there's no help for it; if people have got a mind to build extensions there's no law to prevent 'em, that I'm aware of."

Mrs. Manstey, knowing this, was silent. "There is no help for it," Mrs. Sampson repeated, "but if I *am* a church member, I wouldn't be so sorry if it ruined Eliza Black. Well, good-day, Mrs. Manstey; I'm glad to find you so comfortable."

So comfortable—so comfortable! Left to herself the old woman turned once more to the window. How lovely the view was that day! The blue sky with its round clouds shed a brightness over everything; the ailanthus had put on a tinge of yellow-green, the hyacinths were budding, the magnolia flowers looked more than ever like rosettes carved in alabaster. Soon the wistaria would bloom, then the horse-chestnut; but not for her. Between her eyes and them a barrier of brick and mortar would swiftly rise; presently even the spire would disappear, and all her radiant world be blotted out. Mrs. Manstey sent away untouched the dinner-tray brought to her that evening. She lingered in the window until the windy sunset died in bat-colored dusk; then, going to bed, she lay sleepless all night.

Early the next day she was up and at the window. It was raining, but even through the slanting gray gauze the scene had its charm—and then the rain was so good for the trees. She had noticed the day before that the ailanthus was growing dusty.

"Of course I might move," said Mrs. Manstey aloud, and turning from the window she looked about her room. She might move, of course; so might she be flayed alive; but she was not likely to survive either operation. The room, though far less important to her happiness than the view, was as much a part of her existence. She had lived in it seventeen years. She knew every stain on the wall-paper, every rent in the carpet; the light fell in a certain way on her engravings, her books had grown shabby on their shelves, her bulbs and ivy were used to their window and knew which way to lean to the sun. "We are all too old to move," she said.

That afternoon it cleared. Wet and radiant the blue reappeared through torn rags of cloud; the ailanthus sparkled; the earth in the flower-borders looked rich and warm. It was Thursday, and on Monday the building of the extension was to begin.

On Sunday afternoon a card was brought to Mrs. Black, as she was engaged in gathering up the fragments of the boarders' dinner in the basement. The card, black-edged, bore Mrs. Manstey's name.

"One of Mrs. Sampson's boarders; wants to move, I suppose. Well, I can give her a room next year in the extension. Dinah," said Mrs. Black, "tell the lady I'll be upstairs in a minute."

Mrs. Black found Mrs. Manstey standing in the long parlor garnished with statuettes and antimacassars; in that house she could not sit down.

Stooping hurriedly to open the register, which let out a cloud of dust, Mrs. Black advanced to her visitor.

"I'm happy to meet you, Mrs. Manstey; take a seat, please," the landlady remarked in her prosperous voice, the voice of a woman who can afford to build extensions. There was no help for it; Mrs. Manstey sat down.

"Is there anything I can do for you, ma'am?" Mrs. Black continued. "My house is full at present, but I am going to build an extension, and—"

"It is about the extension that I wish to speak," said Mrs. Manstey, suddenly. "I am a poor woman, Mrs. Black, and I have never been a happy one. I shall have to talk about myself first to—to make you understand."

Mrs. Black, astonished but imperturbable, bowed at this parenthesis.

"I never had what I wanted," Mrs. Manstey continued. "It was always one disappointment after another. For years I wanted to live in the country. I dreamed and dreamed about it; but we never could manage it. There was no sunny window in our house, and so all my plants died. My daughter married years ago and went away—besides, she never cared for the same things. Then my husband died and I was left alone. That was seventeen years ago. I went to live at Mrs. Sampson's, and I have been there ever since. I have grown a little infirm, as you see, and I don't get out often; only on fine days, if I am feeling very well. So you can understand my sitting a great deal in my window—the back window on the third floor—"

"Well, Mrs. Manstey," said Mrs. Black, liberally, "I could give you a back room, I dare say; one of the new rooms in the ex—"

"But I don't want to move; I can't move," said Mrs. Manstey, almost with a scream. "And I came to tell you that if you build that extension I shall have no view from my window—no view! Do you understand?"

Mrs. Black thought herself face to face with a lunatic, and she had always heard that lunatics must be humored.

"Dear me, dear me," she remarked, pushing her chair back a little way, "that is too bad, isn't it? Why, I never thought of that. To be sure, the extension *will* interfere with your view, Mrs. Manstey."

"You do understand?" Mrs. Manstey gasped.

"Of course I do. And I'm real sorry about it, too. But there, don't you worry, Mrs. Manstey. I guess we can fix that all right."

Mrs. Manstey rose from her seat, and Mrs. Black slipped toward the door.

"What do you mean by fixing it? Do you mean that I can induce you to change your mind about the extension? Oh, Mrs. Black, listen to me. I have two thousand dollars in the bank and I could manage, I know I could manage, to give you a thousand if——" Mrs. Manstey paused; the tears were rolling down her cheeks.

"There, there, Mrs. Manstey, don't you worry," repeated Mrs. Black, soothingly. "I am sure we can settle it. I am sorry that I can't stay and talk about it any longer, but this is such a busy time of day, with supper to get——"

Her hand was on the door-knob, but with sudden vigor Mrs. Manstey seized her wrist.

"You are not giving me a definite answer. Do you mean to say that you accept my proposition?"

"Why, I'll think it over, Mrs. Manstey, certainly I will. I wouldn't annoy you for the world——"

"But the work is to begin to-morrow, I am told," Mrs. Manstey persisted.

Mrs. Black hesitated. "It shan't begin, I promise you that; I'll send word to the builder this very night." Mrs. Manstey tightened her hold.

"You are not deceiving me, are you?" she said.

"No——no," stammered Mrs. Black. "How can you think such a thing of me, Mrs. Manstey?"

Slowly Mrs. Manstey's clutch relaxed, and she passed through the open door. "One thousand dollars," she repeated, pausing in the hall; then she let herself out of the house and hobbled down the steps, supporting herself on the cast-iron railing.

"My goodness," exclaimed Mrs. Black, shutting and bolting the hall-door, "I never knew the old woman was crazy! And she looks so quiet and ladylike, too."

Mrs. Manstey slept well that night, but early the next morning she was awakened by a sound of hammering. She got to her window with what haste she might and, looking out, saw that Mrs. Black's yard was full of workmen. Some were carrying loads of brick from the kitchen to the yard, others beginning to demolish the old-fashioned wooden balcony which adorned each story of Mrs. Black's house. Mrs. Manstey saw that she had been deceived. At first she thought of confiding her trouble to Mrs. Sampson, but a settled discouragement soon took possession of her and she went back to bed, not caring to see what was going on.

Toward afternoon, however, feeling that she must know the worst, she rose and dressed herself. It was a laborious task, for her hands were stiffer than usual, and the hooks and buttons seemed to evade her.

When she seated herself in the window, she saw that the workmen had removed the upper part of the balcony, and that the bricks had multiplied since morning. One of the men, a coarse fellow with a bloated face, picked a magnolia blossom and, after smelling it, threw it to the ground; the next man, carrying a load of bricks, trod on the flower in passing.

"Look out, Jim," called one of the men to another who was smoking a pipe, "if you throw matches around near those barrels of paper you'll have the old tinder-box burning down before you know it." And Mrs. Manstey, leaning forward, perceived that there were several barrels of paper and rubbish under the wooden balcony.

At length the work ceased and twilight fell. The sunset was perfect and a roseate light, transfiguring the distant spire, lingered late in the west. When it grew dark Mrs. Manstey drew down the shades and proceeded, in her usual methodical manner, to light her lamp. She always filled and lit it with her own hands, keeping a kettle of kerosene on a zinc-covered shelf in a closet. As the lamp-light filled the room it assumed its usual peaceful aspect. The books and pictures and plants seemed, like their mistress, to settle themselves down for another quiet evening, and Mrs. Manstey, as was her wont, drew up her armchair to the table and began to knit.

That night she could not sleep. The weather had changed and a wild wind was abroad, blotting the stars with close-driven clouds. Mrs. Manstey rose once or twice and looked out of the window; but of the view nothing was discernible save a tardy light or two in the opposite windows. These lights at last went out, and Mrs. Manstey, who had watched for their extinction, began to dress herself. She was in evident haste, for she merely flung a thin dressing-gown over her night-dress and wrapped her head in a scarf; then she opened her closet and cautiously took out the kettle of kerosene. Having slipped a bundle of wooden matches into her pocket she proceeded, with increasing precautions, to unlock her door, and a few moments later she was feeling her way down the dark staircase, led by a glimmer of gas from the lower hall. At length she reached the bottom of the stairs and began the more difficult descent into the utter darkness of the basement. Here, however, she could move more freely, as there was less danger of being overheard; and without much delay she contrived to unlock the iron door leading into the yard. A gust of cold wind smote her as she stepped out and groped shiveringly under the clothes-lines.

That morning at three o'clock an alarm of fire brought the engines to Mrs. Black's door, and also brought Mrs. Sampson's startled boarders to their windows. The wooden balcony at the back of Mrs. Black's house was ablaze, and among those who watched the progress of the flames was Mrs. Manstey, leaning in her thin dressing-gown from the open window.

The fire, however, was soon put out, and the frightened occupants of the house, who had fled in scant attire, reassembled at dawn to find that little mischief had been done beyond the cracking of window panes and smoking of ceilings. In fact, the chief sufferer by the fire was Mrs. Manstey, who was found in the morning gasping with pneumonia, a not unnatural result, as everyone remarked, of her having hung out of an open window at her age in a dressing-gown. It was easy to see that she was very ill; but no one had guessed how grave the doctor's verdict would be, and the faces gathered that evening about Mrs. Sampson's table were awestruck and disturbed. Not that any of the boarders knew Mrs. Manstey well; she "kept to herself," as they said, and seemed to fancy herself too good for them; but then it is always disagreeable to have anyone dying in the house and, as one lady observed to another: "It might just as well have been you or me, my dear."

But it was only Mrs. Manstey; and she was dying, as she had lived, lonely if not alone. The doctor had sent a trained nurse, and Mrs. Sampson, with muffled step, came in from time to time; but both, to Mrs. Manstey, seemed remote and unsubstantial as the figures in a dream. All day she said nothing; but when she was asked for her daughter's address she shook her head. At times the nurse noticed that she seemed to be listening attentively for some sound which did not come; then again she dozed.

The next morning at daylight she was very low. The nurse called Mrs. Sampson and as the two bent over the old woman they saw her lips move.

"Lift me up—out of bed," she whispered.

They raised her in their arms, and with her stiff hand she pointed to the window.

"Oh, the window—she wants to sit in the window. She used to sit there all day," Mrs. Sampson explained. "It can do her no harm, I suppose?"

"Nothing matters now," said the nurse.

They carried Mrs. Manstey to the window and placed her in her chair. The dawn was abroad, a jubilant spring dawn; the spire had already caught a golden ray, though the magnolia and horse-chestnut still slumbered in shadow. In Mrs. Black's yard all was quiet. The charred timbers of the balcony lay where they had fallen. It was evident that since the fire the builders had not returned to their work. The magnolia had unfolded a few more sculptural flowers; the view was undisturbed.

It was hard for Mrs. Manstey to breathe; each moment it grew more difficult. She tried to make them open the window, but they would not understand. If she could have tasted the air, sweet with the penetrating ailanthus savor, it would have eased her; but the view at least was there—the spire was golden now, the heavens had warmed from pearl to blue, day was alight from east to west, even the magnolia had caught the sun.

Mrs. Manstey's head fell back and smiling she died.

That day the building of the extension was resumed.

MANACLED

Stephen Crane

In the First Act there had been a farm scene, wherein real horses had drunk real water out of real buckets, afterward dragging a real wagon off-stage L. The audience was consumed with admiration of this play, and the great Theatre Nouveau rang to its roof with the crowd's plaudits.

The Second Act was now well advanced. The hero, cruelly victimized by his enemies, stood in prison garb, panting with rage, while two brutal warders fastened real handcuffs on his wrists and real anklets on his ankles. And the hovering villain sneered.

"'Tis well, Aubrey Pettingill," said the prisoner. "You have so far succeeded; but, mark you, there will come a time—"

The villain retorted with a cutting allusion to the young lady whom the hero loved.

"Curse you," cried the hero, and he made as if to spring upon this demon; but, as the pitying audience saw, he could only take steps four inches long.

Drowning the mocking laughter of the villain came cries from both the audience and the people in back of the wings. "Fire! Fire! Fire!" Throughout the great house resounded the roaring crashes of a throng of human beings moving in terror, and even above this noise could be heard the screams of women more shrill than whistles. The building hummed and shook; it was like a glade which holds some bellowing cataract of the mountains. Most of the people who were killed on the stairs still clutched their play-bills in their hands as if they had resolved to save them at all costs.

The Theatre Nouveau fronted upon a street which was not of the first importance, especially at night, when it only aroused when the people came to the theatre, and aroused again when they came out to go home. On the night of the fire, at the time of the scene between the enchained hero and his tormentor, the thoroughfare echoed with only the scraping shovels of some street-cleaners, who were loading carts with blackened snow and mud. The gleam of lights made the shadowed pavement deeply blue, save where lay some yellow plum-like reflection.

Suddenly a policeman came running frantically along the street. He charged upon the fire-box on a corner. Its red light touched with flame each of his brass buttons and the municipal shield. He pressed a lever. He had been standing in the entrance of the theatre chatting to the lonely man in the box-office. To send an alarm was a matter of seconds.

Out of the theatre poured the first hundreds of fortunate ones, and some were not altogether fortunate. Women, their bonnets flying, cried out tender names; men, white as death, scratched and bleeding, looked wildly from face to face. There were displays of horrible blind brutality by the strong. Weaker men clutched and clawed like cats. From the theatre itself came the howl of a gale.

The policeman's fingers had flashed into instant life and action the most perfect counter-attack to the fire. He listened for some seconds, and presently he heard the thunder of a charging engine. She swept around a corner, her three shining enthrilled horses leaping. Her consort, the hose-cart, roared behind her. There were the loud clicks of the steel-shod hoofs, hoarse shouts, men running, the flash of lights, while the crevice-like streets resounded with the charges of other engines.

At the first cry of fire, the two brutal warders had dropped the arms of the hero and run off the stage with the villain. The hero cried after them angrily—"Where are you going? Here, Pete—Tom—you've left me chained up, damn you!"

The body of the theatre now resembled a mad surf amid rocks, but the hero did not look at it. He was filled with fury at the stupidity of the two brutal warders, in forgetting that they were leaving him manacled. Calling loudly, he hobbled off-stage L, taking steps four inches long.

Behind the scenes he heard the hum of flames. Smoke, filled with sparks sweeping on spiral courses, rolled thickly upon him. Suddenly his face turned chalk-colour beneath his skin of manly bronze for the stage. His voice shrieked—

"Pete—Tom—damn you—come back—you've left me chained up."

He had played in this theatre for seven years, and he could find his way without light through the intricate passages which mazed out behind the stage. He knew that it was a long way to the street door.

The heat was intense. From time to time masses of flaming wood sung down from above him. He began to jump. Each jump advanced him about three feet, but the effort soon became heart-breaking. Once he fell, and it took time to get upon his feet again.

There were stairs to descend. From the top of this flight he tried to fall feet first. He precipitated himself in a way that would have broken his hip under common conditions. But every step seemed covered with glue, and on almost every one he stuck for a moment. He could not even succeed in falling downstairs. Ultimately he reached the bottom, windless from the struggle.

There were stairs to climb. At the foot of the flight he lay for an instant with his mouth close to the floor trying to breathe. Then he tried to scale this frightful precipice up the face of which many an actress had gone at a canter.

Each succeeding step arose eight inches from its fellow. The hero dropped to a seat on the third step, and pulled his feet to the second step. From this position he lifted himself to a seat on the fourth step. He had not gone far in this manner before his frenzy caused him to lose his balance, and he rolled to the foot of the flight. After all, he could fall downstairs.

He lay there whispering. "They all got out but I. All but I." Beautiful flames flashed above him, some were crimson, some were orange, and here and there were tongues of purple, blue, green.

A curiously calm thought came into his head. "What a fool I was not to foresee this! I shall have Rogers furnish manacles of papier-mâché to-morrow."

The thunder of the fire-lions made the theatre have a palsy.

Suddenly the hero beat his handcuffs against the wall, cursing them in a loud wail. Blood started from under his fingernails. Soon he began to bite the hot steel, and blood fell from his blistered mouth. He raved like a wolf.

Peace came to him again. There were charming effects amid the flames. . . . He felt very cool, delightfully cool. . . . "They've left me chained up."

A STRANGE DEATH

Anonymous

My brother, Walter Kyle, was born a cripple.

This misfortune, this partial helplessness of limb, this forced reliance upon the kindness of others, stimulated my naturally strong love for him, until it became a passion secondary to none, until I married. His was the calm, thoughtful philosophy of a Socrates, that kisses death when it appears, and relinquishes life with a sweet smile upon the lips. He did not murmur because it was doomed that, from birth to death, he should painfully drag his body about by the aid of crutches. Because he thus uncomplainingly bore his sufferings, I thought him a hero. To a stranger, he was a pale-faced cripple, with melancholy eyes; that was all. His health was always delicate; yet he was never seriously ill.

He was twenty when I married, and began practice as a physician. Walter came to me soon afterwards.

"Malcom!" he said, after a few minutes of idle conversation, "I wish you could obtain a situation for me in the city—any place where I could work and be independent."

I reasoned with him until I was vexed, without being able to change his purpose, and subsequently I obtained for him the position of book-keeper in the ship-chandlery of my old friend, Morris Balfour; but I was fearful of the result. Thus far he had been a pure and ingenuous lad. Vicious companions, and the voluptuousness of splendid sin, might suddenly transform him into a sneering cynic, despising morality and ridiculing virtue. It was for him to slay the dragons or be slain.

Shortly after his departure, I moved to a small but thriving village in Wisconsin. He wrote me two or three times a month; his letters were filled with accounts of his success, and vivid descriptions of men and things. Mr. Balfour often added a separate note, commendatory of Walter, expressing, in his blunt way, his gratification at the promptness and ability displayed by him in the discharge of his duties.

Little by little my anxiety for his success diminished, as these letters gave indications of his happiness, and, at the end of the first year of his service, I wrote him a long congratulatory epistle. Six weeks elapsed before his reply came, and I was becoming anxious about him. His letter said that he had been unwell—one of his old nervous attacks—and though not unable to write me, he had lacked the inclination to do that or any thing else. In conclusion, he remarked:

"I am tenderly cared for by kind people, while with whom you need have no fears of my suffering for the slightest comfort. Mr. Balfour bustles around, and overwhelms me with kindness. Then, too, I am in love—with a cat. It is the strongest kind of an affection, my dear Mal."

Here the letter abruptly terminated. My wife and I laughed heartily over the last item of news. Suddenly, my wife observed:

"Malcom! Walter is in love with some woman. Don't you see the dash, after the word love? He was going to make a confession, but changed his mind and the sentence at the same time. See if his next letter don't prove the truth of my prophecy."

That letter never came. There was a great deal of sickness in the village and vicinity, and, in the hurry of my business, a month passed away before I reflected how long it was since I had heard from him.

"Walter must be ill again," I said to my wife.

"I think so; otherwise his silence is inexplicable. You had better write to him or Mr. Balfour."

I wrote that night. The next day's mail brought me a letter from New-York. I tore it open, anxiously, for the superscription was in a strange hand. It was from Mr. Balfour, and informed me that Walter had been found dead in his bed that morning, early, with marks of violence upon his body; that it was a mysterious affair, but that there was no doubt about his having been murdered. I looked at the date of the letter. Two weeks had elapsed since it was written. There were the post-marks of half-a-dozen different towns of the same name on the envelope. Balfour, in his horror and alarm, had omitted to write the name of the State, and the letter had been sent from State to State in search of me.

Naturally, my temperament is somewhat phlegmatic; seldom does any thing excite me, but this was a shock that wrung every nerve. I have forgotten how I passed that mournful day, further than that I locked myself in my study, to which I refused even my wife admittance, though she came to the door many times. That day is a terrible memory in my life; even now I shudder at the thought of the agony I then suffered.

My wife was standing at the study-door when I came out, her head leaning upon her arm against the wall. She stared wildly at me for a second, and then embraced me.

"What *is* the matter, Malcom dear?" she asked, with anxiety. "You've been sobbing and talking to yourself for hours."

I gave her Balfour's letter. In a minute she had read it through, and it dropped from her hands. Her eyes were closed, as if in pain, as she raised her head; her lips moved, but they uttered no word, and her hands aimlessly grasped the air. Before I could reach her, she had fallen, face downwards, upon the floor. That night I started for New-York.

Mr. Balfour's chandlery stood by the most dilapidated of wharves. Intermingled odors of pitch, cordage, canvas, oil-clothing, and heated rubber tarpaulins tainted the atmosphere. It was a low, dilapidated wooden building, with scores of capstans, anchors, barrels of pitch and bales of oakum, piled before it on the side-walk. Within all was gloomy and cheerless. The low, blackened ceiling was crossed by heavy beams, from which hung marline-spikes and balls of twine, capstan-bars and dusty bunting. The little office looked upon the river. Near the window, on brackets, rested a full-rigged ship. It was a bleak, wretched place; but Walter had burrowed in it for a year. I am seldom demonstrative. I had yoked myself to my heavy grief; though it chafed the heart, my body bore up bravely. Yet I felt a tear creeping down my cheek, as I stood sorrowfully viewing a spot hallowed to me by the labors of my dead brother. There was a new clerk at the desk, who permitted me to look into the books Walter had kept; his pen lay upon the desk, thick with ink and dust, and the high stool on which he had sat and worked was put away in a dark corner of the room.

I was looking out of the window, upon the gloomy river, when Mr. Balfour entered. "You here, Mal?" he demanded, as I turned to meet him. "I've been waiting and waiting, thinking you'd come every day, and every day some new perplexity in the affair. I am half insane now, after it is all over."

"All over!" I cried. Then I happened to think that it was nearly three weeks since the letter was written.

"Yes, all over!" repeated Balfour. "The accused man is in a lunatic asylum, and Walter is buried." For a few minutes he walked slowly up and down the office. "I tell you, Malcom," he said, turning to me, "that this murder stabbed my poor old heart until it bleeds all the time. Walter was the noblest, best boy I ever met. He was a son to me." A tear rolled down his cheek, and he went to the door and spitefully brushed it away. It pains my heart to see great, robust men weep; the tears of such men indicate terrible affliction. In my heart I thanked this man, this true friend, for this manifestation of unfeigned love and sympathy. He came back, and seated himself before me.

"Malcom, I come to the office in the morning, early. Sometimes, too often, I forget what has happened, and, seeing the new clerk at the desk, I say: 'Good morning, Walter.' Then the clerk turns slowly about on his stool, and drawls out, 'Good morning, Mr. Balfour,' and awakes me to the truth. I miss him in every thing. I no longer hear his uneven step, his chirrupy voice, his low, musical humming of a gay song. His pale, contented face, always smiling, sick or well, no longer greets me, night and morning, as I come and go. The thought of his being murdered, and no one to suffer for it, is making me desperate. How I envy you your calmness!" he said, hoarsely, striking the arm of his chair heavily with his fist.

"I am calm, because I am ignorant of the particulars. Then, too, I strive to control my feelings. Are you sure Walter was murdered?"

"Sure? I saw him lying dead upon his bed, his face discolored from strangulation, and his hands clenched in the bed-clothes. I saw black marks, the marks of coal-smutted fingers, upon each side of his throat. The doctors said that he was choked to death. Knowing as much, I think he was murdered. So does poor Ellen, who, when I told her about the affair, never shed a tear; but turned white in the face, and fainted. If woman ever loved man, Malcom, she loved Walter."

"Loved Walter!" I cried, in astonishment. "What do you mean? He wrote me about loving a cat, but said nothing about a woman."

"You never received the letter. Mark Baird was the janitor of the building. He is said to have been the murderer of Walter, and is in confinement. Ellen is his daughter. You remember he was ill for five or six weeks—very ill, indeed. She nursed and watched over him then; read to him, brought him flowers, and talked with him. She did him more good than forty doctors. She is good and lovely, and a school-mistress. Just the day before his death, Walter told me that he had written to you that he was going to marry her. I found the letter, the other day, in his drawer."

"Then he was ill, and had recovered, when he was murdered? I want the particulars, Balfour. You have told me nothing about the murder. How did it happen, and why?"

"*Why* it was done, I don't know. There could be no reason. There never was a reason for murder. Walter was just well, and able to work, when he was killed. It was about ten days, from the time he left his bed, to the day of his death. He was weak, and complained of his lungs; but would sleep alone, taking his meals at Mr. Baird's. He performed his duty at the office, though I forbid it, and had hired, temporarily, another book-keeper. Let me say, here, that Baird was a confirmed drunkard; never violent in his drunkenness, but always misty. He had lost a small fortune through drink; it brought him down to what he was, and made him what he is. I don't like to talk about this murder. It breaks my sleep. There is a mystery about it I can't fathom. My brain is dull; yours keen. Perhaps you can make something out of the matter, Malcom. What I don't know, Ellen Baird does. Go and see her!"

There was a profound silence in the little office for minutes. It was getting very dark. The clerk had put up his books, and gone home, soon after my entrance. Balfour was walking rapidly up and down the room.

"Are you ever going to tell me these particulars, Morris?" I quietly asked, though fast becoming incensed at his delay. "How long must I wait? Think of what I am suffering!"

"I forgot that!" he said; "I'd do most any thing rather than tell you. It will make us both sad."

He lighted the gas, and then resumed:

"Three weeks ago to-morrow, Malcom, in the morning, just as I had come into the office, a policeman knocked at the door opening on the dock.

"'Have you a clerk named Walter Kyle?'

"'Yes.'

"'Rooms in Arcade Building?'

"'Yes.'

"'He has just been found dead in his bed. You had better go around there, Sir,' and he walked away.

"I was dizzy for an instant, and sat down; but the vertigo passed away immediately, and I started for Walter's room. Drays and carts thundered over the streets, and their drivers shouted at their beasts and each other; yet to me there was no noise, no bustle. It was profound silence, broken every two or three minutes by those dreadful words: 'He has just been found dead in his bed.' I heard nothing else, thought of nothing else but this revelation. There were several policemen in the room when I arrived, and three or four citizens. Walter lay on the bed. His face was of a dark blue color, and wore an expression of agony. The bed-cover was drawn back. On his neck I saw the black marks of five smutted fingers, four on one side, one on the other. At a glance I comprehended every thing, and was calm. 'Murdered!' I said, to a policeman. He nodded his head. I heard a groan, and, looking around, saw Mr. Baird, held down in a chair by three men. He struggled fiercely; his eyes protruded; his hands worked nervously, now grasping his clothes, now seizing those who held him. He made feeble efforts to cry out, but there only came forth a husky whisper. 'He has the *tremens,* and is arrested for the murder.' A few minutes afterwards he was carried down-stairs, on his way to prison. I don't know how I managed to pass so calmly through this ordeal. It seems like a fearful dream to me, now. Poor Ellen! When she saw the body, she stooped, and kissed again and again its cold lips; but not a tear wet her eyes. I had the corpse removed to my house; and the night before the burial, she was alone with it for four hours. She talked but little about the murder; and then, more to assert her father's innocence than to mourn the loss of her betrothed, for such I understood he was. The coroner's jury, after taking the testimony of several physicians, declared that death was produced by strangulation. They took the testimony of witnesses, and examined it. It showed that Baird entered Walter's room about six o'clock in the morning. Ten minutes afterwards, he was met by a person lodging in the house, going down-stairs, laughing boisterously, and talking to himself about killing somebody or something, which the witness couldn't state. When this lodger came to the landing, he saw Walter's door open, and the occupant lying upon the bed. He called him several times, but receiving no answer, entered, and found him dead. Then the police were called, and Baird was arrested. On being brought into the room where the body was, he began to rave; and he is now a harmless but incurable lunatic. From such evidence, the jury judged that Baird was the murderer. I can't believe it, though, and never will. Somebody else may have done it, and the discovery frightened the old man out of his wits. What puzzles me, under such a supposition, is, that nothing was missing except Toby."

"Who is Toby?" I asked.

"He was a cat; a very large, white, tigerish animal, very fierce, very blood-thirsty, very—in fact, every thing fiendish. He was given to Walter by a captain just in from Calcutta. The sailors had plagued the beast, until it bit one of them so severely that he lost his finger; then they left it alone. Walter managed him very easily, though he now and then showed his teeth. It was double the size of our cats. I told him that the beast would hurt him some day, but these prophecies he always laughed at. Well, Toby was the only thing missing from the room; and he has not been seen from that day to this. But there was one very mysterious circumstance connected with the appearance of the room. Two panes of glass, with the intervening wood or sash, were broken, and blood and short white hair found upon the sill. I said to myself, 'Toby jumped through this window.' But then I thought that he could not have had strength enough to break the wood; and why should he jump through at all? I have only puzzled my head in trying to conjecture the reason of this broken window. You see, Malcom, there is a little mystery about the affair."

I tried to elucidate from the facts thus disorderly arrayed by my friend, some clue to lead to the reason why Mr. Baird should have committed the crime. If he did not, who did, and why? Perplexity succeeded perplexity, and I yielded, in despair, to feelings of grief. I should have sat there all night, in my gloom of heart, had not Balfour taken me by the arm, and led me to his home.

In the mist and fog of the following morning, Rasdale Court, where Miss Baird lived, was very quiet and very dismal. The houses were all one story, but neat and cosy. The jagged trunk of a tree, shattered by lightning, stood just in front of the house I sought. I was looking at the tree, when a young lady, dressed in mourning, came to the gate. If she had been a beautiful woman, I should have admired, not loved her. But she was a modest, intellectual-looking girl of twenty, with eyes whose brilliancy was softened by such afflictions as seldom oppress young hearts. I introduced myself.

"I was going to visit my father," she remarked, as we entered the house. "Though I love him dearly, he must wait for me; for I have been wishing to see and talk with you. I have had no one to talk to, to whom I could confide my thoughts and griefs, except my old housekeeper, Margaret, and she cannot sympathize with me. Mr. Balfour is kind, very kind, but he does not understand me." She had been taking off her bonnet and shawl as she spoke, in a voice low and full of melody. I was sitting by the window, and she came and stood before me.

"You do not resemble Walter," she said. "I should not have recognized you as a relation of his."

"He was much younger than I; his ill-health had effaced the more prominent family characteristics of feature."

Even while she talked, she seemed looking at something invisible to other eyes. Then she gazed vacantly out of the window, till a canary in an adjoining room burst into a thrilling flow of melody, and recalled her wandering thoughts. Suddenly, and almost frantically, she knelt before me, and caught my hands in hers.

"Mr. Kyle, can you, do you believe that my father murdered Walter?" and she looked imploringly into my face. "Oh! pity me! I have afflictions enough to make me mad. No one counsels me, for I am too proud to make confidants of strangers or lukewarm friends. I can't weep away my sorrow; not a tear has moistened my eyes since Walter's death. On my knees, I beg you to tell me you disbelieve this horrid accusation."

"I do not believe it, Miss Baird; though I heard the story, for the first time, last evening. Mr. Balfour told me only what he knew; yet I cannot, from that story, believe your father guilty of Walter's death. Still, I have a favor to ask. Consider me as a brother, as one who would do any thing to serve you, for Walter's sake. Tell me how you came to know him, and to love him. Though I do not think your father guilty, some one else must be. Perhaps, from your story, I may be able to name the assassin, and relieve your father from the charge of murder."

Her head drooped upon her hands, but only for a second.

Rising, she drew up a chair, and sat down beside me.

"You have heard, perhaps, that I am a school-mistress—and I neither like nor dislike the occupation; I am indifferent. Father was janitor of the building in which Walter roomed, and one word expresses our condition: we were ruined.

"The beginning of my acquaintance with Walter was as surprising as the termination was heart-rending.

"One day, father came in great haste, and asked me to come with him, saying, that one of the lodgers in the 'Arcade Buildings' was very ill, and needed a woman's attentions. Then he praised him, and I listened, while plodding wearily onward through the cheerless rain and mud, happy in the thought of pleasing father, and relieving the sufferings of one whom he so much admired. A single glance around the room of the sick man revealed disheartening disorder. A small, emaciated Irish woman was asleep in a rocking-chair, till our voices awakened her; and by the side of Walter, on the bed, was stretched a huge white cat, dappled with yellow spots, like little suns. It uttered a sonorous, angry cry, as I advanced to the bed-side. Walter's eyes flashed, as I told him I had come to attend him, give him his medicine, and be his 'help.' He held out his hand, saying: 'I am confident that we'll be good friends, Miss Ellen. How can I ever repay such unexpected, gratifying kindness?' I thought I saw tears in his eyes, but he turned his face from me, and was silent. 'This woman and your ugly cat must be tedious society,' I said, in the course of the day; and as I spoke, the cat, which had been asleep, opened its eyes, looked steadily at me for a second, rose to its feet, stretched itself as only cats can stretch, walked to the head of the bed, and began to lick the face of its master. Then, with a low laugh at my exclamation of disgust, Walter feebly pushed the cat away, and it jumped upon the floor, where, suddenly fastening its claws in my dress, it once more stretched its huge lithe body. Again your brother laughed, as I shook off the loathsome creature.

"'You see that I have one vigilant friend, Miss Ellen,' he said, with a sigh, and, as it seemed to me, with a shudder. 'But I am unjust. I forget my good, kind employer, Mr. Balfour, who comes every evening to amuse me with accounts of his ludicrous perplexities caused by my absence from the desk. I can see that you are strongly prejudiced against poor Toby; yet this fierce cat, when well behaved—and I acknowledge he is often very naughty—is an affectionate, lovable brute. Often his manners are so outrageous, that their absurdity is attractive. Now and then, in his fierce sportiveness, he hurts me—unintentionally of course.'

"I read and talked for hours; then father came in, followed soon after by Mr. Balfour. Such was my first visit to your brother, and I liked him. Mrs. Daly, the Irish nurse, was a poor companion for an invalid. She was always asleep when I was there, so that I felt more at ease; for I dread the criticism of the vulgar. Walter recovered slowly. He refused to let me write you of his illness, saying you had troubles enough of your own. I believe that he did write to you, though, about a fortnight before he left his room. What most surprised me was the pertinacity with which he clung to his cat, which pompously trod the floor, uttering deep, guttural cries, or reposed beside his master upon the bed. It did not notice me, except by snarling and attempting to bite when I tried to caress it. One day, being unusually spiteful, it scratched my hand. Walter saw the proceeding, and, seizing a stick, gave the brute a whipping, and threw him across the room.

"'Miss Ellen,' he said, apologetically, as, panting with the exertion, he wearily closed his eyes, 'Miss Ellen, I hope you will excuse this show of temper; but really Master Toby is becoming unbearable. His annoyances increase instead of diminish.'

"'Why not give him away?' I asked.

"'I have given him away three or four times. Mrs. Daly took him once. It was parting with an old friend, and it left me lonely. He returned the second day. She would not have him upon any condition. He had scratched the children, broken crockery, and, to finish his vandalism, killed six out of a brood of seven chickens. I really believe he is jealous of you. Poor, untamable Toby!' he said, stroking the cat, which had crept within reach of his master's caressing hand.

"'He is spoiled by your petting,' I said. 'His temper shows that he has not forgotten the sun, and perhaps the jungles of the Indies; for to me he has always seemed a dwarfed tiger. Some day you will strike him too hard, and he will tear you with his claws.'

"'You are severe upon poor Toby, Ellen. I acknowledge he is *outré* in manners. But do you know that I often think he has a soul?'

"Soon after his recovery, Walter and I were betrothed. He made our house his home, sleeping in his old room, with Toby for a companion. In its terrible fulness of sorrow I once more contemplate the last evening of his life; even now I sometimes think I hear his gentle voice telling me his hopes and aspirations, or giving his opinion of passages in a book he was reading. The evening had been very hot and sultry. Father was asleep in his arm-chair. At ten o'clock a terrible thunder-storm broke upon us. The flashes of lightning were almost continuous. Suddenly there was a deep silence for a minute; then a broad, quick flash of lightning, instantaneously followed by sharp, resounding thunder. A vase fell from the shelf behind you, and was shattered. Walter, with hands clasped and upraised, and his face like white marble, rose to his feet. In the quick following darkness he fell heavily upon the floor. He had fainted. Though weak and trembling

with the shock to his nerves, he insisted upon going to his room, and father accompanied him. As we opened the door, we saw that the great elm
in front of the yard had been shattered by the lightning; its limbs and huge
ragged splinters strewed the yard.

"'A narrow escape,' he said, tossing a twig towards me. 'We can never
more sit in its shadow, Ell.' By the dim light of the moon, through the
fleeting clouds, I saw tears upon his cheeks.

"'I am nervous to-night, darling,' he said, brushing his face with his
handkerchief. As he and father passed out of the gate, I saw, with a shudder, that Toby was following them. Father always went to his work early in
the morning, very often not returning until dinner-time. Neither he nor
Walter were at breakfast, about which I was a little alarmed; for your
brother was very punctual in his habits. His illness of the previous evening
might have become so severe as to confine him to his bed; if so, father
would know it, and be with him. This somewhat quieted my fears. Nevertheless, when noon came, and neither were at dinner, my anxiety was so
great that I continually walked the room; now and then going to the window, to look eagerly down the street. At last I saw Mr. Balfour coming, and
walking very fast. I felt a premonition of coming evil, for Mr. Balfour was
ever a slow mover; now he was almost running. By energy almost superhuman I calmed myself, and awaited evil tidings.

"'You have bad news!' I exclaimed. 'Is Walter very ill?' I thought of
nothing worse than that.

"'The most terrible news!' he replied. 'Terrible! terrible!'

"The dumb agony of a frightful dream could not have been more fearful than this man and his words. My heart was like ice.

"'Has any thing happened to my father?' I asked.

"'Alas! my poor girl, it is worse than you imagine—a thousand times
worse.'

"I could not weep or moan. Dull, heavy throbs of pain ran through my
head. In my agony of soul, I gasped and choked for speech. I felt that I was
looking at him with a stony, senseless stare, and that he was standing before me frightened at my manner.

"'Walter is dead!' I said, hoping and praying in my heart that my words
would prove untrue. Mr. Balfour took my hands in his, and besought me
to be calm, for there was worse news than I had imagined.

"'Tell me quickly,' I commanded. 'You cannot kill me, except by torturing me with this delay.' He commenced hesitatingly, apparently dreading the effect of the recital, and gauging my strength by a silence between each word, firmly clasping my hands, and softening his voice that he might render the harshness of the words less distinct:

"'Ellen, Walter—is—dead—murdered; and—and don't look at me in such a fierce way, Ellen. I cannot continue.'

"'Proceed! I am of stone, and have no feeling. My eyes are dry. Is my father dead?'

"'Your father, Ellen—has—been—arrested—as—the—murderer,—and—is—in—prison.'

"I remember that, with the energy of despair, I rose to my feet; then objects seemed to recede into distance; every thing lost identity, and I sank to the floor. My body seems frail; it is only pliant. In a few minutes I recovered.

"I was lying upon the lounge, looking at Mr. Balfour, who was fanning me.

"'I am going to my father,' was all I said. Mr. Kyle, my anguish and heartache were almost insupportable, when, standing in the gloomy corridor of the prison, the creaking bolts were shot back, the heavy bar fell down, and the door of the cell swung open. Father was sitting upon the cot. He slapped his hands together, and cried: 'How it thunders!'

"'Father!' I moaned, throwing my arms around his neck, 'this is terrible.'

"He regarded me with a strange vacant look, for a moment, then held up his hands before him. 'Bah! I am a murderer—of a cat,' he added, as if in doubt. Without noticing me further, he went to the window. Mr. Balfour bent over me, and whispered:

"'I forgot to tell you that he is mad.'

"For a second time I fainted. When I opened my eyes I was lying upon the cot, Mr. Balfour at my side. Papa sat in the deep window, kicking his heels against the wall, and laughing softly to himself. I spoke to him, calling him by every affectionate name I know. As if I annoyed him, he turned from me, and looked out of the window. This act of apparent aversion crushed my heart. I left the cell, joyless, emotionless, and with the despair of a suicide. There is a dumb grief that eats the heart like a corrosive acid. The eyes cannot weep nor the lips mourn. Such is my grief; I have it and I keep it. Physicians having pronounced father incurable, I have been allowed to place him in a private asylum near the city, to which I walk every day when my school is ended. It is needless for me to say that I do not think him guilty of this murder. His whole life is against such a belief."

Her story was ended, so far as she chose to tell it. Her grief for Walter was sacred. Her mourning garb revealed what she had left unspoken.

From the narratives of Ellen and Balfour I deduced certain facts. The story of one without the other would have been worthless. I deemed the mystery of Walter's death solved. One truth only was lacking: if Mr. Baird could not furnish a clue, the case was almost hopeless. In his wandering talk he might thoughtlessly utter this truth. Then I thought and knew I could prove his innocence. The police had failed, because they did not seek a combination of the causes which, through the instrumentality of unsuspected things, had produced Walter's death. To me it was the revelation of a second of time. I did not dare to hope for success, so frail was the prospect of obtaining the conclusive evidence of Baird.

Still it was absolutely necessary to try him.

I said nothing to Ellen of all these hopes, though I again and again assured her that I believed her father entirely innocent.

The next day I accompanied Ellen to the asylum. When we entered the parlor, there stood at the window an old man, with long white hair and beard, and features beautiful even in the painful rigidity of their sharpness; but the eyes, though brilliant, were vacillating in their gaze, and the delicate mouth worked nervously all the time. He was spanning the window-casing with his long, trembling fingers. Ellen embraced him.

He only noticed her caresses because they were obstructions to his employment.

"See, father," Ellen said, leading me to him, "I have brought Walter's brother to see you. You have not forgotten dear Walter, have you?"

As she said this, and for the first time since Walter's death, she wept. It seemed a sudden giving way of the fettered passions. Perhaps her strong sorrow had silently corroded the chains of such unnatural silence, until a sudden pang of grief, the tremor of a bleeding heart at the utterance of the name of her beloved, broke the weakened links of this oppression. Her sobs and moans seemed to fascinate her father for a minute. His eyes became steady in their glances, and filled with a radiance of returning sanity; his lips moved, but there was no sound; his hands were extended over her bowed head as if to bless her. But the shroud of his "death in life" enwrapped him in an instant, and he became a stolid, vacant starer. Gently he smoothed his daughter's hair, then, as if he had not before seen her tears, he exclaimed:

"What! Tears, little birdy? Did you never hear what the lover said?

> "O FATHER! what a hell of witchcraft lies
> In the small orb of one particular tear!"

"Dear, *dear* father!" she cried, putting her arms around his neck. Then he lovingly pushed back from his face his long white hair. "Don't you, don't you remember Walter?" she asked, imploringly.

"Walter! Walter!" he repeated, in a low voice. "Do I remember Walter? Of course I do! Let me think, though! a pale, haggard boy, with large melancholy eyes, and walking with a crutch?"

He looked at me. I nodded my head.

"Yes! yes! He and my daughter were to have been married. Something happened though. Something terrible, I believe. Ah! how very clear it is. I remember perfectly. I killed the cat."

"What was that?" I demanded, grasping his arm. "Say that again, please!"

He looked at me indignantly, and said, "*Sir?*" with a haughty emphasis.

"I beg pardon," I instantly replied, and in intense excitement, fearful of a moody fit of silence. "You were relating a very wonderful story. Could you state how the accident happened? I don't believe that about the cat, though. It is impossible!"

"It is so!" he angrily replied, coming towards me.

"Please don't irritate him," pleaded Ellen, as she strove to calm the old man and get him seated.

"It is all for the best. I am trembling with hope. In his anger he will say what I wish to hear, if ever he says it. He may say how Walter died."

I turned to Mr. Baird. "I will not believe a word of your story unless you tell me how Walter died. Can't you do that?" I spoke roughly. His answer was passionless.

"Yes, I think I can. I'm surprised that I didn't tell you before. It's strange, very strange! The morning was beautiful, I believe; I'm not sure, though." He paused, and put his hands to his head. "Yes! I knocked at his door, and heard a groan. I opened the door, and a cat—I think his name was Toby—I am not quite certain if it were Toby. Let me think!"

There followed a silence of several minutes. He forgot the conversation, and began to hum a song.

"Father! the cat's name *was* Toby," sobbed Ellen. Mr. Baird laughed a foolish laugh. "Don't you think I had forgotten. No! no! Well! Toby lay upon Walter's breast. Walter was dead, quite dead. No! he was dying. I remember now, for when I raised his head he opened his eyes and smiled; then he died. I have quite forgotten the rest; only I know I slung the cat through the window, into the street, and killed it."

The conjectures I had formed, but had not expressed, were verified by the narrative of Mr. Baird. The effect being known, I had sought the cause and found it. There was a joy for a hopeless man and a sorrowful girl.

I had calmly considered the evidence: my judgment was ready to be pronounced. Should it be uttered now, while the dear girl was sobbing out her grief—a grief that had clasped her with a giant's strength? It seemed to me that a delay, while it could harm no one, might be productive of happier results.

Mr. Baird's eyes were closed as if he were asleep. Suddenly he commenced singing, in a shrill voice:

"Roley-Boley sat on a wall:
Roley-Boley had a great fall."

It pained me to listen, so I went into the garden, where Ellen soon joined me.

"To-day is the first time that father has talked about Walter," she said, as we were walking home. "When I have talked about your brother he would not listen to me. But why did you excite him so? Of what good is all that about the cat?"

"Will you listen to me calmly? Joy often kills where grief only numbs."

She grasped my arm, and looked eagerly into my face. "Do you mean that father can recover?"

"I believe your father innocent of my brother's murder."

"Is that all?" she asked coldly. "I never believed him guilty."

"But the public does, and keeps him in prison. I do not believe Walter was murdered by either man or woman."

"Not murdered? Not murdered? I don't understand you."

"You heard your father's story about finding the cat on Walter's breast."

"I can never forget it."

"In days gone by men suffered the *'peine forte et dure'*—that awful death by pressure upon the heart and lungs. You remember it, Ellen. I believe that Walter died such a death."

"But the weight of a cat could not do it."

"Walter's lungs were diseased, his health feeble. His nervous system was shocked, the evening before his death, by that flash of lightning. The cat resumed its old position upon his breast in the night. Walter may have suffered hours of agony; his weakness must have been such as to prevent his moving either himself or the cat; and thus he died, murdered by this cat."

"But the finger-marks on the neck?"

"Were probably made by your father when he raised Walter's head."

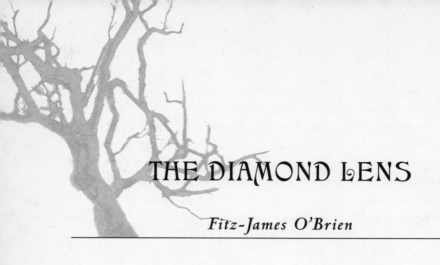

THE DIAMOND LENS

Fitz-James O'Brien

I

The Bending of the Twig

From a very early period of my life the entire bent of my inclinations had been towards microscopic investigations. When I was not more than ten years old, a distant relative of our family, hoping to astonish my inexperience, constructed a simple microscope for me, by drilling in a disk of copper a small hole, in which a drop of pure water was sustained by capillary attraction. This very primitive apparatus, magnifying some fifty diameters, presented, it is true, only indistinct and imperfect forms, but still sufficiently wonderful to work up my imagination to a preternatural state of excitement.

Seeing me so interested in this rude instrument, my cousin explained to me all that he knew about the principles of the microscope, related to me a few of the wonders which had been accomplished through its agency, and ended by promising to send me one regularly constructed, immediately on his return to the city. I counted the days, the hours, the minutes, that intervened between that promise and his departure.

Meantime I was not idle. Every transparent substance that bore the remotest semblance to a lens I eagerly seized upon and employed in vain attempts to realize that instrument, the theory of whose construction I as yet only vaguely comprehended. All panes of glass containing those oblate spheroidal knots familiarly known as "bull's eyes" were ruthlessly destroyed, in the hope of obtaining lenses of marvellous power. I even went so far as to extract the crystalline humor from the eyes of fishes and animals, and endeavored to press it into the microscopic service. I plead guilty to having stolen the glasses from my Aunt Agatha's spectacles, with a dim idea of grinding them into lenses of wondrous magnifying properties—in which attempt it is scarcely necessary to say that I totally failed.

At last the promised instrument came. It was of that order known as Field's simple microscope, and had cost perhaps about fifteen dollars. As far as educational purposes went, a better apparatus could not have been selected. Accompanying it was a small treatise on the microscope—its history, uses, and discoveries. I comprehended then for the first time the "Arabian Nights' Entertainments." The dull veil of ordinary existence that hung across the world seemed suddenly to roll away, and to lay bare a land of enchantments. I felt towards my companions as the seer might feel towards the ordinary masses of men. I held conversations with Nature in a tongue which they could not understand. I was in daily communication with living wonders, such as they never imagined in their wildest visions. I penetrated beyond the external portal of things, and roamed through the sanctuaries. Where they beheld only a drop of rain slowly rolling down the window-glass, I saw a universe of beings animated with all the passions common to physical life, and convulsing their minute sphere with struggles as fierce and protracted as those of men. In the common spots of mould, which my mother, good housekeeper that she was, fiercely scooped away from her jam pots, there abode for me, under the name of mildew, enchanted gardens, filled with dells and avenues of the densest foliage and most astonishing verdure, while from the fantastic boughs of these microscopic forests hung strange fruits glittering with green and silver and gold.

It was no scientific thirst that at this time filled my mind. It was the pure enjoyment of a poet to whom a world of wonders has been disclosed. I talked of my solitary pleasures to none. Alone with my microscope, I dimmed my sight, day after day and night after night poring over the marvels which it unfolded to me. I was like one who, having discovered the ancient Eden still existing in all its primitive glory, should resolve to enjoy it in solitude, and never betray to mortal the secret of its locality. The rod of my life was bent at this moment. I destined myself to be a microscopist.

Of course, like every novice, I fancied myself a discoverer. I was ignorant at the time of the thousands of acute intellects engaged in the same pursuit as myself, and with the advantages of instruments a thousand times more powerful than mine. The names of Leeuwenhoek, Williamson,

Spencer, Ehrenberg, Schultz, Dujardin, Schact, and Schleiden were then entirely unknown to me, or if known, I was ignorant of their patient and wonderful researches. In every fresh specimen of Cryptogamia which I placed beneath my instrument I believed that I discovered wonders of which the world was as yet ignorant. I remember well the thrill of delight and admiration that shot through me the first time that I discovered the common wheel animalcule (*Rotifera vulgaris*) expanding and contracting its flexible spokes, and seemingly rotating through the water. Alas! as I grew older, and obtained some works treating of my favorite study, I found that I was only on the threshold of a science to the investigation of which some of the greatest men of the age were devoting their lives and intellects.

As I grew up, my parents, who saw but little likelihood of anything practical resulting from the examination of bits of moss and drops of water through a brass tube and a piece of glass, were anxious that I should choose a profession. It was their desire that I should enter the counting-house of my uncle, Ethan Blake, a prosperous merchant, who carried on business in New York. This suggestion I decisively combated. I had no taste for trade; I should only make a failure; in short, I refused to become a merchant.

But it was necessary for me to select some pursuit. My parents were staid New England people, who insisted on the necessity of labor; and therefore, although, thanks to the bequest of my poor Aunt Agatha, I should, on coming of age, inherit a small fortune sufficient to place me above want, it was decided, that, instead of waiting for this, I should act the nobler part, and employ the intervening years in rendering myself independent.

After much cogitation I complied with the wishes of my family, and selected a profession. I determined to study medicine at the New York Academy. This disposition of my future suited me. A removal from my relatives would enable me to dispose of my time as I pleased, without fear of detection. As long as I paid my Academy fees, I might shirk attending the lectures, if I chose; and as I never had the remotest intention of standing an examination, there was no danger of my being "plucked." Besides, a metropolis was the place for me. There I could obtain excellent instruments, the newest publications, intimacy with men of pursuits kindred to my own—in short, all things necessary to insure a profitable devotion of my life to my beloved science. I had an abundance of money, few desires that were not bounded by my illuminating mirror on one side and my object-glass on the other; what, therefore, was to prevent my becoming an illustrious investigator of the veiled worlds? It was with the most buoyant hopes that I left my New England home and established myself in New York.

II

The Longing of a Man of Science

My first step, of course, was to find suitable apartments. These I obtained, after a couple of days' search, in Fourth Avenue; a very pretty second-floor unfurnished, containing sitting-room, bedroom, and a smaller apartment which I intended to fit up as a laboratory. I furnished my lodgings simply, but rather elegantly, and then devoted all my energies to the adornment of the temple of my worship. I visited Pike, the celebrated optician, and passed in review his splendid collection of microscopes—Field's Compound, Higham's, Spencer's, Nachet's Binocular (that founded on the principles of the stereoscope), and at length fixed upon that form known as Spencer's Trunnion Microscope, as combining the greatest number of improvements with an almost perfect freedom from tremor. Along with this I purchased every possible accessory—draw-tubes, micrometers, a *camera-lucida*, lever-stage, achromatic condensers, white cloud illuminators, prisms, parabolic condensers, polarizing apparatus, forceps, aquatic boxes, fishing-tubes, with a host of other articles, all of which would have been useful in the hands of an experienced microscopist, but, as I afterwards discovered, were not of the slightest present value to me. It takes years of practice to know how to use a complicated microscope. The optician looked suspiciously at me as I made these wholesale purchases. He evidently was uncertain whether to set me down as some scientific celebrity or a madman. I think he inclined to the latter belief. I suppose I was mad. Every great genius is mad upon the subject in which he is greatest. The unsuccessful madman is disgraced, and called a lunatic.

Mad or not, I set myself to work with a zeal which few scientific students have ever equalled. I had everything to learn relative to the delicate study upon which I had embarked—a study involving the most earnest patience, the most rigid analytic powers, the steadiest hand, the most untiring eye, the most refined and subtle manipulation.

For a long time half my apparatus lay inactively on the shelves of my laboratory, which was now most amply furnished with every possible contrivance for facilitating my investigations. The fact was that I did not know how to use some of my scientific accessories—never having been taught microscopics—and those whose use I understood theoretically were of little avail, until by practice I could attain the necessary delicacy of handling. Still, such was the fury of my ambition, such the untiring perseverance of my experiments, that, difficult of credit as it may be, in the course of one year I became theoretically and practically an accomplished microscopist.

During this period of my labors, in which I submitted specimens of every substance that came under my observation to the action of my lenses, I became a discoverer—in a small way, it is true, for I was very young, but still a discoverer. It was I who destroyed Ehrenberg's theory that the *Volcox globator* was an animal, and proved that his "monads" with stomachs and eyes were merely phases of the formation of a vegetable cell, and were, when they reached their mature state, incapable of the act of conjugation, or any true generative act, without which no organism rising to any stage of life higher than vegetable can be said to be complete. It was I who resolved the singular problem of rotation in the cells and hairs of plants into ciliary attraction, in spite of the assertions of Mr. Wenham and others, that my explanation was the result of an optical illusion.

But notwithstanding these discoveries, laboriously and painfully made as they were, I felt horribly dissatisfied. At every step I found myself stopped by the imperfections of my instruments. Like all active microscopists, I gave my imagination full play. Indeed, it is a common complaint against many such, that they supply the defects of their instruments with the creations of their brains. I imagined depths beyond depths in Nature which the limited power of my lenses prohibited me from exploring. I lay awake at night constructing imaginary microscopes of immeasurable power, with which I seemed to pierce through all the envelopes of matter down to its original atom. How I cursed those imperfect mediums which necessity through ignorance compelled me to use! How I longed to discover the secret of some perfect lens whose magnifying power should be limited only by the resolvability of the object, and which at the same time should be free from spherical and chromatic aberrations, in short from all the obstacles over which the poor microscopist finds himself continually stumbling! I felt convinced that the simple microscope, composed of a single lens of such vast yet perfect power, was possible of construction. To attempt to bring the compound microscope up to such a pitch would have been commencing at the wrong end; this latter being simply a partially successful endeavor to remedy those very defects of the simple instrument, which, if conquered, would leave nothing to be desired.

It was in this mood of mind that I became a constructive microscopist. After another year passed in this new pursuit, experimenting on every imaginable substance—glass, gems, flints, crystals, artificial crystals formed of the alloy of various vitreous materials—in short, having constructed as many varieties of lenses as Argus had eyes, I found myself precisely where I started, with nothing gained save an extensive knowledge of glass-making. I was almost dead with despair. My parents were surprised at my apparent want of progress in my medical studies (I had not attended one lecture since my arrival in the city) and the expenses of my mad pursuit had been so great as to embarrass me very seriously.

I was in this frame of mind one day, experimenting in my laboratory on a small diamond—that stone, from its great refracting power, having always occupied my attention more than any other—when a young Frenchman, who lived on the floor above me, and who was in the habit of occasionally visiting me, entered the room.

I think that Jules Simon was a Jew. He had many traits of the Hebrew character: a love of jewelry, of dress, and of good living. There was something mysterious about him. He always had something to sell, and yet went into excellent society. When I say sell, I should perhaps have said peddle; for his operations were generally confined to the disposal of single articles—a picture, for instance, or a rare carving in ivory, or a pair of duelling-pistols, or the dress of a Mexican *caballero*. When I was first furnishing my rooms, he paid me a visit, which ended in my purchasing an antique silver lamp, which he assured me was a Cellini—it was handsome enough even for that—and some other knick-knacks for my sitting-room. Why Simon should pursue this petty trade I never could imagine. He apparently had plenty of money, and had the *entrée* of the best houses in the city—taking care, however, I suppose, to drive no bargains within the enchanted circle of the Upper Ten. I came at length to the conclusion that this peddling was but a mask to cover some greater object, and even went so far as to believe my young acquaintance to be implicated in the slave-trade. That, however, was none of my affair.

On the present occasion, Simon entered my room in a state of considerable excitement.

"*Ah! mon ami!*" he cried, before I could even offer him the ordinary salutation, "it has occurred to me to be the witness of the most astonishing things in the world. I promenade myself to the house of Madame—— How does the little animal—*le renard*—name himself in the Latin?"

"Vulpes," I answered.

"Ah! yes—Vulpes. I promenade myself to the house of Madame Vulpes."

"The spirit medium?"

"Yes, the great medium. Great Heavens! what a woman! I write on a slip of paper many of questions concerning affairs the most secret—affairs that conceal themselves in the abysses of my heart the most profound: and behold! by example! what occurs? This devil of a woman makes me replies the most truthful to all of them. She talks to me of things that I do not love to talk of to myself. What am I to think? I am fixed to the earth!"

"Am I to understand you, M. Simon, that this Mrs. Vulpes replied to questions secretly written by you, which questions related to events known only to yourself?"

"Ah! more than that, more than that," he answered, with an air of some alarm. "She related to me things—But," he added, after a pause, and suddenly changing his manner, "why occupy ourselves with these follies? It was all the Biology, without doubt. It goes without saying that it has not my credence.—But why are we here, *mon ami*? It has occurred to me to discover the most beautiful thing as you can imagine.—a vase with green lizards on it, composed by the great Bernard Palissy. It is in my apartment: let us mount. I go to show it to you."

I followed Simon mechanically; but my thoughts were far from Palissy and his enamelled ware, although I, like him, was seeking in the dark after a great discovery. This casual mention of the spiritualist, Madame Vulpes, set me on a new track. What if this spiritualism should be really a great fact? What if, through communication with subtiler organisms than my own, I could reach at a single bound the goal, which perhaps a life of agonizing mental toil would never enable me to attain?

While purchasing the Palissy vase from my friend Simon, I was mentally arranging a visit to Madame Vulpes.

III

The Spirit of Leeuwenhoek

Two evenings after this, thanks to an arrangement by letter and the promise of an ample fee, I found Madame Vulpes awaiting me at her residence alone. She was a coarse-featured woman, with a keen and rather cruel dark eye, and an exceedingly sensual expression about her mouth and under jaw. She received me in perfect silence, in an apartment on the ground floor, very sparely furnished. In the centre of the room, close to where Mrs. Vulpes sat, there was a common round mahogany table. If I had come for the purpose of sweeping her chimney, the woman could not have looked more indifferent to my appearance. There was no attempt to inspire the visitor with any awe. Everything bore a simple and practical aspect. This intercourse with the spiritual world was evidently as familiar an occupation with Mrs. Vulpes as eating her dinner or riding in an omnibus.

"You come for a communication, Mr. Linley?" said the medium, in a dry, business-like tone of voice.

"By appointment—yes."

"What sort of communication do you want?—a written one?"

"Yes—I wish for a written one."

"From any particular spirit?"

"Yes."

"Have you ever known this spirit on this earth?"

"Never. He died long before I was born. I wish merely to obtain from him some information which he ought to be able to give better than any other."

"Will you seat yourself at the table, Mr. Linley," said the medium, "and place your hands upon it?"

I obeyed—Mrs. Vulpes being seated opposite me, with her hands also on the table. We remained thus for about a minute and a half, when a violent succession of raps came on the table, on the back of my chair, on the floor immediately under my feet, and even on the window-panes. Mrs. Vulpes smiled composedly.

"They are very strong to-night," she remarked. "You are fortunate." She then continued, "Will the spirits communicate with this gentleman?"

Vigorous affirmative.

"Will the particular spirit he desires to speak with communicate?"

A very confused rapping followed this question.

"I know what they mean," said Mrs. Vulpes, addressing herself to me; "they wish you to write down the name of the particular spirit that you desire to converse with. Is that so?" she added, speaking to her invisible guests.

That it was so was evident from the numerous affirmatory responses. While this was going on, I tore a slip from my pocket-book, and scribbled a name under the table.

"Will this spirit communicate in writing with this gentleman?" asked the medium once more.

After a moment's pause her hand seemed to be seized with a violent tremor, shaking so forcibly that the table vibrated. She said that a spirit had seized her hand and would write. I handed her some sheets of paper that were on the table, and a pencil. The latter she held loosely in her hand, which presently began to move over the paper with a singular and seemingly involuntary motion. After a few moments had elapsed she handed me the paper, on which I found written, in a large, uncultivated hand, the words, "He is not here, but has been sent for." A pause of a minute or so now ensued, during which Mrs. Vulpes remained perfectly silent, but the raps continued at regular intervals. When the short period I mention had elapsed, the hand of the medium was again seized with its convulsive tremor, and she wrote, under this strange influence, a few words on the paper, which she handed to me. They were as follows:—

I am here. Question me.

Leeuwenhoek

I was astounded. The name was identical with that I had written beneath the table, and carefully kept concealed. Neither was it at all probable that an uncultivated woman like Mrs. Vulpes should know even the name of the great father of microscopics. It may have been Biology; but this theory was soon doomed to be destroyed. I wrote on my slip—still concealing it from Mrs. Vulpes—a series of questions, which, to avoid tediousness, I shall place with the responses in the order in which they occurred.

I.—Can the microscope be brought to perfection?

SPIRIT.—Yes.

I.—Am I destined to accomplish this great task?

SPIRIT.—You are.

I.—I wish to know how to proceed to attain this end. For the love which you bear to science, help me!

SPIRIT.—A diamond of one hundred and forty carats, submitted to electromagnetic currents for a long period, will experience a rearrangement of its atoms *inter se*, and from that stone you will form the universal lens.

I.—Will great discoveries result from the use of such a lens?

SPIRIT.—So great, that all that has gone before is as nothing.

I.—But the refractive power of the diamond is so immense, that the image will be formed within the lens. How is that difficulty to be surmounted?

SPIRIT.—Pierce the lens through its axis, and the difficulty is obviated. The image will be formed in the pierced space, which will itself serve as a tube to look through. Now I am called. Good night!

I cannot at all describe the effect that these extraordinary communications had upon me. I felt completely bewildered. No biological theory could account for the *discovery* of the lens. The medium might, by means of biological *rapport* with my mind, have gone so far as to read my questions, and reply to them coherently. But Biology could not enable her to discover that magnetic currents would so alter the crystals of the diamond as to remedy its previous defects, and admit of its being polished into a perfect lens. Some such theory may have passed through my head, it is true; but if so, I had forgotten it. In my excited condition of mind there was no course left but to become a convert, and it was in a state of the most painful nervous exaltation that I left the medium's house that evening. She accompanied me to the door, hoping that I was satisfied. The raps followed us as we went through the hall, sounding on the balusters, the flooring, and even the lintels of the door. I hastily expressed my satisfaction, and escaped hurriedly into the cool night air. I walked home with but one thought possessing me—how to obtain a diamond of the immense size required. My entire means multiplied a hundred times over would have been inadequate to its purchase. Besides, such stones are rare, and become historical. I could find such only in the regalia of Eastern or European monarchs.

IV

The Eye of Morning

There was a light in Simon's room as I entered my house. A vague impulse urged me to visit him. As I opened the door of his sitting-room unannounced, he was bending, with his back towards me, over a carvel lamp, apparently engaged in minutely examining some object which he held in his hands. As I entered, he started suddenly, thrust his hand into his breast pocket, and turned to me with a face crimson with confusion.

"What!" I cried, "poring over the miniature of some fair lady? Well, don't blush so much; I won't ask to see it."

Simon laughed awkwardly enough, but made none of the negative protestations usual on such occasions. He asked me to take a seat.

"Simon," said I, "I have just come from Madame Vulpes."

This time Simon turned as white as a sheet, and seemed stupefied, as if a sudden electric shock had smitten him. He babbled some incoherent words, and went hastily to a small closet where he usually kept his liquors. Although astonished at his emotion, I was too preoccupied with my own idea to pay much attention to anything else.

"You say truly when you call Madame Vulpes a devil of a woman," I continued. "Simon, she told me wonderful things tonight, or rather was the means of telling me wonderful things. Ah! if I could only get a diamond that weighed one hundred and forty carats!"

Scarcely had the sigh with which I uttered this desire died upon my lips, when Simon, with the aspect of a wild beast, glared at me savagely, and rushing to the mantel-piece, where some foreign weapons hung on the wall, caught up a Malay creese, and brandished it furiously before him.

"No!" he cried in French, into which he always broke when excited. "No! you shall not have it! You are perfidious! You have consulted with that demon, and desire my treasure! But I will die first! Me! I am brave! You cannot make me fear!"

All this, uttered in a loud voice trembling with excitement, astounded me. I saw at a glance that I had accidentally trodden upon the edges of Simon's secret, whatever it was. It was necessary to reassure him.

"My dear Simon," I said, "I am entirely at a loss to know what you mean. I went to Madame Vulpes to consult with her on a scientific problem, to the solution of which I discovered that a diamond of the size I just mentioned was necessary. You were never alluded to during the evening, nor, so far as I was concerned, even thought of. What can be the meaning of this outburst? If you happen to have a set of valuable diamonds in your possession, you need fear nothing from me. The diamond which I require you could not possess; or if you did possess it, you would not be living here."

Something in my tone must have completely reassured him, for his expression immediately changed to a sort of constrained merriment, combined, however, with a certain suspicious attention to my movements. He laughed, and said that I must bear with him; that he was at certain moments subject to a species of vertigo, which betrayed itself in incoherent speeches, and that the attacks passed off as rapidly as they came. He put his weapon aside while making this explanation, and endeavored, with some success, to assume a more cheerful air.

All this did not impose on me in the least. I was too much accustomed to analytical labors to be baffled by so flimsy a veil. I determined to probe the mystery to the bottom.

"Simon," I said, gayly, "let us forget all this over a bottle of Burgundy. I have a case of Lausseure's *Clos Vougeot* down-stairs, fragrant with the odors and ruddy with the sunlight of the Côte d'Or. Let us have up a couple of bottles. What say you?"

"With all my heart," answered Simon, smilingly.

I produced the wine and we seated ourselves to drink. It was of a famous vintage, that of 1848, a year when war and wine throve together,— and its pure, but powerful juice seemed to impart renewed vitality to the system. By the time we had half finished the second bottle, Simon's hand, which I knew was a weak one, had begun to yield, while I remained calm as ever, only that every draught seemed to send a flush of vigor through my limbs. Simon's utterance became more and more indistinct. He took to singing French *chansons* of a not very moral tendency. I rose suddenly from the table just at the conclusion of one of those incoherent verses, and fixing my eyes on him with a quiet smile, said:

"Simon, I have deceived you. I learned your secret this evening. You may as well be frank with me. Mrs. Vulpes, or rather, one of her spirits, told me all."

He started with horror. His intoxication seemed for the moment to fade away, and he made a movement towards the weapon that he had a short time before laid down. I stopped him with my hand.

"Monster!" he cried, passionately, "I am ruined! What shall I do? You shall never have it! I swear by my mother!"

"I don't want it," I said; "rest secure, but be frank with me. Tell me all about it."

The drunkenness began to return. He protested with maudlin earnestness that I was entirely mistaken—that I was intoxicated; then asked me to swear eternal secrecy, and promised to disclose the mystery to me. I pledged myself, of course, to all. With an uneasy look in his eyes, and hands unsteady with drink and nervousness, he drew a small case from his breast and opened it. Heavens! How the mild lamp-light was shivered into a thousand prismatic arrows, as it fell upon a vast rose-diamond that glittered in the case! I was no judge of diamonds, but I saw at a glance that this was a gem of rare size and purity. I looked at Simon with wonder, and—must I confess it?—with envy. How could he have obtained this treasure? In reply to my questions, I could just gather from his drunken statements (of which, I fancy, half the incoherence was affected) that he had been superintending a gang of slaves engaged in diamond-washing in Brazil; that he had seen one of them secrete a diamond, but, instead of informing his employers, had quietly watched the negro until he saw him bury his treasure; that he had dug it up, and fled with it, but that as yet he was afraid to attempt to dispose of it publicly—so valuable a gem being almost certain to attract too much attention to its owner's antecedents,—and he had not been able to discover any of those obscure channels by which such matters are conveyed away safely. He added, that, in accordance with Oriental practice, he had named his diamond by the fanciful title of "The Eye of Morning."

While Simon was relating this to me, I regarded the great diamond attentively. Never had I beheld anything so beautiful. All the glories of light, ever imagined or described, seemed to pulsate in its crystalline chambers. Its weight, as I learned from Simon, was exactly one hundred and forty carats. Here was an amazing coincidence. The hand of Destiny seemed in it. On the very evening when the spirit of Leeuwenhoek communicates to me the great secret of the microscope, the priceless means which he directs me to employ start up within my easy reach! I determined, with the most perfect deliberation, to possess myself of Simon's diamond.

I sat opposite him while he nodded over his glass, and calmly revolved the whole affair. I did not for an instant contemplate so foolish an act as a common theft, which would of course be discovered, or at least necessitate flight and concealment, all of which must interfere with my scientific plans. There was but one step to be taken—to kill Simon. After all, what was the life of a little peddling Jew, in comparison with the interests of science? Human beings are taken every day from the condemned prisons to be experimented on by surgeons. This man, Simon, was by his own confession a criminal, a robber, and I believed on my soul a murderer. He deserved death quite as much as any felon condemned by the laws; why should I not, like government, contrive that his punishment should contribute to the progress of human knowledge?

The means for accomplishing everything I desired lay within my reach. There stood upon the mantel-piece a bottle half full of French laudanum. Simon was so occupied with his diamond, which I had just restored to him, that it was an affair of no difficulty to drug his glass. In a quarter of an hour he was in a profound sleep.

I now opened his waistcoat, took the diamond from the inner pocket in which he had placed it, and removed him to the bed, on which I laid him so that his feet hung down over the edge. I had possessed myself of the Malay creese, which I held in my right hand, while with the other I discovered as accurately as I could by pulsation the exact locality of the heart. It was essential that all the aspects of his death should lead to the surmise of self-murder. I calculated the exact angle at which it was probable that the weapon, if levelled by Simon's own hand, would enter his breast; then with one powerful blow I thrust it up to the hilt in the very spot which I desired to penetrate. A convulsive thrill ran through Simon's limbs. I heard a smothered sound issue from his throat, precisely like the bursting of a large air-bubble, sent up by a diver, when it reaches the surface of the water; he turned half round on his side, and as if to assist my plans more effectually, his right hand, moved by some mere spasmodic impulse, clasped the handle of the creese, which it remained holding with extraordinary muscular tenacity. Beyond this there was no apparent struggle. The laudanum, I presume, paralyzed the usual nervous action. He must have died instantaneously.

There was yet something to be done. To make it certain that all suspicion of the act should be diverted from any inhabitant of the house to Simon himself, it was necessary that the door should be found in the morning *locked on the inside.* How to do this, and afterwards escape myself? Not by the window; that was a physical impossibility. Besides, I was determined that the windows *also* should be found bolted. The solution was simple enough. I descended softly to my own room for a peculiar instrument which I had used for holding small slippery substances, such as minute spheres of glass, etc. This instrument was nothing more than a long slender hand-vice, with a very powerful grip, and a considerable leverage, which last was accidentally owing to the shape of the handle. Nothing was simpler than, when the key was in the lock, to seize the end of its stem in this vice, through the keyhole, from the outside, and so lock the door. Previously, however, to doing this, I burned a number of papers on Simon's hearth. Suicides almost always burn papers before they destroy themselves. I also emptied some more laudanum into Simon's glass—having first removed from it all traces of wine—cleaned the other wine-glass, and brought the bottles away with me. If traces of two persons drinking had been found in the room, the question naturally would have arisen, Who was the second? Besides, the wine-bottles might have been identified as belonging to me. The laudanum I poured out to account for its presence in his stomach, in case of a *post-mortem* examination. The theory naturally would be, that he first intended to poison himself, but, after swallowing a little of the drug, was either disgusted with its taste, or changed his mind from other motives, and chose the dagger. These arrangements made, I walked out, leaving the gas burning, locked the door with my vice, and went to bed.

Simon's death was not discovered until nearly three in the afternoon. The servant, astonished at seeing the gas burning—the light streaming on the dark landing from under the door—peeped through the keyhole and saw Simon on the bed. She gave the alarm. The door was burst open, and the neighborhood was in a fever of excitement.

Every one in the house was arrested, myself included. There was an inquest; but no clue to his death, beyond that of suicide, could be obtained. Curiously enough, he had made several speeches to his friends the preceding week, that seemed to point to self-destruction. One gentleman swore that Simon had said in his presence that "he was tired of life." His landlord affirmed, that Simon, when paying him his last month's rent, remarked that "he would not pay him rent much longer." All the other evidence corresponded—the door locked inside, the position of the corpse, the burnt papers. As I anticipated, no one knew of the possession of the diamond by Simon, so that no motive was suggested for his murder. The jury, after a prolonged examination, brought in the usual verdict, and the neighborhood once more settled down into its accustomed quiet.

V

Animula

The three months succeeding Simon's catastrophe I devoted night and day to my diamond lens. I had constructed a vast galvanic battery, composed of nearly two thousand pairs of plates—a higher power I dared not use, lest the diamond should be calcined. By means of this enormous engine I was enabled to send a powerful current of electricity continually through my great diamond, which it seemed to me gained in lustre every day. At the expiration of a month I commenced the grinding and polishing of the lens, a work of intense toil and exquisite delicacy. The great density of the stone, and the care required to be taken with the curvatures of the surfaces of the lens, rendered the labor the severest and most harassing that I had yet undergone.

At last the eventful moment came; the lens was completed. I stood trembling on the threshold of new worlds. I had the realization of Alexander's famous wish before me. The lens lay on the table, ready to be placed upon its platform. My hand fairly shook as I enveloped a drop of water with a thin coating of oil of turpentine, preparatory to its examination—a process necessary in order to prevent the rapid evaporation of the water. I now placed the drop on a thin slip of glass under the lens, and throwing upon it, by the combined aid of a prism and a mirror, a powerful stream of light, I approached my eye to the minute hole drilled through the axis of the lens. For an instant I saw nothing save what seemed to be an illuminated chaos, a vast luminous abyss. A pure white light, cloudless and serene, and seemingly limitless as space itself, was my first impression. Gently, and with the greatest care, I depressed the lens a few hairs' breadths. The wondrous illumination still continued, but as the lens approached the object, a scene of indescribable beauty was unfolded to my view.

I seemed to gaze upon a vast space, the limits of which extended far beyond my vision. An atmosphere of magical luminousness permeated the entire field of view. I was amazed to see no trace of animalculous life. Not a living thing, apparently, inhabited that dazzling expanse. I comprehended instantly, that, by the wondrous power of my lens, I had penetrated beyond the grosser particles of aqueous matter, beyond the realms of Iufusoria and Protozoa, down to the original gaseous globule, into whose luminous interior I was gazing, as into an almost boundless dome filled with a supernatural radiance.

It was, however, no brilliant void into which I looked. On every side I beheld beautiful inorganic forms, of unknown texture, and colored with the most enchanting hues. These forms presented the appearance of what might be called, for want of a more specific definition, foliated clouds of the highest rarity; that is, they undulated and broke into vegetable formations, and were tinged with splendors compared with which the gilding of our autumn woodlands is as dross compared with gold. Far away into the illimitable distance stretched long avenues of these gaseous forests, dimly transparent, and painted with prismatic hues of unimaginable brilliancy. The pendant branches waved along the fluid glades until every vista seemed to break through half-lucent ranks of many-colored drooping silken pennons. What seemed to be either fruits or flowers, pied with a thousand hues lustrous and ever varying, bubbled from the crowns of this fairy foliage. No hills, no lakes, no rivers, no forms animate or inanimate were to be seen, save those vast auroral copses that floated serenely in the luminous stillness, with leaves and fruits and flowers gleaming with unknown fires, unrealizable by mere imagination.

How strange, I thought, that this sphere should be thus condemned to solitude! I had hoped, at least, to discover some new form of animal life—perhaps of a lower class than any with which we are at present acquainted—but still, some living organism. I find my newly discovered world, if I may so speak, a beautiful chromatic desert.

While I was speculating on the singular arrangements of the internal economy of Nature, with which she so frequently splinters into atoms our most compact theories, I thought I beheld a form moving slowly through the glades of one of the prismatic forests. I looked more attentively, and found that I was not mistaken. Words cannot depict the anxiety with which I awaited the nearer approach of this mysterious object. Was it merely some inanimate substance, held in suspense in the attenuated atmosphere of the globule? or was it an animal endowed with vitality and motion? It approached, flitting behind the gauzy, colored veils of cloud-foliage, for seconds dimly revealed, then vanishing. At last the violet pennons that trailed nearest to me vibrated; they were gently pushed aside, and the Form floated out into the broad light.

It was a female human shape. When I say "human," I mean it possessed the outlines of humanity—but there the analogy ends. Its adorable beauty lifted it illimitable heights beyond the loveliest daughter of Adam.

I cannot, I dare not, attempt to inventory the charms of this divine revelation of perfect beauty. Those eyes of mystic violet, dewy and serene, evade my words. Her long lustrous hair following her glorious head in a golden wake, like the track sown in heaven by a falling star, seems to quench my most burning phrases with its splendors. If all the bees of Hybla nestled upon my lips, they would still sing but hoarsely the wondrous harmonies of outline that enclosed her form.

She swept out from between the rainbow-curtains of the cloud-trees into the broad sea of light that lay beyond. Her motions were those of some graceful Naiad, cleaving, by a mere effort of her will, the clear, unruffled waters that fill the chambers of the sea. She floated forth with the serene grace of a frail bubble ascending through the still atmosphere of a June day. The perfect roundness of her limbs formed suave and enchanting curves. It was like listening to the most spiritual symphony of Beethoven the divine, to watch the harmonious flow of lines. This, indeed, was a pleasure cheaply purchased at any price. What cared I, if I had waded to the portal of this wonder through another's blood? I would have given my own to enjoy one such moment of intoxication and delight.

Breathless with gazing on this lovely wonder, and forgetful for an instant of everything save her presence, I withdrew my eye from the microscope eagerly—alas! As my gaze fell on the thin slide that lay beneath my instrument, the bright light from mirror and from prism sparkled on a colorless drop of water! There, in that tiny bead of dew, this beautiful being was forever imprisoned. The planet Neptune was not more distant from me than she. I hastened once more to apply my eye to the microscope.

Animula (let me now call her by that dear name which I subsequently bestowed on her) had changed her position. She had again approached the wondrous forest, and was gazing earnestly upwards. Presently one of the trees—as I must call them—unfolded a long ciliary process, with which it seized one of the gleaming fruits that glittered on its summit, and sweeping slowly down, held it within reach of Animula. The sylph took it in her delicate hand, and began to eat. My attention was so entirely absorbed by her, that I could not apply myself to the task of determining whether this singular plant was or was not instinct with volition.

I watched her, as she made her repast, with the most profound attention. The suppleness of her motions sent a thrill of delight through my frame; my heart beat madly as she turned her beautiful eyes in the direction of the spot in which I stood. What would I not have given to have had the power to precipitate myself into that luminous ocean, and float with her through those groves of purple and gold! While I was thus breathlessly following her every movement, she suddenly started, seemed to listen for a moment, and then cleaving the brilliant ether in which she was floating, like a flash of light, pierced through the opaline forest, and disappeared.

Instantly a series of the most singular sensations attacked me. It seemed as if I had suddenly gone blind. The luminous sphere was still before me, but my daylight had vanished. What caused this sudden disappearance? Had she a lover, or a husband? Yes, that was the solution! Some signal from a happy fellow-being had vibrated through the avenues of the forest, and she had obeyed the summons.

The agony of my sensations, as I arrived at this conclusion, startled me. I tried to reject the conviction that my reason forced upon me. I battled against the fatal conclusion,—but in vain. It was so. I had no escape from it. I loved an animalcule!

It is true, that, thanks to the marvelous power of my microscope, she appeared of human proportions. Instead of presenting the revolting aspect of the coarser creatures, that live and struggle and die, in the more easily resolvable portions of the water-drop, she was fair and delicate and of surpassing beauty. But of what account was all that? Every time that my eye was withdrawn from the instrument, it fell on a miserable drop of water, within which, I must be content to know, dwelt all that could make my life lovely.

Could she but see me once! Could I for one moment pierce the mystical walls that so inexorably rose to separate us, and whisper all that filled my soul, I might consent to be satisfied for the rest of my life with the knowledge of her remote sympathy. It would be something to have established even the faintest personal link to bind us together—to know that at times, when roaming through those enchanted glades, she might think of the wonderful stranger, who had broken the monotony of her life with his presence, and left a gentle memory in her heart!

But it could not be. No invention, of which human intellect was capable, could break down the barriers that Nature had erected. I might feast my soul upon her wondrous beauty, yet she must always remain ignorant of the adoring eyes that day and night gazed upon her, and, even when closed, beheld her in dreams. With a bitter cry of anguish I fled from the room, and, flinging myself on my bed, sobbed myself to sleep like a child.

VI

The Spilling of the Cup

I arose the next morning almost at daybreak, and rushed to my microscope. I trembled as I sought the luminous world in miniature that contained my all. Animula was there. I had left the gas-lamp, surrounded by its moderators, burning, when I went to bed the night before. I found the sylph bathing, as it were, with an expression of pleasure animating her features, in the brilliant light which surrounded her. She tossed her lustrous golden hair over her shoulders with innocent coquetry. She lay at full length in the transparent medium, in which she supported herself with ease, and gambolled with the enchanting grace that the Nymph Salmacis might have exhibited when she sought to conquer the modest Hermaphroditus. I tried an experiment to satisfy myself if her powers of reflection were developed. I lessened the lamp-light considerably. By the dim light that remained, I could see an expression of pain flit across her face. She looked upwards suddenly, and her brows contracted. I flooded the stage of the microscope again with a full stream of light, and her whole expression changed. She sprang forward like some substance deprived of all weight. Her eyes sparkled, and her lips moved. Ah! if science had only the means of conducting and reduplicating sounds, as it does the rays of light, what carols of happiness would then have entranced my ears! what jubilant hymns to Adonaïs would have thrilled the illumined air!

I now comprehended how it was that the Count de Gabalis peopled his mystic world with sylphs—beautiful beings whose breath of life was lambent fire, and who sported forever in regions of purest ether and purest light. The Rosicrucian had anticipated the wonder that I had practically realized.

How long this worship of my strange divinity went on thus I scarcely know. I lost all note of time. All day from early dawn, and far into the night, I was to be found peering through that wonderful lens. I saw no one, went nowhere, and scarce allowed myself sufficient time for my meals. My whole life was absorbed in contemplation as rapt as that of any of the Romish saints. Every hour that I gazed upon the divine form strengthened my passion—a passion that was always overshadowed by the maddening conviction, that, although I could gaze on her at will, she never, never could behold me!

At length I grew so pale and emaciated, from want of rest, and continual brooding over my insane love and its cruel conditions, that I determined to make some effort to wean myself from it. "Come," I said, "this is at best but a fantasy. Your imagination has bestowed on Animula charms which in reality she does not possess. Seclusion from female society has produced this morbid condition of mind. Compare her with the beautiful women of your own world, and this false enchantment will vanish."

I looked over the newspapers by chance. There I beheld the advertisement of a celebrated *danseuse* who appeared nightly at Niblo's. The Signorina Caradolce had the reputation of being the most beautiful as well as the most graceful woman in the world. I instantly dressed and went to the theatre.

The curtain drew up. The usual semicircle of fairies in white muslin were standing on the right toe around the enamelled flower-bank, of green canvas, on which the belated prince was sleeping. Suddenly a flute is heard. The fairies start. The trees open, the fairies all stand on the left toe, and the queen enters. It was the Signorina. She bounded forward amid thunders of applause, and lighting on one foot remained poised in air. Heavens! was this the great enchantress that had drawn monarchs at her chariotwheels? Those heavy muscular limbs, those thick ankles, those cavernous eyes, that stereotyped smile, those crudely painted cheeks! Where were the vermeil blooms, the liquid expressive eyes, the harmonious limbs of Animula?

The Signorina danced. What gross, discordant movements! The play of her limbs was all false and artificial. Her bounds were painful athletic efforts; her poses were angular and distressed the eye. I could bear it no longer; with an exclamation of disgust that drew every eye upon me, I rose from my seat in the very middle of the Signorina's *pas-de-fascination*, and abruptly quitted the house.

I hastened home to feast my eyes once more on the lovely form of my sylph. I felt that henceforth to combat this passion would be impossible. I applied my eye to the lens. Animula was there—but what could have happened? Some terrible change seemed to have taken place during my absence. Some secret grief seemed to cloud the lovely features of her I gazed upon. Her face had grown thin and haggard; her limbs trailed heavily; the wondrous lustre of her golden hair had faded. She was ill!—ill, and I could not assist her! I believe at that moment I would have gladly forfeited all claims to my human birthright, if I could only have been dwarfed to the size of an animalcule, and permitted to console her from whom fate had forever divided me.

I racked my brain for the solution of this mystery. What was it that afflicted the sylph? She seemed to suffer intense pain. Her features contracted, and she even writhed, as if with some internal agony. The wondrous forests appeared also to have lost half their beauty. Their hues were dim and in some places faded away altogether. I watched Animula for hours with a breaking heart, and she seemed absolutely to wither away under my very eye. Suddenly I remembered that I had not looked at the water-drop for several days. In fact, I hated to see it; for it reminded me of the natural barrier between Animula and myself. I hurriedly looked down on the stage of the microscope. The slide was still there,—but, great heavens! the water-drop had vanished! The awful truth burst upon me; it had evaporated, until it had become so minute as to be invisible to the naked eye; I had been gazing on its last atom, the one that contained Animula— and she was dying!

I rushed again to the front of the lens, and looked through. Alas! the last agony had seized her. The rainbow-hued forests had all melted away, and Animula lay struggling feebly in what seemed to be a spot of dim light. Ah! the sight was horrible: the limbs once so round and lovely shrivelling up into nothings; the eyes—those eyes that shone like heaven—being quenched into black dust; the lustrous golden hair now lank and discolored. The last throe came. I beheld that final struggle of the blackening form—and I fainted.

When I awoke out of a trance of many hours, I found myself lying amid the wreck of my instrument, myself as shattered in mind and body as it. I crawled feebly to my bed, from which I did not rise for months.

They say now that I am mad; but they are mistaken. I am poor, for I have neither the heart nor the will to work; all my money is spent, and I live on charity. Young men's associations that love a joke invite me to lecture on Optics before them, for which they pay me, and laugh at me while I lecture. "Linley, the mad microscopist," is the name I go by. I suppose that I talk incoherently while I lecture. Who could talk sense when his brain is haunted by such ghastly memories, while ever and anon among the shapes of death I behold the radiant form of my lost Animula!

HER STORY

Harriet Prescott Spofford

Wellnigh the worst of it all is the mystery.

If it was true, that accounts for my being here. If it wasn't true, then the best thing they could do with me was to bring me here. Then, too, if it was true, they would save themselves by hurrying me away; and if it wasn't true— You see, just as all roads lead to Rome, all roads led me to this Retreat. If it was true, it was enough to craze me; and if it wasn't true, I was already crazed. And there it is! I can't make out, sometimes, whether I am really beside myself or not; for it seems that whether I was crazed or sane, if it was true, they would naturally put me out of sight and hearing—bury me alive, as they have done, in this Retreat. They? Well, no—he. She stayed at home, I hear. If she had come with us, doubtless I should have found reason enough to say to the physician at once that she was the mad woman, not I—she, who, for the sake of her own brief pleasure, could make a whole after-life of misery for three of us. She— Oh no, don't rise, don't go. I am quite myself, I am perfectly calm. Mad! There was never a drop of crazy blood in the Ridgleys or the Bruces, or any of the generations behind them, and why should it suddenly break out like a smothered fire in me? That is one of the things that puzzle me—why should it come to light all at once in me if it wasn't true?

Now, I am not going to be incoherent. It was too kind in you to be at such trouble to come and see me in this prison, this grave. I will not cry out once: I will just tell you the story of it all exactly as it was, and you shall judge. If I can, that is—oh, if I can! For sometimes, when I think of it, it seems as if Heaven itself would fail to take my part if I did not lift my own voice. And I cry, and I tear my hair and my flesh, till I know my anguish weighs down their joy, and the little scale that holds that joy flies up under the scorching of the sun, and God sees the festering thing for what it is. Ah, it is not injured reason that cries out in that way: it is a breaking heart!

How cool your hand is, how pleasant your face is, how good it is to see you! Don't be afraid of me: I am as much myself, I tell you, as you are. What an absurdity! Certainly any one who heard me make such a speech would think I was insane and without benefit of clergy. To ask you not to be afraid of me because I am myself!—isn't it what they call a vicious circle? And then to cap the climax by adding that I am as much myself as you are myself! But no matter—you know better. Did you say it was ten years? Yes, I knew it was as much as that—oh, it seems a hundred years! But we hardly show it: your hair is still the same as when we were at school; and mine— Look at this lock—I cannot understand why it is only sprinkled here and there: it ought to be white as the driven snow. My babies are almost grown women, Elizabeth. How could he do without me all this time? Hush now! I am not going to be disturbed at all; only that color of your hair puts me so in mind of his: perhaps there was just one trifle more of gold in his. Do you remember that lock that used to fall over his forehead and he always tossed back so impatiently? I used to think that the golden Apollo of Rhodes had just such massive, splendid locks of hair as that; but I never told him, I never had the face to praise him: she had. She could exclaim how like ivory the forehead was—that great wide forehead—how that keen aquiline was to be found in the portrait of the Spencer of two hundred years ago. She could tell of the proud lip, of the fire burning in the hazel eye: she knew how, by a silent flattery, as she shrank away and looked up at him, to admire his haughty stature, and make him feel the strength and glory of his manhood and the delicacy of her womanhood.

She was a little thing—a little thing, but wondrous fair. Fair, did I say? No: she was dark as an Egyptian, but such perfect features, such rich and splendid color, such great soft eyes—so soft, so black—so superb a smile; and then such hair! When she let it down, the backward curling ends lay on the ground and she stood on them, or the children lifted them and carried them behind her as pages carry a queen's train. If I had my two hands twisted in that hair! Oh, how I hate that hair! It would make as good a bowstring for her neck as ever any Carthaginian woman's made. Ah, that is too wicked! I am sure you think so. But living all these lonesome years as I have done seems to double back one's sinfulness upon one's self. Because one is sane it does not follow that one is a saint. And when I think of my innocent babies playing with that hair that once I saw him lift and pass across his lips! But I will not think of it!

Well, well! I was a pleasant thing to look at myself once on a time, you know, Elizabeth. He used to tell me so: those were his very words. I was tall and slender, and if my skin was pale it was clear, and the lashes of my gray eyes were black as shadows; but now those eyes are only the color of tears.

I never told any one anything about it—I never could. It was so deep down in my heart, that love I had for him: it slept there so dark and still and full, for he was all I had in the world. I was alone, an orphan—if not friendless, yet quite dependent. I see you remember it all. I did not even sit in the pew with my cousin's family, that was so full, but down in one beneath the gallery, you know. And altogether life was a thing to me that hardly seemed worth the living. I went to church one Sunday, I recollect, idly and dreamingly as usual. I did not look off my book till a voice filled my ear—a strange new voice, a deep sweet voice, that invited you and yet commanded you—a voice whose sound divided the core of my heart, and sent thrills that were half joy, half pain, coursing through me. And then I looked up and saw him at the desk. He was reading the first lesson: "Fear not, for I have redeemed thee, I have called thee by thy name: thou art mine." And I saw the bright hair, the bright upturned face, the white surplice, and I said to myself, It is a vision, it is an angel; and I cast down my eyes. But the voice went on, and when I looked again he was still there. Then I bethought me that it must be the one who was coming to take the place of our superannuated rector—the last of a fine line, they had been saying the day before, who, instead of finding his pleasure otherwise, had taken all his wealth and prestige into the Church.

Why will a trifle melt you so—a strain of music, a color in the sky, a perfume? Have you never leaned from the window at evening, and had the scent of a flower float by and fill you with as keen a sorrow as if it had been disaster touching you? Long ago, I mean—we never lean from any windows here. I don't know how, but it was in that same invisible way that this voice melted me; and when I heard it saying, "But thou hast not called upon me, O Jacob, but thou hast been weary of me, O Israel," I was fairly crying. Oh, nervous tears, I dare say. The doctor here would tell you so, at any rate. And that is what I complain of here: they give a physiological reason for every emotion—they could give you a chemical formula for your

very soul, I have no doubt. Well, perhaps they were nervous tears, for certainly there was nothing to cry for, and the mood went as suddenly as it
came—changed to a sort of exaltation, I suppose—and when they sang
the psalm, and he had swept in, in his black gown, and had mounted the
pulpit stairs, and was resting that fair head on the big Bible in his silent
prayer, I too was singing—singing like one possessed:

> Awake, my glory; harp and lute,
> No longer let your strains be mute;
> And I, my tuneful part to take,
> Will with the early dawn awake!

And as he rose I saw him searching for the voice unconsciously, and our
eyes met. Oh, it was a fresh young voice, let it be mine or whose. I can hear
it now as if it were somebody else' singing. Ah, ah, it has been silent so
many years! Does it make you smile to hear me pity myself? It is not myself I am pitying: it is that fresh young girl that loved so. But it used to re-
joice me to think that I loved him before I laid eyes on him.

He came to my cousin's in the week—not to see Sylvia or to see Laura:
he talked of church-music with my cousin, and then crossed the room and
sat down by me. I remember how I grew cold and trembled—how glad,
how shy I was; and then he took me into the music-room to sing; and at
first Sylvia sang with us, but by and by we sang alone—I sang alone. He
brought me yellow old church music, written in quaint characters: he said
those characters, those old square breves, were a text guarding secrets of
enchantment as much as the text of Merlin's book did; and so we used to
find it. Once he brought a copy of an old Roman hymn, written only in
the Roman letters: he said it was a hymn which the ancients sang to Maia,
the mother-earth, and which the Church fathers adopted, singing it stealthily in the hidden places of the Catacombs; and together we translated it
into tones. A rude but majestic thing it was.

And once— The sunshine was falling all about us in the bright lonely
music-room, and the shadows of the rose leaves at the window were dancing over us. I had been singing the Gloria while he walked up and down
the room, and he came up behind me: he stooped and kissed me on the
mouth. And after that there was no more singing, for, lovely as the singing
was, the love was lovelier yet. Why do I complain of such a hell as this is
now? I had my heaven once—oh, I had my heaven once! And as for the
other, perhaps I deserve it all, for I saw God only through him: it was he

that waked me up to worship. I had no faith but Spencer's faith: if he had been a heathen, I should have been the same, and creeds and systems might have perished for me had he only been spared from the wreck. And he had loved me from the first moment that his eyes met mine. "When I looked at you," he said, "singing that Easter hymn that day, I felt as I do when I look at the evening star leaning out of the clear sunset lustre: there is something in your face as pure, as remote, as shining. It will always be there," he said, "though you should live a hundred years." He little knew, he little knew!

But he loved me then—oh yes, I never doubted that. There were no happier lovers trod the earth. We took our pleasure as lovers do: we walked in the fields; we sat on the river's side; together we visited the poor and sick; he read me the passages he liked best in his writing from week to week; he brought me the verse from which he meant to preach, and up in the organ-loft I improvised to him the thoughts that it inspired in me. I did that timidly indeed: I could not think my thoughts were worth his hearing till I forgot myself, and only thought of him and the glory I would have revealed to him, and then the great clustering chords and the full music of the diapason swept out beneath my hands—swept along the aisles and swelled up the raftered roof as if they would find the stars, and sunset and twilight stole around us there as we sat still in the succeeding silence. I was happy: I was humble too. I wondered why I had been chosen for such a blest and sacred lot. It seemed *that* to be allowed to be the minister of one delight to him. I had a little print of the angel of the Lord appearing to Mary with the lily of annunciation in his hand, and I thought— I dare not tell you what I thought. I made an idol of my piece of clay.

When the leaves had turned we were married, and he took me home. Ah, what a happy home it was! Luxury and beauty filled it. When I first went into it and left the chill October night without, fires blazed upon the hearths; flowers bloomed in every room; a marble Eros held a light up, searching for his Psyche. "Our love has found its soul," said he. He led me to the music-room—a temple in itself, for its rounded ceiling towered to the height of the house. There were golden organ-pipes and banks of keys fit for St. Cecilia's hand; there were all the delightful outlines of violin and piccolo and horn for any comers who knew how to use them; there was a pianoforte near the door for me—one such as I had never touched before; and there were cases on all sides filled with the rarest musical works. The floor was bare and inlaid; the windows were latticed in stained glass, so that no common light of day ever filtered through, but light bluer than the sky, gold as the dawn, purple as the night; and then there were vast embowering chairs, in any of which he could hide himself away while I made my incantation, as he sometimes called it, of the great spirits of song. As I tried the piano that night he tuned the old Amati which he now and then played upon himself, and together we improvised our own epithalamium. It was the violin that took the strong assuring part with strains of piercing sweetness, and the music of the piano flowed along in a soft cantabile of undersong. It seemed to me as if his part was like the flight of some white and strong-winged bird above a sunny brook.

But he had hardly created this place for the love of me alone. He adored music as a regenerator; he meant to use it so among his people: here were to be pursued those labors which should work miracles when produced in the open church. For he was building a church with the half of his fortune—a church full of restoration of the old and creation of the new: the walls within were to be a frosty tracery of vines running to break into the gigantic passion-flower that formed the rose-window; the lectern was a golden globe upon a tripod, clasped by a silver dove holding on outstretched wings the book.

I have feared, since I have been here, that Spencer's piety was less piety than partisanship: I have doubted if faith was so much alive in him as the love of a great perfect system, and the pride in it I know he always felt. But I never thought about it then: I believed in him as I would have believed in an apostle. So stone by stone the church went up, and stone by stone our lives followed it—lives of such peace, such bliss! Then fresh hopes came into it—sweet trembling hopes; and by and by our first child was born. And if I had been happy before, what was I then? There are some compensations in this world: such happiness ought not to come twice as there was in that moment when I lay, painless and at peace, with the little cheek nestled beside my own, while he bent above us both, proud and glad and tender. It was a dear little baby—so fair, so bright! and when she could walk she could sing. Her little sister sang earlier yet; and what music their two shrill little voices made as they sat in their little chairs together at twilight before the fire, their curls glistening and their red shoes glistening, while they sang the evening hymn, Spencer on one side of the hearth and I upon the other! Sometimes we let the dear things sit up for a later hour in the music-room—for many a canticle we tried and practiced there that hushed hearts and awed them when the choir gave them on succeeding Sundays—

and always afterward I heard them singing in their sleep, just as a bird stirs in his nest and sings his stave in the night. Oh, we were happy then; and it was then she came.

She was the step-child of his uncle, and had a small fortune of her own, and Spencer had been left her guardian; and so she was to live with us—at any rate, for a while. I dreaded her coming. I did not want the intrusion; I did not like the things I heard about her, I knew she would be a discord in our harmony. But Spencer, who had only seen her once in her childhood, had been told by some one who traveled in Europe with her that she was delightful and had a rare intelligence. She was one of those women often delightful to men indeed, but whom other women—by virtue of their own kindred instincts, it may be, perhaps by virtue of temptations overcome— see through and know for what they are. But she had her own way of charming: she was the being of infinite variety—to-day glad, to-morrow sad, freakish, and always exciting you by curiosity as to her next caprice, and so moodish that after a season of the lowering weather of one of her dull humors you were ready to sacrifice something for the sake of the sun- shine that she knew how to make so vivid and so sweet. Then, too, she brought forward her forces by detachment. At first she was the soul of do- mestic life, sitting at night beneath the light and embossing on weblike muslin designs of flower and leaf which she had learned in her convent, listening to Spencer as he read, and taking from the little wallet of her work-basket apropos scraps which she had preserved from the sermon of some Italian father of the Church or of some French divine. As for me, the only thing I knew was my poor music; and I used to burn with indignation when she interposed that unknown tongue between my husband and my- self. Presently her horses came, and then, graceful in her dark riding-habit, she would spend a morning fearlessly breaking in one of the fiery fellows, and dash away at last with plume and veil streaming behind her. In the early evening she would dance with the children—witch-dances they were— with her round arms linked above her head, and her feet weaving the mea- sure in and out as deftly as any flashing-footed Bayadere might do—only when Spencer was there to see: at other times I saw she pushed the little hindering things aside without a glance.

By and by she began to display a strange dramatic sort of power: she would rehearse to Spencer scenes that she had met with from day to day in the place, giving now the old churchwarden's voice and now the sexton's, their gestures and very faces; she could tell the ailments of half the old women in the parish who came to see me with them, in their own tone and manner to the life; she told us once of a street-scene, with the crier crying a lost child, the mother following with lamentations, the passing strangers questioning, the boys hooting, and the child's reappearance, followed by a tumult, with kisses and blows and cries, so that I thought I saw it all; and presently she had pierced the armor and found the secret and vulnerable spot of every friend we had, and could personate them all as vividly as if she did it by necromancy.

One night she began to sketch our portraits in charcoal: the likenesses were not perfect; she exaggerated the careless elegance of Spencer's attitude, perhaps the primness of my own; but yet he saw there the ungraceful trait for the first time, I think. And so much led to more: she brought out her portfolios, and there were her pencil-sketches from the Rhine and from the Guadalquivir, rich water-colors of Venetian scenes, interiors of old churches, and sheet after sheet covered with details of church architecture. Spencer had been admiring all the others—in spite of something that I thought I saw in them, a something that was not true, a trait of her own identity, for I had come to criticise her sharply—but when his eye rested on those sheets I saw it sparkle, and he caught them up and pored over them one by one.

"I see you have mastered the whole thing," he said: "you must instruct me here." And so she did. And there were hours, while I was busied with servants and accounts or with the children, when she was closeted with Spencer in the study, criticising, comparing, making drawings, hunting up authorities; other hours when they walked away together to the site of the new church that was building, and here an arch was destroyed, and there an aisle was extended, and here a row of cloisters sketched into the plan, and there a row of windows, till the whole design was reversed and made over. And they had the thing between them, for, admire and sympathize as I might, I did not *know.* At first Spencer would repeat the day's achievement to me, but the contempt for my ignorance which she did not deign to hide soon put an end to it when she was present.

It was this interest that now unveiled a new phase of her character: she was devout. She had a little altar in her room; she knew all about albs and chasubles; she would have persuaded Spencer to burn candles in the chancel; she talked of a hundred mysteries and symbols; she wanted to embroider a stole to lay across his shoulders. She was full of small church sentimentalities, and as one after another she uttered them, it seemed to me that her belief was no sound fruit of any system—if it were belief, and not a mere bunch of fancies—but only, as you might say, a rotten windfall of the Romish Church: it had none of the round splendor of that Church's creed, none of the pure simplicity of ours: it would be no stay in trouble, no shield in temptation. I said as much to Spencer.

"You are prejudiced," said he: "her belief is the result of long observation abroad, I think. She has found the need of outward observances: they are, she has told me, a shrine to the body of her faith, like that commanded in the building of the tabernacle, where the ark of the covenant was enclosed in the holy of holies."

"And you didn't think it profane in her to speak so? But I don't believe it, Spencer," I said. "She has no faith: she has some sentimentalisms."

"You are prejudiced," he repeated. "She seems to me a wonderful and gifted being."

"Too gifted," I said. "Her very gifts are unnatural in their abundance. There must be scrofula there, to keep such a fire in the blood and sting the brain to such action: she will die in a madhouse, depend upon it." Think of my saying such a thing as that!

"I have never heard you speak so before," he replied coldly. "I hope you do not envy her her powers."

"I envy her nothing," I cried, "for she is as false as she is beautiful." But I did—oh I did!

"Beautiful?" said Spencer. "Is she beautiful? I never thought of that."

"You are very blind, then," I said with a glad smile.

Spencer smiled too. "It is not the kind of beauty I admire," said he.

"Then I must teach you, sir," said she. And we both started to see her in the doorway, and I, for one, did not know till shortly before I found myself here how much or how little she had learned of what we said.

"Then I must teach you, sir," said she again. And she came deliberately into the firelight and paused upon the rug, drew out the silver arrows and shook down all her hair about her, till the great snake-like coils unrolled upon the floor.

"Hyacinthine," said Spencer.

"Indeed it is," said she—"the very color of the jacinth, with that red tint in its darkness that they call black in the shade and gold in the sun. Now look at me."

"Shut your eyes, Spencer," I cried, and laughed.

But he did not shut his eyes. The firelight flashed over her: the color in

her cheeks and on her lips sprang ripe and red in it as she held the hair
away from them with her rosy finger-tips; her throat curved small and
cream-white from the beautiful half-bare bosom that the lace of her
dinner-dress scarcely hid; and the dark eyes glowed with a great light as
they lay full on his.

"You mustn't call it vanity," said she. "It is only that it is impossible,
looking at the picture in the glass, not to see it as I see any other picture.
But for all that, I know it is not every fool's beauty: it is no daub for the
vulgar gaze, but a masterpiece that it needs the educated eye to find. I
could tell you how this nostril is like that in a famous marble, how the
curve of this cheek is that of a certain Venus, the line of this forehead like
the line in the dreamy Antinous' forehead. Are you taught? Is it beautiful?"

Then she twisted her hair again and fastened the arrows, and laughed
and turned away to look over the evening paper. But as for Spencer, as he
lay back in his lordly way, surveying the vision from crown to toe, I saw
him flush—I saw him flush and start and quiver, and then he closed his
eyes and pressed his fingers on them, and lay back again and said not a
word.

She began to read aloud something concerning services at the recent
dedication of a church. I was called out as she read. When I came back, a
half hour afterward, they were talking. I stopped at my work-table in the
next room for a skein of floss that she had asked me for, and I heard her
saying, "You cannot expect me to treat you with reverence. You are a married priest, and you know what opinion I necessarily must have of married
priests." Then I came in and she was silent.

But I knew, I always knew, that if Spencer had not felt himself weak,
had not found himself stirred, if he had not recognized that, when he
flushed and quivered before her beauty, it was the flesh and not the spirit
that tempted him, he would not have listened to her subtle invitation to
unnatural austerity. As it was, he did. He did—partly in shame, partly in
punishment; but to my mind the listening was confession. She had set the
wedge that was to sever our union—the little seed in a mere idle cleft that
grows and grows and splits the rock asunder.

Well, I had my duties, you know. I never felt my husband's wealth a reason why I should neglect them any more than another wife should neglect
her duties. I was wanted in the parish, sent for here and waited for there:
the dying liked to see me comfort their living, the living liked to see me

touch their dead; some wanted help, and others wanted consolation; and where I felt myself too young and unlearned to give advice, I could at least give sympathy. Perhaps I was the more called upon for such detail of duty because Spencer was busy with the greater things, the church-building and the sermons—sermons that once on a time lifted you and held you on their strong wings. But of late Spencer had been preaching old sermons. He had been moody and morose too: sometimes he seemed oppressed with melancholy. He had spoken to me strangely, had looked at me as if he pitied me, had kept away from me. But she had not regarded his moods: she had followed him in his solitary strolls, had sought him in his study; and she had ever a mystery or symbol to be interpreted, the picture of a private chapel that she had heard of when abroad, or the ground-plan of an ancient one, or some new temptation to his ambition, as I divine; and soon he was himself again.

I was wrong to leave him so to her, but what was there else for me to do? And as for those duties of mine, as I followed them I grew restive; I abridged them, I hastened home; I was impatient even with the detentions the children caused. I could not leave them to their nurses, for all that, but they kept me away from him, and he was alone with her.

One day at last he told me that his mind was troubled by the suspicion that his marriage was a mistake; that on his part at least it had been wrong; that he had been thinking a priest should have the Church only for his bride, and should wait at the altar mortified in every affection; that it was not for hands that were full of caresses and lips that were covered with kisses to break sacramental bread and offer praise. But for answer I brought my children and put them in his arms. I was white and cold and shaking, but I asked him if they were not justification enough; and I told him that he did his duty better abroad for the heartening of a wife at home, and that he knew better how to interpret God's love to men through his own love for his children; and I laid my head on his breast beside them, and he clasped us all and we cried together, he and I.

But that was not enough, I found; and when our good bishop came, who had always been like a father to Spencer, I led the conversation to that point one evening, and he discovered Spencer's trouble, and took him away and reasoned with him. The bishop was a power with Spencer, and I think that was the end of it.

The end of that, but only the beginning of the rest. For she had accustomed him to the idea of separation from me—the idea of doing without me. He had put me away from himself once in his mind: we had been one soul, and now we were two.

One day, as I stood in my sleeping-room with the door ajar, she came in. She had never been there before, and I cannot tell you how insolently she looked about her. There was a bunch of flowers on a stand that Spencer himself placed there for me every morning: he had always done so, and there had been no reason for breaking off the habit; and I had always worn one of them at my throat. She advanced a hand to pull out a blossom. "Do not touch them," I cried: "my husband puts them there."

"Suppose he does?" said she lightly. "What devotion!" Then she overlooked me with the long sweeping glance of search and contempt, shrugged her shoulders, and with a French sentence that I did not understand turned back and coolly broke off the blossom she had marked and hung it in her hair. I could not take her by the shoulders and put her from the room: I could not touch the flowers that she had desecrated. I left the room myself, and left her in it, and went down to dinner for the first time without the flower at my throat. I saw Spencer's eye note the omission: perhaps he took it as a release from me, for he never put the flowers in my room again after that day.

Nor did he ask me any more into his study, as he had been used, or read his sermons to me: there was no need of his talking over the church-building with me—he had her to talk it over with; and as for our music, that had been a rare thing since she arrived, for her conversation had been such as to leave but little time for it, and somehow when she came into the music-room and began to dictate to me the time in which I should take an Inflammatus and the spirit in which I should sing a ballad, I could not bear it. Then, too, to tell you the truth, my voice was hoarse and choked with tears full half the time.

It was some weeks after the flowers ceased that our youngest child fell ill. She was very ill—I don't think Spencer knew how ill. I dared not trust her with any one, and Spencer said no one could take such care of her as her mother could; so, though we had nurses in plenty, I hardly left the room by night or day. I heard their voices down below, I saw them go out for their walks. It was a hard fight, but I saved her.

But I was worn to a shadow when all was done—worn with anxiety for her, with alternate fevers of hope and fear, with the weight of my responsibility as to her life; and with anxiety for Spencer too, with a despairing sense that the end of peace had come, and with the total sleeplessness of many nights. Now, when the child was mending and gaining every day, I could not sleep if I would.

The doctor gave me anodynes, but to no purpose: they only nerved me wide awake. My eyes ached, and my brain ached, and my body ached, but it was of no use: I could not sleep. I counted the spots on the wall, the motes upon my eyes, the notes of all the sheets of music I could recall; I remembered the Eastern punishment of keeping the condemned awake till they die, and wondered what my crime was; I thought if I could but sleep I might forget my trouble, or take it up freshly and master it. But no, it was always there—a heavy cloud, a horror of foreboding. As I heard that woman's step go by the door I longed to rid the house of it, and I dinted my palms with my nails till she had passed.

I did not know what to do. It seemed to me that I was wicked in letting the thing go on, in suffering Spencer to be any longer exposed to her power; but then I feared to take a step lest I should thereby rivet the chains she was casting on him. And then I longed so for one hour of the old dear happiness—the days when I and the children had been all and enough. I did not know what to do; I had no one to counsel with; I was wild within myself, and all distraught. Once I thought if I could not rid the house of her I could rid it of myself; and as I went through a dark passage and chanced to look up where a bright-headed nail glittered, I questioned if it would bear my weight. For days the idea haunted me. I fancied that when I was gone perhaps he would love me again, and at any rate I might be asleep and at rest. But the thought of the children prevented me, and one other thought—I was not certain that even my sorrows would excuse me before God.

I went down to dinner again at last. How she glowed and abounded in her beauty as she sat there! And I—I must have been very thin and ghastly: perhaps I looked a little wild in all my bewilderment and hurt. His heart smote him, it may be, for he came round to where I sat by the fire afterward and smoothed my hair and kissed my forehead. He could not tell all I was suffering then—all I was struggling with; for I thought I had better put him out of the world than let him, who was once so pure and good, stay in it to sin. I could have done it, you know. For though I slept still with the little girl, I could have stolen back into our own room with the chloroform, and he would never have known. I turned the handle of the door one night, but the bolt was slipped. I never thought of killing her, you see: let her live and sin, if she would. She was the thing of slime and sin, a splendid tropical growth of passionate heat and the slime: it was only her nature. But then we think it no harm to kill reptiles, however splendid.

But it was by that time that the spirits had begun to talk with me—all night long, all day. It was they, I found, that had kept me so sleepless. Go where I might, they were ever before me. If I went to the woods, I heard them in the whisper of every pine tree; if I went down to the seashore, I heard them in the plash of every wave; I heard them in the wind, in the singing of my ears, in the children's breath as I hung above them, for I had decided that if I went out of the world I would take the children with me. If I sat down to play, the things would twist the chords into discords; if I sat down to read, they would come between me and the page. Then I could see them: they had wings like bats. I did not dare to speak of them, though I fancied she suspected me, for once she said, as I was kissing my little girl, "When you are gone to a madhouse, don't think they'll have many such kisses." I did not answer her, I did not look up: I suppose I should have flown at her throat if I had.

I took the children out with me on my long rambles: we went for miles; sometimes I carried one, sometimes the other. I took such long, long walks to escape those noisome things: they would never leave me till I was quite tired out. Now and then I was gone all day; and all the time that I was gone he was with her, I knew, and she was tricking out her beauty and practicing her arts.

I went to a little festival with them, for Spencer insisted. And she made shadow-pictures on the wall, wonderful things with her perfect profile and her perfect arms and her supple curves—she out of sight, the shadow only seen. Now it was Isis, I remember, and now it was the head and shoulders and trailing hair of a floating sea-nymph. And then there were charades in which she played; and I can't tell you the glorious thing she looked when she came on as Helen of Troy with all her "beauty shadowed in white veils," you know—that brown and red beauty with its smiles and radiance under the wavering of the flower-wrought veil. I sat by Spencer, and I felt him shiver. He was fighting and struggling too within himself, very likely; only he knew that he was going to yield after all—only he longed to yield while he feared. But as for me, I saw one of those bat-like things perched on her ear as she stood before us, and when she opened her mouth to speak I saw them flying in and out. And I said to Spencer, "She is tormenting me. I cannot stay and see her swallowing the souls of men in this way." And I would have gone, but he held me down fast in my seat. But if I was crazy then—as they say I was, I suppose—it was only with a metaphor, for she was sucking Spencer's soul out of his body.

But I was not crazy. I should admit I might have been if I alone had seen those evil spirits. But Spencer saw them too. He never exactly told me so, but I knew he did; for when I opened the church door late, as I often did at that time after my long walks, they would rush in past me with a whizz, and as I sat in the pew I would see him steadily avoid looking at me; and if he looked by any chance, he would turn so pale that I have thought he would drop where he stood, and he would redden afterward as though one had struck him. He knew then what I endured with them, but I was not the one to speak of it. Don't tell me that his color changed and he shuddered so because I sat there mumbling and nodding to myself: it was because he saw those things mopping and mowing beside me and whispering in my ear. Oh what loathsomeness the obscene creatures whispered!—foul quips and evil words I had never heard before, ribald songs and oaths; and I would clap my hands over my mouth to keep from crying out at them. Creatures of the imagination, you may say. It is possible, but they were so vivid that they seem real to me even now: I burn and tingle as I recall them. And how could I have imagined such sounds, such shapes, of things I had never heard or seen or dreamed?

And Spencer was very unhappy, I am sure. I was the mother of his children, and if he loved me no more, he had an old kindness for me still, and my distress distressed him. But for all that the glamour was on him, and he could not give up that woman and her beauty and her charm. Once or twice he may have thought about sending her away, but perhaps he could not bring himself to do it—perhaps he reflected it was too late, and now it was no matter. But every day she stayed he was the more like wax in her hands. Oh, he was weaker than water that is poured out. He was abandoning himself, and forgetting earth and heaven, and hell itself, before a passion—a passion that soon would cloy, and then would sting.

It was the spring season then: I had been out several hours. The sunset fell while I was in the wood, and the stars came out; and at one time I thought I would lie down there on last year's leaves and never get up again; but I remembered the children, and went home to them. They were both in bed and asleep when I took off my shoes and opened the door of their room—breathing so sweetly and evenly, the little yellow heads close together on one pillow, their hands tossed about the coverlid, their parted lips, their rosy cheeks. I knelt to feel the warm breath on my own cold cheek, and then the spirits began whispering again: "If only they never waked! they never waked!"

And all I could do was to spring to my feet and run from the room. I ran shoeless down the great staircase and through the long hall. I thought I would go to Spencer and tell him all—all my sorrows, all the suggestions of the spirits, and maybe in the endeavor to save me he would save himself. And I ran down the long dimly-lighted drawing-room, led by the sound I heard, to the music-room, whose doors were open just beyond. It was lighted only by the pale glimmer from the other room and by the moonlight through the painted panes. And I paused to listen to what I had never listened to there—the sound of the harp and a voice with it. Of course they had not heard me coming, and I hesitated and looked, and then I glided within the door and stood just by the open piano there.

She sat at the harp singing—the huge gilded harp. I did not know she sang—she had kept that for her last reserve—but she struck the harp so that it sang itself, like some great prisoned soul, and her voice followed it—oh so rich a voice! My own was white and thin, I felt, beside it. But mine had soared, and hers still clung to earth—a contralto sweet with honeyed sweetness—the sweetness of unstrained honey that has the earth-taste and the heavy blossom-dust yet in it—sweet, though it grew hoarse and trembling with passion. He sat in one of the great arm-chairs just before her: he was white with feeling; with rapture, with forgetfulness; his eyes shone like stars. He moved restlessly, a strange smile kindled all his face: he bent toward her, and the music broke off in the middle as they threw their arms around each other, and hung there lip to lip and heart to heart. And suddenly I crashed down both my hands on the keyboard before me, and stood and glared upon them.

And I never knew anything more till I woke up here. And that is the whole of it. That is the puzzle of it—was it a horrid nightmare, an insane vision, or was it true? Was it true that I saw Spencer, my white, clean lover, my husband, a man of God, the father of our spotless babies,—was it true that I saw him so, or was it only some wild, vile conjuration of disease? Oh, I should be willing to have been crazed a lifetime, a whole lifetime, only to wake one moment before I died and find that that had never been!

Well, well, well! When time passed and I became more quiet, I told the doctor here about the spirits—I never told him of Spencer or of her—

and he bade me dismiss care: he said I was ill—excitement and sleeplessness had surcharged my nerves with that strange magnetic fluid that has
worked so much mischief in the world. There was no organic disease, you
see; only when my nerves were rested and right, my brain would be. And
the doctor gave me medicines and books and work, and when I saw the
spirits again I was to go instantly to him. And after a little while I was not
sure that I did see them; and in a little while longer they had ceased to
come altogether, and I have had no more of them. I was on my parole then
in the parlor, at the table, in the grounds. I felt that I was cured of whatever had ailed me: I could escape at any moment that I wished.

And it came Christmas-time. A terrible longing for home overcame
me—for my children. I thought of them at this time when I had been used
to take such pains for their pleasure; I thought of the little empty stockings, the sad faces; I fancied I could hear them crying for me. I forgot all
about my word of honor. It seemed to me that I should die, that I might
as well die, if I could not see my little darlings, and hold them on my
knees, and sing to them while the chimes were ringing in the Christmas
Eve; and winter was here and there was so much to do for them. And I
walked down the garden, and looked out at the gate, and opened it and
went through. And I slept that night in a barn—so free, so free and glad;
and the next day an old farmer and his sons, who thought they did me a
service, brought me back, and of course I shrieked and raved; and so
would you.

But since then I have been in this ward and a prisoner. I have my work,
my amusements. I send such little things as I can make to my girls; I read;
sometimes of late I sing in the Sunday service. The place is a sightly place;
the grounds, when we are taken out, are fine; the halls are spacious and
pleasant. Pleasant—but ah, when you have trodden them ten years! And so,
you see, if I were a clod, if I had no memory, no desires, if I had never
been happy before, I might be happy now. I am confident the doctor thinks
me well, but he has no orders to let me go. Sometimes it is so wearisome;
and it might be worse if lately I had not been allowed a new service, and
that is to try to make a woman smile who came here a year ago. She is a little woman, swarthy as a Malay, but her hair, that grows as rapidly as a fungus grows in the night, is whiter than leprosy: her eyebrows are so long and
white that they veil and blanch her dark dim eyes, and she has no front
teeth. A stone from a falling spire struck her from her horse, they say—the
blow battered her and beat out reason and beauty. Her mind is dead: she

remembers nothing, knows nothing, but she follows me about like a dog: she seems to want to do something for me, to propitiate me. All she ever says is to beg me to do her no harm. She will not go to sleep without my hand in hers. Sometimes, after long effort, I think there is a gleam of intelligence, but the doctor says there was once too much intelligence, and her case is hopeless. Hopeless, poor thing!—that is an awful word: I could not wish it said for my worst enemy. In spite of these ten years I cannot feel that it has yet been said for me. If I am strange just now, it is only the excitement of seeing you, only the habit of the strange sights and sounds here. I should be calm and well enough at home. I sit and picture to myself that some time Spencer will come for me—will take me home to my girls, my fireside, my music. I shall hear his voice, I shall rest in his arms, I shall be blest again. For, oh, Elizabeth, I do forgive him all! Or if he will not dare to trust himself at first, I picture to myself how he will send another—some old friend who knew me before my trouble—who will see me and judge, and carry back report that I am all I used to be—some friend who will open the gates of heaven to me, or close the gates of hell upon me—who will hold my life and my fate. If—oh if it should be you, Elizabeth!

THE YELLOW WALL-PAPER

Charlotte Perkins Gilman

It is very seldom that mere ordinary people like John and myself secure ancestral halls for the summer.

A colonial mansion, a hereditary estate, I would say a haunted house, and reach the height of romantic felicity—but that would be asking too much of fate!

Still I will proudly declare that there is something queer about it.

Else, why should it be let so cheaply? And why have stood so long untenanted?

John laughs at me, of course, but one expects that in marriage.

John is practical in the extreme. He has no patience with faith, an intense horror of superstition, and he scoffs openly at any talk of things not to be felt and seen and put down in figures.

John is a physician, and *perhaps*—(I would not say it to a living soul, of course, but this is dead paper and a great relief to my mind—) *perhaps* that is one reason I do not get well faster.

You see he does not believe I am sick!

And what can one do?

If a physician of high standing, and one's own husband, assures friends and relatives that there is really nothing the matter with one but temporary nervous depression—a slight hysterical tendency—what is one to do?

My brother is also a physician, and also of high standing, and he says the same thing.

So I take phosphates or phosphites—whichever it is, and tonics, and journeys, and air, and exercise, and am absolutely forbidden to "work" until I am well again.

Personally, I disagree with their ideas.

Personally, I believe that congenial work, with excitement and change, would do me good.

But what is one to do?

I did write for a while in spite of them; but it *does* exhaust me a good deal—having to be so sly about it, or else meet with heavy opposition.

I sometimes fancy that in my condition if I had less opposition and more society and stimulus—but John says the very worst thing I can do is to think about my condition, and I confess it always makes me feel bad.

So I will let it alone and talk about the house.

The most beautiful place! It is quite alone, standing well back from the road, quite three miles from the village. It makes me think of English places that you read about, for there are hedges and walls and gates that lock, and lots of separate little houses for the gardeners and people.

There is a *delicious* garden! I never saw such a garden—large and shady, full of box-bordered paths, and lined with long grape-covered arbors with seats under them.

There were greenhouses, too, but they are all broken now.

There was some legal trouble, I believe, something about the heirs and co-heirs; anyhow, the place has been empty for years.

That spoils my ghostliness, I am afraid, but I don't care—there is something strange about the house—I can feel it.

I even said so to John one moonlight evening, but he said what I felt was a *draught*, and shut the window.

I get unreasonably angry with John sometimes. I'm sure I never used to be so sensitive. I think it is due to this nervous condition.

But John says if I feel so, I shall neglect proper self-control; so I take pains to control myself—before him, at least, and that makes me very tired.

I don't like our room a bit. I wanted one downstairs that opened on the piazza and had roses all over the window, and such pretty old-fashioned chintz hangings! but John would not hear of it.

He said there was only one window and not room for two beds, and no near room for him if he took another.

He is very careful and loving, and hardly lets me stir without special direction.

I have a schedule prescription for each hour in the day; he takes all care from me, and so I feel basely ungrateful not to value it more.

He said we came here solely on my account, that I was to have perfect rest and all the air I could get. "Your exercise depends on your strength, my dear," said he, "and your food somewhat on your appetite; but air you can absorb all the time." So we took the nursery at the top of the house.

It is a big, airy room, the whole floor nearly, with windows that look all ways, and air and sunshine galore. It was nursery first and then playroom and gymnasium, I should judge; for the windows are barred for little children, and there are rings and things in the walls.

The paint and paper look as if a boys' school had used it. It is stripped off—the paper—in great patches all around the head of my bed, about as far as I can reach, and in a great place on the other side of the room low down. I never saw a worse paper in my life.

One of those sprawling flamboyant patterns committing every artistic sin.

It is dull enough to confuse the eye in following, pronounced enough to constantly irritate and provoke study, and when you follow the lame uncertain curves for a little distance they suddenly commit suicide—plunge off at outrageous angles, destroy themselves in unheard of contradictions.

The color is repellant, almost revolting; a smouldering unclean yellow, strangely faded by the slow-turning sunlight.

It is a dull yet lurid orange in some places, a sickly sulphur tint in others.

No wonder the children hated it! I should hate it myself if I had to live in this room long.

There comes John, and I must put this away—he hates to have me write a word.

☆   ☆   ☆   ☆   ☆   ☆

We have been here two weeks, and I haven't felt like writing before, since that first day.

I am sitting by the window now, up in this atrocious nursery, and there is nothing to hinder my writing as much as I please, save lack of strength.

John is away all day, and even some nights when his cases are serious.

I am glad my case is not serious!

But these nervous troubles are dreadfully depressing.

John does not know how much I really suffer. He knows there is no *reason* to suffer, and that satisfies him.

Of course it is only nervousness. It does weigh on me so not to do my duty in any way!

I meant to be such a help to John, such a real rest and comfort, and here I am a comparative burden already!

Nobody would believe what an effort it is to do what little I am able—to dress and entertain, and order things.

It is fortunate Mary is so good with the baby. Such a dear baby!

And yet I *cannot* be with him, it makes me so nervous.

I suppose John never was nervous in his life. He laughs at me so about this wall-paper!

At first he meant to repaper the room, but afterwards he said that I was letting it get the better of me, and that nothing was worse for a nervous patient than to give way to such fancies.

He said that after the wall-paper was changed it would be the heavy bedstead, and then the barred windows, and then that gate at the head of the stairs, and so on.

"You know the place is doing you good," he said, "and really, dear, I don't care to renovate the house just for a three months' rental."

"Then do let us go downstairs," I said, "there are such pretty rooms there."

Then he took me in his arms and called me a blessed little goose, and said he would go down cellar, if I wished, and have it whitewashed into the bargain.

But he is right enough about the beds and windows and things.

It is an airy and comfortable room as any one need wish, and, of course, I would not be so silly as to make him uncomfortable just for a whim.

I'm really getting quite fond of the big room, all but that horrid paper.

Out of one window I can see the garden, those mysterious deep-shaded arbors, the riotous old-fashioned flowers, and bushes and gnarly trees.

Out of another I get a lovely view of the bay and a little private wharf belonging to the estate. There is a beautiful shaded lane that runs down there from the house. I always fancy I see people walking in these numerous paths and arbors, but John has cautioned me not to give way to fancy in the least. He says that with my imaginative power and habit of story-making, a nervous weakness like mine is sure to lead to all manner of excited fancies, and that I ought to use my will and good sense to check the tendency. So I try.

I think sometimes that if I were only well enough to write a little it would relieve the press of ideas and rest me.

But I find I get pretty tired when I try.

It is so discouraging not to have any advice and companionship about my work. When I get really well, John says we will ask Cousin Henry and Julia down for a long visit; but he says he would as soon put fireworks in my pillow-case as to let me have those stimulating people about now.

I wish I could get well faster.

But I must not think about that. This paper looks to me as if it *knew* what a vicious influence it had!

There is a recurrent spot where the pattern lolls like a broken neck and two bulbous eyes stare at you upside down.

I get positively angry with the impertinence of it and the everlastingness. Up and down and sideways they crawl, and those absurd, unblinking eyes are everywhere. There is one place where two breaths didn't match, and the eyes go all up and down the line, one a little higher than the other.

I never saw so much expression in an inanimate thing before, and we all know how much expression they have! I used to lie awake as a child and get more entertainment and terror out of blank walls and plain furniture than most children could find in a toy-store.

I remember what a kindly wink the knobs of our big, old bureau used to have, and there was one chair that always seemed like a strong friend.

I used to feel that if any of the other things looked too fierce I could always hop into that chair and be safe.

The furniture in this room is no worse than inharmonious, however, for we had to bring it all from downstairs. I suppose when this was used as a playroom they had to take the nursery things out, and no wonder! I never saw such ravages as the children have made here.

The wall-paper, as I said before, is torn off in spots, and it sticketh closer than a brother—they must have had perseverance as well as hatred.

Then the floor is scratched and gouged and splintered, the plaster itself is dug out here and there, and this great heavy bed which is all we found in the room, looks as if it had been through the wars.

But I don't mind it a bit—only the paper.

There comes John's sister. Such a dear girl as she is, and so careful of me! I must not let her find me writing.

She is a perfect and enthusiastic house-keeper, and hopes for no better profession. I verily believe she thinks it is the writing which made me sick!

But I can write when she is out, and see her a long way off from these windows.

There is one that commands the road, a lovely shaded winding road, and one that just looks off over the country. A lovely country, too, full of great elms and velvet meadows.

This wall-paper has a kind of sub-pattern in a different shade, a particularly irritating one, for you can only see it in certain lights, and not clearly then.

But in the places where it isn't faded and where the sun is just so—I can see a strange, provoking, formless sort of figure, that seems to skulk about behind that silly and conspicuous front design.

There's sister on the stairs!

*   *   *   *   *   *

Well, the Fourth of July is over! The people are all gone and I am tired out. John thought it might do me good to see a little company, so we just had mother and Nellie and the children down for a week.

Of course I didn't do a thing. Jennie sees to everything now.

But it tired me all the same.

John says if I don't pick up faster he shall send me to Weir Mitchell in the fall.

But I don't want to go there at all. I had a friend who was in his hands once, and she says he is just like John and my brother, only more so!

Besides, it is such an undertaking to go so far.

I don't feel as if it was worth while to turn my hand over for anything, and I'm getting dreadfully fretful and querulous.

I cry at nothing, and cry most of the time.

Of course I don't when John is here, or anybody else, but when I am alone.

And I am alone a good deal just now. John is kept in town very often by serious cases, and Jennie is good and lets me alone when I want her to.

So I walk a little in the garden or down that lovely lane, sit on the porch under the roses, and lie down up here a good deal.

I'm getting really fond of the room in spite of the wall-paper. Perhaps *because* of the wall-paper.

It dwells in my mind so!

I lie here on this great immovable bed—it is nailed down, I believe—and follow that pattern about by the hour. It is as good as gymnastics, I assure you. I start, we'll say, at the bottom, down in the corner over there where it has not been touched, and I determine for the thousandth time that I *will* follow that pointless pattern to some sort of a conclusion.

I know a little of the principle of design, and I know this thing was not arranged on any laws of radiation, or alternation, or repetition, or symmetry, or anything else that I ever heard of.

It is repeated, of course, by the breadths, but not otherwise.

Looked at in one way each breadth stands alone, the bloated curves and flourishes—a kind of "debased Romanesque" with *delirium tremens*—go waddling up and down in isolated columns of fatuity.

But, on the other hand, they connect diagonally, and the sprawling outlines run off in great slanting waves of optic horror, like a lot of wallowing seaweeds in full chase.

The whole thing goes horizontally, too, at least it seems so, and I exhaust myself in trying to distinguish the order of its going in that direction.

They have used a horizontal breadth for a frieze, and that adds wonderfully to the confusion.

There is one end of the room where it is almost intact, and there, when the crosslights fade and the low sun shines directly upon it, I can almost fancy radiation after all—the interminable grotesque seem to form around a common centre and rush off in headlong plunges of equal distraction.

It makes me tired to follow it. I will take a nap I guess.

*   *   *   *   *   *

I don't know why I should write this.

I don't want to.

I don't feel able.

And I know John would think it absurd. But I *must* say what I feel and think in some way—it is such a relief!

But the effort is getting to be greater than the relief.

Half the time now I am awfully lazy, and lie down ever so much.

John says I mustn't lose my strength, and has me take cod liver oil and lots of tonics and things, to say nothing of ale and wine and rare meat.

Dear John! He loves me very dearly, and hates to have me sick. I tried to have a real earnest reasonable talk with him the other day, and tell him how I wish he would let me go and make a visit to Cousin Henry and Julia.

But he said I wasn't able to go, nor able to stand it after I got there; and I did not make out a very good case for myself, for I was crying before I had finished.

It is getting to be a great effort for me to think straight. Just this nervous weakness I suppose.

And dear John gathered me up in his arms, and just carried me upstairs and laid me on the bed, and sat by me and read to me till it tired my head.

He said I was his darling and his comfort and all he had, and that I must take care of myself for his sake, and keep well.

He says no one but myself can help me out of it, that I must use my will and self-control and not let any silly fancies run away with me.

There's one comfort, the baby is well and happy, and does not have to occupy this nursery with the horrid wall-paper.

If we had not used it, that blessed child would have! What a fortunate escape! Why, I wouldn't have a child of mine, an impressionable little thing, live in such a room for worlds.

I never thought of it before, but it is lucky that John kept me here after all, I can stand it so much easier than a baby, you see.

Of course I never mention it to them any more—I am too wise—but I keep watch of it all the same.

There are things in that paper that nobody knows but me, or ever will.

Behind that outside pattern the dim shapes get clearer every day.

It is always the same shape, only very numerous.

And it is like a woman stooping down and creeping about behind that pattern. I don't like it a bit. I wonder—I begin to think—I wish John would take me away from here!

*   *   *   *   *   *

It is so hard to talk with John about my case because he is so wise, and because he loves me so.

But I tried it last night.

It was moonlight. The moon shines in all around just as the sun does.

I hate to see it sometimes, it creeps so slowly, and always comes in by one window or another.

John was asleep and I hated to waken him, so I kept still and watched the moonlight on that undulating wall-paper till I felt creepy.

The faint figure behind seemed to shake the pattern, just as if she wanted to get out.

I got up softly and went to feel and see if the paper *did* move, and when I came back John was awake.

"What is it, little girl?" he said. "Don't go walking about like that—you'll get cold."

I thought it was a good time to talk, so I told him that I really was not gaining here, and that I wished he would take me away.

"Why, darling!" said he, "our lease will be up in three weeks, and I can't see how to leave before.

"The repairs are not done at home, and I cannot possibly leave town just now. Of course if you were in any danger, I could and would, but you really are better, dear, whether you can see it or not. I am a doctor, dear, and I know. You are gaining flesh and color, your appetite is better, I feel really much easier about you."

"I don't weigh a bit more," said I, "nor as much; and my appetite may be better in the evening when you are here, but it is worse in the morning when you are away!"

"Bless her little heart!" said he with a big hug, "she shall be as sick as she pleases! But now let's improve the shining hours by going to sleep, and talk about it in the morning!"

"And you won't go away?" I asked gloomily.

"Why, how can I, dear? It is only three weeks more and then we will take a nice little trip of a few days while Jennie is getting the house ready. Really dear you are better!"

"Better in body perhaps—" I began, and stopped short, for he sat up straight and looked at me with such a stern, reproachful look that I could not say another word.

"My darling," said he, "I beg of you, for my sake and for our child's sake, as well as for your own, that you will never for one instant let that idea enter your mind! There is nothing so dangerous, so fascinating, to a temperament like yours. It is a false and foolish fancy. Can you not trust me as a physician when I tell you so?"

So of course I said no more on that score, and we went to sleep before long. He thought I was asleep first, but I wasn't, and lay there for hours trying to decide whether that front pattern and the back pattern really did move together or separately.

*   *   *   *   *   *

On a pattern like this, by daylight, there is a lack of sequence, a defiance of law, that is a constant irritant to a normal mind.

The color is hideous enough, and unreliable enough, and infuriating enough, but the pattern is torturing.

You think you have mastered it, but just as you get well underway in following, it turns a back-somersault and there you are. It slaps you in the face, knocks you down, and tramples upon you. It is like a bad dream.

The outside pattern is a florid arabesque, reminding one of a fungus. If you can imagine a toadstool in joints, an interminable string of toadstools, budding and sprouting in endless convolutions—why, that is something like it.

That is, sometimes!

There is one marked peculiarity about this paper, a thing nobody seems to notice but myself, and that is that it changes as the light changes.

When the sun shoots in through the east window—I always watch for that first long, straight ray—it changes so quickly that I never can quite believe it.

That is why I watch it always.

By moonlight—the moon shines in all night when there is a moon—I wouldn't know it was the same paper.

At night in any kind of light, in twilight, candlelight, lamplight, and worst of all by moonlight, it becomes bars! The outside pattern I mean, and the woman behind it is as plain as can be.

I didn't realize for a long time what the thing was that showed behind, that dim sub-pattern, but now I am quite sure it is a woman.

By daylight she is subdued, quiet. I fancy it is the pattern that keeps her so still. It is so puzzling. It keeps me quiet by the hour.

I lie down ever so much now. John says it is good for me, and to sleep all I can.

Indeed he started the habit by making me lie down for an hour after each meal.

It is a very bad habit I am convinced, for you see I don't sleep.

And that cultivates deceit, for I don't tell them I'm awake—O no!

The fact is I am getting a little afraid of John.

He seems very queer sometimes, and even Jennie has an inexplicable look.

It strikes me occasionally, just as a scientific hypothesis—that perhaps it is the paper!

I have watched John when he did not know I was looking, and come into the room suddenly on the most innocent excuses, and I've caught him several times *looking at the paper!* And Jennie too. I caught Jennie with her hand on it once.

She didn't know I was in the room, and when I asked her in a quiet, a very quiet voice, with the most restrained manner possible, what she was doing with the paper—she turned around as if she had been caught stealing, and looked quite angry—asked me why I should frighten her so!

Then she said that the paper stained everything it touched, that she had found yellow smooches on all my clothes and John's, and she wished we would be more careful!

Did not that sound innocent? But I know she was studying that pattern, and I am determined that nobody shall find it out but myself!

✳ ✳ ✳ ✳ ✳ ✳

Life is very much more exciting now than it used to be. You see I have something more to expect, to look forward to, to watch. I really do eat better, and am more quiet than I was.

John is so pleased to see me improve! He laughed a little the other day, and said I seemed to be flourishing in spite of my wall-paper.

I turned it off with a laugh. I had no intention of telling him it was *because* of the wall-paper—he would make fun of me. He might even want to take me away.

I don't want to leave now until I have found it out. There is a week more, and I think that will be enough.

✳ ✳ ✳ ✳ ✳ ✳

I'm feeling ever so much better! I don't sleep much at night, for it is so interesting to watch developments; but I sleep a good deal in the daytime.

In the daytime it is tiresome and perplexing.

There are always new shoots on the fungus, and new shades of yellow all over it. I cannot keep count of them, though I have tried conscientiously.

It is the strangest yellow, that wall-paper! It makes me think of all the yellow things I ever saw—not beautiful ones like buttercups, but old foul, bad yellow things.

But there is something else about that paper—the smell! I noticed it the moment we came into the room, but with so much air and sun it was not bad. Now we have had a week of fog and rain, and whether the windows are open or not, the smell is here.

It creeps all over the house.

I find it hovering in the dining-room, skulking in the parlor, hiding in the hall, lying in wait for me on the stairs.

It gets into my hair.

Even when I go to ride, if I turn my head suddenly and surprise it—there is that smell!

Such a peculiar odor, too! I have spent hours in trying to analyze it, to find what it smelled like.

It is not bad—at first, and very gentle, but quite the subtlest, most enduring odor I ever met.

In this damp weather it is awful, I wake up in the night and find it hanging over me.

It used to disturb me at first. I thought seriously of burning the house—to reach the smell.

But now I am used to it. The only thing I can think of that it is like is the *color* of the paper! A yellow smell.

There is a very funny mark on this wall, low down, near the mopboard. A streak that runs round the room. It goes behind every piece of furniture, except the bed, a long, straight, even *smooch*, as if it had been rubbed over and over.

I wonder how it was done and who did it, and what they did it for. Round and round and round—round and round and round—it makes me dizzy!

*   *   *   *   *   *

I really have discovered something at last.

Through watching so much at night, when it changes so, I have finally found out.

The front pattern *does* move—and no wonder! The woman behind shakes it!

Sometimes I think there are a great many women behind, and sometimes only one, and she crawls around fast, and her crawling shakes it all over.

Then in the very bright spots she keeps still, and in the very shady spots she just takes hold of the bars and shakes them hard.

And she is all the time trying to climb through. But nobody could climb through that pattern—it strangles so; I think that is why it has so many heads.

They get through, and then the pattern strangles them off and turns them upside down, and makes their eyes white!

If those heads were covered or taken off it would not be half so bad.

      *   *   *   *   *   *

I think that woman gets out in the daytime!

And I'll tell you why—privately—I've seen her!

I can see her out of every one of my windows!

It is the same woman, I know, for she is always creeping, and most women do not creep by daylight.

I see her in that long shaded lane, creeping up and down. I see her in those dark grape arbors, creeping all around the garden.

I see her on that long road under the trees, creeping along, and when a carriage comes she hides under the blackberry vines.

I don't blame her a bit. It must be very humiliating to be caught creeping by daylight!

I always lock the door when I creep by daylight. I can't do it at night, for I know John would suspect something at once.

And John is so queer now, that I don't want to irritate him. I wish he would take another room! Besides, I don't want anybody to get that woman out at night but myself.

I often wonder if I could see her out of all the windows at once.

But, turn as fast as I can, I can only see out of one at one time.

And though I always see her, she *may* be able to creep faster than I can turn!

I have watched her sometimes away off in the open country, creeping as fast as a cloud shadow in a high wind.

      *   *   *   *   *   *

If only that top pattern could be gotten off from the under one! I mean to try it, little by little.

I have found out another funny thing, but I shan't tell it this time! It does not do to trust people too much.

There are only two more days to get this paper off, and I believe John is beginning to notice. I don't like the look in his eyes.

And I heard him ask Jennie a lot of professional questions about me. She had a very good report to give.

She said I slept a good deal in the daytime.

John knows I don't sleep very well at night, for all I'm so quiet!

He asked me all sorts of questions, too, and pretended to be very loving and kind.

As if I couldn't see through him!

Still, I don't wonder he acts so, sleeping under this paper for three months.

It only interests me, but I feel sure John and Jennie are secretly affected by it.

✻   ✻   ✻   ✻   ✻   ✻

Hurrah! This is the last day, but it is enough. John to stay in town over night, and won't be out until this evening.

Jennie wanted to sleep with me—the sly thing! but I told her I should undoubtedly rest better for a night all alone.

That was clever, for really I wasn't alone a bit! As soon as it was moonlight and that poor thing began to crawl and shake the pattern, I got up and ran to help her.

I pulled and she shook, I shook and she pulled, and before morning we had peeled off yards of that paper.

A strip about as high as my head and half around the room.

And then when the sun came and that awful pattern began to laugh at me, I declared I would finish it to-day!

We go away to-morrow, and they are moving all my furniture down again to leave things as they were before.

Jennie looked at the wall in amazement, but I told her merrily that I did it out of pure spite at the vicious thing.

She laughed and said she wouldn't mind doing it herself, but I must not get tired.

How she betrayed herself that time!

But I am here, and no person touches this paper but me,—not *alive!*

She tried to get me out of the room—it was too patent! But I said it was so quiet and empty and clean now that I believed I would lie down again and sleep all I could; and not to wake me even for dinner—I would call when I woke.

So now she is gone, and the servants are gone, and the things are gone, and there is nothing left but that great bedstead nailed down, with the canvas mattress we found on it.

We shall sleep downstairs to-night, and take the boat home to-morrow.

I quite enjoy the room, now it is bare again.

How those children did tear about here!

This bedstead is fairly gnawed!

But I must get to work.

I have locked the door and thrown the key down into the front path.

I don't want to go out, and I don't want to have anybody come in, till John comes.

I want to astonish him.

I've got a rope up here that even Jennie did not find. If that woman does get out, and tries to get away, I can tie her!

But I forgot I could not reach far without anything to stand on!

This bed will *not* move!

I tried to lift and push it until I was lame, and then I got so angry I bit off a little piece at one corner—but it hurt my teeth.

Then I peeled off all the paper I could reach standing on the floor. It sticks horribly and the pattern just enjoys it! All those strangled heads and bulbous eyes and waddling fungus growths just shriek with derision!

I am getting angry enough to do something desperate. To jump out of the window would be admirable exercise, but the bars are too strong even to try.

Besides I wouldn't do it. Of course not. I know well enough that a step like that is improper and might be misconstrued.

I don't like to *look* out of the windows even—there are so many of those creeping women, and they creep so fast.

I wonder if they all come out of that wall-paper as I did?

But I am securely fastened now by my well-hidden rope—you don't get *me* out in the road there!

I suppose I shall have to get back behind the pattern when it comes night, and that is hard!

It is so pleasant to be out in this great room and creep around as I please!

I don't want to go outside. I won't, even if Jennie asks me to.

For outside you have to creep on the ground, and everything is green instead of yellow.

But here I can creep smoothly on the floor, and my shoulder just fits in that long smooch around the wall, so I cannot lose my way.

Why there's John at the door!

It is no use, young man, you can't open it.

How he does call and pound!

Now he's crying for an axe.

It would be a shame to break down that beautiful door!

"John dear!" said I in the gentlest voice, "the key is down by the front steps, under a plantain leaf!"

That silenced him for a few moments.

Then he said—very quietly indeed, "Open the door, my darling!"

"I can't," said I. "The key is down by the front door under a plantain leaf!"

And then I said it again, several times, very gently and slowly, and said it so often that he had to go and see, and he got it of course, and came in. He stopped short by the door.

"What is the matter?" he cried. "For God's sake, what are you doing!"

I kept on creeping just the same, but I looked at him over my shoulder.

"I've got out at last," said I, "in spite of you and Jane! And I've pulled off most of the paper, so you can't put me back!"

Now why should that man have fainted? But he did, and right across my path by the wall, so that I had to creep over him every time!

About the Editors

Elizabeth Terry was raised in the South, but has spent more than half her adult life north of the Mason-Dixon line. She works in publishing and currently lives in New York City with her husband and a huge chair in which she read lots of eerie stories for this collection.

Terri Hardin prowls libraries and antiquarian bookstores to uncover forgotten or little known writers. She is the editor of such anthologies as *Legends & Lore of the American Indians*, *A Treasury of American Folklore*, and *Supernatural Tales from Around the World*. She currently works in New York City and resides in New Jersey.